Her gaze con... gorgeous pair of hazel eyes.

At that moment Crystal knew it was Bane. She was about to open the door when she remembered the note. *Trust no one*. But this wasn't just anyone. This was Bane.

She unlocked the door and stepped back. Soft porch light poured into her foyer as Bane stepped in. He'd always been tall, but the man entering her house appeared a lot taller than she remembered. And he was no longer slender. He was all muscles, perfectly proportioned to his height and weight. And when her gaze settled on his face, she drew in a sharp breath. He even looked different. Rougher. Tougher.

He closed the door behind him and her heart pounded. A part of her wanted to race to him, tell him how glad she was to see him, how much she had missed him, but she couldn't. Her legs refused to move and she knew why.

For some reason this Bane was like a stranger to her. Had five years of separation done that to them?

* * *

Bane
is part of *New York Times* bestselling author
Brenda Jackson's The Westmorelands series:
a family bound by loyalty. . .and love!

BANE

BY
BRENDA JACKSON

Published in Great Britain 2015
by Mills & Boon, an imprint of Harlequin (UK) Limited,
Eton House, 18-24 Paradise Road, Richmond, Surrey, TW9 1SR

© 2015 Brenda Streater Jackson

ISBN: 978-0-263-25288-0

51-1215

Harlequin (UK) Limited's policy is to use papers that are natural, renewable and recyclable products and made from wood grown in sustainable forests. The logging and manufacturing processes conform to the legal environmental regulations of the country of origin.

Printed and bound in Spain
by CPI, Barcelona

Brenda Jackson is a *New York Times* bestselling author of more than one hundred romance titles. Brenda lives in Jacksonville, Florida, and divides her time between family, writing and traveling.

Email Brenda at authorbrendajackson@gmail.com or visit her on her website at www.brendajackson.net.

To the man who will always and forever be
the love of my life, Gerald Jackson, Sr.

So then, my beloved brethren, let every man be
swift to hear, slow to speak, slow to wrath.
—James 1:19

Prologue

"You wanted to see me, Dil?" Brisbane Westmoreland asked, walking into his eldest brother Dillon's home office.

The scenic view out the window was that of Gemma Lake, the main waterway that ran through the rural part of Denver the locals referred to as Westmoreland Country. For Bane, this was home. This wasn't Afghanistan, Iraq or Syria, which meant he didn't have to worry about booby traps, enemies hiding behind trees and bushes or the boat dock being wired with explosives set to go off the second someone stepped on it. Westmoreland Country was a place where he felt safe. All in all, he was glad to be back home.

Thanksgiving dinner had ended hours ago, and keeping with family traditions, everyone had gathered outside for a game of snow volleyball. Now the females in the Westmoreland family had gathered in the sitting room to watch a holiday movie with the kids, and the men had gone upstairs for a card game.

"Yes, come on in, Bane."

Bane stopped in front of Dillon's desk. He knew Dillon was studying him with that sharp eye of his, taking in every detail. And he could imagine what his brother was thinking. Bane was not the same habitual troublemaker who had left Westmoreland Country five years ago to make something of himself.

Bane would be the first to admit that a lot in his life had changed. He was now military through and through, both mentally as well as physically. Since graduating from the naval academy and becoming a navy SEAL, he'd learned a lot, seen a lot and done a lot...all in the name of the United States government.

"I want to know how you're doing," Dillon inquired, interrupting Bane's thoughts.

Bane drew in a deep breath. He wished he could answer truthfully. Under normal circumstances he would say he was in prime fighting condition, but that was not the case. During his team's last covert operation, an enemy's bullet had nearly taken him out, leaving him flat on his back in a hospital bed for nearly two months. But he couldn't tell Dillon that. It was confidential. So he said, "I'm fine, although my last mission took a toll on me. I lost a team member who was also a good friend."

Dillon shook his head sadly. "I'm sorry to hear that."

"Me, too. Laramie Cooper was a good guy. One of the best. We went through the academy together." Bane knew Dillon wouldn't ask for specifics. Bane had explained to his family early on that all his covert ops were classified and linked to national security and couldn't be discussed.

Dillon didn't say anything for a minute and then he

asked, "Is that why you're taking a three-month military leave? Because of your friend's death?"

Bane eased down in the leather armchair across from Dillon's desk. When their parents, aunt and uncle had gotten killed in a plane crash over twenty years ago, Dillon, the eldest of the Denver Westmorelands, had acquired the role of guardian of his six brothers—Micah, Jason, Riley, Stern, Canyon and Bane—and his eight cousins—Ramsey, Zane, Derringer, Megan, Gemma, the twins Adrian and Aidan, and Bailey. As far as Bane was concerned Dillon had done an outstanding job in keeping the family together and making sure they each made something of themselves. All while making Blue Ridge Land Management Corporation, founded by their father and uncle, into a Fortune 500 company.

Since Dillon was the eldest, he had inherited the main house in Westmoreland Country along with the three hundred acres it sat on. Everyone else, upon reaching the age of twenty-five, received one hundred acres to call their own. Thanks to Bailey's creative mind, each of their spreads were given names—Ramsey's Web, Zane's Hideout, Derringer's Dungeon, Megan's Meadows, Gemma's Gem, Jason's Place, Stern's Stronghold, Canyon's Bluff and Bane's Ponderosa. It was beautiful land that encompassed mountains, valleys, lakes, rivers and streams.

Again, Bane thought about how good it was to be home, and safe here talking with his brother.

"No, that's not the reason," Bane said. "All my team members are on leave because our last operation was one from hell. However, I'm using my leave for a specific purpose, and that is to find Crystal."

Bane paused before adding somberly, "If nothing

else, Coop's death showed me how fragile life is. You can be here today and gone tomorrow."

Dillon would never know that Bane wasn't just referring to Coop's life, but also how close he'd come to losing his own more than a few times.

Bane watched as Dillon came around and sat on the edge of his desk to face him, unsure of how his brother had taken what he'd just said about finding Crystal. Especially since she was the main reason Dillon, and the rest of Bane's family, had supported his decision to join the navy. During their teen years, Bane and Crystal had been obsessive about each other in a way that had driven her family, as well as his, out of their wits.

"Like I told you when you came home for Jason's wedding…" Dillon said. "When the Newsomes moved away they didn't leave a forwarding address. I think their main objective was to put as much distance between you and Crystal as they could." He paused, then said, "But after your inquiry, I hired a private investigator to locate their whereabouts, and I'm not sure if you know it but Carl Newsome passed away."

Bane shook his head. Although he definitely hadn't been Mr. Newsome's favorite person, the man had been Crystal's father. She and her dad hadn't always seen eye to eye, but Crystal had loved him nonetheless. "No, I didn't know he had died."

Dillon nodded. "I called and spoke to Emily Newsome, who told me about Carl's death from lung cancer. After offering my condolences, I asked about Crystal. She said Crystal was doing fine, working on her master's degree at Harvard with plans to get a PhD in biochemistry from there, as well."

Bane tipped his head to the side. "That doesn't surprise me. Crystal was pretty smart. If you recall she was two grades ahead and was set to graduate from high school at sixteen."

What he wouldn't bring up was that she would have done just that if she hadn't missed so many days of school playing hooky with him. That was something everyone, especially the Newsomes, blamed him for. Whenever Crystal had attended school steadily she'd made good grades. There was no doubt in his mind she would have graduated at the top of her class. That was one of the reasons he hadn't tried to find her for all these years. He'd wanted her to reach her full potential. He'd owed her that much.

"So you haven't seen or heard from Crystal since that day Carl sent her to live with some aunt?"

"No, I haven't seen her. You were right at the time. I didn't have anything to offer Crystal. I was a hothead and Trouble was my middle name. She deserved better and I was willing to make something of myself to give her better."

Dillon just stared at him for a long moment in silence, as if contemplating whether or not he should tell him something. Bane suddenly felt uneasy. Had something happened to Crystal that he didn't know about?

"Is there something else, Dil?"

"I don't want to hurt or upset you Bane, but I want to give you food for thought. You're planning to find Crystal, but you don't know what her feelings are for you now. The two of you were young. First love doesn't always mean last love. Although you might still care about her, for all you know she might have moved on, gotten on with her life without you. It's been five years. Have you considered that she might be involved with someone else?"

Bane leaned back in his chair, considering Dillon's

words. "I don't believe that. Crystal and I had an understanding. We have an unbreakable bond."

"But that was years ago," Dillon stressed. "You just said you haven't seen her since that day Carl sent her away. For all you know she could be married by now."

Bane shook his head. "Crystal wouldn't marry anyone else."

Dillon lifted a brow. "And how can you be so sure of that?"

Bane held his brother's stare. "Because she's already married, Dil. Crystal is married to me and I think it's time to go claim my wife."

Dillon was on his feet in a flash. "Married? You? Crystal? B-but how? When?"

"When we eloped."

"But you and Crystal never made it to Vegas."

"Weren't trying to," Bane said evenly. "We deliberately gave that impression to send everyone looking for us in the wrong direction. We got married in Utah."

"Utah? You have to be eighteen to marry without parental consent and Crystal was seventeen."

Bane shook his head. "She was seventeen the day we eloped, but turned eighteen the next day."

Dillon stared at him. "Then, why didn't the two of you say something? Why didn't she tell her parents that she was your wife or why didn't you tell us? You let them send her away."

"Yes, because I knew that although she was my wife, I could still be brought up on kidnapping charges. I violated the restraining order from that judge when I set foot on her parents' property. If you recall, Judge Foster was pissed about it and wanted to send me to the prison farm for a year. And knowing Mr. Newsome, had I mentioned anything about me and Crystal being married, he would have demanded that Judge Foster send me away for even longer. Once I was gone, Newsome would have found a way to have our marriage annulled or forced Crystal into divorcing me. She and I both knew that so we decided not to say anything about our marriage no matter what…even if it meant being apart for a short while."

"A short while? You've been apart for five years."

"I hadn't planned for it to be this long. We figured her old man would keep her under lock and key for a while. We were prepared for that seven-month separation because it would give Crystal a chance to finish high school. We hadn't figured on him sending her away. But then something you said that day stuck with me. At the time I had nothing to offer Crystal. She was smart and deserved more than a dumb ass who enjoyed being the town's troublemaker."

Bane didn't say anything for a minute before adding, "I told you earlier that I hadn't seen Crystal, but what I didn't say is that I managed to talk to her after she left town."

Dillon frowned. "You made contact with Crystal?"

"Only once. A few months after she was sent away."

"But how? Her parents made sure no one knew where she'd gone."

"Bailey found out for me."

Dillon shook his head. "Now, why doesn't that surprise me? And how did Bailey find out where Crystal was?"

Bane held his brother's gaze. "Are you sure you want to know?"

Dillon rubbed his hand down his face. "Does it involve breaking the law?"

Bane shrugged his shoulders. "Sort of."

Bailey was their female cousin who was a couple of years younger than Bane and the baby in the Denver Westmoreland family. While growing up, the two of them, along with the twins, Adrian and Aidan, had been extremely close, thick as thieves, literally. The four used to get into all kinds of trouble with the law. Bane knew that Dillon's close friendship with Sheriff Harper was what had kept them out of jail.

Now the twins were Harvard graduates. Adrian had a PhD in engineering and Aidan was a cardiologist at Johns Hopkins Research Hospital. And both were happily married. Bailey, who had her MBA, was marrying Walker Rafferty, a rancher from Alaska, on Valentine's Day and moving to live on his spread. That announcement had definitely come as a shock to Bane and everyone else since Bailey had always sworn she would never, ever leave Westmoreland Country. Bane had met Rafferty today and immediately liked the ex-marine. Bane had a feeling Rafferty would not only handle Bailey but would make Bane's cousin happy.

"So if you knew where she was, what stopped you from going to her?" Dillon asked, holding Bane's gaze.

"I didn't know where she was and I made Bailey promise not to tell me. I just needed to talk to her and Bailey arranged a call between me and Crystal that lasted about twenty minutes. I told her about my decision to join the navy and I made her a promise that while we were apart I would honor our marriage vows, and for her to always believe that one day I would come back for her. That was the last time we talked to each other."

Bane remembered that phone call as if it had been yesterday. "Another reason I needed to talk to Crystal was to be certain she hadn't gotten pregnant during the time we eloped. A pregnancy would have been a game changer for me. I would not have gone into the navy. Instead, I would have gone to her immediately."

Dillon nodded. "Do you know where she is now?"

"I didn't know up until a few hours ago. Bailey lost contact with Crystal a year and a half ago. Last week I hired someone to find her, and I got a call that she's been found. I'm heading out in the morning."

"To where?"

"Dallas, Texas."

One

Leaving her job at Seton Industries, Crystal Newsome quickly walked to her car, looking over her shoulder when she thought she heard footsteps behind her. She tried ignoring the sparks that moved up her arms, while telling herself she was probably getting all worked up for nothing. And all because of that note someone had left today in her desk drawer.

Someone wants the research you're working on. I suggest you disappear for a while. No matter what, don't trust anyone.

After reading it she had glanced around the lab. Her four colleagues seemed preoccupied, busy working on their individual biochemistry projects. She wondered who'd given her the warning and wished she could dismiss the note as a joke, but she couldn't. Especially not after the incident yesterday.

Someone had gotten inside her locker. How the person had known her combination she wasn't sure, since there hadn't been any signs of forced entry. But whoever it was had taken the time to leave things almost exactly as she'd left them.

And now the anonymous note.

Reaching her car, she unlocked the door and got inside, locking it again behind her. After checking her surroundings and the other cars parked close by, she maneuvered out of the parking lot and onto the street. When she came to a stop at the first traffic light, she pulled the typed note from her purse and reread it.

Disappear? How could she do that, even if she wanted to?

She was currently working on her PhD as a biochemist, and was one of five chosen nationally to participate in a yearlong research program at Seton Industries. Crystal knew others were interested in her research. Case in point: just last month she'd been approached by two government officials who wanted her to continue her PhD research under the protection of Homeland Security. The two men had stressed what could happen if her data got into the wrong hands, namely those with criminal intent. She had assured them that even with the documented advances of her research, her project was still just a theoretical concept. But they had wanted to place her in a highly collaborative environment with two other American chemists working on similar research. Although their offer had been tempting, she had turned it down. She was set to graduate from Harvard with her PhD in the spring and had already received a number of job offers.

But now she wondered if she should have taken the men's warning seriously. Could someone with criminal intent be after the findings she'd already logged?

She glanced in her rearview mirror and her heart pounded. A blue car she'd noticed several traffic lights back was still there. Was she imagining things?

A short while later she knew she wasn't. The car was staying a few car lengths behind her.

Crystal knew she couldn't go home. The driver of that blue car would follow her. So where could she go? Who could she call? The four other biochemists were also PhD students, but she stayed to herself the majority of the time and hadn't formed relationships with any of them.

Except for Darnell Enfield. He'd been the one intent on establishing a relationship with her. She had done nothing to encourage the man and had told him countless times she wasn't interested. When that hadn't deterred him, she'd threatened to file a complaint with the director of the program. In anger, Darnell had accused her of being stuck-up, saying he hoped she had a lonely and miserable life.

Crystal had news for him. She had that already. On most days she tried not to dwell on just how lonely the past five years had been. But as far as she was concerned, Loneliness had been her middle name for further back than five years.

Born the only child to older, overprotective parents, she'd been homeschooled and rarely allowed to leave the house except to attend church or accompany them to the grocery store. For years, her parents wouldn't even allow her to go outside and play. She remembered when one of the neighbor kids had tried befriending her, the most she could do was talk to the little girl through her bedroom window.

It was only after their pastor had encouraged her parents to enroll Crystal in public school to enhance her social skills that they did so. By then she was fifteen and starving for friends. But she'd discovered just how cruel the world was when the other girls had snubbed her and the guys had made fun of her because she'd been advanced in all her studies. They'd called her a genius freak. She had been miserable attending school until she'd met Bane.

Brisbane Westmoreland.

The man she had secretly married five years ago on her eighteenth birthday. And the man she hadn't seen since.

As a teenager, Bane had been her best friend, her sounding board and her reason for existing. He'd understood her like no other and she'd felt she had understood him. Her parents made the four-year difference in their ages a big issue and tried keeping them apart. The more her parents tried, the more she'd defied them to be with him.

Then there was the problem of Bane being a Westmoreland. Years ago, her and Bane's great-grandfathers had ended their friendship because of a dispute regarding land boundaries, and it seemed her father had no problem continuing the feud.

When Crystal came to another traffic light she pulled out a business card from her purse. It was the card those two government officials had left with her. They'd asked her to call if she changed her mind or if she noticed any funny business. At the time she'd thought their words were a scare tactic to make her give their offer more consideration. But could they have been right? Should she contact them? She replaced the card in her purse and looked at the note again.

No matter what, don't trust anyone.

So what should she do? Where could she go? Since

her father's death, her mother was now a missionary in Haiti. Should Crystal escape to Orangeburg, South Carolina, where her aunt Rachel still lived? The last thing Crystal wanted was to bring trouble to her elderly aunt's doorstep.

There was another place she could hide. Her childhood home in Denver. She and her mother had discovered, after going through her father's papers, that he'd never sold their family homestead after her parents moved to Connecticut. And even more shocking to Crystal was that he'd left the ranch to her. Had that been his way of letting her know he'd accepted that one day she would go back there?

She nibbled her bottom lip. Should she go back now? And face all the memories she'd left behind? What if Bane was there? What if he'd hooked up with someone else despite the promises he'd made to her?

She didn't want to believe that. The Bane Westmoreland she had fallen in love with had promised to honor their wedding vows. Before marrying someone else he would seek her out to ask for a divorce.

She thought about the other promise he'd made and wondered if she was the biggest fool on earth. He'd vowed he would come back for her. That had been five years ago and she was still waiting. Was she wasting her life on a man who had forgotten about her? A lot could have happened since he'd made that promise. Feelings and emotions could change. People could change. Why was she refusing to let go of teenage memories with a guy who might have moved on with his life?

Legally she was a married woman, but all she had to show for it was a last name she never used and a husband who'd left her with unfulfilled promises. Her last contact with him after her father had sent her away was when he'd called to let her know he was joining the navy. Did he expect her to wait until he got tired of being a sailor, moving from one port to the next? What if an emergency had come up and she'd needed him?

She knew the answer to that without much thought. Had an emergency arisen, she could have reached him through his family. Although the Westmorelands had no idea where she lived now, she'd always known where they were. She could have picked up the phone and called Dillon, Bane's eldest brother, if she'd ever truly wanted or needed to contact Bane. Several times she'd come close to doing that, but something had always held her back. First of all, she knew the Westmorelands blamed her for a lot of the trouble Bane had gotten into.

As teens, her and Bane's relationship had been obsessive and she didn't want to think about the number of times they'd broken the law to be together. She'd had resorted to cutting school, and regardless of what her parents had assumed, the majority of the time it had been her idea and not his. Nothing her parents or his family said or did had torn them apart. Instead, their bond had gotten stronger.

Because of the difference in their ages, her parents had accused Bane of taking advantage of her, and her father had even put a restraining order in place and threatened Bane with jail time to keep him away from her. But that hadn't stopped her or Bane from being together. When they'd gotten tired of their families' interference, they had eloped.

She reached inside her shirt and pulled out the sterling-silver heart-shaped locket Bane had given her instead of a wedding ring he couldn't afford. When he'd placed the locket around her neck he'd said it had belonged to his deceased mother. He'd wanted her to have it, to always wear it as a reminder of their love. His love. She swallowed a thick lump in her throat. If he loved her so much, then why hadn't he kept his promise and come back for her?

Her mother had mentioned that Bane's eldest brother, Dillon, had called a year ago when he'd heard about her father's death. According to her mother, the conversation had been brief, but Dillon had taken the time to inquire about how she was doing. According to her mother the only thing he'd said about Bane was that he was in the navy. Of course her mother thought her daughter was doing just fine now that Bane was out of her life, and the Westmorelands probably felt the same way since she was out of Bane's. What if her mother was right and Bane *was* doing just fine without her?

Drawing in a deep breath, Crystal forced her thoughts back to the car following her. Should she call the police for help? She quickly dismissed the idea. Hadn't the note warned her not to trust anyone? Suddenly an idea popped into her head. It was the start of the holiday shopping season and shoppers were already out in large numbers. She would drive to the busiest mall in Dallas and get lost in traffic. If that didn't work she would come up with plan B.

The one thing she knew for certain was that she would not let the person tail her home. When she got there, she would quickly pack her things and disappear for a while. She would decide where she was going once she got to the airport. The Bahamas sounded pretty good right about now.

What would Seton Industries think when she didn't show up for work as usual? At present that was the least of her worries. Staying safe was her top priority.

Half an hour later she smiled, satisfied that plan A

had worked. All it took was to scoot her car in and out of all those tenacious shoppers a few times, and the driver of the blue car couldn't keep up. But just to be certain, she drove around for a while to make sure she was no longer being tailed.

She had fallen in love with Dallas but had no choice except to leave town for a while.

Sitting in the SUV he had rented at the airport, Bane tilted his Stetson off his eyes and shifted his long legs into a more comfortable position. He checked his watch again. The private investigator's report indicated Crystal was employed with Seton Industries as a biochemist while working on her PhD, and that she usually got off work around four. It was close to seven and she hadn't gotten home yet. So where was she?

It *was* the holiday season and she could have gone shopping. And she must have girlfriends, so she could very well be spending time with one of them. He just had to wait.

None of his family members had been surprised when he'd announced he was going after Crystal. However, except for Bailey, who knew the whole story, all of them were shocked to learn he'd married Crystal when they had eloped. His brother Riley had claimed he'd suspected as much, but all the others hadn't had a clue.

Bailey had given Bane a huge hug and whispered that it was about time he claimed his wife. Of course others, like Dillon, had warned Bane that things might be different and not to expect Crystal to be the eighteen-year-old he'd last seen. Just like he had changed over the years, so had she.

His cousin Zane, who was reputed to be an expert on women, had gone so far as to advise Bane not to expect

Crystal to readily embrace her role as loving wife or his role as long-lost husband. Zane had cautioned him not to do anything stupid like sweeping her off her feet and carrying her straight to the bedroom. They would have to get to know each other all over again, and he shouldn't be surprised if she tried putting up walls between them for a while.

Zane had reiterated that regardless of the reason, Bane hadn't made contact with his wife in almost five years and doubts would have crossed Crystal's mind regarding Bane's love and faithfulness.

He had appreciated everyone's advice. And while he wished like hell he could sweep Crystal off her feet and head straight for the nearest bedroom when he saw her, he had enough sense to know they would have to take things slow. After all, they had been apart all this time and there would be a lot for them to talk about and sort out. But he felt certain she knew he would come back for her as he'd promised; no matter how long it had taken him to do so.

He was back in her life and didn't intend to go anywhere. Even if it meant he lived with her in Dallas for a while. As a SEAL he could live anywhere as long as he was ready to leave for periodic training sessions or covert operations whenever his commanding officer called. And as long as there was still instability in Iraq, Afghanistan and Syria, his team might be needed.

Thinking of his team made him think about Coop. It was hard to believe his friend was gone. All the team members had taken Coop's death hard and agreed that if it was the last thing they did, they would return to Syria, find Coop's body and bring him home. His parents deserved that and Coop did, too.

For the longest time, Bane had thought he could keep

his marriage a secret from his team. But he found it hard to do when the guys thought it was essential that he got laid every once in a while. Things started getting crazy when they tried fixing him up with some woman or another every chance they got.

He'd finally told them about his marriage to Crystal. Then he wished he hadn't when they'd teased him about all the women they were getting while he wasn't getting any. He took it all in stride because he only wanted one woman. His team members accepted that he intended to adhere to his wedding vows and in the end they all respected and admired him for it.

Now the SEAL in him studied his surroundings, taking notice. The one thing he appreciated was that Crystal's home appeared to be in a safe neighborhood. The streets were well lit and the houses spaced with enough distance for privacy yet with her neighbors in reach if needed.

The brick house where she lived suited her. It looked to be in good condition and the yard was well manicured. One thing he did notice was that unlike all the other houses, she didn't have any Christmas decorations. There weren't any colorful lights around her windows or animated objects adorning her lawn. Did she not celebrate the holidays anymore? He recalled a time when she had. In fact the two most important days to her had been her birthday and Christmas.

He'd made her birthday even more special by marrying her on it. A smile touched his lips when he recalled how, over the years, he had bought her birthday cards and anniversary cards, although he hadn't been able to send them to her. He'd even bought her Valentine's Day cards and Christmas cards every year. He had stored them in a trunk, knowing one day he would give them to her. Well, that day had finally arrived and he had all of them packed in his luggage. He had signed each one and taken the time to write a special message inside. Then there were all those letters he'd written. Letters he'd never mailed because he hadn't a clue where to send them.

He'd made Bailey promise not to tell him because if he'd known how to get to Crystal he would have gone to her and messed up all the effort he'd made in becoming the type of man who could give her what she deserved in life.

Five years was a long time and there had been times he'd thought he would lose his mind from missing her so much. It had taken all he had, every bit of resolve he could muster, to make it through. In the end, he knew the sacrifice would be worth it.

He figured he would give Crystal time to get into the house before he got out of the car and knocked on the door, so as not to spook her. No need to give her neighbors anything to talk about, either, especially if no one knew she was married. And from the private investigator's report, her marital status was a guarded secret. He understood and figured it wouldn't be easy to explain a husband who'd gone AWOL.

His phone rang and a smile tugged at the corner of his mouth when he recognized the ringtone. It was Thurston McRoy, better known to the team as Mac. All Bane's team members' names had been shortened for easy identification during deployment. Cooper was Coop. McRoy was Mac. And because his name was Brisbane, the nickname his family had given him was already a shortened version, so his team members called him Bane like everyone else.

"What's up, Mac?"

"Have you seen her yet?"

He had spoken to Mac on his way to the airport to let him know his whereabouts, just in case the team was needed somewhere. "No, not yet. I'm parked outside her place. She's late getting off work."

"When she gets there, don't ask a lot of questions and please don't go off on her as if you've been there for the past five years. You may think she's late but it might be her usual MO to get delayed every once in a while. Women do have days they like to get prettied up. Get their hair and nails done and stuff."

Bane chuckled. He figured Mac would know since he was one of the married team members. And Mac would tell them that after every extended mission, he would go home to an adjustment period, where he would have to get to know his wife all over again and reclaim his position as head of the house.

When Bane saw car lights headed toward where he was parked, he said, "I think this is her pulling up now."

"Great. Just remember the advice I gave you."

Yours and everybody else's, Bane thought. "Whatever. I know how to handle my business."

"See that you do." Then without saying anything else, Mac clicked off the phone.

As Bane watched the headlights get closer, he couldn't stop the deep pounding of his heart. He wondered what changes to expect. Did Crystal wear her hair down to her shoulders like she had years ago? Did she nibble her bottom lip when she was nervous about something? And did she still have those sexy legs?

It didn't matter. He intended to finally claim her as his. His wife.

Bane watched as she pulled into her yard and got out of the car. The moment his gaze latched on to her all the emotion he hadn't been able to contain over the years washed over him, putting an ache in his gut.

The streetlight shone on her features. Even from the distance, he could see she was beautiful. She'd grown taller and her youthful figure had blossomed into that of a woman. His pulse raced as he studied how well her curves filled out her dark slacks and how her breasts appeared to be shaped perfectly beneath her jacket.

As he watched her, the navy SEAL in him went on alert. Something wasn't right. He had been trained to be vigilant not just to his surroundings but also to people. Recognizing signs of trouble had kept him alive on more than one mission. Maybe it was the quickness of her steps to her front door, the number of times she looked back over her shoulder or the way she kept checking the street as if to make certain she hadn't been followed.

When she went inside and closed the door he released the breath he only realized now that he'd been holding. Who or what had her so antsy? She had no knowledge that he was coming, so it couldn't be him. She seemed more than just rattled. Terrified was more like it. Why? Even if she'd somehow found out he was coming, she had no reason of be afraid of him. Unless...

He scowled. What if she assumed he wasn't coming back for her and she'd taken a lover? What if she was the mother of another man's child? What if...

He cleared his mind. Each of those thoughts was like a quick punch to his gut, and he refused to go there. Besides, the private investigator's report had been clear. She lived alone and was not involved with anyone.

Still, something had her frightened.

After waiting for several minutes to give her time to

get settled after a day at work, he opened the door to the SUV. It was time to find out what the hell was going on.

With her heart thundering hard in her chest, Crystal began throwing items in the suitcase open on her bed. Had she imagined it or had she been watched when she'd entered her home tonight? She had glanced around several times and hadn't noticed anything or anyone. But still...

She took a deep breath, knowing she couldn't lose her cool. She had to keep a level head. She made a decision to leave her car here and a few lights burning inside her house to give the impression she was home. She would call a cab to take her to the airport and would take only the necessities and a few items of clothing. She could buy anything else she needed.

But this, she thought, studying the photo album she held in her hand, went everywhere with her. She had purchased it right after her last phone call with Bane. Her parents had sent Crystal to live with Aunt Rachel to finish out the last year of school. They'd wanted to get her away from Bane, not knowing she and Bane had married.

Before they'd returned home after eloping, Bane had convinced Crystal it was important for her to finish school before telling anyone they'd gotten married. He'd told her that if her parents tried keeping them apart that he would put up with it for a few months, which was the time it would take for her to finish school. They hadn't counted on her parents sending her away. But still, she believed that Bane would come for her once the school year ended, no matter where she was.

But a couple of months after she left Denver, she'd gotten a call from him. She'd assumed he was calling to let her know he couldn't stand the separation and was coming for her. But his real purpose had been twofold. He'd wanted to find out if she had gotten pregnant when they eloped, and he'd told her he'd enlisted in the navy and would be leaving for boot camp in Great Lakes, Illinois, in a few weeks. He'd said he needed to grow up, become responsible and make something out of himself. She deserved a man who could be all that he could be, and after he'd accomplished that goal he would come for her. He'd also promised that while they were apart he would honor their wedding vows and she'd promised him the same. And she had.

She'd figured he would be in the navy for four years. Preparing for the separation, she'd decided to make something of herself, as well. He deserved that, too. So after completing high school she'd enrolled in college. She had taken a placement test, which she'd aced. Instead of being accepted as a freshman, she had entered as a junior.

Sitting on the edge of the bed now, she flipped through the album, which she had dedicated to Bane. She'd even had his name engraved on the front. While they were apart she'd kept this photo journal, chronicling her life without him. There were graduation pictures from high school and college, random pictures she'd taken just for him. She'd figured that by the time she saw him she would have at least two to three years' worth of photos. She hadn't counted on the bulky album containing five years of photographs. The last thing she'd assumed was that they would be apart for this long without any contact.

She thought of him often. Every day. What she tried not to think about was why it was taking him so long to come back for her, or how he might be somewhere enjoying life without her. Forcing those thoughts from her mind, she packed the album in her luggage. Her destination was the Bahamas. She had done an online bank transfer to her "fun" account, which had accumulated a nice amount due to the vacations she'd never gotten around to taking. And in case her home was searched, she'd made sure not to leave any clues about where she was headed.

Was she being impulsive by heeding what the note had said when she didn't even know who'd written it? She could report it, what happened to her locker and that she'd noticed someone following her to those two government officials. If she couldn't trust her own government, then who could she trust? She shook her head, deciding against making that call. Maybe she'd watched too many TV shows where the government had turned out to be the bad guy.

Crystal thought about calling her mother and Aunt Rachel, and then decided against it. Whatever she was involved with, it would be best to leave them out of it. She would contact them later when she felt doing so would be safe. Moments later, she had rolled her luggage out of her bedroom into the living room and was calling for a cab when her doorbell rang.

She went still. Nobody ever visited her. Who would be doing so now? She crept back into the shadows of her hallway, hoping whoever was at the door would think she wasn't home. She held her breath when the doorbell sounded again. Had the person on the other side seen her enter her house and knew she was there?

Moments passed and the doorbell did not sound again. She sighed in relief—and then there was a hard knock. She swallowed. The person hadn't gone away. Either she answered it or continued to pretend she wasn't there. Since the latter hadn't worked so far, she rushed into her bedroom and grabbed her revolver out of the nightstand drawer.

She'd grown up around guns, and thanks to Bane she knew how to use one. This neighborhood was pretty safe, and even though she'd figured she'd never need to use it, she had bought the gun anyway. A woman living alone needed to be cautious.

By the time she'd made it back to the living room, there was a second knock. She moved toward the door, but stopped five feet away. She called out, "Who is it?" and tightened her hands on the revolver.

There was a moment of silence. And then a voice said, "It's me, Crystal. Bane."

Two

The revolver Crystal held almost fell from her hand.

Bane? My Bane? No way, she thought, backing up. It had to be an impostor. It didn't even sound like Bane. This voice was deeper, huskier.

If it was a trick, who knew of her relationship with Brisbane Westmoreland? And if it really was Bane, why had he shown up on her doorstep now? Why tonight of all nights?

It just wasn't logical for her to have been thinking about him only moments ago and for him to be here now. She would go with her first assumption. The person at the door claiming to be Bane wasn't him.

"You aren't Bane. Go away or I'll call the police," she threatened loudly. "I have a gun and will shoot if I have to."

"Crystal Gayle, it *is* me. Honest. It's Bane."

Crystal Gayle? She sucked in a deep breath. Nobody

called her that but her parents…and Bane. When she was young, she had hated being called by her first and middle names, which her father had given her, naming her after his favorite country singer. But Bane had made her like it when he'd called her that on occasion. Could it really be him at the door?

Lowering the gun, she looked out the peephole. Her gaze connected to a gorgeous pair of hazel eyes with a greenish tint. They were eyes she knew. It *was* Bane.

She was about to open the door when she remembered the note. *Trust no one.* But this wasn't just anyone, she reasoned with herself. This was Bane.

She unlocked the door and stepped back. Soft porch light poured into her foyer as Bane eased open the door. He'd always been tall and lanky, but the man entering her house appeared a lot taller than she remembered. And he was no longer slender. He was all muscles and they were in perfect proportion to his height and weight. It was obvious he worked out a lot to stay in shape. His body exemplified endurance and strength. And when her gaze settled on his face, she drew in a deep, sharp breath. He even looked different. Rougher. Tougher.

The eyes were the same but she'd never seen him with facial hair before. He'd always been handsome in a boyish sort of way, but his features now were perfectly masculine. They appeared chiseled, his lips sculpted. She was looking into the most handsome face she'd ever seen.

He not only looked older and more mature, but he also looked military—even while wearing jeans, a chambray shirt, a leather bomber jacket, Western boots and a Stetson. There was something about the way he stood, upright and straight. And all this transformation had come from being in the navy?

He closed the door behind him, staring at her just as she was staring at him. Her heart pounded. A part of her wanted to race over to him, tell him how glad she was to see him, how much she had missed him…but she couldn't. Her legs refused to move and she knew why. This Bane was like a stranger to her.

"Crystal."

She hadn't imagined it. His voice had gotten deeper. Sounded purely sexy to her ears. "Bane."

"You look good."

She blinked at his words and said the first thing that came to her mind. "You look good, too. And different."

He smiled and her breath caught. He still had that Brisbane Westmoreland smile. The one that spread across a full mouth and showed teeth that were perfectly even and sparkling white against mocha-colored skin. The familiarity warmed her inside.

"I am different. I'm not the same Bane. The military has a way of doing that to you," he said, in that husky voice she was trying to get used to hearing.

He was admitting to being different.

Was this his way of saying his transformation had changed his preferences? Like his taste in women? He was older now, five years older, in fact. Had he shown up on her doorstep tonight of all nights to let her know that he wanted a divorce?

Fine, she would deal with it. She had no choice. Besides, she wasn't sure if she would like the new Bane anyway. He was probably doing her a favor.

"Okay," she said, placing her revolver on the coffee table. "If you brought any papers with you that require my signature, then give them to me."

He lifted a brow. "Papers?"

"Yes."

"What kind of papers?"

Instead of answering, she glanced at her watch. She needed to call a cab to the airport. The plane to the Bahamas would take off in three hours.

"Crystal? What kind of papers are you talking about?"

She glanced back over at him. And why did her gaze automatically go to his mouth, the same mouth that had taught her how to kiss and given her so much pleasure? And why was she recalling a lot of those kisses right now? She drew in a deep, shallow breath. "Divorce papers."

"Is that why you think I'm here?"

Was she imagining things or had his voice sounded brisk? She shrugged. Why were they even having this conversation? Why couldn't he just give her the papers and be on his way so she could be on hers? After all, it had been five years. She got that. Did it matter that she had spent all that time waiting for him to show up?

"Crystal? Is that why you think I'm here? To ask for a divorce?" He repeated the question and she noticed his tone still had a brusque edge.

She held his gaze. "What other reason could there be?"

He shoved his hands into the pockets of his jeans and braced his legs apart in a stance that was as daunting as it was sexy. It definitely brought emphasis to his massive shoulders, the solidness of chest and his chiseled good looks.

"Did you consider that maybe I'm here to keep that promise I made about coming back for you?"

She blinked, not sure she'd heard him correctly. "You aren't here to ask for a divorce?"

"No. What makes you think I'd want to divorce you?"

She could give him a number of reasons once her

head stopped spinning. Instead, she said what was in the forefront of her mind. "Well, it has been five years, Bane."

"I told you I'd come back for you."

She placed her hands on her hips. "Yes, but I hadn't counted on it being *five* years. Five years without a single word from you. Besides, you just said you've changed."

The look in his eyes indicated he was having a hard time keeping up with her. "I *have* changed, Crystal. Being a SEAL has a way of changing you, but that has nothing to do—"

"SEAL? You're a navy SEAL?"

"Yes."

Now she was the one having a hard time keeping up. "I knew you'd joined the navy, but I figured you'd been assigned to a ship somewhere."

He nodded. "I would have been if my captain in boot camp hadn't thought I would be a good fit for the SEALs. He cut through a lot of red tape for me to go to the naval academy."

That was another surprise. "You attended the naval academy?"

"Yes."

Jeez. She was realizing just how little she knew about what he'd been doing over the past five years. "I didn't know."

He shifted his stance and her gaze followed the movement, taking in his long, denim-clad, boot-wearing legs.

"Bailey said the two of you lost contact with each other a couple of years ago," he said.

Now was the time to come clean and say losing contact with Bailey had been a deliberate move. The periodic calls from his cousin had become depressing since they'd agreed Crystal wouldn't ask about Bane. Just as he wouldn't ask Bailey any questions about Crystal.

That had been Bane's idea. He'd figured the less they knew about the other's lives, the less chance they had of reneging on their promise not to seek the other out before he could meet his goals.

During one of those conversations Bailey had informed her Bane had set up a bank account for her, in case she ever needed anything. She never had and to this day she'd never withdrawn any funds.

"Even if Bailey and I had kept in touch, she would not have told me *what* you were doing, just *how* you were doing. That was the agreement, remember, Bane?"

"You could have called Dil," he said as he raked his gaze over her.

He was probably taking note of how she'd changed as she'd done with him. He could clearly see she was no longer the eighteen-year-old he'd married, but was now a twenty-three-year-old woman. Her birthday had been two weeks ago. She wondered if he'd remembered.

"No, I couldn't call your brother, or any other member of your family for that matter, and you know why. They blamed me for you getting into trouble."

Crystal glanced at her watch again. He'd said he was here to fulfill his promise. If he was doing it because he felt obligated then she would release him from it. Although asking for a divorce might not have been his original intent, she was certain it was crossing his mind now. Why wouldn't it? They were acting like strangers instead of two people who'd once been so obsessed with each other they'd eloped. Why weren't they all over each other? Why was he over there and she still standing over here? The answer to both questions was so brutally clear she had to force tears from her eyes.

Like he said, he had changed. He was a SEAL. Something other than her was number one in his life now. More than likely it had been his missions that had kept him away all this time. He'd chosen what he really wanted.

"Crystal, I have a question for you."

His words interrupted her thoughts. "What?"

"Why did you come to the door with a gun?"

It had taken every ounce of Bane's control not to cross the room and pull his wife into his arms. How often had he dreamed of this moment, wished for it, yearned for it? But things weren't playing out like he'd hoped.

Although he'd taken heed to Zane's warning and not swept her off her feet and headed for the nearest bedroom, he hadn't counted on not getting at least a kiss, a hug…something. But she stood there as if she wasn't sure what to make of his appearance here tonight. And he still couldn't grasp why she assumed he wanted a divorce just because he'd told her he'd changed. He'd changed for the better, not only for himself but also for her. Now he had something to offer her. He could give her the life she deserved.

Crystal nibbled her bottom lip, which had always been an indication she was nervous about something. Damn, she looked good. Time had only enhanced her beauty, and where in the hell had all those curves come from?

She had changed into a pair of skinny jeans, a pullover sweater and boots. She looked all soft and feminine. So gorgeous. Her hair was not as long as it used to be. Instead of flowing past her shoulders it barely touched them. The new style suited her. How had she managed to keep the guys away? He was certain that with her beauty there had been a number of men who'd come around over the years.

Even now Bane's hands itched to touch her all over like he used to. He would give anything to run his fingers across the curve of her hips and buttocks and cup her breasts.

"The gun?"

Her question pulled his concentration back to their conversation. Probably for the best, since the thought of what he wanted to do with his hands was turning him on big-time. "Yes. I watched you get out of your car to come into the house and you seemed nervous. Is something going on? Is some man harassing you or stalking you?"

She lifted a brow. "A man stalking me? What makes you think that?"

He held her gaze. "I told you. I noticed you were nervous and—"

"Yes, I got that part," she interrupted to say. "But what makes you think any man would stalk me?"

Had she looked in the mirror lately? If she'd asked him *why* he thought she was being stalked, then he could have told her that his SEAL training had taught him how to zero in on certain things. But her question had been what made him think *any man* would want to stalk *her*. That was a different question altogether. He could see a man becoming obsessed with her. Hadn't Bane?

"You're a very beautiful woman. You've always been beautiful, Crystal. You're even more so now."

She shook her head. "Beautiful? You're laying it on thick, aren't you, Bane?"

"No, I don't think so. Level with me. Is there some man stalking you? Is that why you had the gun? And what's with the luggage? You're going someplace?"

She broke eye contact with him to shrug. "The gun is to protect myself."

Bane had a feeling that wasn't all there was to it. When he'd first walked into her house he'd seen the luggage, but his mind had been solely on her, entranced with her beauty. This older version of Crystal sent his heart pounding into overdrive. It had been a long time. Too long.

He turned his concentration back to what she'd just told him. "You have the gun to protect yourself... I can buy that, although this seems to be a pretty safe neighborhood," he said. "But that doesn't explain why you were ready to shoot. Has your home been broken into before?"

"No."

"Then what's going on?"

Even after all this time he still could read her like a book. She had a tendency to lick her lips when she was nervous, and unconsciously shift her body from side to side while standing on the balls of her feet. He could tell she was trying to decide how to answer his question. That didn't sit well with him. In the past, he and Crystal never kept secrets from each other. So why was she doing so now?

"After all this time, you don't have the right to ask me anything, Bane."

You're wrong about that, sweetheart.

Without thinking about what he was doing, he closed the distance separating them to stand directly in front of her. "I believe I do have that right. As long as we're still legally married, Crystal, I have every right."

She lifted her chin and pinched her lips together. "Fine. Then, we can get a divorce."

"Not happening." He rubbed his hand down his face. What the hell was going on here? Not only was this reunion not going the way he'd wanted, it had just taken a bad turn.

He looked at her, somewhat bewildered by her refusal to answer his question. "I'm asking again, Crystal. What's going on with you? Why the gun and the packed luggage?"

When she didn't answer, standing there with a mutinous expression on her face, he then asked the one question he hadn't wanted to ask, but needed to know. And he hoped like hell he was wrong.

"Are you involved with someone who's causing you problems?"

Three

That question set Crystal off. She took the final step to completely close the distance between them. "Involved with someone? Are you accusing me of being unfaithful?"

"Not accusing you of anything," he said in a tone that let her know her outrage had fueled his. "But I find it odd you won't answer my question. Why are you acting so secretive? You've never acted that way with me before."

No, she hadn't. But then the Bane she used to know, the one she'd loved more than life itself, would not have forgotten her for five years. He would have moved heaven, hell and any place in between to have her with him so the two of them could be together.

"You're not the only one who's changed. Just like you're not the same, I'm not the same."

They faced off. She didn't see him move, but suddenly his body brushed against hers and she drew in a sharp breath. The touch had been electric, sending a sizzle through her. Suddenly, her mind was filled with memories of the last time they'd touched. Really touched. All over. Naked. Those memories were enough to ignite a fire in the pit of her stomach.

"You may not be the same," he said, breaking into the silence between them, speaking in a low tone, "but you kept your wedding vows."

He spoke with such absolute certainty, she wondered how he could be so sure. But of course he was right. "Yes, I kept them."

He nodded. "And before doubt starts clouding that pretty little head of yours, let me go on record to say that I might not be the same, but I kept my wedding vows, as well."

There was no way. Not that she didn't think he would have tried, but she knew when it came to sex, some men classified it as a *must have*. She of all people knew how much the old Bane had enjoyed it. There was no reason to think the new and different Bane wouldn't like it just as much. Just look at him. He was more masculine, more virile—so macho. Even if he hadn't targeted women, they would definitely have targeted him.

"Now that we have that cleared up…"

Did they? "Not so fast," she said, trying to ignore it when his body brushed against hers again. Had it been intentional? And why hadn't one of them taken a step back? "What kept you sane?"

"Sane?"

"Yes. You know. From climbing the walls and stuff. I heard men need sex every so often."

He smiled and the force of it sent her senses reeling. "Remind me to give you all the details one day. Now, back to our earlier topic, why did you come to the door with a gun and why the packed bags?"

They were back to that?

But then maybe they should be. She needed to call a cab and get to the airport. And just like she didn't want to involve her mother and Aunt Rachel in whatever was going on, she definitely didn't want to involve Bane. Maybe she should have lied and said she was involved with someone else. Then he would have gotten angry and left, and she would be free to do as the note advised and disappear. Whatever was going on was her issue and not his.

She nibbled her lips as she tried coming up with something that would sound reasonable. Something that wasn't too much of a lie. So she said, "The reason for the packed luggage is because I'm taking a trip."

He looked at her as if to say *duh*. Instead, he held her gaze and asked, "Business or pleasure?"

"Business."

"Where are you headed?"

If she told him the Bahamas, he would question if it really was a business trip, so she said, "Chicago."

"Fine. I'll go with you."

She blinked, suddenly feeling anxiety closing in on her. "Go with me?"

"Yes. I'm on leave so I can do that," he said calmly. "Besides, it's time I got to know you again, and I want you to get to know me."

She drew in a breath, feeling her control deteriorating. Those hazel eyes had always been her weakness.

She knew she was a goner when he asked in a husky voice, "You do want to get to know me all over again, don't you, Crystal Gayle?"

Getting to know Brisbane Westmoreland the first

time around had been like a roller coaster, and she'd definitely enjoyed the ride. There was no doubt that getting to know the new Bane would be even more exhilarating. Now she could enjoy the ride as a woman in control of her own destiny and not as a girl whose life was dictated by her parents. A woman who was older, mature and could appreciate the explosiveness of a relationship with him.

As if he knew what she was thinking and wanted to drive that point home, he caressed the side of her face with the tip of his finger. "I definitely want to get to know you again, Crystal."

Then he brought her body closer to his. She felt his erection pressing hard against her middle and a craving she'd tried to put to rest years ago reared its greedy head, making her force back a moan. When his finger left her face to tug on a section of her hair, sensations she hadn't felt in years ran rampant through her womb.

She stared into his eyes. Hazel eyes that had literally branded her the first time she'd gazed into them. Eyes belonging to Bane. *Her* Bane. And he had admitted just moments ago to keeping their vows all this time. That meant he had five years of need and hunger stored inside him. The thought sent heated blood racing through her veins.

Then he shifted. The movement nudged his knees between hers so she could feel his hard bulge even more. Intentional or not, she wasn't sure. The only thing she was certain about was that if she didn't get her self-control back, she would jump his bones without a second thought. And that wasn't good. She didn't even know him anymore.

He leaned in slowly—too slowly, which let her know this side of Bane wasn't different…at least when it came to this. He'd always let her establish the pace, so as not to take advantage of the difference in their ages and experience levels. She'd always known she hadn't been Bane's first girl, but he'd been her first guy. And he'd always handled her with tenderness.

Bane was letting her take the lead now, and she intended to take it to a whole other level. At that moment, she didn't care that they'd both changed; she wanted his hands on her and his tongue in her mouth. To be totally honest, she needed more but she would settle for those two things now...even if she knew there probably wouldn't be a later.

He bent his head closer, and she refused to consider anything other than what she wanted, needed and had gone five years without. She clutched tight to his shoulders and leaned up on tiptoes to cover his mouth with hers.

Bane wasn't sure what was more dangerous. Storming an extremist stronghold in the middle of the night, or having his way with Crystal's mouth after all these years of going without her taste. But now was not the time to dwell on it. It was time to act.

The way their mouths mated seemed as natural as breathing, and he was glad time had not diminished the desire they'd always shared.

When she slid her tongue inside his mouth, memories of the last time they'd kissed flooded his mind. It had been on their wedding day, during their honeymoon in a small hotel in Utah. He recalled very little about the room itself, only what they'd done within those four walls. And they'd done plenty.

But now, this very minute, they were making new memories. He had dreamed about, thought about and wished for this moment for so long. She took the kiss deeper and he wrapped his arms around her waist and pulled her closer, loving the feel of her body plastered against his.

He loved her taste. Always had and always would. When she sucked on his tongue, his heartbeat thundered in his chest and his erection throbbed mercilessly behind his zipper. He was tempted to devour her and tried like hell to keep his self-control in check. But it became too much. Five years without her had taken its toll.

Suddenly he became the aggressor, taking her mouth with a hunger he felt all the way to the soles of his feet. He wanted her to feel him in every part of her body. And when he finally caught her wriggling tongue, he feasted on it.

The one thing that had consumed his mind on their wedding day was the same thing consuming his mind right now. Crystal was his. Undeniably, unquestionably and indisputably his.

He thrust his tongue even deeper into her mouth. He knew he had to pull back; otherwise he would consume her whole. Especially now, when he was filled with the need to do the one thing he shouldn't do, which was to sweep her off her feet and head for the nearest bedroom. He had wanted this moment for so long… Kissing her filled him with sensations so deliciously intoxicating that he could barely think straight.

Bane knew he was embarking on a mission more dangerous than any he'd gone on as a SEAL. Crystal had always been both his weakness and his strength. She was an ache he'd always had to ease. Some way, somehow, he had to show her, prove to her, that any changes he'd made over the past five years were all good and would benefit both of them. Otherwise, the time they'd spent apart would have been for nothing. He refused to accept that.

Reluctant to do so but knowing he should, Bane ended the kiss. But he wasn't ready to release her yet and his hands moved from her waist to boldly cup her backside. And while she was snuggled so close to him, his hands moved up and down the length of her spine before returning to cup her backside again. Now that she was back in his life, he couldn't imagine her being out of it again.

That thought drove him to reiterate something he'd said earlier. "I'm going to Chicago with you."

Slowly recovering from their kiss, Crystal tilted her head back and gazed up at Bane. Her lips had ground against his. Her tongue had initiated a dance inside his mouth that had been as perfect as anything she'd ever known. And he had reciprocated by kissing her back with equal need. Waves of passion had consumed her, nearly drowning her.

But now she had reclaimed her senses and the words he'd spoken infiltrated her mind. She knew there was no way he could go anywhere with her. She was about to open her mouth to tell him so when her cell phone rang. She tensed. Who could be contacting her? She seldom got calls.

"You plan on getting that?" Bane murmured the question while placing a kiss on the side of her neck.

She swallowed. Should she? It could be the airline calling her for some reason. She had left them her number in case her flight was delayed or canceled. "Yes," she said, quickly moving away from him to grab the phone off the table, right next to where she had laid the gun. Seeing the weapon was a reminder of what she had to do and why she couldn't let Bane sidetrack her.

She clicked on her cell phone. "Hello?"

"Don't try getting away, Ms. Newsome. We will find you." And then she heard a click ending the call.

Crystal's heart thumped painfully in her chest. Who was the caller? How did the person get her private number? How did the person know she was trying to get away? She turned toward Bane. Something in her eyes must have told him the call had troubled her because he quickly crossed the room to her. "Crystal, what's wrong?"

She took a deep breath, not knowing what to do or say. She stared up at him as she nervously bit her lip. Should she level with Bane and tell him everything that was going on? The note had said not to trust anyone, but how could she not trust the one and only person she'd always trusted?

"I don't know what's wrong," she said quietly.

She pulled away to reach for her purse and retrieve the note. "I got this note at work today," she said, handing it to him. "And I don't know who sent it."

She waited while he read it and when he glanced back up at her, she said, "Yesterday someone broke into my locker at work, and I noticed someone following me home today."

"Following you?"

"Yes. I thought maybe I was imagining things at first, but when the driver stayed discreetly behind me, I knew that I wasn't. I deliberately lost the car in all the holiday shoppers at one of the busiest malls."

"What about that phone call just now?" he asked, studying her.

She told him what the caller had said. "I don't know who it was or how they got my number."

Bane didn't say anything for a minute. "Is that the reason for the packed bags? You're doing what the note said and disappearing?"

"Yes. Those guys said craziness might start happening and—"

Bane frowned. "What guys?"

"Last month while I was eating lunch at a restaurant near work, I was approached by two government men. They showed me credentials to prove it. They knew about the project I'm working on at Seton and said Homeland Security was concerned about my research getting into the wrong hands. They offered me a chance to work for the government at some lab in DC, along with two other chemists who're working on similar research."

"And?"

"I turned them down. They accepted my answer, but warned me that there were people out there with criminal intent who would do just about anything to get their hands on my research. They gave me their business card and told me to call them if any craziness happened."

"Have you called them?"

"No. After reading the note I wasn't sure who I could trust. At this point that includes Homeland Security."

"Do you still have the business card those guys gave you?"

"Yes."

"May I see it?"

"Yes." She reached for her purse again. She handed the card to him and watched him study it before snapping several pictures of it with his mobile phone.

"What are you doing?"

He glanced over at her. "Verifying those guys are who they say they are. I'm sending this to someone who can do that for me." He then handed her back the card. "Just what kind of research are you working on?"

She paused a moment before saying. "Obscured Reality, or OR as it's most often called."

"Obscured Reality?"

She nodded. "Yes. It's the ability to make objects invisible."

Four

Bane lifted a brow. "Did you say your research was finding a way to make objects invisible?"

"Yes. Although it hasn't been perfected yet, it won't be long before I perform the first test."

Because he was a SEAL, Bane was aware of advances in technology that most people didn't know about, especially when it came to advanced weapons technology. But he'd never considered that objects could become invisible to the naked eye. He could imagine the chaos it would cause if such a thing fell into the wrong hands.

"And you think this note is legit?" he asked.

"If I doubted it before, that phone call pretty much proved otherwise. That's why I'm leaving."

He nodded. "And that's why I'm going with you."

She shook her head. "You can't go with me, Bane, and I don't have time to argue with you about it. I need to get to the airport."

Argue?

It suddenly dawned on him that in all the years he and Crystal had been together, mostly sneaking around to do so, they'd never argued. They had always been of one accord, always in sync with their thoughts, plans and ideas. The very concept of them not agreeing about something just couldn't compute with him. Of course it would be logical not to be in complete harmony since they were different people now.

Even so, him going with her was not up for discussion.

"How were you planning to get to the airport? Drive?" he asked her.

She shook her head. "No. I was going to call a cab and leave my car here."

"Then, I will take you. We can talk some more on the way."

"Okay, let me close up everything. Won't take but a second."

His gaze followed her movements as she went from room to room turning off lights and unplugging electrical items. Her movements were swift, yet sexy as hell and his body responded to them. She'd always had a cute shape, but this grown-up Crystal was rocking curves like he couldn't believe.

Earlier she had asked how he'd maintained his sanity without sex. He wondered how she'd maintained hers. They had enjoyed each other and he was convinced the only reason she hadn't gotten pregnant was because when it came to her, he'd always been responsible. A teenage pregnancy was something neither of them had needed to deal with.

She leaned down to pick up something off the floor and the way the denim stretched across her shapely backside sent heat rushing through him. He drew in a deep breath. Now was not the time to think about how hot his wife was. What should be consuming his mind was finding out the identity of the person responsible for her fleeing her home. Whoever was messing with her would definitely have to deal with him.

"At least I'm going where there's plenty of sunshine."

His brow furrowed. Did she honestly think there was sunshine in Chicago this time of the year? She met his gaze and he knew from the uh-oh look on her face that she'd unintentionally let that slip.

He was reminded now that although they'd never argued, they had lied quite a few times. But never to each other. Mainly the fibs had been for their families. They'd gotten good at it, although Dillon would catch Bane in his lies more often than not.

Crossing the room, Bane stopped in front of her. "You lied to me about where you're going, didn't you?"

She took a deep breath and he could hear the beats of her heart. They were coming fast and furious. Bane wasn't sure whether her heart was pounding because he was confronting her about the lie or because his nearness unnerved her like hers did him. Even when he should be upset about her lying to him, all he wanted to do was lean in closer and taste her again.

"Yes, I lied. I'm not going to Chicago but to the Bahamas. But when I lied about it, it was for your own good."

"For my own good?" he repeated as if making sure he'd heard her right.

"Yes. In the past I was the reason you got into trouble. Now you're a SEAL and I won't be responsible for you getting into more trouble on my account."

He stared at her. Didn't she know whatever he'd done

in the past had been of his own free will? During those days he would have done anything to be with her. There was no way he could have stayed away as her father had demanded. Her parents hadn't even given them a chance just because Bane's last name was Westmoreland. Although Carl Newsome had claimed Bane's age had been the major factor, Bane often wondered if that was true.

Everyone knew how much he'd loved Crystal. Members of his family had thought he was insane, and in a way he had been. Insanely in love. Hadn't his brother Riley even told him once that no man should love any female that much? Bane wondered if Riley was singing that same tune now that he was married to Alpha. Bane doubted it. All it took was to see his brother and Alpha together to know Riley now understood how deeply a man could love a woman.

"Crystal?" he said, trying to keep his voice on a serious note because he knew she actually believed what she'd said. "Stop thinking you're the reason I was such a badass back in the day. When I met you I was already getting into trouble with the law. After I hooked up with you, I actually got in less trouble."

She rolled her eyes. "That's not the way I remember it."

"You remember it the way your parents wanted you to remember it. Yes, I deliberately defied your father whenever he tried keeping us apart, but it wasn't as if I was a gangster or anything."

A smile curved his lips as he continued, "At least not after meeting you. With you I was on my best behavior. You even nailed the reason I behaved that way. You're the one who pointed out it had everything to do with the loss of my parents and aunt and uncle in that plane crash. The depth of our grief overpowered me, Bailey and the twins, and getting into trouble was our outlet. That just goes to show how smart you were even back then, and your theory made sense. Remember all those long talks we used to have?"

She nodded. "Yes, by the side of the road or in our private place. Our family thought all those times the sheriff found us that we were making out in your truck or something. And all we'd been doing was talking. I tried telling my parents that but they wouldn't listen. You were a Westmoreland and they wanted to think the worst. They believed I was sexually active when I wasn't."

He recalled those times. Yes, they had been caught parking, and cutting school had become almost the norm, but all they'd done was spend time together talking. He'd refused to go all the way with her until she was older. The first time they'd had sex was when she'd turned seventeen. By then they'd been together almost two years.

At least Dillon had believed Bane when he'd told his brother he hadn't touched her. However, given their relationship, it would have been crazy to think they wouldn't get around to making love one day, and Dillon had had the common sense to know that. Instead of giving Bane grief about it, his older brother had lectured him about being responsible and taking precautions.

Bane would never forget the night they'd finally made love. And it hadn't been in the backseat of his truck. He had taken her to the cabin he'd built as a gift for her seventeenth birthday. He'd constructed it on the land he was to inherit, Bane's Ponderosa.

It was a night he would never forget. Waiting had almost done them in, but in the end they'd known they'd done the right thing. That night had been so unbelievably special and he'd known she would be his forever. He knew on that night that one day he would make her his wife.

In fact it had been that night when he'd asked her to marry him once she finished school, and she'd agreed. And that had been the plan until her parents made things even worse for them after she'd turned seventeen.

Crystal had retaliated by refusing to go to school. And when her parents had threatened to have him put in jail if he came on their property, he and Crystal had eloped. He hadn't counted on her parents sending her away the moment Sheriff Harper found them.

Bane had come close to telling everyone they'd gotten married; no one had the right to separate them. But something Dillon had said about the future had given him pause.

Once he'd revealed they were married, he'd known Crystal would not go back to school. And he of all people had known just how smart she was.

That was when he'd decided to make the sacrifice and let her go. That had been the hardest decision he'd ever made. Lucky for him, Bailey had put her pickpocketing skills to work and swiped old man Newsome's cell phone to get Crystal's aunt's phone number.

"I need to go, Bane," Crystal said, intruding into his memories. "I'll give you my number and we can talk when I get to where I'm going."

Then in a rush, she added, "I'll call to let you know when I arrive in the Bahamas so you'll know I'm okay."

He stared at her. Evidently she didn't get it and it was about time that she did. "Crystal," he said in what he hoped was a tone that grabbed her absolute attention. When she stared at him he knew it had. "If you think I'm going to let you disappear on your own, then you really don't know me. The old Bane did let you disappear when your father sent you away. But at the time I figured it was for your own good. But those days are over. There's no way in hell you're disappearing on me again."

From her blistering scowl he could tell she didn't appreciate what he'd said. When she opened her mouth to reply, he quickly held up his hand. "I know it's been five years and that we have changed. But there's something with us that hasn't changed."

"What?" she asked in an annoyed tone.

"No matter what happens, we're in this together. That's how things have always been with us, right?"

"Yes, but that was then, Bane."

"And that's how it is now. We're married," he said, touching the locket he'd given her on their wedding day. Just knowing she was still wearing it meant everything to him. "We're in this together, Crystal. Got that?"

For a minute Crystal didn't say anything and then through clenched teeth, she snapped, "Yes, I got it."

There was no way she could *not* get it when he'd spoken so matter-of-factly. She'd never liked being bossed around and he knew that, which was why he'd never done it before. They had understood each other so well. And in the past they'd made decisions together, especially those that defied anyone trying to keep them apart, whether it was her family or his.

But this Bane was difficult to deal with. Didn't he understand it was not in his best interest to go anywhere with her?

Without saying anything else she walked away, leaving him standing in the middle of her living room while she went into the kitchen to check the locks on the back door. She needed time alone. Time away from him. His unexpected arrival had torpedoed her world.

As soon as she was out of his view, she leaned against the kitchen counter and released a sigh as blood pounded through her body. The man she'd loved was back after five years. One moment she'd been rushing around, trying to disappear, and the next she was opening the door for Bane. They had been separated for so long she'd thought… What?

That he wasn't going to come for her. But if she'd really thought that then why hadn't she gotten on with her life?

There were a lot of other whys she needed answered. Why had he decided to become a SEAL? Placing his life at risk with each mission? Better yet, why had he wanted to be involved in something that would keep him from her longer? And why had he shown up today of all days, when her normal life was turned upside down?

On top of everything else, he wanted to take over, as if he'd been here all the time. As if she didn't know what she was doing. As if she hadn't taken care of her own business for the past five years without him.

"Need help in there?" he called out.

Crystal gritted her teeth. "No, I've got this." She crossed the kitchen floor to check the locks on the back door.

What did he expect of her? Of them?

And of all things, within ten minutes of being inside her house they had kissed. A kiss she'd initiated. He might have made the first move by lowering his head, but she had been the one to make the connection. The memory of their mouths locking and tongues tasting had her feeling all hot inside. It had definitely proved they were still attracted to each other. That kiss had snatched all her senses and made her weak in the knees. She was certain she could still taste him on her lips.

She pushed a strand of hair back from her face and walked out of the kitchen and stopped in the living room. Bane's back was to her as he stood in front of her fireplace, staring at the framed photographs on her mantel. Except for one picture of her parents, all the rest were of him or of her and him. Most had been taken when they'd dated and the others when they'd eloped.

He turned around and their gazes met. She almost forgot to breathe. Was that heat in her stomach? And why was her heart beating a mile a minute? She drew in a deep breath wondering what he was thinking. Had he remembered each and every moment in those pictures? Did he remember how in love they'd been? Did he realize, married or not, they were different people now and needed to get to know each other all over again?

Should they?

Could they?

She broke eye contact to look at where her luggage had been. Then she glanced back at him. "You've taken my bags out already?"

"Yes."

"I didn't hear anything. Not even the door open."

A smile tugged at the corner of his lips. "That's the way a SEAL operates."

Oh, God. That smile was turning her insides to mush.

A part of her wanted to race across the room and throw herself in his arms like she used to do. But she couldn't. As far as she was concerned, too much stood in the way, keeping them apart.

Five

"I was sorry to hear about your dad, Crystal," Bane said, after easing the car onto the interstate. "Although the two of us never got along, he was still your father."

He felt her gaze on him, and he wanted to take his eyes off the road and look at her but decided not to. She was gorgeous and every time he gazed at her he felt desire seep into his bones. He needed to keep his self-control so he could convince her that he was coming with her when she left town.

"Thanks. Sending me away to live with Aunt Rachel widened the chasm between us but we made amends before he died…as best we could, considering everything." She was quiet for a moment before continuing, "He even told me he loved me, Bane. And I told him I loved him, as well. Dad leaving me the ranch was a shocker because he said he would be selling it to make sure I never had a reason to return to Denver. But after he died I found out he had left it to me. I wasn't aware he still owned it and assumed he'd sold it like he said he would do."

Bane had assumed Mr. Newsome had sold it, as well. Whenever he came home, Dillon had mentioned that the Newsome place was still deserted, but Bane had assumed the repairs needed around the place hadn't made it an easy sale. But there was something else he'd wanted to tell her. "It's admirable that you're working on your PhD, Crystal. For someone who claimed they hated school, that's quite an accomplishment."

"No big deal. Since I didn't have a life I decided to go to school full-time. All year-round. Nonstop. And when I took a placement test, there were classes I didn't have to take. My parents were happy that I was focusing on my studies again."

And not on him, he thought, and then asked her the question that had nagged at him since he'd first seen her tonight. "How did you do it?"

"Do what?"

"Keep the guys away. You're a very beautiful woman so I'm sure plenty tried hitting on you."

He glanced over and saw the compliment had made her blush. He meant it. She had the kind of beauty he'd never been able to explain with words.

"The guys stayed away because they thought I was gay."

Bane almost swerved into another lane. Placing a tight grip on the steering wheel, he glanced over at her again. "They thought what?"

"That I was gay. I didn't have a boyfriend so what else were they to think? The rumor started in college when I refused all their advances, even the guys on the football team, who were in such high demand on campus. They figured if I wasn't into them, then I must be into females."

"Why didn't you tell them you were a married woman?"

"What good would that have done with a husband who never came around?"

He could imagine how she'd felt knowing a rumor was circulating about her. One that was false.

"I thought about you every day, Crystal."

"Did you?"

He heard the skepticism in her tone. Did she not believe him? He was about to question her when she said, "This isn't the way to the airport, Bane."

"We aren't going to the airport."

"Not going to the airport? And just when did you decide that?"

"When I noticed we were being followed."

They were being followed?

Crystal glanced over at Bane. "How do you know?"

"Because although the driver is trying to be inconspicuous, that blue car has been tailing us for a while."

"Blue car?"

"Yes."

Her muscles trembled. "The car that followed me earlier was blue. But how would he know to follow you when we're not in my car?"

"Evidently someone saw us getting into mine."

The feel of goose bumps moved up her neck. "If the person saw us leave that means he knows where I live."

"Pretty much. But don't worry about it."

His calm unnerved her. How could he tell her not to worry? It was her home they were talking about. Whoever was after her would probably trash her house looking for something that wasn't there.

As if Bane read her mind, he said, "The reason I told you not to worry is because Flip is watching your place for me."

She stared over at him. "Someone you know is watching my house?"

He exited off the interstate. "Yes. David Holloway is one of my team members, who happens to live here in Dallas. His code name is Flipper because he's the best diver on the team. I contacted him when my plane landed to let him know I was in town. I called him again when I took out your luggage. I noticed a strange car in the driveway across the street."

Crystal was trying hard to keep up. He didn't live in her neighborhood, so how could he tell when some car was out of place? "How did you know it was a strange car?"

"I sat in front of your place for two hours waiting for you to come home and it wasn't parked there then," he said, turning another corner.

She noticed they were driving in an area she wasn't familiar with and wondered where in the heck they were going. "That's it? You figured it was out of place because it hadn't been there earlier?"

"That was enough. I'm trained to take stock of my surroundings."

Evidently, she thought. "And this Flipper guy went to my house after we left?"

"He got there just as we were leaving. Flip and his brothers will be keeping an eye on the place while you're gone."

She arched a brow. "Brothers?"

Bane looked over at her when he brought the car to a stop at a traffic light. "Yes, he has four. All SEALs. Your place is in good hands for now."

She was glad to hear that, but she couldn't help wishing the only hands her house was in were hers. Granted, she leased it rather than owned it, but it was the only house she'd lived in since moving to Dallas. When she noticed him glancing in the rearview mirror and grinning she asked, "What's so funny?"

"Ambush. I deliberately had the driver of the blue car follow us here and Flip's brothers were waiting."

"How did they know?"

"When Flip's brothers noticed I was being followed, they followed the blue car. Then one of Flip's brothers passed the blue car and got in the front of us to lead me off the interstate. The others went ahead and were ready to stop the guy at that intersection back there."

Nervousness danced around in her stomach. "So now we can continue to the airport?"

"No," he said, pulling the car into what appeared to be the parking lot of an abandoned warehouse. After parking the car and turning off the lights, he grabbed the mobile phone he'd placed on the dashboard. He glanced down at it for a minute before looking back at her. "There might be others looking for us there."

"Why would you think that?"

He pushed back in the seat to stretch out his legs. "Remember those two men who approached you about coming to work for Homeland Security?"

"Yes, what about them?"

"It seems *they* are the bad guys."

Bane wished he could kiss the shocked look right off Crystal's face, beginning at her eyes and moving slowly downward to her lips.

"That's not possible," she said. "I saw their credentials."

"Whatever credentials they had were faked. The department they claimed to work for under Homeland Security doesn't even exist."

"Are you sure?"

"Positive. I texted a copy of that business card to a friend at Homeland Security and a few minutes ago he verified what I'd suspected."

He watched her nibble her bottom lip and wished seeing her do so didn't have such an arousing effect on him. He had to stay focused. "The mystery of that note bothers me."

"How so?"

"Did the person who wrote it have your best interest at heart, or did he or she advise you to disappear for a reason, hoping when you did it would make it easier for those guys to find you?"

She lifted a brow. "You think someone at Seton Industries, the person who put that note in my desk, is in cahoots with those two guys?"

"You have to admit that's a strong possibility. You said someone broke into your locker. Who would have access to that area other than another employee?"

Bane didn't like this. He and Crystal should be at her place talking about their future and how they would get beyond the five years they'd spent apart.

He started to say something else when his mobile phone rang with Flipper's ringtone. He grabbed it off his dashboard. "What you got, Flip?"

"A bunch of crazies, man. No sooner than you and the blue car pull off, a black sedan pulled up and two goons got out. It was like watching a scene out of *Men in Black* with both of them dressed in black suits and all. Not sure how they planned to break into your wife's place but there's no doubt in my mind that was their intent. Until…"

Bane lifted a brow. "Until what?"

"Until they noticed the infrared beam Mark had leveled in the center of their chests. I guess knowing we could blow their guts out freaked them, especially since we could see them but they couldn't see us. I've never seen two men run back to their car so fast."

Bane shook his head. "You and your brothers are having fun with this, aren't you?"

"Yes, I guess you can say that."

Flip would. Although Bane hadn't met any of Flipper's brothers, he'd heard about them. They had inherited their thirst for excitement and danger from their father, who'd retired as a SEAL. "What about the driver of the blue car?"

"He got out and hauled ass. Left the car running. You said not to shoot anybody so my brothers let him go. Sure you don't want to involve the cops?"

"Not yet." Bane told Flipper about who he figured the men in black were.

"Impersonating government officials isn't good," Flipper said.

Bane had to agree. He glanced over at Crystal and saw she'd been trying to follow his conversation. "You're right. But at least you put the fear of God in them. However, don't be surprised if they come back."

"We'll be ready. Take care of yourself and your lady."

Bane nodded. "I intend to."

He had barely clicked off the phone when Crystal asked, "They broke into my house?"

Her shoulders sagged and he wished he had told Flipper it was okay for his brothers to shoot the bastards after all. He hated that she was going through this. "No, but that had been their intent. Flipper and his brother ran them off." There was no need telling her the method they'd used to do so. "They'll be back if they believe you have information or data stored somewhere in your house."

"I don't."

"I doubt they know that, and the first place they'll look is your computer."

"So what now? Where do we go?"

He checked his watch. It was late. "Find a hotel."

She narrowed her eyes. "Why?"

Not for the reason I want, he thought, again remembering the last time he'd been in a hotel room with her. The memory of her naked on that bed and all they'd been doing before the sheriff had shown up was what had kept him sane during dangerous missions.

"We're going to a hotel to sleep and put a plan of action in place, Crystal. As much as I want to make love to you, I've got a feeling the want isn't mutual."

Which meant it would be a long night.

Six

Crystal broke eye contact with Bane to look out the car window. Of course going to a hotel made sense, but still…

She'd seen the way he'd looked tonight, and she knew that look. Had even fantasized about it a number of times over the years. The memories of what followed that look always made her hot inside. But she wasn't sure she could trust herself alone with him. Her attraction to him was stronger than ever.

"Or we can stay here. Parked," he said, interrupting her thoughts.

She looked over at him. "All night?"

He gave her a smile that had heat swirling in her stomach. "Won't be anything new for us. In fact, it would be just like old times."

Why did he have to go there? Being in a parked car with him would definitely be like old times, but she was no longer a teenager who thought she could never get enough of Bane Westmoreland. She was a woman on the run with a husband she no longer knew. "We're too old for parked cars, Bane."

"I know. That's why I suggested a hotel."

She turned toward him. It was time to burst his bubble. "If we go to a hotel we get separate rooms."

"Why? We're married."

She tried to ignore the sexiness of his voice. And she definitely didn't need to notice the electricity sizzling in the air between them. Yes, they were married, but hadn't it already been established that things had changed? That *they* had changed? For starters, she was no longer a dreamer but a realist. And he was no longer the guy who claimed she would always be his love for life. Apparently the navy had booted her aside.

"Legally yes, we are married, but that's about all. Five years is a long time. We've already established that we're different people now. You may not like the new me, and for all I know I may not like the new you."

"I don't *like* you, Crystal. Never have. I fell in love with you the first time I saw you."

Now, why would he go and say something like that? If he really felt that way, wouldn't he have come back long before now? And why was she now remembering that day when she had been walking home from school, minding her own business, and he'd passed her on his motorcycle. He'd made a U-turn and the moment he'd stopped his bike, taken off his helmet and turned those hazel eyes on her, she'd been lost. So if he wanted to say that he'd fallen in love with her the moment he'd first seen her, she could certainly make that same claim about him.

But there were still those five years apart between them.

"Will it make you feel better if there were two beds in the room?"

Crystal took a breath. *Not really.* Even after being separated for five years she still found him captivating. Even now, tingles of awareness were invading her entire body. She couldn't look at any part of him without getting naughty thoughts. Being in close quarters with him all night would only be asking for trouble. She shook her head. "Doubt that will work, Bane."

He shrugged broad shoulders. "It will have to work, because I don't plan on letting you out of my sight until we get to the bottom of what's going on."

Her gaze narrowed on him. She was about to tell him that when it came to her he didn't make any decisions, when his cell phone went off again. He quickly reached for it. "Yes?"

Crystal studied his face. Whatever the caller was saying was making him angry. She could tell by the fire she saw forming in the depths of his eyes, the tightening of his jaw and the way his fingers gripped the phone. And she couldn't miss the abrasive tone of his voice.

She was certain the call was about her, which was why his gaze flicked to her time and time again. Gone was that hot and steamy I-can't-wait-to-get-some-of-you look in his eyes. It had been replaced with a look that clearly said that if pushed, Brisbane Westmoreland was liable to hurt somebody.

She pushed her hair back from her face and silently tapped her fingers on the car's console. She couldn't wait for the call to end so she could find out what was going on.

As soon as she heard him click off the phone she turned, ready to inquire, but he held up a finger to silence her. Already he had clicked someone else's number. He then quickly barked the words into his phone. "Code purple. Will enlighten everyone in a few."

As soon as he disconnected the call she asked, "What was that about?"

He didn't say anything for a long moment. He just stared at her as if he was trying to make up his mind about something.

She frowned and said, "And don't you dare think about not telling me what's going on, Bane."

Bane had contemplated doing just what she'd accused him of. But he knew he couldn't. Crystal was too intelligent, too quick to figure out things. Besides, she needed to know what they were up against and the caution they would have to take.

But more than anything, he needed her to trust him and to believe that he would never let anyone touch a single hair on her head.

"Bane?"

He took a deep breath. "First, give me your cell phone."

"My cell phone?"

"Yes."

She stared at him for a second, then went into her purse to retrieve her phone. He took it and then got out of the car. Throwing the phone on the pavement and ignoring her shocked gasp, he used his foot to stomp it into pieces.

"Are you crazy? What do you think you're doing?" she asked in outrage after getting out of the car to save her phone. Of course it was too late.

"I'm destroying your phone."

She placed her hands on her hips and glared up at him. "I see that. What I want to know is why."

"There's a chance a tracking device is on it."

"What are you talking about?"

"Things are more serious than I thought or what you might know, Crystal."

She stiffened her spine. "Well, I've got news for you. I don't know anything other than what I received in that note today and that my locker was tampered with and a blue car has been following me."

He glanced around. "Come on, let's get back inside the car. I'll tell you what I know."

She looked down at her smashed phone in disgust before going around the front of the SUV to get back inside. As soon as they had gotten inside the car, she said, "Tell me."

She touched his arm and a surge of desire rushed through him. Evidently it shone in his eyes because she quickly snatched her hand away. "Sorry."

He grabbed her hand, entwined their fingers and met her gaze. "Don't ever apologize for touching me."

Instead of a response, she nervously swiped her tongue across her bottom lip and his own tongue tingled, dying to mate with hers. Since he figured he couldn't kiss her anytime soon, he would tell her what she wanted to know. What she needed to know.

Ignoring the thud in his chest from holding her hand in his, he said, "My contact at Homeland Security did some more digging, even went so far as to tap into classified information. It seems you've been watched for a while."

She lifted a brow. "By who?"

"Mainly the government. They are aware of the research you're working on."

She shrugged. "I figured they were. Seton sent periodic reports to them as part of national security. Besides, the funding for my research was a grant subsidized by the government."

"Well, it seems the report got into the hands of someone it shouldn't have. To make a long story short, a plan was devised to kidnap you and the two other biochemists working on similar projects. They were to take the three of you to a lab underground somewhere and force you to work together and perfect a formula they'd use to their advantage."

Crystal shook her head. "That plan is preposterous."

Bane wished she wouldn't do that. Shake her head and make her hair fan across her face and place more emphasis on her dark eyes. Momentarily he lost his concentration. He couldn't afford any distractions now. There was too much at stake. "Whoever came up with the idea evidently didn't think so. And now you're the missing link."

She leaned back and frowned. "What do you mean I'm the missing link?"

His hand tightened on hers. "The other two chemists were abducted yesterday. One was leaving his home for work and the other chemist was leaving the gym around noon. The plan was to kidnap the three of you within hours of each other. However, their plan to grab you was foiled. But since they are determined to get their hands on the formula, they won't give up."

The spark in her eyes told him she clearly understood what he was saying. She was vital to these guys' plans and they didn't intend to fail. That spark also told him something else. She would like to see them try to grab her. He still had the ability to read her mind sometimes. She still had the spunk he'd always admired in her.

He swallowed hard when she eased her hand from his and broke eye contact to gaze out of the car's windshield. She was thinking, trying to come up with her own plan. One that didn't include him. More for his safety than anything else, he figured. And while she was spending that time thinking, he was spending his time feeling possessive, protective and proactive. If anyone thought they would grab her from him, then they didn't know Bane Westmoreland.

She looked back at him and because he had a feeling he knew what she was about to say, he cut her off before she could start. "I won't leave you unprotected, so forget it."

When she just continued to look at him, he added, "I need you to trust my ability to keep us safe."

A ripple of awareness floated between them and he tried to ignore it. Knowing he had her trust was more important at the moment.

"It's going to be hard, Bane," she said softly. "I've been on my own for a long time."

Five years. And not for the first time he wondered if he'd done the right thing in staying away. She had been his wife, yet he'd left her believing that living apart was the best thing for both of them. That they'd both needed to grow up and mature. Especially him. And he had. But what if he hadn't shown up today? What if she'd gotten kidnapped like those other two chemists? What if—

"I will trust you in this, Bane."

Her words intruded into his thoughts. He nodded. He was more than ready to be the husband she deserved, but he had to show her that she could trust him. Not just to keep her safe, but to build a life with her.

"So…" she said with a heavy sigh. "What now?"

A smile touched his lips. "Now we show them that together we're a force to reckon with."

A force to reckon with.

Crystal couldn't help but smile. That was how Sheriff Harper used to describe them. Nothing, not even the threat of jail time, could keep Bane from her or her from him. They'd been that fixated on each other.

Bane's cell phone signaled a text massage had come through and he grabbed the phone off the dashboard. Out the car window she saw they were parked in an unlit area. The only illumination was from the stars and moon overhead. Bane read the text with his full attention while her full attention was on him. She couldn't help but admire the way his wide shoulders fit his leather jacket and the casual way he sat in his seat. He had pushed the seat back to accommodate his long legs. And speaking of those long legs…

She loved how they looked bare, whenever he went swimming, and when they were covered in jeans, like they were now. Or when he rode his motorcycle or one of the horses from his family ranch. She'd known how to ride when she met him, but with his help, she had perfected the skill. He'd also taught her how to ride a motorcycle, shoot a gun and climb mountains. She had shared his love for the outdoors and they would spend time together outside whenever they could.

She swept her gaze over him from head to toe, thinking he was definitely sheer male perfection, the epitome of every woman's fantasy. It was only when he'd cleared his throat that she realized he had finished reading the text and had caught her ogling him.

"Yes? Did you say something?"

He chuckled. "No. Just wanted you to know that our ride will be here in a few minutes."

She lifted a brow. "Our ride?"

"Yes. We're changing vehicles. Chances are the people looking for you have already ID'd this one, so we need to swap it out."

"So who's bringing us another vehicle?" she asked,

glancing out the window. Other than a huge vacant building, the parking lot was empty.

"Flip's dad."

She frowned. "His dad?"

"Yes. He's an ex-SEAL."

Moments later Crystal heard the sound of another vehicle pull up and noted the driver had turned out the headlights. Bane looked over at her.

"That's our ride."

Seven

Bane gathered their belongings out of the SUV so they could place them in the trunk of the car Mr. Holloway had delivered.

Flip favored his father. Same shade of blue eyes and blond hair, although the older man had streaks of gray. It was easy to tell the man had been a SEAL. A commanding officer. He was still alert and wore an intense look on his face. And it was quite obvious that even at the age of sixty-five, he was in great shape physically. He was ready for anything and could probably still hold his own.

"Don't need to know where you're headed. The less people who know the better. Just be safe," the older man said, handing Bane the keys.

"I will, and thanks for everything, Mr. Holloway. I owe you and your family."

Mr. Holloway waved off his words. "No, you don't.

David told me and his brothers what happened during your last mission when you saved his life. Besides, any friend of my boys is a friend of mine. If you get in a pinch, just give us a call."

Bane didn't plan on getting in a pinch, but figured it was best to accept the offer just the same. "I will, and thanks."

Crystal was already seated inside the new car with her seat belt snapped in place. The older man followed Bane's gaze. "I understand that's your wife who you haven't seen in a while."

Bane nodded as he looked back at the man. "Yes, that's right."

"And she waited for you to come back for all that time?"

Bane nodded, remembering what Crystal had told him. She had kept her promise like he'd kept his. "Yes, she waited."

The older man smiled. "Then, you're a very lucky man. Take care of yourself and your wife."

His wife. He liked the sound of that. He was ready to finally claim her as his wife—but he had to keep her safe first. "I will. Again, thanks for all you and your sons have done. Are still doing." He knew Flip and his brothers would be keeping an eye on Crystal's place for a while.

"Don't mention it." Mr. Holloway gave him a supportive pat on the shoulder before getting into the SUV to drive off.

Bane quickly walked to the car, got inside, closed the door and locked it.

Crystal glanced over at him. "Where to now?"

He could hear the exhaustion in her voice. It was close to eleven. Probably past her bedtime. "A hotel, but not here in Dallas. Get some sleep. We'll be riding for a while."

"Okay."

She didn't ask where they were headed and as he started the ignition, he watched her lower her seat into a reclining position. He couldn't stop his appreciative gaze from sweeping over her, taking in how the denim molded to her hips and thighs. At eighteen she'd had a slender figure. Now she was amazingly curvy with a small waist. Forcing his eyes off her, he adjusted the car's temperature to a comfortable setting. It had gotten pretty cold outside.

As he pulled out of the parking lot he saw her starting to doze off. She looked just as beautiful with her eyes closed as she did when they were open. This was what he had dreamed about, what he had craved. The two of them together again.

Bane had driven a few miles and had made it to their first traffic light when he heard the sound of her chuckle. He glanced over at her and saw that her eyes were closed, yet a smile had formed on her lips. Was she having a dream or something? No sooner had that thought entered his mind than she opened her eyes, saw him looking at her and shifted upright in her seat. "What's wrong?" she asked.

"Nothing is wrong with me. You chuckled in your sleep just now."

A smile touched her lips. "I wasn't asleep. Just resting my eyes. And I got to thinking that this is getting to be the norm for us."

"What?"

"Being on the run. The last time we were together we eloped and were running from Sheriff Harper. Remember?"

"Yes, I remember." How could he forget? They had intentionally led everyone on a wild-goose chase thinking they were headed to Vegas when they'd married in Utah.

"Now we're on the run from heaven knows who."

"Doesn't matter. We're together again," he said.

She didn't say anything, and when the traffic light changed, he moved forward. After a while he figured she'd dozed off…or as she put it, had gone back to resting her eyes, when she asked, "For how long, Bane?"

Grateful for another traffic light, he brought the car to a stop and glanced over at her. "How long?"

"Yes, how long will we be together before you leave? Before I'm all alone again? You're a SEAL. That means you'll be gone a lot, right?"

He hesitated for a moment, giving thought to how he would respond. If she thought he would allow her to use his being a SEAL against him, against them, then she was definitely wrong. "Yes, I might be gone on missions whenever my CO calls."

"Your CO?"

"Commanding officer."

"And what if he calls now? You'll have to go, won't you?"

He tightened his grip on the steering wheel. Was she trying to insinuate that when it came to her he wasn't dependable? "Unless there's a national threat of some kind, it won't happen. I'm on military leave. My entire team is."

"Why?"

Now, this was where things got kind of sticky. He had to let her know that parts of his job weren't up for discussion, but he'd save that heart-to-heart conversation for later. Right now he merely said, "We were due one." That was the truth, although he wasn't telling her everything.

"You take risks. Put your life in danger."

Now it was his turn to chuckle.

"What's so funny?" she asked.

"I was just thinking that right now it's not my life that's in danger. I'd say we both have unusual occupations."

"There's nothing unusual about mine. I just happen to be working on research that's pretty sensitive."

He smiled, figuring that was one way of looking at it. "I guess you can say I work on things that are pretty sensitive, as well."

"There's no comparing what we do so don't even try, Bane."

Okay, so she had a point. But still, like he'd told her, he wasn't the one in danger now. "I'm well trained in what I do. Six months ago I made master sniper." That had been a major accomplishment for someone who was new on the team. But Bane's skills as a sharpshooter were what had caught the eye of his chief in boot camp. When he discovered Bane could hit a bull's-eye target with one eye closed, the man had put the thought of becoming a SEAL in Bane's head. The chief had made the captain aware of Bane's skill and the captain had pulled a lot of strings to get him into the naval academy.

"Master sniper? That doesn't surprise me. You were the one who taught me and Bailey how to shoot. And you always held your own against JoJo."

Yes, he had, he remembered proudly. And the Westmorelands sure knew how to shoot. He hadn't been surprised when he'd gotten home and everyone had told him about that grizzly bear Bailey had taken down in Alaska last month. And Crystal had been just as good a shot as Bailey. Only person better than those two was JoJo, who was now married to his brother Stern.

"And you want me to think your job isn't dangerous, Bane?"

"I admit it's dangerous, but it's also rewarding."

He heard her snort before she said, "I can see you think it's rewarding because it gives you an excuse to kick ass in the name of your country."

He laughed, and considering everything, it felt good to laugh. Especially with her. She always had a knack for bringing humor to any situation, although he was convinced what she'd just said hadn't been meant to be funny.

"You're making a career out of it, though, aren't you?"

Was she seriously asking or did she think she had everything figured out already? "Not sure. It's a decision we will have to make together."

"Oh, no, don't pull me into this, Bane. I won't let you blame me for making your life miserable."

Making his life miserable? What was she talking about? "Define what you mean."

"Gladly. I can see you as a SEAL, and a darn good one. What I don't see is you going into the office at Blue Ridge Management every day. You'd go stark crazy sitting behind a desk. And you'd never forgive me if you saw me as the reason you had to go work there."

She knew him well and was right about his not wanting to work at his family's company. Although his brothers—Dillon, Riley, Canyon and Stern—as well as his cousin Aidan were a perfect fit for Blue Ridge Land Management, he wasn't.

"I could join Jason, Derringer and Zane in their horse-training business," he said. Honestly, he couldn't imagine doing that, either. He didn't have the same love of horses that his brother and two cousins had.

"Bailey told me about their company the last time we talked."

"But she wouldn't tell you anything about me," he said in a gruff tone.

Crystal frowned at him. "That was the rule, Bane, and need I remind you that it was your idea." She broke eye contact with him to glance out the side window.

Yes, it had been. And it was time they talked about it. He suddenly felt the tension flowing in the car between them and didn't like it. "You know why I made my decision, Crystal."

"The decision to desert me?"

He quickly swerved off the road and whipped into the parking lot of what looked like an all-night truck stop. He pulled in between two tractor trailers, which concealed them from the view of anyone driving by. He brought the car to a stop and turned off the ignition.

"Are you trying to kill us, Bane?" she asked, trying to catch her breath.

Instead of answering, he unsnapped his seat belt and turned toward her. "I know you didn't just say that I deserted you."

Crystal could tell Bane was furious. She'd seen him angry before, but his anger had never been directed at her. Now it was. He was glaring at her to the point where the color of his eyes seemed to take on a Saint Patrick's Day green. But she had a feeling it was not her lucky day. Not backing down, she lifted her chin. "And what if I did?"

"Then, we need to talk."

"Too late for that. Nothing you say will make me change the way I feel."

"Then, you need to tell me why you feel that way."

He really didn't know? She would find the whole thing amusing but instead she wanted to cry. She had loved him so much. He had been her world. The yang to her yin. The one person she'd thought would never hurt her or let her down. But he had.

"Crystal?"

Fine, if he wanted to pretend he didn't know why she felt the way she did then she'd tell him. "I understand why you let my father send me away after we eloped but—"

"It was for the best. You were going to drop out of school, Crystal. I couldn't let you do that. I couldn't interfere with your education. It was November. All you had to do was make it to June to graduate."

"I know all that," she snapped. "So I let my father think he was calling the shots when he sent me to live with Aunt Rachel." The memory of that day still scorched her brain whenever she thought about it. "I figured I could put up with it because you would come and get me in June after I finished high school."

She saw the look in his eyes, knew the exact moment he figured out where she was going with this. She took a deep breath and plunged forward. "When you finally called me in January, I thought it was to tell me you couldn't live without me and had decided to come for me early. And that I could finish school back in Denver while we lived together in the cabin you had built for me. As man and wife."

"Dammit, Crystal, I know you. If I had come for you early, you would have come up with all kinds of excuses not to go back to school. Plus, I wouldn't have been able to support you. I wasn't old enough to claim my land or my trust fund. When I finished high school, my income came from working odd jobs. I walked off the job Dillon gave me at Blue Ridge at the end of the first week. I didn't like my supervisor telling me what to do. I was a Westmoreland. My family owned the damn company and I figured that gave me the right to do whatever the hell I wanted."

"I would have gone back to school, Bane. I promised you that I would. And as far as you not having a stable income, we would have made it work."

"You deserved more."

"I thought I deserved you. I was your wife."

"Why can't you understand that I needed to make something of myself?" he asked in an agitated tone. "As your husband, I owed that to you. Why can't you see that you deserved better than what I was at the time? I was an undisciplined man without any goals in life. I enjoyed defying authority."

"Those things didn't matter to me, Bane."

"They should have."

She narrowed her gaze at him. "Your family got to you, didn't they? Convinced you we didn't belong together. So you told no one we were married. No one but Bailey."

She watched him rub his hands down his face in frustration. As far as she was concerned, he had no right to be frustrated. She was the one he'd forgotten about when he'd chosen a career as a SEAL over her.

"You're wrong about my family, Crystal. They knew how much I loved you, but they saw what we refused to see. They knew we couldn't keep going the way we were headed. So I made a decision that I felt was best for us. And I want to believe that it was. Look at you now.

You not only finished high school, but you went on to college and got your master's degree and are working on your PhD. You were always smart and I was holding you back. Had I been selfish enough to claim you as my wife, I would have taken you to that cabin and made a pitiful life for you there. And it would have been just our luck if you'd gotten pregnant. What sort of future would our kid have had?"

She quickly turned her face away so he wouldn't see the tears in her eyes, but she hadn't been quick enough. Bane knew her. He could read her when she didn't want to be read. And she knew he was doing it now when he reached out, used his finger to turn her face back toward him. He studied her features intently.

Moments later he narrowed his gaze. "What's wrong? What aren't you telling me, Crystal?"

She knew she had to tell him. There was no reason to keep her secret any longer. "That day when you called and told me you had decided to go into the navy, you asked me if I was pregnant and I told you no."

He didn't say anything for a minute and a part of her knew he'd already guessed what she was about to say. "But you lied, didn't you? You *were* pregnant, weren't you?" he said in an accusing tone.

She didn't say anything for a long moment and then answered, "I didn't lie. When you asked, I wasn't pregnant…any longer. I had miscarried our baby, Bane. A few days before. The day you called was the day Aunt Rachel brought me home from the hospital."

Eight

Bane literally buckled over as if he'd been kicked in the gut. In a way he had. He drew in a deep breath as if doing so would ease the pain. It took a few moments for him to get himself together, and when he looked over at Crystal, she was sitting up straight in her car seat and the first thing he noticed were the tears streaming down her face.

His breath caught. He'd always been a sucker for tears…especially hers. But a part of him couldn't ignore that she'd been pregnant with their child and hadn't told him. Although he hadn't known where her parents had sent her, other than to live with some aunt, she had known how to reach him. And she hadn't even tried.

He recalled the days he had waited by the phone, figuring she would get around to contacting him somehow to let him know where she was. And when she hadn't, he'd figured her parents had probably talked the same sense into her that Dillon had talked into him. It was then and only then, that he had made the decision to follow Dillon's advice and make something of himself before going to claim her.

Trying to pull himself together and keep the anger out of his voice, he asked, "How could you not tell me?"

She looked over at him. "I didn't tell you because you'd already made up your mind about what you wanted to do."

"Dammit, Crystal, I only went into the navy because—"

"You thought I deserved more. You've said that."

A muscle in his jaw ticked. When had she developed such a damn attitude? He felt anger beginning to roll around in his stomach and he worked hard to control it because he'd never lost his temper with her. "Yes, I said it and I will keep on saying it."

Neither of them spoke for a while and the silence between them was thick, full of the tension he knew they both felt. "When did you know you were pregnant?" he finally asked her.

Tears reappeared in her eyes and she swiped them away. "That's the thing, Bane. I didn't know. I was late but I'd been late before, you know that. So I really didn't think anything about it. I was trying to fit into a new school and was focusing on my studies. It was nearing the end of January and I was looking forward to you coming to get me by June. Silly me, I figured even if you didn't know where I was that you would look for me until you found me.

"Anyway, I got really bad stomach pains one night. When I went to the bathroom I noticed I was bleeding profusely and woke up my aunt. She took me to the emergency room and after checking me over, the doctor told me I'd been pregnant and had lost the baby.

They kept me in the hospital overnight because I'd lost a lot of blood."

She swiped at her eyes again. "How can a woman be pregnant and not know it? How could I have carried your baby—our baby—in my body and not know it? That seemed so unfair, Bane. So unfair. The doctor was a nice woman. She said miscarriages weren't uncommon and usually happen within the early weeks of pregnancy. I figured I'd gotten pregnant on our wedding night so I was less than eight weeks along. She assured me it wasn't because of anything I did, and that my next pregnancy should go smoothly."

A deep pain sliced through Bane. It had been his baby as well, and at that moment he mourned for the loss of a life that would never be. A baby that had been a part of him and a part of her. He wanted to reach out and pull Crystal into his arms. Hold her. Share the pain. He felt he had every right to do that. But then he also felt she'd put an invisible wall between them and he would need to tear it down, piece by piece.

"I'm sorry about our baby," he said, meaning every word. It was true he'd gotten careless on their wedding night. It had been the first time they'd ever spent the entire night together, wrapped in each other's arms, and he had been so overjoyed he'd gotten carried away and hadn't used a condom. "I never deserted you, Crystal. I could no more do that than cut off my arm. Do you have any idea what I went through when we were apart?" he asked softly. "How much I suffered each day not knowing where you were?"

"I called you."

"When?"

"As soon as I could get away from my parents. They kept an eye on me during the entire plane trip to South

Carolina, but when the plane landed I went into the ladies' room and asked some woman to use her cell phone. It was around five hours after we parted."

Bane frowned. He hadn't gotten her call. But then he figured it out. "I know the reason why you couldn't reach me," he said, remembering that day. "I was at the cabin, and there's no phone reception out there."

He paused and then added, "After Sheriff Harper told me you'd left Denver, I stormed out of the police station and got into my truck and went to your parents' place and found it deserted. I drove around awhile, getting angrier by the minute. Somehow I ended up at the cabin and I stayed there for two whole days. On the third day Riley came and convinced me to go home with him."

She nodded. "That's probably why I still couldn't reach you the next night, either. I waited until everyone had gone to bed and sneaked downstairs and used my aunt's phone. I couldn't get you, which was just as well because Dad caught me trying. He got upset all over again, and said he knew I would try calling you and figured it was time for me to know the truth."

Bane frowned. "What truth?"

"That he and your brother Dillon had met when we first went missing and made a deal."

"What kind of a deal?"

"The two of them agreed that when we were found, Dillon would keep you away from me and Dad was to keep me away from you."

"That's a damn lie!" Bane said bluntly, feeling red-hot anger flow through him.

"How can you be so sure?"

Her question only infuriated him more. "First of all, Dil doesn't operate that way. Second, Dillon wasn't even in Denver when we eloped. He was somewhere in Wyoming following up on leads to learn more about my great-grandfather Raphel. Ramsey called Dil but he didn't get home until after we were found."

Bane angrily rubbed his hand over his head. "I can't believe you fell for what your dad said. You knew how much he despised the Westmorelands. Did you honestly think he and Dillon sat down and talked about anything?"

She lifted her chin. "I didn't want to believe it but…"

"But what?"

"I called you twice and you didn't take my calls."

"I didn't take them because I didn't get them," he said.

"Well, I didn't know that."

"You should have."

"Well, I didn't. And when you finally called me… two months later…it was to tell me you were going into the navy and it would be best for us to go our separate ways."

His frown deepened. "The reason it was two months later was because it took me that long to find out where you'd gone. And Bailey had to pickpocket your dad's phone to find out then. And as far as saying it was best for us to go our separate ways, that's *not* what I said."

"Pretty much sounded like it to me."

Had it? Frustrated, he leaned back in his seat, trying to recall what he'd said. Joining the navy had been a hard decision, but he'd made it after talking to his cousin Dare, who'd been in the marines. He'd also talked to Riley's best friend Pete. Pete's brother, Matthew, had joined the navy a few years before, and Pete had told Bane how much money Matthew had saved and how the military had trained him to work on aircrafts. Bane had figured going into the navy would not only teach him a skill but also get him out of Denver for a while. Being there without Crystal had made him miserable.

As he recalled all he'd said to her that day, he could see why she'd assumed it was a break-up call, considering the lie her father had told her. His only saving grace had been the promises he'd made to her that he would keep his wedding vows and would come back for her. That made him wonder…

"You think I deserted you. Did you not believe me when I told you that I would come for you once I made something of myself? And that I would keep my wedding vows?" he asked.

She glanced out the window before looking over at him. "Yes, at the time I believed you, although I sort of resented you for putting me out of your life even for a little while, for whatever the reason."

Her words took him by surprise. How could she think he would do such a thing? And she had said, "at the time I believed you." Did that mean at some point in time she had stopped believing? Now he wondered if he'd made a grave mistake not keeping the lines of communication open between them.

"I never put you out of my life and I had every intention of coming back for you. That never changed, Crystal. I thought about you every day. Sometimes every hour, minute and second. I longed for you. I went to bed every night needing you. There were days when I wasn't sure I could go on without you and wanted to give up. That's why I made sure Bailey didn't tell me where you were. Had I known, I would have given up for sure and come after you. And had you told me about your miscarriage, nothing would have stopped me from coming for you. Navy or no navy."

Unable to stop himself, he released his seat belt and reached out and unfastened hers before pulling her across the console to hold her in his arms.

Crystal buried her face in Bane's chest. She couldn't stop her tears from flowing and was surprised she had any tears left to shed. She'd figured she had gone through all of them when the doctor had broken the news to her that day that she had lost her baby. And then getting Bane's call, the same day she'd come home from the hospital, had been too much.

Her aunt Rachel had been wonderful and understanding, the one to hold Crystal each time she wept. And when she'd begged her aunt not to tell her parents about the baby, her aunt had given Crystal her word that she wouldn't. Whether it had been his intention or not, his phone call that day had made her feel as if he was turning his back on them and their love. Deserting her. It had been her aunt who had persuaded her to pull herself together and make decisions about her life…with or without Bane. So she had made them without him. But each time Bailey had called after that, a part of her had hoped it was Bane instead of his cousin. Then, when it had gotten too much for her to deal with, she'd had her number changed.

After listening to Bane's words just now, she remembered all too well how she had thought about him every day, sometimes every hour, minute and second, as well. He had longed for her, gone to bed needing her, and she had done the same for him. At one point she had been tempted to go to Denver to find him. But then she'd known he wouldn't be there and hadn't a clue where he would be. And at some point, how had he expected her not to doubt he still cared when he hadn't contacted her in five years?

"I'm fine now, Bane," she said, pushing back from him and wiping away her tears.

He looked down at her with an intense scrutiny that sent shivers through her body. "Are you, Crystal? Are you fine? Or will you hold it against me for wanting to give you the best of me?"

"I thought I already had the best of you, Bane. You didn't hear me complaining, did you?"

He didn't say anything and she used that time to scramble out of his lap and back into her seat. She stared out the window and could see from the reflection in the glass that he was staring at her.

Without turning back around to him, she asked, "Have you decided where we're going?"

He started the ignition. "Yes, I know where we're going."

Instead of telling her where, he pulled the car out of the parking spot and headed back to the main road.

Nine

"I'll take the bed closer to the door, Crystal," Bane said, dropping his luggage on the floor by the bed.

Instead of answering him, she merely nodded and rolled her luggage over to the other bed. Figuring that she had missed dinner, he'd stopped at an all-night diner to grab orders of chicken and waffles. Then he had driven four hours before finally settling at this hotel for the night. During that time she hadn't said one word to him, not a one. And her silence bothered the hell out of him. How could she be upset with him for wanting to give her a better life? How could she think he'd deserted her? It now seemed that not keeping in contact with her had been a mistake, but what she failed to understand was that she was his weakness.

She said she would have been satisfied with him just the way he was. Flaws and all. But she deserved more. Deserved better. No matter what she thought, he would

always believe that. He would admit he had been separated from her longer than he'd planned, and for that
he would take the blame. Five years was a long time to
expect her to put her life on hold. But that was just it.
He hadn't expected her to put her life on hold. He had
expected her to make something worthwhile out of it,
like he had been doing with his. And she had. She had
finished high school, earned both bachelor and master's
degrees and was now working on her PhD. All during
the five years he'd been gone. Why couldn't she understand that when he'd decided to go into the navy, he'd
believed that he was giving them both the chance to be
all that they could be, while knowing in the end they
would be together? They would always be together.
Although he'd loved her more than life, he had been
willing to make the sacrifice. Why hadn't she? Had he
been wrong to assume that no matter what, their love
would be strong enough to survive anything? Even a
long separation?

"I need to take a shower."

His heart nearly missed a beat upon hearing the
sound of her voice again. At least she was back to talking to him. "All right. I figure we'll check out after
breakfast and head south."

"South?"

"Yes, but that might change depending on any reports I get from people I have checking on a few things."

"Is that what that Code Purple was all about?"

So she had been listening. "Yes. That's a code for
my team. It means one of us is in trouble and all hands
on deck."

"Oh, I see."

She then opened her luggage and dismissed him
again. He placed his own travel bag on the bed and

opened it. The first thing he came to was the satchel containing all the cards and letters he'd saved for her over the years. He had looked forward to finally giving them to her. But now…

"You haven't heard anything else about my home, have you?"

He looked over at her. Although she'd taken several naps while he'd been driving, she still looked tired and exhausted. However, fatigued or not, to him she looked beautiful. "No. Flip has everything under control."

She nodded before gathering a few pieces of clothing under her arms and heading for the bathroom, closing the door behind her. Deciding he would really try hard to not let her attitude affect his, he took the satchel and walked over to place it on her bed. It was hers. He had kept it for her and had lived for years just waiting for the day when he could give it to her. He wouldn't let the bitterness she felt keep him from giving it to her.

His phone beeped, letting him know he'd received a text message. He glanced at his watch. It was two in the morning. He pulled his phone from his jacket and read Flip's message. All quiet here.

He texted back. Let's hope things stay that way.

He tried to ignore the sound of running water. He could just imagine Crystal stripping off her clothes for her shower. He would love being in there with her, taking pleasure in stepping beneath the spray of water with her, lathering her body and then making love to her. He would press her against the wall, lift her up so her legs encircled his waist and then he would ease inside her. How many nights had he lain in bed and fantasized of doing that very thing?

To take his mind off his need to make love to his wife, he glanced around the hotel room, checking things out in case they needed to make a quick get-away. This room was definitely a step up from the one they'd shared on their wedding night. He'd taken her to a nice enough hotel in Utah, but tonight's room was more spacious. The beds looked warm and inviting and the decor eye-catching.

Crystal had accompanied him inside when he'd booked the room. He could feel her body tense up beside him when he'd told the hotel clerk he wanted one room. He'd then heard her sigh of relief when he'd added that he wanted a room with two beds.

He lifted a brow when his cell phone went off and he recognized the ringtone. It was a call from home. Dillon. He pulled his phone out of his back pocket again. "Yes, Dil?"

"You didn't call to let us know you'd made it to Dallas. Is everything okay?"

How could he tell his brother that no, everything wasn't okay? "Yes, I made it to Dallas. Sorry, I didn't call but things got kind of crazy."

"Crazy? Were you able to find Crystal?"

"Yes, went straight to her place but…"

"But the warm, cozy, loving reception that you had expected isn't what you got."

He shook his head. His brother could say that again. "I figured we would have to work through some issues, but I didn't expect her to open the door with a loaded gun in her hand, her luggage packed and a bunch of bad guys trying to kidnap her."

There was a pause and then Dillon said, "I think you need to start from the beginning, Bane."

Crystal toweled herself off and tried not to think of the man on the other side of the door. The man she had shared her first kiss with. Her body. The man who had been her best friend. The one who'd defied her father's threat of jail time just to be with her. And the man who was her husband.

She glanced at herself in the mirror. Did Bane see the changes? Did he like what he saw? She couldn't attribute her figure to spending time in the gym or anything. The changes had just happened. One day she was thin and then the next, right after she'd turned twenty, the curves had come. The guys at college had noticed it, too, and tried causing problems. That was when she wished she'd had a wedding ring on her finger that would have deterred their interest. Instead, she had this, she thought, glancing at her locket.

She brought it to her lips and kissed it. It had been what had kept her sane over the past five years. She would look at it and think of Bane and remember the promise. Even on those days she hadn't wanted to remember or thought he'd possibly forgotten.

Her heart began thumping in her chest when she recalled how he had looked at her a few times tonight. The last had been when she'd told him she was going to take a shower. Nobody could turn her on quicker with a mere look than Brisbane Westmoreland. When he had leveled those hazel eyes on her, she could feel her skin get flushed. He was the only one in his family with that eye color, which he'd inherited from his great-grandmother.

She slid into a pair of sweats and then pulled on an oversize T-shirt. Looking into the mirror again, she nervously licked her lips as she thought of Bane. *What a man. What a man.* She even used her hands to fan herself. A number of times on the ride tonight she had pretended to be asleep just so she could study him without him knowing she was doing so. If his eyes weren't bad enough, he had an adorable set of lashes. Almost too long to be a man's. He had taken off his jacket and she couldn't help but appreciate the breadth of his shoulders. Bane was so well toned that it was obvious he lifted weights or something. SEALs were known to stay in shape. If it was required of them, then he was passing that test with flying colors.

Knowing she had spent more time than she needed in the bathroom, she gathered up her clothes in her arms and slowly opened the door. She saw Bane sitting at the desk staring at a laptop.

A laptop? How many times in the past when she'd tried showing him how to surf the net had he claimed he was technology challenged and just couldn't get the hang of using a computer? She sniffed the air and picked up the smell of coffee. Evidently he'd made a pot while she was taking a shower. Coffee was something she'd never acquired the taste for. She preferred hot chocolate or herbal tea.

Crystal cleared her throat. "I'm finished."

"Okay."

He didn't even turn around, but kept his back to her as he stared at the computer screen. Shoving the clothes she'd taken off earlier into the small travel laundry bag, she turned to put it into her luggage and saw the satchel on the bed. She picked it up. "You left something on my bed."

It was then that he looked over his shoulder at her and at that moment she wished he hadn't. Having those hazel eyes trained on her was sending spikes of desire up her spine. "I put it there. It's yours."

She lifted a brow. "Mine?"

"Yes." He turned back to his computer.

She glanced down at the satchel. "What's in it?"

Without turning back around to her he said, "Why don't you look inside and see?"

Bane returned his attention to the computer screen, or at least he pretended to. He'd known the moment Crystal had walked out of the bathroom. Hearing the door open had sent all kinds of arousing sensations through him. The last thing he needed was to glance over at her. His control wasn't all that great. Going without her for five years was playing havoc on his brain cells. Although he kept his eyes glued to the computer, he could hear her ease the leather strap of his satchel open. His wife never could resist her curiosity, and he'd known it.

"There are cards in here. A lot of cards and envelopes," he heard her say. Yet he still refused to turn around.

"Yes. I remembered your birthday, our wedding anniversary, Valentine's Day and Christmas every year. Although I couldn't mail them to you, I bought them anyway and tucked them inside my satchel. I knew one day, when we got back together again, I'd have them for you."

He could hear her shuffling through all those sealed envelopes. "There are letters in here, as well," she said.

"Yes. Most of the other guys had wives or significant others to write home to, but again, I couldn't do the same for you. So I got in the habit of writing you a letter whenever you weighed heavily on my mind." He hoped she could tell from the number of letters he'd written that she'd consumed his mind a lot of the time.

"Thanks, Bane. This is a surprise. I hadn't expected you to do this...for me."

This time he couldn't help but turn around when he said, "I would do just about anything for you, Crystal."

It never ceased to amaze him how easily he could make her blush. At least that hadn't changed. He could actually feel her gaze moving across his face as she held his stare and he wondered if she could feel him doing the same thing. Suddenly, she broke eye contact with him while drawing in a deep breath. He could see the nipples of her breasts pressing against the T-shirt she had on. It was supposed to fit large on her, but she still looked sexy as hell wearing it.

She glanced back down at the satchel. "I can't wait to read the cards and letters."

He nodded and then turned his attention back to his laptop just when the shrill ring of his mobile phone got his attention. He grabbed it off the desk. "This is Bane."

He nodded and his jaw tightened as he listened to what his friend was telling him. Nick Stover, who used to be a member of his SEAL team, had decided to leave the field and go work for Homeland Security when his wife gave birth to triplets. Bane appreciated his friend's inside scoop. But what he was telling him now had his temper rising.

When Nick was done, Bane said, "Okay. Thanks for letting me know so I can get in touch with Flip."

He clicked off the phone and immediately called Flipper. There was no doubt Crystal had stopped whatever she was doing to listen to his conversation. He would have to tell her what was going on. But first, he had a question for her. He turned around and saw her staring at him.

"Is there anything in your home you want saved?"

She frowned. "What?"

"I asked if there's anything in your house that you want to save."

He could tell by the look on Crystal's face that she was trying to figure out why he would ask her such a thing. Before he could explain himself further, he heard Flip pick up the phone. "This is Bane." He knew Nick had already relayed the same information to Flip that he'd just told him.

"Yes, there are some things she wants to save." Since Crystal hadn't answered his question, just continued to look at him like he'd grown a set of horns or something, he said to Flip, "I know for certain she'll want to save all the photographs on her fireplace mantel."

Crystal crossed the room to stand next to him. "Hold it! Why are you telling him that, Bane? What's happening to my house?"

Bane spoke into the phone. "I'll call you back in a sec, Flip." He then clicked off the phone and placed it back on the desk.

He regretted having to answer her question, but knew he had to. "In a couple of hours or so, your house will get burned down to the ground."

Ten

Crystal felt the room spinning and wondered if she was about to fall flat on her face. Bane was obviously wondering the same thing because he was out of his chair in a flash and had grabbed hold of her arm to steady her.

"I think you need to sit down, Crystal," he said, trying to ease her down into the chair he'd just vacated.

"No. I won't sit down," she said, telling herself she'd just imagined what he'd said about her house burning down. There was no way he could have said that. But all it took was to see the concerned look on his face to know she hadn't imagined anything at all.

"Why would anyone want to burn my house down?" She just couldn't fathom such a thing.

"Actually, it's not just anyone. The order came from Homeland Security."

Shock took over her features. "Homeland Security? Why would the government do something like that?"

"I told you about those other two chemists who were kidnapped. And now the kidnappers are trying to get their hands on you. It's a serious situation, Crystal, and you're talking about national security. As long as there's a possibility something is in your house connected to the project you're working on, then—"

"But I told you there wasn't. I never bring work home."

"The Department of Homeland Security can't take any chances. Without you the bad guys will try to piece together what they need, and DHS can't let them do that."

"Fine. Get them on the phone."

"Get who on the phone?"

"Someone at Homeland Security. Evidently you have their number. If they don't believe you, then maybe they will believe me."

"I can't do that."

"Why not?"

There was a moment of silence before he said, "Because right now we can't trust anyone. Not even Homeland Security. At least until they find out what's going on. Evidently, there's a mole within the organization. Otherwise, how else would your project come under such close scrutiny?"

He moved around her to the cabinet that held the coffeepot, poured a cup and took a sip. He leaned back against the cabinet and added, "Homeland Security has no idea where you are. All they know is the bad guys haven't nabbed you yet because they're still trying to find you. Obviously, the person who sent you that note is one of the good guys and figured out what was about to go down, which is why he or she told you to disappear. For all they know, that's what you did."

He took another sip of his coffee. "So beside those framed photographs over your fireplace, is there anything else in your house you want to save?"

Crystal drew in a deep breath. Technically, it wasn't her house since she was leasing it. But it was where she'd made a home for the past year, putting her own signature on it with the decorating she'd done. What she'd liked most about her home was the screened-in patio. She could sit out there for hours and read. That made her realize that all the furniture she did own would probably be destroyed because it was too big to move out without attracting attention. The impact of that made her slide down in the chair. It was still warm from when Bane had sat in it.

"We don't have much time, Crystal."

She sat upright, glad she'd already packed her marriage license and placed it inside the photo album she'd kept for Bane. "My family Bible," she said with resolve. "It's in the nightstand drawer. And there are more pictures in a small trunk under my bed."

"Okay."

He returned to the desk and when he reached for his phone, his arm brushed against hers. The feel of their skin coming into contact made her draw in a sharp breath. He looked at her, holding her gaze for a minute, and she knew he'd felt the sizzle, as well. He continued to hold her gaze, letting her know she had his full attention while he talked on the phone. "Flip, check the nightstand drawer next to her bed and grab her family Bible. And there's a small trunk under her bed."

Moments later he clicked off the phone. "I see you haven't outgrown that."

"What?"

"Blushing."

"Was I supposed to outgrow it?"

He smiled. "I have no complaints. In fact I've always enjoyed watching you blush."

She tried to give him a small smile, but in all honesty, she had very little to smile about right now.

"I didn't ask if you wanted a cup of coffee. Since you didn't order a cup at that diner earlier tonight, I figured you're still not a coffee drinker."

She nodded. "And I see that you still are."

"Yep."

She frowned and broke eye contact with him to look at the cup he held in his hand. "Too much caffeine isn't good for you."

He chuckled. "So you've always said."

"And so I know. Especially now that I've become a biochemist. It's not good for your body."

Why had she said that? And why after saying it did her gaze automatically move up and down his solid frame? Bane Westmoreland was so overwhelmingly sexy. He'd always possessed a magnetism that could draw her in. The man was such a perfect hunk of carved mahogany, it was a crying shame.

She moved her gaze off his body and up to his face, thinking his facial hair gave him a sexier look. He gave her a roguish smile and she could feel her cheeks flush. "Looking at me like that can get you in a lot of trouble, Crystal Gayle," he murmured in a deep husky voice.

He was standing close, so close she could inhale his scent. Manly. Deliciously provocative. "Then, I won't look at you," she said, cutting her eyes elsewhere. Namely to her bed and all the cards and letters she'd pulled out of the satchel. "I don't need any more trouble than I'm already in. It's pretty bad when you have the government burning down your house. I'd like to see how they explain their actions to the insurance company."

"They won't have to. They will handle it in a way that makes it look like an electrical fire or something. It definitely won't appear intentional."

She lifted her chin. "Still, I don't like it." She eased up out of the chair, assuming he would step back and give her space. He didn't, and it brought their bodies within touching distance of each other.

"You look good in your T-shirt and sweats, by the way," he said softly. They were standing so close the heat of his words seemed to fan across her face.

She looked down at herself, thinking he had to be kidding. Both garments were old and ratty looking, but she remembered her manners and glanced up and said, "Thank you."

The moment she looked into his face, she wished she hadn't. The intense desire in the hazel eyes staring back at her was so profoundly sensual she felt a tug in the middle of her stomach.

Setting his coffee cup down, he moved closer. Before she knew what he was doing he reached out and placed his hands at her waist. But he didn't stop there. As he inched his hands upward and gently caressed the curve of her body, he said, "I can't get used to these. Where did all these curves come from?"

She shrugged. "Wish I knew. I just woke up one morning and they were there." Why wasn't she telling him to keep his hands to himself? Why did his touch feel so good?

He chuckled. "Only you would think these curves were an overnight thing."

Although a part of her wished he didn't do that, she kind of liked the way he would subtly remind her that they had a past. And she needed that because at times he seemed like such a stranger to her.

"Well," she said, making a move to scoot around him. But he held tight to her waist and when he began lowering his head, she could just imagine how their tongues would mingle.

The moment he took hold of her mouth, his lips ground against hers and she was powerless to do anything but kiss him back.

Bane loved kissing Crystal. Always had and figured he always would. Their kisses weren't just hot, they were flaming red-hot, and in no time he was shivering with desire. And like in the past, he had to taper his lust; otherwise he would have her spread out on that bed in no time. And he doubted she was ready for that just yet.

So he enjoyed this. The way she was provocatively returning his kiss. The way his mouth seemed to be in sync with hers, feeding off hers with a hunger he felt in every part of his body. As when he'd kissed her earlier tonight, it felt as if he'd finally come home to the woman he loved. He had been hungry for her taste for five years. He'd tried to remember just how delicious it was and knew his memories hadn't come close. The intensity was clouding his mind and he could tell she wasn't holding back, pouring everything into the kiss like he was doing.

She suddenly pulled her mouth away and drew in a deep breath. When she licked her bottom lip, he was tempted to kiss her again, take his own tongue and lick her lips.

"We should not have done that, Bane," she said softly. And the look of distress in her eyes touched him.

"Don't see why not. You're my wife."

"I don't feel like your wife."

"That can be remedied, sweetheart," he said in a provocative drawl.

"I know," she said, looking at him with a serious expression. "But sleeping with you won't make me feel as if I know you any better. I need time, Bane. I don't need you to rush me into anything."

"I won't."

She crossed her arms over her chest and he wished she hadn't done that when he saw her nipples pressed against her T-shirt. "Then, what was that kiss about just now?"

He smiled. "Passion. You can't deny you felt it. I want you so much, Crystal." He saw uneasiness line her pupils. "Relax, baby. You will let me know when you're ready. One day you will realize that no matter how long it's been, I'm still your husband."

She shook her head. "But we haven't seen each other in five years."

He frowned. Was she saying that because she wasn't sure she still loved him after all this time? He refused to believe that. "Trust me, Crystal," he heard himself say softly. "After reading all my cards and letters to you, I have no doubt you'll see what I mean."

His cell phone rang and when he turned to pick it up, she used that time to quickly move away from him and back to the bed.

"This is Bane." He nodded a few times. "Okay, Flip. Thanks and I owe you." He then clicked off the phone.

He looked over at her. "That was Flip. He wanted to let me know he collected all the items you wanted saved. And by the way. Did you know your house was bugged?"

* * *

Crystal was experiencing one shock after another. First Bane returned after five years. Then she was on the run from men who wanted to kidnap her. Then the government wanted to burn her house down. And now she was being told it was bugged?

"That's not possible. Nobody I work with has ever been invited to my home. They consider me a recluse."

Bane nodded. "Where did the stuffed giraffe come from?"

She frowned. "The stuffed giraffe?"

"Yes."

She thought for a minute. "It was a gift from one of my coworkers, who took a trip to South Africa earlier this year. She brought everyone souvenirs back."

"Who was this generous person?"

"A biochemist by the name of Jasmine Ross."

"Well, yours was given to you with a purpose. Flip saw it on your dresser and figured it would be something you'd want to keep, as well. When his sensor went off he knew it contained an audio bugging device. He proved his suspicions true when he gutted it. I guess someone thought they could catch you saying something about your research on the phone or something."

"Well, they were wrong." Things were getting crazier by the minute and she couldn't believe it. "Were there others?"

Bane shook his head. "Flip and his brothers combed the rest of the house and didn't detect anything. Now you see why Homeland Security wants to burn it down to the ground?"

No, she still didn't see it. "They could have found another way."

"Evidently not."

She didn't like Bane's attitude, as if he was perfectly fine with someone torching the place where she lived. Turning her back to him, she angrily began shoving all the cards and envelopes back into the satchel. She was in no mood to read anything now. All she wanted to do was get into bed and rest her brain.

"I'll take my shower now."

"Fine." Crystal was tempted to turn around but refused to do so. She planned to be in bed and dead asleep by the time he came out of the bathroom.

When she heard the bathroom door close she released a deep sigh. How were she and Bane going to share a hotel room without…

She shook her head. The thought of them making love was driving her nuts. All of a sudden the memories of their last time together were taking hold of her. They had been happy. They had just gotten married and thought the future was theirs to grab and keep.

When she heard the water from his shower she couldn't help but recall when they had showered together. All the things he had taught her to do. Bane had been the best teacher, and he'd always been easy and gentle with her.

As she drew the bedcovers back and then slid beneath them, she tried to not think of Bane. Instead, she thought of her house and how at that very minute it could be going up in flames.

Eleven

Twenty minutes later Bane walked out of the bathroom and glanced over at the bed where Crystal lay sleeping. Or was she? He found it amusing that she was pretending to be asleep while checking out his bare chest and the way his sweats rode low on his hips. He had no problem with her ogling him; she could even touch him if she liked. Better yet, he would love for her to invite him to her bed. He would love to slide between the sheets with her.

Intending to give her more to look at, he decided he might as well get on the floor and do his daily exercises. He'd begin with push-ups after a five-minute flex routine that included bending to touch his toes. Maybe a vigorous workout would work out all the desire that was overtaking his senses and at the same time arouse her enough that she would want him to make love to her. It was worth a try.

Less than thirty minutes into his exercises he wondered if she realized her breathing had changed. He most certainly had noticed. Now he was off the floor and running in place. His sweats had ridden even lower on his hips and his bare chest was wet from sweat. Now for a few crunches.

"What you're doing doesn't make sense, Bane."

He forced himself not to smile. "I thought you were asleep," he said, lying, when he knew she'd been peeking through a slightly closed eye at him.

"How could I sleep with all that racket you're making down there on the floor?"

"Sorry if I disturbed you. And what doesn't make sense?"

"For a person to take a shower only to get all sweaty again."

He chuckled. "I'll take another shower. No problem."

She had shifted in bed to lie on her side and look over at him. "You did three hundred push-ups. Who does that?"

"A SEAL who needs to stay in shape." Evidently she'd been counting right along with him but had missed a few. "And I did three hundred and twenty-five." He wondered where her concentration had been when he'd done the other twenty-five.

"Whatever. I just hope that's the last of it."

"For tonight. I do the same thing each morning. But I'll try to be a little quieter so as not to disturb you."

The sound of him exercising wasn't what was disturbing her, Crystal thought, trying not to let her gaze roam all over Bane. Jeez. How could sweat look so good on a man? It was such a turn-on. All that testosterone being worked up like that. Rippling muscles. Bulging biceps. Firm abs. Mercy! She'd gone without sex for five years and it had never bothered her before. But now it did. Only because the man here with her now was Bane.

She had pretended to be asleep when he'd come out of the bathroom. But seeing him bare chested and wearing sweats was just too much. She had tried closing her eyes and holding them shut. Tight. But the sounds of him grunting sent all kinds of fantasies through her mind and she'd begun peeking. And definitely getting an eyeful. If she didn't know better she'd think he'd deliberately gone after her attention.

"I've worked up an appetite. Do you want something?"

She had worked up an appetite watching him as well, but it wasn't for food. She definitely wanted something, but it was something she'd best do without—it was just too soon since Bane had come for her, and she needed to stay focused until she was out of danger. "No thanks. I'm still full from those waffles and chicken we ate earlier. But you can order room service if you like. The hotel clerk did say the kitchen was open twenty-four hours." But who wanted to eat at four in the morning?

He glanced at the clock on the nightstand separating the beds. "I think I'll order something up. Nothing heavy. If I do it now, it will probably arrive by the time I get out of the shower. But if they come while I'm in the shower, don't open the door for anyone. They can wait a few minutes. If they can't, then they can take it back to the kitchen."

She wondered if all that was necessary. But then all she had to remember was her house was probably getting burned to the ground about now. "Fine." She hoped by the time he got out of the shower for a second time that night she would be asleep for real. But that hadn't worked during his first shower—the sound of running water and picturing him naked beneath that water had kept her awake.

She watched as he moved over to the desk and picked up the phone to order a steak dinner with potatoes. At four in the morning? She lifted a brow. Hadn't he said nothing heavy? If that wasn't heavy then what was his definition?

And speaking of heavy...

Why had her breathing suddenly gone that way? Could it be because her gaze had now landed on the perspiration dripping off his hard chest, past those chiseled muscles, and making a path toward the waistband of his sweats? And why did the thought of licking it before the drops of sweat could disappear beneath the waistband actually appeal to her?

He had grabbed more clothes and was about to go into the bathroom when his cell phone rang. "That's Nick," Bane said, turning and heading back toward the desk.

Crystal felt a tightening of her stomach. It seemed that whenever this guy Nick called, he was the bearer of bad news. "Maybe they changed their minds about burning down my house."

The look Bane gave her all but said not to count on it. "Yes, Nick?"

She saw the tightening of Bane's jaw and the dark and stormy look in his eyes. And when he said, "Damn" three times she felt uneasy and suspected the news wasn't good.

"Thanks for letting me know. We're on the road again. Contact Viper. He'll know what to do."

Crystal had eased up on the side of the bed. As soon

as he clicked off the phone she was about to ask what was wrong when he asked, "Where's your jacket?"

She lifted a brow. "My jacket?"

"Yes."

"Hanging up in the closet. Why?"

"It has a tracking device on it."

"What!"

Already Bane had reached the closet and jerked her jacket off the hanger. She watched in horror as he took a pocketknife and ripped through a seam. "Bingo." He pulled out a small item that looked like a gold button.

She drew in a deep breath and met Bane's gaze when he looked over at her. "Does that mean…"

"Yes. Someone has been keeping up with our whereabouts all this time, and chances are they know we're here."

"But how did someone get my jacket?"

"Probably at work. Do you keep it on during the day?"

"No. I always take it off, hang it up and put on my lab coat."

He nodded. "Then, you have your answer. And I suspect the person who put this tracker in your coat is the same person who gave you the stuffed giraffe." He rubbed his hands down his face. "Come on. Let's pack up and get the hell out of here."

"But what about your food? Your shower?"

"I'll stop somewhere later to grab something, but for now we need to put as much distance between us and this place as we can. As for my shower, you'll just have to put up with sharing a car with a musky man."

"I can handle it." She was already on her feet and pulling out her luggage. She considered how Bane hadn't expected all this drama when he'd come looking for her. "I'm sorry, Bane." She glanced over at him and saw he was doing likewise with his luggage.

He paused in tossing items into his duffel bag and looked back at her. "For what?"

"For being the cause of so much trouble. I guess you hadn't figured on all of this."

"No, but it doesn't matter, Crystal. You're my wife, and I will protect you with my life if it came to that."

She shivered at the thought and hoped it didn't. But still, the words he'd just spoken had a profound impact on her. She pushed several locks of hair back from her face to focus on Bane as he continued to pack. Surprisingly, it wasn't Bane's sexiness that was wearing her down, but his ability to still want her in spite of everything.

"Ready?"

She nodded. "Yes."

"We need to be aware of our surroundings more than ever and make sure we aren't being tailed. There's a pretty good chance someone is sitting and waiting for us in the parking lot, which is why I'm putting plan B in place."

"What's plan B?"

"You'll see."

After Bane checked up and down the hallway, they left the hotel room, moving quickly toward the stairwell instead of the elevator. She followed his lead and didn't ask any questions. And when they came to a locked door that led to the courtyard, he used what looked like a knitting needle to pick the lock.

"Still doing that, I see," she said.

He shrugged. "Not as much as I used to."

In no time the lock gave way and she saw they were in the courtyard, which was located on the other side of the building from the parking lot. "How will we get to our car?"

"We won't."

She was about to ask what he meant when suddenly a white SUV pulled up, tailed by a dark sedan. Since Bane didn't seemed alarmed by the two vehicles, she figured he knew the occupants. When the door to the SUV opened and a big bruiser of a man got out, she saw Bane's lips ease into a smile.

When the man came to a stop in front of them, Bane said. "Crystal, I want you to meet Gavin Blake, better known as Viper. Another one of my teammates."

Bane wasn't bothered by the way Viper was checking out Crystal. He was curious, as most of his teammates were. They had wondered what kind of woman could keep a man faithful to a wife he hadn't seen in five years. Bane could tell that Viper, a known ladies' man, was in awe, if his stare was anything to go by.

Moments later, Viper switched his intense gaze from Crystal back to Bane. "She's beautiful, Bane."

"You forgot to check out my teeth," Crystal said, frowning.

Viper let out a deep laugh. "And she has a good sense of humor," he added. "I like that. She's definitely a keeper."

"Yes, she is." Bane had known that the first day he'd met Crystal. "Did you check out the parking lot?"

Viper nodded. "Yes, and it was just like you figured. A car with two men inside is parked beside the one you were driving. I phoned in the description and the license plates to Nick, and according to him, it's the same vehicle an eyewitness saw in the area when one of the other biochemists was kidnapped. So you did the right thing by having Nick call me."

Viper nodded toward the SUV. "Here's your new ride. Chances are those guys don't know you're onto them. They probably planned to snatch your wife the minute you checked out of the hotel tomorrow morning."

"Like hell."

"That's what I said," Viper said, chuckling. "I figured they don't have a clue who they're messing with. I'm going to keep those guys busy while you and your lady get a head start. This ought to be fun."

Bane frowned. "Don't enjoy yourself too much."

"I won't. I brought my marine cousin with me to make sure I stay out of trouble. At least as much as I can," Viper said, handing Bane the keys to the SUV. "Do you have a plan from here?"

Bane nodded. "Yes. My brother is calling in family members with connections to law enforcement."

Viper nodded. "That's good. There's nothing like family backing you when you're in a pinch." He then turned his attention back to Crystal and smiled. "It was nice finally getting to meet you. You have a good man here. And, Bane, if you need my help again, just call." With those words, Viper walked away and got inside the dark sedan before the driver pulled off.

Bane watched him leave before turning his attention to Crystal. "Come on, let's get the hell out of here before those guys sitting in the parking lot figure out we're one up on them." He opened the trunk and placed their luggage inside.

"Do you want me to drive, Bane? You have to be tired."

He smiled when he opened the SUV's door for her to

get in. What he was enduring was nothing compared to missions he and his teammates typically encountered. "No, I'm fine. We're together, and that's all that matters to me."

We're together, and that's all that matters to me.

A half hour later, as Bane took the interstate with a remarkable amount of ease for a man who hadn't gotten much rest, Crystal couldn't help but continue to recall those words. Shouldn't that be all that mattered to her, as well? The one thing she knew for certain was that she was glad he was here with her. No telling what her fate would be if he wasn't. She wouldn't have known where to go or what to do. Her plans had been to head for the Bahamas, not knowing someone would have been there, waiting for her at the airport to grab her before she could get on the plane.

But Bane had known. Through his intricate network of teammates, he'd been able to stay one step ahead of the bad guys. What had gone down at the hotel was too close for comfort. She would never have known a tracker had been sewn inside her jacket.

She was surprised Jasmine Ross was involved. The woman was a few years older than she and seemed perky enough. Jasmine had even tried to befriend her a few times, but Crystal hadn't been ready to become the woman's friend. She hadn't thought anything about the stuffed giraffe, since Jasmine had given everyone working in the lab a gift. And as for her jacket, Crystal hung it on the coatrack like everyone else, so Jasmine had access to it. She could have sneaked off with it and placed a tracker inside without being detected.

Crystal wondered what would entice a person to be on the wrong side of the law. What was in it for the woman? Crystal didn't want to think about what those other two chemists were enduring against their will. They'd been separated from their families and probably didn't know if anyone would find and rescue them. Were they even still in this country?

"You okay over there?"

She glanced at Bane. As far as she was concerned, she should be asking him that. At least she'd gotten a couple hours of sleep earlier tonight. "Yes, I'm fine. What about you?"

He chuckled. "I'm great."

To a degree, she believed him. Bane was definitely in his element. This was a different Bane. More in control. Disciplined. Not impulsive, irresponsible or reckless. The Bane she remembered would have gone out to the parking lot to confront those guys, ready to kick ass. The old Bane had an attitude and detested anyone telling him what to do, especially when it involved her. That was why he'd butted heads with her father countless times and defied the law.

And defied his family. She recalled how often his brother Dillon had sat them down and talked to them, urging her to stay in school. He had lectured them to stop acting impulsively and to start thinking of someone other than themselves.

Deciding to continue the conversation with the goal of keeping him awake, she asked, "So what's going on with your family? Are your brothers and cousins still single?"

His laugh was rich and filled the car's interior. The sound filled her as well, and she wondered how the deep throatiness of his voice could do that to her. "Not hardly. In fact, after Valentine's Day when Bailey ties the knot, that will take care of everyone."

"Bailey is getting married?"

"Yes, and she's moving to Alaska. Her husband-to-be owns a huge spread on an island there."

Crystal was shocked. "Bailey always swore that she would never marry and move away."

"Well, evidently Walker Rafferty was able to change her mind about that. I got a chance to meet him over Thanksgiving. A pretty nice guy. Ex-marine."

The man must really be something if Bane approved of him. As the youngest two Westmorelands, Bane and Bailey had been close growing up. They'd done a lot of things together. Even got into trouble. "I'm happy for her."

"So am I."

She then listened as he brought her up-to-date on his other siblings and cousins and the women and men they had married. His cousins Zane and Derringer, and his brother Riley were also shockers. She remembered they had reputations around Denver as being ladies' men.

She shifted to get comfortable in her seat as Bane continued to fill her in on his family. She loved hearing the sound of his voice and could tell he was proud of everyone in the Westmoreland family. He also told her about more cousins his family had tracked down in Alaska with the last name of Outlaw.

As she continued to listen to him, she didn't think to question where they were headed. Like he'd said earlier, they were together, and that was all that mattered. She felt safe with him, and at the moment she couldn't imagine being anyplace else.

Twelve

"I'm taking the bed closer to the door again."

"All right."

Bane tossed his duffel bag on the bed and glanced around the hotel room. This one was roomier than the last and the bed looked inviting as hell. The first thing he intended to do was take a shower. He had driven for nine hours and he had to hand it to Crystal, she had tried keeping him company by engaging him in conversation about his family and his job as a SEAL. He had explained that due to the highly classified nature of what he did, there was a lot about his missions he couldn't divulge. She understood and seemed fascinated by what he had been able to tell her.

He glanced over at her and could tell she was exhausted, as well. It was daylight outside but he figured as long as they kept the curtains drawn the room would have the effect of nighttime. Right now he doubted his body cared that it was just two in the afternoon. As long as he could get a little sleep, he would be ready for the next phase of his mission to keep his wife safe.

He turned to place his cell phone on the night-stand. He'd received text messages from Flip letting them know Crystal's house had been burned down to the ground, which probably infuriated those thinking she had data stored somewhere inside it. And then Viper had texted to say that before turning those guys in the parking lot over to Homeland Security, he and his cousin had given them something to think about. Bane hadn't asked for details, thinking it was best not to know. But he figured the men wanting Crystal had to be insanely mad when their plans were derailed time and time again. Hopefully, if those guys were the same ones who had kidnapped the other two chemists, it would be just a matter of time before they were found.

"Do you want me to order you something to eat? That way when you get out of the shower your food will be here," Crystal asked.

He glanced back over at her. "That would be nice. Thanks."

"Anything in particular you want?"

It was close to the tip of his tongue to answer and say, *Yes, you. You are what I want*. Instead, he said, "Whatever looks good. I'm game." Grabbing some fresh clothes out of the duffel bag, he went into the bathroom and closed the door behind him. And then he leaned against it and drew in a deep breath.

Needing a shower was just an excuse. What he really needed was breathing space away from Crystal. Sharing a room with her, being in close proximity to her after all this time was playing havoc on every part of his body. Every time he looked at her he was filled with desire

so deep, the essence of it seemed to drench his pores.
And he couldn't ignore the sensations he felt knowing
they were finally together after being apart for so long.

The sound of his phone alerted him to a text message
from Nick. Pulling the phone out of his back pocket, he
quickly read the lengthy text before placing his phone
on the vanity.

Stripping off his clothes, he stepped into the shower.
A cold one. And he didn't so much as flinch when
the icy cold water bore down on his skin. Instead, he
growled, sounding like a male calling out for a mate he
wanted but couldn't have.

Deciding to focus on something else to get his mind
off Crystal for the time being, he mentally ran through
all the information Nick had texted him. Crystal's co-
worker, Jasmine Ross, was nowhere to be found. Rumor
within Homeland Security indicated she'd had help from
inside, and for that reason Nick agreed with Bane's way
of thinking to not let anyone, especially Homeland Security, know of his connection to Crystal. Right now
everyone was trying to figure out where she'd gone.

The plan was for him and Crystal to stay put at this
hotel until tomorrow. Then they would drive overnight
to the Alabama and Georgia line and meet with some of
his family members. Namely his cousins Dare, Quade,
Cole and Clint Westmoreland. Dare, a former FBI agent,
was currently sheriff of College Park, a suburb of Atlanta. Clint and Cole were former Texas Rangers and
Quade still dabbled from time to time in secretive as-
signments for a branch of government connected directly to the White House.

Bane stepped out of the shower and began toweling himself off, ready to have something to eat and
then finally get some sleep. After slipping into a pair

of jeans and a T-shirt, he grabbed his phone and slid it into his back pocket. He then opened the bathroom door and walked out to find Crystal pacing the hotel room. "What's wrong?"

She paused and looked over her shoulder at him. "What makes you think something is wrong?"

"You're pacing."

"So I was." She moved to the desk and sat down in the black leather armchair. "Too much nervous energy, I guess. I don't want to bother you."

"You aren't bothering me," he said, moving to his duffel bag to discard the clothes he'd just taken off. "I just don't want you to wear yourself out."

"You're worried about me wearing myself out? You? Who barely got any sleep or ate a decent meal in the past twenty-four hours?"

"I've survived before on less."

"Well, I prefer not hearing about it."

He wondered if she was ready to hear what Nick had texted him earlier. "Jasmine Ross is missing."

"Missing?"

"Yes. Nick thinks she might have suspected DHS is onto her and went into hiding." At that moment there was a knock on the door, followed by a voice that said, "Room service."

"Great timing," Bane said as he headed for the door. Deciding not to take any chances, he grabbed his gun off the table and then looked through the peephole before opening the door.

After the attendant had rolled in a cart loaded down with a variety of foods, arranged everything and left, Bane smiled over at Crystal. "The food looks good. You're joining me, right?"

She nodded. "Yes, I'm joining you."

* * *

"I doubt if I can eat another bite, Bane," Crystal said, sliding her chair back from the table. Her goal had been to make sure he got something to eat and not the other way around. But he'd had other ideas and had practically fed her off his plate. She recalled how they used to do stuff like that years ago. Until now, she hadn't realized just how intimate it was.

"Mmm, you've got to try this. The piecrust is so flaky it nearly melts in your mouth," he said, reaching over and offering her his fork with a portion of apple pie on it.

It slid easily between her lips and she closed her eyes and moaned. He was right. It was delicious. In fact, everything was. Instead of ordering an entrée, she had chosen a variety of appetizers she thought he might like. And from the way he'd dived in, he had been pretty hungry. She was glad he had enjoyed all her selections.

She watched him finish off the last of the pie and tried ignoring the way her own stomach fluttered. He even looked sexy while he ate. Seriously, how totally ridiculous was that? Sighing, she glanced around the hotel room, deciding she could handle looking at just about anything right now except Bane. More than once she'd noticed him looking at her and had recognized that glint in his eyes. He'd always had that look when he wanted her. And why was she having such a hard time getting past that look?

"It's hard to believe the sun is about to go down already."

She glanced over at him and saw he was looking out the window. She had opened the blinds while he was taking a shower so the room wouldn't look so dark. The light coming through the window had helped, but now they would be losing that daylight soon.

"We'll make the twenty-four-hour mark in a few hours."

She lifted a brow. "Twenty-four-hour mark?"

He smiled and stared at her for what seemed like a minute or two before saying, "We will have spent the past twenty-four hours together. That's a pretty good start, don't you think?"

Pretty good start? Considering everything, he could think that? "I suppose." She glanced at her watch. "Now it's my turn to shower. I plan on getting into bed early."

"So do I."

She glanced at him and saw gorgeous hazel eyes staring back at her across the rim of a coffee cup. She couldn't help but return his stare. Okay, what was going on here and why was she encouraging it? He shouldn't be looking at her like that and she certainly shouldn't be returning the look. She should be saying something… or better yet, shouldn't she be getting up from her chair and heading for the bathroom? Yes, that was exactly what she should be doing.

She cleared her throat before easing to her feet. And because she felt she needed to say something she said, "Umm, I think I'll take a tub bath instead of a shower. I feel the need to soak my body in bubbles for a while." She frowned. Seriously? Wasn't that too much information?

She knew it probably had been when she saw his smile. It wasn't just any old smile but one that was so sexy it had sparks of desire shooting all through her.

"Sounds nice. Mind if I join you?"

Why had he had to ask her that? And why had his gaze just lowered to her chest just now? And why were her nipples stiffening into buds and feeling achy against her T-shirt? "You took a shower earlier. Besides, you'd be bored to tears."

His rich chuckle filled the room. "Bored to tears? In a bathtub with you? I seriously doubt that, sweetheart. In fact, I know for sure that won't be the case."

She raked her eyes over him from head to toe. She had a feeling that wouldn't be the case as well, but would never confess that to him. "But I'm sure such a macho SEAL wouldn't want to smell like vanilla," she said, moving quickly to the bed where she'd laid out a change of clothes.

Grabbing the items off the bed, she dashed into the bathroom and closed the door behind her.

Bane took the last sip of his coffee as he continued to stare at the closed door. Did he have his wife running scared? He grinned, thinking how he'd at least asked about taking a bath with her...even if she'd turned him down. Already he heard the sound of running water and his mind was beginning to work overtime, conjuring up all kinds of fantasy scenarios involving Crystal's naked body and a bathtub full of bubbles.

He had it bad. Yes, he most certainly did. But hell, that could be expected. He was a full-grown man who hadn't shared a woman's bed in five years, and the woman he'd been holding out for was behind that closed door without a stitch of clothes on, playing with bubbles and smelling like vanilla.

He shifted his gaze from the closed door to glance out the window. He might as well get up and close the blinds, since it was getting dark outside. However, instead of moving, he continued to gaze thoughtfully out of the window. He wondered how long it would be before he could officially bring Crystal out of hiding. According to Nick's text messages, two arrests had been made, but so far those guys weren't talking.

Just then, his phone went off. He picked it up when he recognized the ringtone. "Yes, Bay?"

"Just checking on you and Crystal. Dillon told us what's going on."

Bane leaned back in his chair. "So far so good, considering someone had sewn a tracker inside Crystal's jacket. Luckily, we were able to stay ahead of them anyway."

"Dillon said you're headed south. Why not come home to Westmoreland Country?"

"Can't do that. The last thing the family needs is for me to deliver trouble to everyone's doorstep."

"We can handle it, Bane."

"It's not the old days, Bay. My brothers and cousins have wives and kids now. We're dealing with a bunch of crazies and there's no telling what they might do. I can't take the chance."

"Then, come to Kodiak. Walker told me to tell you that you and Crystal are welcome there. We're leaving for home tomorrow and won't be returning to Westmoreland Country until a week before Christmas."

Bane smiled. "Did you hear what you just said?"

"About what?"

"Kodiak, Alaska. You said that you and Walker were leaving for *home* tomorrow. It's strange hearing you think of anywhere other than Denver as home."

Bailey chuckled. "I guess I'm beginning to think of wherever Walker is as home for me."

Bane nodded. "You really love the guy, don't you?"

"Yes. Now I know how you and Crystal felt all those years ago. Especially the obsession. I can't imagine my life without Walker." She paused a moment and then asked, "And how are things going with you and Crystal? You guys still love each other, right?"

"Why wouldn't we?"

"The two of you haven't seen each other in five years, Bane. That's a long time to not have any kind of communication with someone."

Yes, it was, but he'd known the moment he'd seen Crystal that for him nothing had changed. But could he say the same about her feelings for him?

Before his cousin could ask him any more sensitive questions, he said, "I need to make a call, Bay. Thank Walker for the offer and tell him if I decide to take him up on it, I'll let him know."

"Okay. Stay safe and continue to keep Crystal safe."

"I can't handle my business any other way."

He ended the call, then stood and closed the blinds before wheeling the table and dishes out into the hall. Once back inside he reached for his phone, figuring now was a good time to check in with Nick before calling it a night. His friend picked up on the second ring. "What's going on, Nick?"

"Glad you called. I was about to text you. Jasmine Ross has been found."

Crystal drew in a deep breath as she slid into her bathrobe. She felt good and refreshed. Soaking in the tub for almost an hour had definitely relaxed her mind. Hopefully Bane was asleep by now and she would be soon, too. They both needed a good ten hours' worth before heading out again.

Opening the bathroom door she allowed her eyes to adjust to the semidarkness. The first thing she noticed was that Bane was not in bed sleeping as she had hoped but was sitting at the desk with his back to her.

He turned around when he heard her and she could tell from the look on his face that something was wrong.

"Bane? What's going on?"

He stood and stuck his hands into the pockets of his jeans. "I talked to Nick a short while ago."

Nick, who was usually the bearer of bad news, she thought, tightening the belt of her robe around her. "And?"

"They found Jasmine Ross."

"Really?" she said, moving toward Bane with a feeling of excitement flowing through her. "That's good news, right? Hopefully Jasmine will confess her part in all this and work out a plea deal or something. Maybe they'll get her to tell them where those other two chemists are being held."

"Unfortunately, Jasmine won't be telling anyone anything."

Crystal frowned. "Why?"

"Because she's dead. She was shot in the head and dumped in a lake. A couple of fishermen came across her body a few hours ago."

Thirteen

"Here. Drink this."

Crystal's fingers tightened on the glass Bane placed in her hand, and she fought hard to hold it steady. Jasmine was dead? Suddenly everything seemed so unreal. So unbelievable.

She glanced down into the liquid. It was alcohol, and the smell alone was so strong it had her straightening up a little in her chair. "Whoa. What is it?"

"Scotch."

She lifted an arched brow. "Where did Scotch come from?"

"I ordered it from room service after I talked with Nick. I figured you'd need a glass."

"I don't drink, Bane."

"You need to drink this. It will help with the shock of what I told you."

Crystal nodded, took a sip and frowned. Like coffee, liquor was a taste she'd never acquired. She drew in a deep breath as her gaze flickered around the room.

"She brought it on herself, Crystal," she heard Bane say. "Evidently, the woman didn't have any problem setting you up. Don't forget she placed a bugging device in a gift she gave you and a tracker inside your jacket."

"I know, but it's still hard to believe she'd do something like that. She was nice most of the time. At least she pretended to be," Crystal said, leaning forward to place her glass on the desk. One sip had been enough for her. "How could she have gotten mixed up in something so devious?"

Bane shrugged. "Who knows what makes people do what they do? Unfortunately, she got in too far over her head. And the people she thought she could trust saw her as a threat instead of an asset."

Shivers passed through Crystal, and when Bane touched her arm she nearly jumped out of her skin. "You okay?" he asked softly.

She tipped her head all the way back to gaze up at the ceiling before lowering it to look at him. "Not really. It was bad enough to know one of my coworkers was involved in heaven knows what, but then to find out she lost her life because of it is a little too much."

"Are you sure you're okay?"

She glanced at Bane. "Yes, pretty much. But I think I'll go to bed now and try to get some sleep."

Crystal stood up. Without saying anything else and feeling Jasmine's death weighing her down, she moved across the room, threw back the covers and slid into bed. She turned her back to Bane so he wouldn't be able to see her tears.

Bane came awake with a start. First there was a small whimper from the bed next to his. Then he heard a rumbled, emotional plea. "Please don't! Don't shoot him. Please don't."

It took only a second to realize Crystal was thrashing around in her bed having a bad dream. He was out of his bed in a flash and flipped on the small lamp on the nightstand, bathing the room in a soft glow. He sat on the edge of her bed, gently shaking her awake. "Crystal, it's okay. Wake up, baby. You're having a bad dream. Wake up."

He watched as her eyes flew open just seconds before she threw herself into his arms. Automatically he held her tight and used his hands to gently stroke her back. "It's okay, Crystal."

"Bane."

She whispered his name against his neck and the heat from her breath set off a fire in the pit of his stomach. Her arms tightened around him and he refused to let this moment pass. She needed him and he wanted to be needed.

"I'm here, baby."

She pulled back slowly, meeting his gaze and holding it. "It was an awful dream. They came for us, and you wouldn't let them take me. You put yourself in front of me. To protect me. And the man raised his gun to shoot. They were going to shoot you and I felt so helpless."

He slid one hand to the back of her neck and used the other to push several strands of hair back from her face. He saw fear in her eyes, and more than anything he wanted to take that look away. "It was just a dream, Crystal. No one is here but us, and no one is going to shoot me."

"B-but I…"

"Shh, baby. It's okay. I'm okay. We're okay."

He leaned in close to kiss the corners of her lips but

she tipped her head at an angle and his mouth landed over hers. Instinctively, she parted her lips at the moment of impact and he swept his tongue inside her mouth to kiss her fully.

They'd kissed a couple of times over the past twenty-four hours, but nothing like this. There had been a hunger, but tonight this was about taking care of an ache. He deepened the kiss to taste her more fully as desire quickened inside him. She whimpered, and the sound was so unlike the one that had awakened him earlier. This one sent sensations jolting through him, filling him with the awareness of a sexual need that he felt all over.

And when she reached up and wrapped her arms around his neck it became the kind of kiss that curled a man's toes and made his entire body get hard. She tangled her tongue with his in a way that made every cell in his body come alive and he could only moan out loud.

A swirl of heat combined with a heavy dose of want overtook him as he continued to ply her mouth with hungry, languorous strokes of his tongue. There was only so much of her he could take without craving more, and his desire for more was nearly eating him alive, driving him insane.

And he didn't want to just kiss her. He wanted to make love to her the way a husband would want to make love to his wife. He wanted to taste her all over. Feel his hands touching every inch of her. And reacquaint himself with being inside her.

Exploring her mouth this way was making his already aroused body that much more unrestrained. It was hard to remain in his good-guy lane and stay in control. Especially when she was returning his kiss with just as much bone-melting fire as he was putting into it. Explosive chemistry was something they'd always shared. Nothing had changed. The taste of her was incredibly pleasurable as always. To his way of thinking, even more so.

Unable to take any more, he broke off the kiss and pressed his forehead to hers while releasing pent-up breath from deep in his lungs. "Crystal." He wasn't sure why he needed to whisper her name at that particular moment, but he did.

"I'm here, Bane."

Yes, she most certainly was, he thought, breathing hard. He briefly considered giving her another kiss before tucking her under the covers and returning to his bed, but for some reason he couldn't do that. He wanted to continue holding her in his arms, so she would know she was safe here with him.

Bane shifted their bodies so they were stretched out together in the bed, and as they lay there beside each other, he wrapped his arms around her. "Sleep now," he whispered softly, trying to ignore how the angle of her backside was smacked up against his groin. He had a hard-on and there was no way she couldn't feel it.

She began writhing around in the bed trying to get comfortable, and each time she did so he felt his engorged erection get that much harder. Finally, after gritting his teeth a few times, he reached out and cupped a firm hold to her thigh. "I wouldn't do that too often if I were you," he warned.

"Why? Because you want me?"

With a guttural hiss, he positioned her body so that she was lying flat on her back. He loomed over her and looked down into her eyes. "What do you think?"

She broke eye contact with him for a mere second before returning his gaze. "I think I might not be as good with that as I used to be."

"Why would you think that?"

"It's been a while. Five years."

A smile curved his lips. "Are you saying that because you think that I might not be as good as I used to be, as well?"

Surprise leaped into her eyes and she exhaled sharply. "No. That never crossed my mind."

"Good. And just for the record, the thought that you're not as good as you used to be never crossed mine, either."

"Not even once?"

He stared at her in the lamplight. Her features were beautiful, the look in her eyes intense as she waited on his answer. "Not even once," he said, meaning every word. "But I have been wondering about something, though," he added, breathing her scent deep into his nostrils.

She lifted a brow. "What?"

"Can my tongue still make you come?"

Bane's words caused Crystal to squeeze her eyes shut as sensations, namely memories of him doing that very thing, assailed her. She always thought Bane's mouth should be outlawed. And it didn't take much to recall everything he used to do, while licking her from the top of her head to the bottom of her feet, paying close attention to those areas in between.

Especially those areas in between.

"Open your eyes, sweetheart."

She did and her gaze met his. Held it. She felt the sexual tension mounting between them, easing them into a comfortable and mutual existence where memories were surrounding them in ways they couldn't ignore or deny. And at the exact moment his fingers shifted from her thigh to settle between her legs, she knew just what he'd found.

A woman who was hot and ready.

Crystal wasn't exactly sure when the amount of time they'd been apart no longer mattered to her. The only thing that mattered was that he still wanted her after so long. That he hadn't been with another woman just like she hadn't been with another man. It was as if her body was his and his was hers. They had known it, accepted it and endured the loneliness. She hadn't wanted any other man but him, and now her body was demanding to have what it had gone without for quite some time.

"Do you know how many times I lay in bed at night and envisioned touching you this way, Crystal?" Bane whispered.

He shifted his hand and his fingers began moving, sliding inside her, and automatically her thighs eased apart. "No, how many?" she asked, loving how the tip of his fingers stroked up and down her clit.

"Too many. Those were the times I had to take matters into my own hands. Literally. That's how I kept from going insane. But I like this better," he said as he continued working his fingers inside her, causing a deep ache to spread through her. "The real thing. No holds barred."

No holds barred. As he stroked the juncture between her thighs, Crystal couldn't recall the last time she had felt so electrified. For so long, she had mostly ignored her body's demands, except for those rare occasions when she couldn't and had resorted to self-pleasure the way he had.

But Bane's fingers were not toys. They were real, and what they were doing to her was as real as it could get. The sensations being generated inside her were so intense she actually felt air being ripped right out of her lungs with every breath she took. Her heart rate had picked up, and she felt as if she was being driven off the edge, falling headfirst into one powerful wave of pleasure.

"You like this?"

Before she could answer, he reached down, sliding his free hand beneath her shirt and settling it on the center of her stomach. She felt the heat radiating from his touch and began writhing. "Hey, it's okay, baby. It's just me and my touch. I want to put my imprint on you everywhere," he whispered.

Did he think his imprint wasn't already there? She was convinced his fingertips had burned into her skin years ago. And when he pushed her T-shirt up, she felt a whoosh of air touch her skin, especially her breasts. She wasn't wearing a bra and could feel the heat of his gaze as he stared down at the twin globes.

"Hmm, beautiful. Just as I remembered. Do you have any idea how much I used to enjoy sucking these?"

Yes, she had an idea because he used to do so all the time. At one point she'd been convinced his mouth was made just for her nipples. And now, when he used his tongue to lick his lips just moments before lowering his head toward her breasts, she could actually feel a fire ignite inside her. She felt her nipples harden even more. And all it took was one look into his eyes to know he was about to devour her alive.

He buried his face in her chest and took her nipple easily between his lips. Then he began sucking hard. She wasn't sure if it was his fingers working inside her below or his mouth torturing her nipples that would do her in first. When it happened, she had a feeling it was both.

"Bane!"

An orgasm tore through her immediately and she couldn't hold back the scream. But he was there, capturing her mouth with his, smothering her deep moans with his kiss. Still, he didn't let up, his fingers continuing to work her, rebuilding a degree of passion within her that she could not contain. And when he released her mouth, he began licking her skin from the base of her chin, all over her breasts, down past her stomach all the way to where his mouth met his fingers. He pulled his fingers out of her only to lift her hips to bring the essence of her toward his mouth. The moment his tongue slid inside her she shuddered, filled to the rim with flames of erotic desire.

She pushed on his shoulders but he wasn't letting up. It was as if he was a hungry beast who intended to get his fill, and when another orgasm ripped through her, she cried out his name again. For a fraction of a second, she was convinced she had died and gone to heaven.

But she was quickly snatched back to earth when she felt him lower her hips and remove his mouth from her. Then she watched through languid eyes as he stood and began stripping off his clothes before reaching down to practically tear off hers. A raw, primitive need was overtaking him. It stirred the air, and she could see it in the passion-glazed eyes staring down at her. She felt the heat in every part of her body.

"That was just the beginning," he whispered as he slid a condom on his engorged erection. "Just the beginning."

And then he was back, spreading her thighs, looming over her, and when their gazes met, she saw what she'd always seen when he'd made love to her. Love. Pure, unadulterated love. Bane still loved her and she knew at that moment that no matter what they'd gone through and what they were going through now, she still loved him, as well.

She reached out and slid her hands up his back, feeling the deep cords of his muscles and flinching when she came to several scars that hadn't been there before. But before she could even imagine what story those scars told, he was taking her mouth again, pulling her in and consuming her with a need that was demanding her full concentration. On them. On this. Never had she been filled with such overwhelming desire, need and passion. She wanted him. Her husband. The man who had been her first and only best friend. The man who'd always had her back and had defied anyone who'd tried keeping them apart.

He ended the kiss to stare down at her. "You ready?"

She looked up at him, dragging in a deep whoosh of air filled with their heated scents. "Yes, I'm ready."

And then, holding tight to her hips, spreading her thighs even wider, he slid inside her.

Bane pushed into Crystal all the way until he couldn't go any farther, not sure where his body began and hers ended. The only thing he knew was this was home. He was home. He had been gone five years and that was five years too long. But now he was back and intended to remind her just how good they were together. Remind her why she was his and he was hers.

His blood was boiling, and at that moment it seemed as though all of it had rushed to the head of his erection buried deep inside her. He felt compelled to move, to mate, to drown even deeper into her sweet, delicious depths. He felt her inner muscles clamp down on him, begin milking him, and he threw his head back and growled. Then he began moving, pumping into her, thrusting over and over again until her climax hit so hard that he was convinced they would have tumbled to the floor had he not been holding on to her tight.

"Bane!"

"Crystal!"

Never had he wanted any woman more than he wanted her. Nothing had changed. But in a way, things *had* changed. They were older, wiser and in control of who they were and what they wanted. No one could dictate when and where they could love. The sky was now their limit. And as he continued to rock his hips against hers, thrusting in and out of her, working them both into yet another orgasm, he knew that this was just the beginning, just like he'd told her.

He wanted her to feel every hard, solid inch of him; he wanted to rebrand her, reclaim her. And when another climax hit them both, this one more earth-shattering and explosive than the last, he met her gaze just moments before claiming her mouth, kissing her with a hunger he knew she felt. The ecstasy was bone-deep, mind-blowing, erotic.

And when he released the kiss and she screamed his name once again, he knew that no matter what, Crystal Gayle Newsome Westmoreland was his destiny. He knew it with all his heart.

Fourteen

Crystal slowly opened her eyes and squinted against the bright morning sun coming through the open window blinds. She shifted her gaze to Bane, who was down on the floor doing push-ups. She watched and listened to him keeping count. He was up to three hundred and eighty and his entire body was glistening with sweat. She dragged in a deep breath, thinking the man had more energy than anyone she knew.

That was just the beginning...

He had been deadly serious when he'd issued that warning last night. He had proved that yes, he could still make her come with his tongue. Nothing had changed there. And what he was packing between those fine legs of his wasn't so bad, either. She had barely recovered from one orgasm before he'd had her hurling into another. She didn't recall him having the ability to do all that before. At least not in such rapid succession.

She switched her gaze to the clock on the nightstand and saw that it was almost nine. She had slept late and didn't have to wonder why. It had been a late night and early morning with Bane. He had the ability to make her body want him over and over again, to satisfy her each and every time.

This morning she felt sore, but at the same time she felt so gratified and contented she had to force back a purr. She couldn't stop smiling as she shifted in bed to stretch out her limbs, feeling the way her body was still humming with pleasure. If his goal had been to make up for all their lost time, he definitely had succeeded.

"Good morning. It's nice seeing you smile this morning."

She glanced back at Bane. His deep, husky voice sent erotic shivers down her spine. He had finished exercising and was standing across the room with a cup of coffee in his hand. His feet were braced apart, his sweats hung low on his hips and his chest was bare.

"Good morning to you, too, Bane. You gave me a lot to smile about last night," she said honestly.

"Glad you think so."

From his smile she knew he was pleased by her admission. She saw no reason to pretend regret when there wasn't any. And Bane of all people knew there had never been a shy bone in her body. However, seeing him two days ago after all those years had given her pause. She had to take things slow and get to know him all over again. It would be a process and, as far as she was concerned, making love was part of the process.

"I wanted to wait for you to wake up before ordering breakfast," he said, placing the coffee cup aside to come sit on the edge of her bed.

She pulled herself up, being careful to keep the

bedsheet over her naked body. "You didn't have to do that. I'm sure with everything…and especially those exercises…that you must be hungry."

"Starving."

"Then, let's order."

"Okay, but this first."

He leaned down and pulled her into his arms. It didn't bother her one iota that her naked body was revealed in the daylight. She recalled having a problem with Bane seeing her naked before since she'd always thought she didn't have enough curves to show off. Now she did.

He kissed her and she wrapped her arms around his neck and returned the kiss. She could feel every hard inch of him, all solid muscles, and immediately thought back to last night. Her pulse began hammering inside her veins. Only his kisses had the ability to do that to her. If she didn't put a halt to things, she was liable to short-circuit. Like she had last night.

Typically, she wasn't a demonstrative person, not in the least. However, last night had been a different story. She could blame it on the fact that she'd gone a long time without having sex, and once she was getting some, she was like a woman starving for more and more. Bane was a man who had no problem delivering, and she had experienced one orgasm after another. Yes, she could definitely say last night had been off the charts in more ways than one.

She broke off the kiss at the sound of her stomach growling. She chuckled. "I guess that's my tummy's way of letting me know it needs to be fed."

"Then, I'll order breakfast," Bane said, standing and reaching for the phone on the nightstand. "Anything in particular that you want?"

"Pancakes if they have them. Blueberry ones prefer-ably. Maple syrup and bacon. Crisp bacon. A scrambled egg would be nice and a glass of orange juice."

He looked at her and grinned. "Anything else?"

"Umm, not at the moment. And while I'm waiting, I'll take a shower and put on some clothes."

"If you want to walk around naked, I wouldn't mind."

After last night she could definitely see where he wouldn't mind. "I'd rather put on clothes."

"Your choice."

As he placed their order, she slipped out of bed and looked around for the clothes he'd taken off her last night. But she didn't see them. When she found his T-shirt under a pillow she slid it over her head.

"Nice fit."

She looked down at herself. "It will do in a pinch." She looked back at him. "Any calls this morning?"

"No. I think we got enough excitement yesterday."

She nodded as she began pulling clean clothes from her luggage. "What are the plans for today?"

"We stay here most of the day and rest up. When it gets dark then we'll leave."

"And go where?"

"We'll meet up with my cousins Quade, Dare, Clint and Cole near the Alabama-Georgia border."

She nodded, recalling having met those particular cousins at a family get-together around the time that the Denver Westmorelands had discovered they had rela-tives living in Georgia, Texas and Montana.

Crystal glanced over her shoulder. Bane was back to doing his exercises, and the woman in her couldn't help but admire the way his muscular hips rocked while he ran in place. Drops of perspiration trickled off his face and rolled down his neck and shoulders toward his bare chest.

She drew in a deep breath as she imagined her tongue licking each drop and the way his skin would taste. But she wouldn't stop there. She would take her hands and run them all over his body, touching places she might have missed out on last night, although she doubted there were any. She had been pretty thorough.

But still…

What if there were places she had missed and—

"Anything wrong?"

She blinked and realized she'd been standing there staring. Swallowing deeply she said, "No, nothing is wrong." She wanted to turn and rush off toward the bathroom to take her shower, but for some reason she couldn't get her feet to move. It was if they were glued to the floor.

Now he was the one staring at her. She could actually feel his gaze on every part of her. Any place it landed made her body sizzle. She closed her eyes to fight off the desire that threatened to overwhelm her but when she saw it was no use, she opened them again and let them roam over every single, solid inch of him. He was so muscular, and so big and hard. She glanced down at his middle. Umm, did she say big and hard?

She drew in a deep breath when she saw him moving slowly toward her. She wanted to back up but again her feet wouldn't cooperate. All she could do was stand there and watch all six foot three of him gaining ground on her. She felt herself breathing faster with every step he took and her hands actually began shaking. Her fingertips were even tingling, but what she noticed most of all was how the juncture of her thighs seemed to throb like crazy.

When had her desire for him become so potent? Had making love to him all night suddenly turned her into a lustful woman? A woman whose needs dictated how she behaved with him? She could only imagine. But then she thought, no, she really couldn't. She hadn't been with a man taking up her space and time for so long, she wasn't sure how to deal with Bane now.

"Are you sure nothing is wrong, Crystal?" Bane had come to a stop directly in front of her. He was standing so close it wouldn't take much to reach out and touch him, feel those hard muscles, that solid chest glistening with sweat.

"Nothing's wrong, Bane. I'm fine."

He gave her a knowing grin, which put her on notice that he knew she was lying. She wasn't fine. Thanks to him she had gotten a taste of what she'd been missing for five years, and just how well he could still deliver. But it was more than just sex when it came to him. She'd always known it, ever since they'd held out those two years before even making love.

During that time they had developed a closeness and an understanding she knew very few couples shared. She had thought that maybe it hadn't survived their separation, but it seemed to have. Of course she knew better than to expect everything to go back to the way it had always been between them. They weren't the same people. They still needed to work out a few things, make adjustments and get a greater understanding of who they were now. But it could be done.

"May I offer a suggestion?" he asked her.

She licked her lips. It was either doing that or giving in to temptation and leaning over and licking him. "What?"

"Let's shower together."

Now, why had he suggested that? All kinds of hot and searing visions begin flooding her brain. "Shower together?"

"Yes. I suggested that same thing the night before last but you sort of turned me down."

Yes, she had. "I wasn't ready."

He took a step closer. "What about now, Crystal? Are you ready now? After last night, are you ready to give your husband some more playtime?"

It wasn't his request that caused her mind to shatter. It was his reference to himself as *her* husband. Because at that moment it hit her that he was hers and had been since her eighteenth birthday, probably even before then.

Bane had always told her she was his, regardless of what her parents or his family thought about it. And she had believed him. At no time had she doubted his words. Until that day he'd called to tell her he had decided to go into the navy. But now he was back and was letting her know that although he might have changed in some ways, he was the same in the way that mattered to her. He was still hers.

"That shower isn't very big," she decided to say. "And it might get messy with water sloshing all over the place."

"I'll clean it up," he said.

His smile made her weak in the knees, it was so darn sexy. "Well, if you don't mind doing that, then who am I to argue?" And without saying anything else, she forced her feet to move and walked toward the bathroom. But she didn't close the door behind her. When she turned toward the vanity to look in the mirror, out of the corner of her eye she saw that he was still standing in the same spot staring at her. So she figured that she might as well give him something to look at.

"Down boy," Bane muttered under his breath, trying to get his hard-on under control as he watched Crystal strut off toward the bathroom. As he stood there watching, she proceeded to wash her face and brush her teeth. When had seeing a woman doing basic morning tasks become a turn-on? He could answer that easily. The woman was his wife, and the times he'd seen her do those things had been few and far between.

So he watched her and began getting harder. He couldn't help noticing how his T-shirt clung to her breasts as she leaned toward the sink to rinse out her mouth, how the hem of the shirt had inched up and barely covered her thighs. The same thighs he'd ridden hard last night.

And back to her breasts... He could clearly see how hard the buds were and how well defined the twin globes looked. They were a nice size and nice shape. And he knew for certain they had one hell of a nice taste. As far as he was concerned everything about Crystal was nice. The word *nice* wasn't good enough. He could come up with a number of better ways to describe his wife. *Shapely. Sexy. Mesmerizing. Hot. Tasty.*

Did he need to go on? He doubted it. Instead, as he stood there and watched her take a washcloth to wet her face, he was suddenly turned on in a way he'd never been turned on before. Hell, it was worse than last night, and he hadn't believed that could be possible.

Feeling like a man who needed his wife and needed her now, he moved toward the bathroom. She had to know he was coming, but she didn't turn and look his way. Instead, she began removing his T-shirt and then tossed it aside. By the time he reached her she was naked.

Bane moved behind her and looked into the mirror, holding her gaze in the reflection. He moved closer and took hold of her backside, settling his groin against it. Perfect fit. And when he began grinding, feeling his engorged erection working against her buttocks, the contact nearly sent him over the edge. He broke eye contact with her in the mirror to lean over to lap her shoulder, licking it from one end to the other, taking a few nibbles of her flesh in between. He liked the way her skin tasted this morning. Salty. Womanly.

"I haven't taken a shower yet," she whispered in a voice that let him know the effect his mouth had on her.

"We'll eventually get around to it. No rush."

Then he remembered there was a certain spot on her body, right underneath her left ear, that when licked and sucked could make the raw hunger in her come out. So he licked and sucked there and immediately her body began shivering in a way that sent a violent need slamming through him.

"Bane…"

"I know, baby," he whispered. "Trust me, I know. And I want you just as much. Now. I need to be inside you. Bad. I got five years of want and need stored up just for you."

"And last night?" she asked in that same sexy whisper.

"Just the beginning. One night can't alleviate everything. To be honest, I doubt one hundred nights can."

"Oh, my."

"Oh, yes."

And with that said, he turned her around to face him,

lifted her off her feet and sat her on the vanity. "Spread your legs for me, Crystal."

As if they had a will of their own, her thighs parted. He pulled a condom pack out of the side pocket of his sweats and moved back only far enough to ease the sweats down his legs.

"You don't have to use that unless you want to," she said softly. "After I lost the baby my aunt suggested I go on the pill. More to help keep me regulated than anything else."

He nodded. So in other words she was letting him know that this time or any time they felt like it, they could go skin to skin, flesh to flesh. Just the thought made his entire body feel as if it was on fire. "Then, I won't use one."

With his pants out of the way, he got back into position between her spread legs. His shaft was ready, eager to mate and greedier than he'd ever felt it to be. He cupped himself to lead it home.

"Let me."

He looked up and gazed into her eyes. The thought that she'd asked to guide him inside her almost made him weak in the knees. "All right."

When she reached out and took hold of him, he felt himself harden even more in her hands. And then she led him to her center, and it was as if a thousand watts of electricity jolted through her nerve endings to him. And instinctively he pushed forward, thrusting into her hard and deep, all the way to the hilt. Reaching out, he grabbed hold of her hips, and began moving inside her like crazy.

Needing even more of a connection with her, he leaned forward to capture her lips with his. She had the minty taste of whatever mouthwash she'd used and he intended to lick the taste right from her mouth. She returned the kiss and he deepened it as much as he could while thrusting even more deeply into her body. Setting the same rhythm for both, the same beat. The same drive.

And the beat went on. He could hear her whispering in a choppy breath for him not to stop. So he didn't. He couldn't. It seemed that everything was out of his control. He was out of control. His entire body was ablaze for her.

"Bane!"

She screamed his name and tightened her legs around his waist. He thrust harder in response and before he could catch his next breath, his body exploded. But he wasn't done.

"Hold on, Crystal. I'm coming again."

"Bane!"

He threw his head back and sucked in a deep gulp of air that included a whiff of her scent. He practically lifted her hips off the vanity as he pushed deeper, and he came again with a primal need that made his entire body tremble. Now he knew that this woman who'd gotten under his skin so many years ago, who'd been his world, still was. And would always be so.

Fifteen

There was a knock on their hotel room door. "That should be dinner."

Crystal felt an immediate sense of loss when Bane separated his limbs from hers. Had they gone through breakfast and lunch? A part of her knew they had but the only thing she could recall with clarity was their seemingly nonstop lovemaking sessions. They'd only taken time out to grab something to eat and indulge in a couple of power naps in between.

She watched as he quickly slid into his jeans. When he grabbed his gun off the desk and inserted it into his waistband, it was a stark reminder of the situation they were in. There was a group of people out there who wanted her, and Bane was just as determined that they would not get her.

"Yes?" Bane asked as he looked out the door's peephole.

"Room service."

"Just a minute." He looked over his shoulder at her. "Decent?"

She was pulling his T-shirt over her head. "Now I am." But she still slid beneath the covers and pulled the bedsheet practically up to her chin.

He opened the door to a smiling young woman who couldn't help roaming her gaze all over Bane as she pushed a cart into their hotel room. "Everything you ordered, sir."

"Thanks."

Once the woman left, Crystal slid out of bed and glanced at the food. The cart was set like a table for two. Bane was finally getting his steak and potatoes, and as far as she was concerned, he deserved it. She was certain he'd worked up an appetite over the past few hours.

"I need to wash my hands first."

"So do I."

"But not together. I'll go first," she said, racing off toward the bathroom and closing the door behind her. Every time she and Bane entered the bathroom together they ended up making out all over the place. He had taken her on the vanity and in the shower just before breakfast. And then again in the shower right before lunch.

After washing her hands she quickly dried them off before opening the bathroom door, only to find him standing right there waiting. "My turn now," he said, grinning. "If you want to keep me company, I won't mind."

Yes, she just bet he wouldn't. "No thanks. I'll be okay out here waiting for you. I promise not to start without you."

"I won't be long because I'm sure you're hungry,

too," he said with a grin. He went into the bathroom and closed the door behind him.

Crystal rubbed her hand down her face. Jeez. This new Bane was almost too much for her. He'd always had a pretty hefty sexual appetite, but in the past, due to her lack of experience, he'd always kept that appetite under control. Now it was obvious he wasn't holding anything back. In a way she couldn't help but smile about that because now he was treating her as an equal in the bedroom. He'd taken off the kid gloves and wasn't treating her like a piece of china that could easily break.

"I'm back."

She glanced up and thought that yes, he was back, looking sexy as ever and easily transforming her into one huge bundle of sexual need. "Umm, maybe I should change clothes. Keeping on your T-shirt might not be a good idea."

He moved around her toward the cart. "Don't know why you think so. Besides, we'll both be changing soon enough since we'll be moving out in a few hours."

That was right. He had mentioned that to her. They'd be meeting up with his cousins. When she approached the cart, Bane pulled out a chair for her. She wasn't surprised. One thing about those Westmoreland men, they might have been hell-raisers a time or two, but they always knew how to act proper and show respect.

"Thanks, Bane," she said, taking her seat.

"You're welcome." He leaned down and placed a kiss on her lips. "Eat up."

"Do you know what the plan is after we meet with your cousins?"

He took a sip of coffee and shook his head. "Not sure. Quade has connections with the White House. He may have some insight into the mole at Homeland Security."

Crystal didn't say anything as she began eating, but she couldn't help wondering what could be done to keep her safe. She doubted Bane could continue to protect her on the run. What if he had orders for an assignment? Then where would she be?

"You're frowning. You think the food isn't good or something?"

She glanced over at him. "The food is good," she said of the grilled chicken salad she'd ordered. "I was just wondering about something."

"What?"

"What happens if you get that phone call?"

"What phone call?"

"The one from your commander that you're needed on one of those covert operations."

He shrugged. "Like I told you, my team and I are on military leave for a while. However, if something comes up, I'll let my commander know I can't go. You're my wife and I won't be going anywhere until I know for certain that you're safe."

"Because of your sense of duty and obligation?" she asked, needing to know.

He stared at her as a moment of silence settled between them. Then, he spoke. "I'm not sure what it's going to take for you to realize something, Crystal."

"What?"

"That you're more than an obligation to me. I love you. Always have and always will. That's why I joined the navy five years ago instead of hanging around in Denver and getting into more trouble. In all honesty, I think had I claimed you as my wife back then we might very well be divorced by now."

His words almost snatched the air from her lungs. "Why do you think that?"

"Because there is more to life than what we had back then."

"We had love."

"Yes," he agreed. "And it was our love that would have held things together for a while. But I could see things eventually falling apart. I had a high school education and barely two years of college, and you were determined not to go back to school to get a diploma. All you wanted was to be my wife and the mother of my kids."

"And you saw something wrong with that?" she asked, not sure what he was getting at.

"No, not at the time. But think about it. How far would we have gotten on our own without finally asking your family or mine for help? And eventually I would have resented having to ask anyone for handouts. Granted, I had my land, though legally it didn't belong to me until I turned twenty-five, which meant we would have had to live in the cabin, but only if Dillon agreed to it. But then I doubt the cabin would have been enough. I would have wanted to build a house just as big as my brothers'. One large enough to raise our kids in."

He paused a moment before adding, "And we talked about having a house full of kids without really giving any consideration to how we would take care of them."

She nodded. Although a part of her didn't want to admit it, she knew what he was saying was true. After her miscarriage she had cried for months because she'd lost his baby. After all, they'd talked so often of having a child together one day. But neither had talked about how they would take care of one financially. She'd known the Westmorelands had money, and her young, immature mind had assumed that whatever she and Bane needed his family would eventually take care of. He was right; all she had wanted to do was marry him and have his babies. And she had hated school. Or so she'd thought. The kids had been mean and hateful and resented her ability to ace every test with flying colors. After a while she'd gotten tired of being the class star and having the haters on her back. She'd finally convinced herself that going to school was a waste of her time. Her family had blamed Bane for that decision but it had been hers and hers alone.

She glanced over at him. He had gotten quiet again as he cut into his steak. *Her Bane.* And then a part of her finally got it. He had loved her back then and he loved her now and had told her so several times since he'd walked through her front door. Bane had wanted to give her a better life five years ago because he loved her enough to believe that she and his kids deserved the best of anything. And to give them that, he had made sacrifices. And one of those sacrifices had been her. But she could finally say she understood why he'd made them.

He had wanted to grow up, but he'd also given her a chance to grow up, as well. And she had. She knew how to think for herself, she had two college degrees and was working on her PhD. That had been a lot to accomplish in five years' time and she had done it thanks to him. He had practically forced her to realize her full potential.

"That steak was good."

She glanced over at his plate. It was clean. "You want some of my salad?"

He shook his head and grinned. "No, thanks. I'm good."

Yes, she agreed inwardly. Bane Westmoreland was definitely good. "Bane?"

He pushed his plate aside and glanced over at her. "Yes?"

"I've finally taken my blinders off, and do you know what I see?"

He leaned back in his chair and stared at her. "No. What?"

"A man who loves me. A man who truly loves me even after five years of not seeing me or talking to me. A man who was willing to give me up to give me the best. And for that I want to give you my thanks."

Instead of the smile she'd expected, she watched as a muscle twitched in his jaw. "I really don't want your thanks, Crystal."

No, he wouldn't want her thanks, she thought. He would want her love. Pushing her chair back, she eased from her seat and went to him. Ignoring the look of surprise on his face, she slid down into his lap and turned around to face him. Wrapping her arms around his neck she leaned up and slanted her mouth over his.

He let her kiss him but didn't participate. That was fine with her because she needed him to understand something with this kiss. She'd know the moment he got it, the moment he understood. So she kissed him, putting everything she had into it, and when she heard his breathless moan, she knew he'd almost gotten it. He then returned her kiss with as much passion as she was giving and she felt his hand slide down to her thighs before moving underneath the T-shirt to caress her naked skin.

She knew things could turn sexual between them real quick if she didn't take control. If she didn't let him know what was on her mind...and in her heart. So she pulled back, breaking off the kiss. But that didn't slow up his hands, which were still moving. One was still underneath her T-shirt and the other was sliding up and down her back, stroking the length of her spine.

"I love you, too, Bane," she whispered against his

lips. "I guess you can say I never knew how much until now. And you never stopped loving me like I never stopped loving you. I get that now."

"No, baby. I never stopped loving you," he whispered back against her lips. Then he tightened his arms around her as he stood with her and headed toward the bed.

After placing her there, without saying a word he tucked his fingers into the hem of the T-shirt she was wearing and took it off her.

She watched him step back and ease his jeans down his thighs and legs. Her gaze roamed up and down his naked form. Good thing she wasn't wearing any panties or they would be drenched. She wanted him just that much. And she could tell from the look in his eyes that he wanted her with all the passion he'd stored up for five years. He'd told her as much a number of times, had proved it last night and all day today. She saw it now while looking at his engorged erection and could hear it in his breathing.

He came back toward the bed, and before he could make another move, she reached out and wrapped her fingers around his swollen sex. It fit perfectly in her hand. "Nice," she said, licking her lips.

She heard Bane groan deep in his throat before saying, "Glad you think so."

"I do. Always have thought so."

When she began stroking him with her fingers, even using her fingernail to gently scrape along the sensitive skin, he threw his head back and released a growl that seemed to come from deep within his gut. And when she leaned down and swirled her tongue over him, she felt his fingers dig through her hair to her scalp. That drove her to widen her mouth and draw the full length of him between her lips.

* * *

Pleasure ripped through Bane to all parts of his body. Crystal was using her mouth to build a roaring fire inside him. A fire that was burning him from the inside out. And when she used her fingers to stroke the thatch of curly hair covering his groin, he could feel his erection expanding in her mouth. That pushed her to suck on him harder and he fought hard not to explode right then and there. Instead, he reached down and entwined his fingers in the silky strands of her hair before wrapping a lock around his fist. And then he began moving his hips, pumping inside her mouth. The more he did so the more she stroked him before using those same fingers to gently squeeze his testicles.

Was she trying to kill him? Did she have any idea what she was doing to him? Did she know how hard it was to hold back and not come in her mouth? He knew if he allowed her to continue at this rate, she was liable to soon find out.

"Crystal," he whispered, barely able to get her name past his lips as his heart raced and blood pulsed through his veins. "Stop, baby. You need to stop now."

She was ignoring him, probably because he hadn't said it with much conviction. And honestly, there was no way he could with all the pleasurable sensations tearing through him. Her desire to please him this way meant more than anything because even with her inexperience she was doing one hell of a job making him moan.

When he could no longer hold back, he shouted her name and tried pushing her away, but she held tight to his thighs until the last sensation had swept through his body. He should have felt drained but instead he felt even more needy. Desperate to get inside her body, he jerked himself out of her mouth and eased her back on the bed.

He felt her body shudder the moment he entered her. She was wet, drenched to the core, which made it easy to thrust deep, all the way to her womb. Then he positioned them so that her legs were wrapped around his waist and back.

He stared down into her face. "I love you. I love your scent. I love your taste. I loved making love to you. I love coming inside you. And I love being buried inside you so deep it's unreal. Heaven. Over-the-top wonderful."

"Oh, Bane."

He was certain she would have said more, but when he began moving, she began moaning. He lifted her hips and began thrusting in and out of her with rapid strokes, taking her over and over again, and intentionally driving her over the edge the way she'd done earlier to him.

He couldn't get enough of her, and when she screamed his name and he felt the heels of her feet dig deep into his back, he knew she was coming. However, he refused to go there yet. But it was the feel of her inner muscles clamping down on him, trying to pull everything out of him that was the last straw, and he couldn't hold back his explosion any longer.

"Crystal!"

He was a goner as he emptied himself completely inside her, filling her in a way that had his entire body shuddering uncontrollably. He could feel her arms wrapped around him and could hear her softly calling his name. Moments later when the earth stopped shaking and his world stopped spinning, he managed to lift his head to stare down at her before crashing his mouth down on hers.

And the words that filled his mind as he kissed her
with a hunger he couldn't contain were the same ones
he'd said a number of times recently.

This is just the beginning.

Sixteen

"Wake up, sleepyhead."

Crystal slowly opened her eyes and looked out the car's windshield. They were parked at what appeared to be a truck stop decorated with a zillion Christmas lights that were blinking all over the place, although she could see the sun trying to peek out over the mountains.

They had checked out of the hotel around six the night before, which meant that they'd been on the road for twelve hours or so. They'd only stopped twice for bathroom breaks. Otherwise, most of the time she'd been sleeping and he'd been driving. She had offered to share the driving time, but he had told her he could handle things and he had.

He probably figured she needed her rest and she was grateful for that. Before getting dressed, the two of them had taken a third shower. The third in a single day, but all that physical activity had called for it. Besides, she enjoyed taking showers with Bane. He could be so creative when they were naked together under a spray of water. The memories of all they'd done had her body tingling.

Pulling herself up in her seat, she glanced over at him. "We're here already?"

"Yes, but plans changed. Instead of meeting up at the Alabama-Georgia line, we're meeting here."

She glanced around and lifted a curious brow. "And where is here exactly?"

"North Carolina."

North Carolina? No wonder they were surrounded by mountains so huge they reminded her of Denver. "Why the change?"

"They preferred meeting at Delaney's cabin but didn't say why. My guess is because it's secluded, and the way Jamal has things set up, you can spot someone coming for miles around."

"I see." And honestly she did. She had met his cousin Delaney once and recalled hearing how she'd met this prince from the Middle East at a cabin in the North Carolina mountains. To make a long story short, the two had fallen in love and married. "I read an article about her in *Essence* a couple of years back."

"Did you?"

"Yes. And she and her prince are still together."

"Yes, they are. Only thing is that now Jamal is king. He gave the cabin where they met to Delaney as a wedding gift. Since she lives outside the country most of the time, she's given us permission to use it whenever we like."

Bane's phone went off and he quickly pulled it out of the pocket of his jacket and answered it. "This is Bane." After a few seconds he said, "We're here." Then several moments later he said, "Yes, I recall how to get there. I'll see you guys in a little while."

After he hung up the phone he glanced over at her. "I know this has to be both taxing and tiring for you, Crystal, but hopefully the guys and I will come up with some sort of plan."

She nodded. "Still no word on the whereabouts of those other two chemists?"

"No. None. I spoke to Nick while you were sleeping and he's not sure what the hell is going on now. It seems that with the revelation of a mole in the agency, everyone is keeping their lips sealed."

Crystal figured that didn't bode well for her, since Nick had been Bane's source of information from the inside. She bit back an exasperated sigh and leaned back against the headrest.

"Everything is going to be all right," Bane said, reaching over and taking her hand in his. Not waiting for her to respond he asked, "Did you enjoy yourself yesterday and last night?"

That brought a smile to her lips as the pleasant memories washed over her. Hot and spicy memories that made her nipples suddenly become hard and sensitive against her blouse. "Yes, I did. What about you?"

"Yes, I thought it was nice. Best time I've had in a long time."

She was glad he thought so because she definitely felt the same way. The chemistry they'd always shared had been alive and kicking. It didn't even take a touch between them. A look sufficed. At one point he'd lain across his bed and she'd lain across hers with the television going. She had been trying to take a power nap and had felt his gaze on her. When she'd looked over at him and their eyes connected, she couldn't recall who had moved first. All she knew was that the glance had sparked a reaction between them. A reaction that had them tearing off their clothes again.

He brought her hand to his lips and kissed her fingers. "I can't wait to get you back home."

"Home?" She thought of her house that had been set on fire.

"Yes, back in Denver."

She nodded. Although she realized there was nothing back in Dallas for her now, it had been a long time since she'd thought of Denver as home. "What's the hurry?"

"I can't wait for everyone to see you, and to finally introduce you to them as my wife. And we'll have a house to design and build."

Instead of saying anything, she met his gaze and couldn't ignore the flutter that passed through her stomach or the way her pulse quickened at that precise moment. She watched his gaze roam over her, and noticed how his eyes were drawn to her chest. Specifically, the hardened buds pressing against her blouse.

Releasing her hand he turned on the car's ignition. "Come on. We better find Delaney's cabin, and if I figure right, it's about a half hour drive from here. If it was left up to me we'd check into another hotel and have another play day."

Crystal glanced over at him. His eyes were on the road and he was concentrating on their surroundings. She should be, too, but at the moment she couldn't help but concentrate on him.

Brisbane Westmoreland had always seemed bigger than life to her. The past five years hadn't been easy for either of them, but they were back together and that was all that mattered. Now, if they could only stop the men who were trying to kidnap her, everything would be great.

When he brought the car to a stop at a traffic light he glanced over at her and smiled. "You okay, baby?"

She nodded, smiling back at him. Releasing her seat belt, she leaned toward him and placed a quick kiss on his lips. "You're here with me, and as far as I'm concerned that's all that matters now."

She rebuckled her seat belt and sat back. Satisfied.

"What the hell?" Bane muttered through clenched teeth.

Crystal looked over at him and then sat up straight in her seat and glanced out the SUV's window. "What's wrong, Bane?"

He shook his head and stared out at all the cars, trucks and motorcycles that were parked in front of the cabin they'd pulled up to. "I should have known."

"Should have known what?"

"That it would be more than just Quade, Dare, Clint and Cole meeting us today. Some Westmorelands will find just about any excuse to get together."

Chuckling, he brought the car to a stop and turned off the ignition before unbuckling his seat belt. He then reached over and unbuckled hers. "Before going inside, there's something I need to give you."

"What?"

"This," he said, pulling a small black velvet box from his jacket. When he flipped open the lid, he heard her breath catch at the sight of the diamond solitaire ring with a matching gold wedding band.

"Oh, Bane, it's beautiful."

"A beautiful ring for a beautiful woman," he said,

taking the ring out of the box and sliding it on her finger. "It looks good on you, as if it's where it belongs."

She held up her hand and the diamond sparkled in the sunlight. "But when did you get it? How?"

He smiled. "I got it in New York. I had a layover there for a couple of days due to bad weather, and to kill time I checked out some of the jewelry stores. When we got married I couldn't afford to give you anything but this," he said, reaching out and touching the locket she still wore. "I figured it was time I get you something better. It was time I put my ring on your finger."

He got quiet for a moment and then said, "You don't know how much it bothered me knowing you were out there not wearing a ring. I wondered how you were keeping the men away."

"I told you what they thought."

Yes, she had, which he still found hard to believe, but at least it had kept the men at bay.

He lifted her hand and brought it to his lips and kissed it. He then leaned over and lowered his head to kiss her. And he needed this kiss. He hadn't made love to her in over twelve hours, and it was too long.

How had he gone without her for five years? That showed he had willpower he hadn't known he had.

And the one thing he liked most about kissing her was the way she would kiss him back, just like he'd taught her all those years ago to do. Some women's mouths were made for kissing, and he thought hers was one of them. She tasted just as good as she looked and smelled. And that was another thing about her: her scent. His breath would quicken each and every time he took a sniff of her.

His cousin Zane swore that a woman's natural scent was a total turn-on for most men. It had something to do with pheromones. Bane wasn't sure about all that, but the one thing he did know was that Crystal's scent could literally drive him over the edge. And her scent was a dead giveaway that she wanted him regardless of whether she admitted it or not.

There was a loud knock on the truck's window, and he broke off the kiss to glare at the intruder, who said, "Knock it off, Bane."

Rolling his eyes, Bane returned his gaze to Crystal, mainly to focus on her wet lips. "Go away, Thorn."

"Not until I check you over to make sure you're all in one piece. I'm on my way to a benefit bike race in Daytona and in a hurry, so get out of the car."

Bane shook his head as he eased his car seat back. But then in a surprise move he reached across and pulled Crystal over the console and into his arms. He opened the door with her in his arms and got out.

"Bane! Put me down," Crystal said, trying to wriggle free in his arms.

"In a minute," he said, holding her a little longer before sliding her down his body so her feet could touch the ground.

He then turned to Thorn. "Good seeing you, Thorn."

"Good seeing you, too," Thorn said, giving Bane a bear hug. Thorn then reached out to Crystal and pulled her to him, as well. "You too, Crystal. It's been a while."

Bane watched the exchange and knew Thorn's comment had surprised her. Thorn Westmoreland was the celebrity in the family, a well-known, award-winning motorcycle racer who as far as Bane was concerned also built the baddest bikes on earth. He had several movie stars and sports figures as clients.

Crystal and Thorn had only met once at a Westmoreland family reunion, but Bane knew that when it came to his family, Crystal had assumed they saw her as the reason he'd gotten into trouble all those times.

"Thanks, Thorn. It's good seeing you again, as well," Crystal said, as Bane pulled her closer to his side. "How is your family?"

"Fine. Tara's inside along with all the others."

"And just who are *all* the others?" Bane asked.

No sooner than he'd asked that question, the door to the cabin opened and his family members began filing out. The one person Bane hadn't expected to see was Dillon. His older brother stepped out onto the porch along with their cousin Dare. Bane shook his head, not for the first time, at how much Dillon and Dare favored each other.

Bane smiled as his family kept coming out of the cabin. There was Dare and Thorn's brother Stone, and Quade's brother Jared. And besides Dillon, Bane saw his brothers Riley and Canyon, as well as his twin cousins, Aidan and Adrian. He'd just seen the latter four in Denver for Thanksgiving.

"Hey, what's going on?" he asked chuckling. "Last time I looked, Crystal and I were on the run and not dropping by to socialize."

"Doesn't matter," his cousin Dare said, grinning. "We all wanted to see for ourselves that the two of you were okay."

"And we're ready to take anyone on who thinks they can snatch Crystal away from us," Riley said.

"From *us*?" Bane asked, looking at his brother. He knew that of all his siblings and cousins, Riley had been bothered the most by Bane's relationship with Crystal. Riley was afraid that Bane's quest to find her might prove painful if she hadn't waited for him those five years the way Bane had waited for her.

"Yes. *Us*. She's a Westmoreland and we take care of what's ours" was Riley's response.

Bane looked over at Crystal and pulled her closer to his side. "Yes, she is a Westmoreland."

Quade came forward. "Most of the men arrived yesterday. Figured we would get some fishing in while we waited for you to get here. The women showed up this morning and are out back on the porch frying the fish. First we eat breakfast, then we talk about putting a plan together. There're a couple of others we're waiting on."

Bane wondered who the others were but didn't ask. Instead, he said, "Fried fish in the morning? Hey, lead the way."

Crystal had never felt as much a part of the Westmoreland family as she did now. And she knew she had the women to thank for that. They had oohed and aahed over her ring, telling her how much they liked it and how good it looked on her finger. And they had congratulated her on her marriage to Bane and officially welcomed her to the family.

This was her first time meeting Dillon's wife, Pam. In fact, the last time she'd seen Dillon, he was a single man on a quest to find out more about his great-grandfather Raphel. It seemed that pursuit had landed him right on Pam's doorstep, and it had meant nothing to Dillon that Pam was engaged to marry another man at the time.

And then there was Tara, Thorn's wife, whose sister, Trinity, was married to Bane's cousin Adrian. Crystal thought it was pretty neat that two sisters were married to two cousins. And the same thing went for Pam and her sister, Jillian. Jillian was married to Bane's cousin Aidan. Crystal also enjoyed getting to know

Dare's wife, Shelly, Stone's wife, Madison, Jared's wife, Dana, and Canyon's wife, Keisha.

Quade's wife, Cheyenne, was back home in Charlotte with their triplets—a son and two daughters. The girls had dance class today; otherwise, he said his wife would have come with him.

All the women were friendly and the men were, as well. Crystal fought back tears when they welcomed her to the family in a toast. And when Bane's brother Dillon pulled her aside and said that as far as he was concerned, she'd always been part of the family, and that he was glad she and Bane were back together again, she had to excuse herself for a minute to compose herself. Coming from Dillon, that had meant everything.

After going inside for a quick second to get a beer out of the refrigerator, Bane found her sitting on the dock by the lake. Without saying anything, he pulled her up into his arms. "You okay, baby?"

She looked up at him and nodded. "Yes. Everyone is so nice to me."

He smiled and reached out and caressed her cheek. "And why wouldn't they be nice to you? You're a nice person."

"B-but you and I used to cause your family so many headaches. We did some crazy stuff and got into a lot of trouble."

"Yes." He nodded. "We did. But look at us now, Crystal. I finished the naval academy and I'm a SEAL, and you're just a few months shy of getting your PhD. I think Dr. Crystal Westmoreland will sound damn good, don't you?"

Swiping tears away from her eyes, she said, "Yes. I think so, as well."

"All I'm saying is that you and I have changed, Crystal. We aren't the same people we were back then. We're older, better and more mature, although I'll admit we still have a lot of growing to do. But above all, what didn't change was our love for each other. That's the one thing that remained constant."

Crystal knew Bane was right. Their love *had* been the one thing to remain constant. "I love you, Bane," she whispered.

"And I love you back, baby."

Standing on tiptoe, she slanted her mouth over his, doubting that she could or would ever tire of kissing him. And when he wrapped his arms around her and returned her kiss, she knew she could stay in his arms like that forever. Or maybe not, she thought, when she began feeling weak in the knees.

It was the sound of a car door slamming that made them pull their mouths apart. They both turned to look toward the clearing at the people getting out of the cars that had just pulled up. There were three men and a woman. The only person Crystal recognized was the woman. It was Bane's cousin Bailey.

"I'll be damned," Bane said. "That guy... The one in the black leather jacket sure does look like—"

"Riley," she finished for him. "Riley doesn't have a twin, so who is he?" she asked staring.

"That has to be Garth Outlaw. I never met him but I'd heard how he and his five siblings look just like the Westmorelands. And they *are* Westmorelands. I told you we found out that my great-grandfather Raphel had a son he hadn't known about who was adopted by the Outlaws as a baby."

"Well, if anyone doubts Garth Outlaw is related to your family all they have to do is put him and Riley side by side."

"That's true," Bane agreed. "And the man with Bailey is her fiancé, Walker Rafferty. I wonder why they decided to come here instead of flying back to Alaska. When I talked to her the other day that's where they were headed. And I have no idea who the third guy is. The one in the dark suit."

Bane took Crystal's hand in his. "Come on. Quade is beckoning us to join them."

A few moments later when they reached Quade, introductions were made. Just as Bane said, Riley's lookalike was one of their newfound cousins from Alaska, the Outlaws, and the man with Bailey was her fiancé, Walker. However, the third man, the one in the dark suit, was just what Crystal had figured him to be—a government man. She wasn't surprised when Quade said, "Bane and Crystal, this here is Hugh Oakwood. He was recently appointed by the president to head a special agency under the Department of Defense."

Bane raised a brow. "Department of Defense? I don't understand why this would involve the DOD. Their primary concern is with military actions abroad. The Department of Homeland Security's role is to handle things domestically."

Hugh Oakwood nodded as he glanced from Bane to Crystal. "Typically that would be true, but what's going on here isn't typical. We think we're dealing with an international group. And it's highly likely that some of our own people at Homeland Security are involved. That's why the president has authorized my agency to handle things."

The man glanced around and saw he had an audience. Clearing his throat, he asked, "Is there someplace where we can talk privately?"

Quade spoke up and said, "Yes, come this way, Hugh. I got just the place."

Seventeen

Bane had heard that after Jamal had purchased the cabin for Delaney, he'd hired a builder to quadruple the size of it to expand the kitchen, add three additional bedrooms, three more bathrooms, a huge family room and a study. The spacious study was where they were now.

He couldn't imagine anyone getting any studying done in here. Not with the gorgeous view of the mountains and the lake. And if those two things didn't grab you then there was the room itself, with its oak walls and beautiful rustic decor. A floor-to-ceiling bookshelf took up one wall and another wall consisted entirely of a large plate-glass window.

Bane sat beside Crystal on a sofa facing the huge fireplace. Dillon, Quade, Clint, Cole and Dare grabbed chairs around the room. It seemed that Hugh Oakwood preferred standing, which made perfect sense since he had the floor. It was obvious that everyone was interested in what he had to say.

The man turned to Crystal. "I read the report and you, Dr. Westmoreland, have a brilliant mind."

Bane noticed that everyone's gaze had settled on Crystal and she seemed uncomfortable with all the attention she was getting. They were realizing what he'd always known. His wife was a very smart woman.

Crystal blushed. "I wouldn't say that. And officially I'm not a doctor yet."

"I *would* say that. And it's only a matter of months before you get your PhD. After going over all your research, at least what I have access to, there's no doubt that you'll get it," Oakwood said. "And if you don't mind, although I noted you've never used the Westmoreland name, I prefer using it now."

"No, I don't mind," she said. "Bane and I decided years ago to keep our marriage a secret."

Oakwood nodded. "That in itself might be a blessing in disguise. Because no one knows of your marriage, the group that's looking for you has no leads as to where you might be right now."

He paused a moment, then said, "In your research you've basically come up with a formula to make items invisible. Similar testing and research have been done by others, but it seems you might have perfected it to the degree where it's almost ready to use."

"So what does all this mean?" Bane asked.

"It means that in the wrong hands it can be a threat to national security. Right now one particular terrorist group, PFBW, which stands for People for a Better World, sees it as a way to smuggle things in and out of countries undetected."

"Things like what?"

"Drugs, bombs, weapons, you name it. Right, Dr. Westmoreland?"

Crystal nodded. "Yes. Although there's quite a bit of research that still needs to be done before that can happen."

Oakwood nodded. "PFBW have already nabbed the other two chemists, as you all know, and would have grabbed you if your husband hadn't intervened."

"I got that note from someone as a warning," Crystal said.

"Yes, you did. PFBW started recruiting members a few years ago. But we managed to infiltrate the group. That's the only way we know what's going on. When you join, you join for life and the only way to get out is death. We're lucky that our informant hasn't been identified so far."

He paused a minute and then added, "The best we can figure is that although Jasmine Ross started out as part of the group, somewhere along the way she had a change of heart and is the one who slipped you that note. It seems that she tried to disappear as well but wasn't as lucky as you. They found her."

And Bane was sure everyone in the room was aware of the outcome of that. "My wife can't continue to hide out and be on the run forever."

"I agree," Oakwood said. "The problem we're facing is not knowing who we can trust in Homeland Security. The one thing we do know is that PFBW still wants you, Dr. Westmoreland. You're the missing link. The other chemists' work can only go so far. You have researched a key component they lack, and it's your work that's needed to put their scheme in place."

"Sorry, but they won't be getting her," Bane said through clenched teeth as he wrapped his arms around Crystal's shoulders.

"That's why we have a plan," Oakwood said, finally taking a chair.

"What's the plan?" Bane asked, removing his arm from around Crystal to lean forward.

From the looks exchanged between Quade and Oakwood, Bane had a feeling whatever plan Oakwood had come up with, he wasn't going to like it.

Bane was off the sofa in a flash. "No! Hell no! No one is using my wife as bait!"

Crystal reached out and touched Bane's arm. "Calm down, Bane. It doesn't sound too bad."

Bane stared down at her. "They want to set you up someplace and then tell PFBW where you are so they can grab you and—"

"When they do come for me, it sounds as if Oakwood and his men will be ready to arrest them."

Bane rolled his eyes. As a SEAL, he of all people knew things didn't always go as planned. "But what if something goes wrong? What if they fail to protect you? What if—"

"Their mission is successful?" Crystal asked, still trying to calm her husband down. "I have to take the chance their plan will work. Like you said, I can't be on the run for the rest of my life."

Bane pulled her up into his arms. "I know, baby, but I can't take a chance with your life. I can't have you back just to lose you."

Crystal heard the agony in his voice, but she needed to make him understand. "And I can't have you back just to lose you, either, but every time you'll leave to go on covert operations as a SEAL I'll face that possibility."

"It's not the same. I'm trained to go into risky places. You aren't."

He was right; she wasn't. "But I'll be well guarded from a distance. Right, Mr. Oakwood?"

The man nodded. "Right. And we do have an informant on the inside."

A muscle twitched in Bane's jaw. "Not good enough," he said, bracing his legs apart and crossing his arms over his chest. "She won't be alone. I will be with her."

Oakwood shook his head. "That won't work. The people looking for her expect her to be alone."

Bane frowned. "Damn their expectations. I refuse to let my wife go anywhere alone. At some point they'll suspect she had help. They probably already do from the way we've successfully eluded them up to now. I don't like your plan, Oakwood, and the only way I'll even consider it is if I'm the one protecting my wife."

"May I make a suggestion?" Everyone in the room glanced over at Quade.

"What's your suggestion, Quade?" Crystal asked when it was obvious neither Bane nor Oakwood was going to. Tension was so thick in the room you could cut it with a knife.

"Oakwood ran his idea by me earlier and knowing Bane like I do, I figured he wouldn't go along with it, so I came up with a plan B, which I'm hoping everyone will accept. It still requires using Crystal as bait, but at least Bane will get to stay with her."

Oakwood stared at Quade for a moment and then said, "Okay, what's your plan?"

Quade stood. "Before I explain things, I need to get two other people in here who will be instrumental to the success of this plan. The three of us discussed it last night and feel it will work."

He then went to the door, opened it and beckoned for someone. Moments later, Bailey's fiancé, Walker Rafferty, and the Westmorelands' newfound cousin Garth Outlaw entered the room.

Crystal studied Walker and could see how Bailey had fallen for him. He was a looker, but so was Bane. In Crystal's mind, no man looked better. And Garth Outlaw looked so much like Riley it was uncanny. And she found out that like Walker, Garth was an ex-Marine.

Garth began talking. "Quade brought me up-to-date as to what's going on. If you want to set a trap by using Crystal as bait then I suggest you do it in Alaska."

"Alaska?" Bane asked, frowning. "Why Alaska?"

"Because the Outlaws happen to own a cabin on Kodiak Island and it's in a very secluded area. But it's also secured and the cabin has an underground tunnel," Garth said.

Quade moved forward. "If word intentionally leaks out as to where Crystal is, then the people wanting her won't lose any time going after her."

"In Alaska?" Now it was Crystal's turn to ask doubtfully.

"Yes, in Alaska," Oakwood said, rubbing his chin, as if giving plan B serious thought. "They will check things out to make sure it's not a trap, though. Why would Dr. Westmoreland escape to Alaska? The dots will have to connect."

"They will," Garth spoke up and said. "I understand Crystal attended Harvard. Coincidentally, my brother Cash went there at the same time. He was working on his master's degree. Who says their paths didn't cross?"

"I'm following you," Oakwood said thoughtfully. "The people looking for Dr. Westmoreland will assume that their paths *did* cross, and that in desperation, Dr. Westmoreland, you reached out to Outlaw and he offered you safe haven at a cabin he owns in Alaska."

"Exactly," Quade said. "And from what Garth says, this cabin will be perfect. It's in a secluded location on Outlaw property, and the underground tunnel will provide an escape route if needed."

"And in addition to all of that," Garth said, smiling, "thanks to those strong Westmoreland genes, Bane and Cash look alike. Probably just as much as me and Riley resemble each other. That will work in our favor if someone knows Crystal had help and has gotten a glimpse of the guy she's been seen with. They would expect that same guy to be there with her, still protecting her. They will think it's Cash when it will be Bane."

Dillon spoke up. "That plan will work if no one knows that Crystal is married to Bane. Are you guys absolutely certain no one knows?"

"So far that's a guarded secret," Oakwood said. "I checked and Dr. Westmoreland never indicated Brisbane Westmoreland as her husband on any official school records or other documentation. I wasn't even aware of the marriage until Quade brought it to my attention. However, on the other hand," he said, shifting in his chair, "Brisbane Westmoreland has always indicated on any of his official paperwork that he was married and Crystal Newsome Westmoreland is listed as his wife."

Bane shrugged. "I needed to make sure Crystal was taken care of if anything ever happened to me," he said, pulling her closer to him and placing a kiss on her forehead. "I also have medical coverage on her as well, just in case she ever needed it, and I established a bank account in her name."

"All traceable if someone really started to dig," Dare said. It was obvious his former FBI agent's mind was at work.

"Let's hope no one feels the need to dig that far,"

Clint Westmoreland said. He then looked over at Oak-wood. "Can't that information be blocked?"

"Yes, but because I don't know who's the mole at Homeland Security and how high up in the department he or she is, blocking it might raise a red flag," Oak-wood said. "Our main goal is to try to flush out the mole. Right now he is a danger to our national secu-rity. To know he might be someone in authority is even more of a reason for concern."

Neither Bane nor Crystal said anything as everyone looked over at them. The decision was theirs.

"It's a big decision. You might want to sleep on it," Cole suggested.

Crystal stood. "Thanks, but there's no need to sleep on it. And I appreciate everyone wanting to help me. However, what concerns me more than anything is that those people want me alive, but they won't think twice about taking out Bane if he gets in their way. For that reason, I prefer that Bane not be with me."

"Like hell!"

When Bane stood up to object further, Crystal reached out and placed a finger over his lips. "I fig-ured that would be your reaction, Bane." She shook her head. "There's no way you'll let me put my life at risk without trying to protect me, is there?"

He removed her finger from his lips and stared down at her with an unwavering expression on his face. "No."

She released a deep breath. "Then, I guess that means we'll be together in Alaska."

A gusty winter's breeze caused Bane to pull his jacket tighter as he wrapped his arms around Crystal and they walked inside the hotel. It was late. Close to midnight. After making the decision that they would be traveling to Alaska, they'd needed to put in place concrete plans. Crystal had trusted him to handle things and asked to be excused to join the ladies who'd been outside sitting on the patio.

In a way he was glad she'd left when she had, because more than once he'd ripped into Oakwood. Too often it appeared that the man was so determined to find out the identity of the mole at Homeland Security that he was willing to overlook Crystal's safety. And Bane wasn't having that.

It had taken Dillon, Quade and Dare to soothe his ruffled feathers and remove the boiling tension in the room by assuring him that Crystal's safety was the most important thing. Only after that could they finally agree on anything.

He still didn't like it, but more than anything he wanted to bring those responsible to justice so that he and Crystal could have normal lives…something they hadn't had since the day they married.

"You've been quiet, Bane," Crystal said a short while later after they'd checked into the hotel and gone to their room.

"Been thinking," he said, glancing around at the furnishings. They were staying at the Saxon Hotel, and it was as if they'd walked right into paradise.

Dare had offered them the use of one of the bedrooms at Delaney's cabin, but since some of his kin also planned to stay there for the night, he had opted out. He preferred having Crystal to himself, and was not up to sharing space with anyone, not even his family. After he said that he and Crystal would spend the night at a hotel in town, Quade had offered him his room at the Saxon Hotel. The penthouse suite.

It just so happened Quade's brother-in-law was Dominic Saxon, the owner of the luxurious five-star Saxon Hotels and the Saxon Cruise Line. Quade had a standing reservation at any Saxon Hotel, but since his wife, Cheyenne, hadn't accompanied him on this trip, he preferred hanging out with his cousins and brother at the cabin, figuring a card game would be taking place later.

"Wow! This place is simply gorgeous," Crystal said.

Bane leaned back against the door as she walked past him to stand in the middle of the hotel room and glance around.

"Yes, it is that," he said, thinking the room wasn't the only gorgeous thing he was looking at. Before leaving the cabin she had showered and changed clothes. Now she was wearing a pair of dark slacks and a pullover sweater. Whether she was wearing jeans and a T-shirt or dressed as she was now, as far as he was concerned, she was the epitome of sexy.

Since her original destination had been the Bahamas, most of the items she'd packed were summer wear. Luckily she and Bailey were similar in size and height, so Bailey had loaned Crystal several outfits that would be perfect for the harsh Alaska weather.

"Come on, let's explore," she said, coming back to him, grabbing his hand and pulling him along.

He wished this could have been the kind of hotel he'd taken her to on their wedding night. As far as he was concerned, it was fit for a king and queen. There was a state-of-the-art kitchen, and according to the woman at the check-in desk, the suite came with its own chef who was on call twenty-four hours a day.

Then there was the spacious living room with a beautiful view of the Smokey Mountains. He figured the furnishings alone in the place cost in the millions. There was a private bar area that came with your own personal bartender if you so desired, and a connecting theater room that had box-office movies at the press of a button.

But what really had his pulse racing was the bedroom, which you entered through a set of double doors. The room was huge and included a sitting area and game nook. He was convinced the bed was created just for lovemaking. Evidently Crystal thought so, as well. He watched as she crossed the room to sit on the edge of the bed and bounced a few times as if to test the mattress.

"It will work."

He lifted a brow, pretending he didn't know what she was referring to. "Work for what?"

"For us. I think that last hotel probably had to replace the mattresses on the beds after we left."

He chuckled, thinking he wouldn't be surprised if they had. He and Crystal had definitely given both beds major workouts. He continued to stare across the room at her. There was just something about seeing Crystal sitting on the bed that was causing a delicious thrill to flow through him. When their gazes met and held, he decided there was something missing from the picture of her sitting on the bed.

Him.

Eighteen

Crystal leaned back on her arms and gazed through watchful eyes as Bane moved from the doorway and headed in the direction of the bed. Straight toward her.

As much as she tried, she couldn't dismiss the flutter in her tummy or the way her pulse was beating out of control. All she could do was watch him, knowing what he had in mind, because it was what she had in mind, as well. He was taking slow, sexy and seductive steps with an intensity that filled the room with his sexual aura. There seemed to be some kind of primitive force surrounding him and she could only sit there, stare and feel her panties get wet.

As if he knew what she was thinking, what she wanted, without breaking his stride he eased his leather jacket from his shoulders and tossed it aside. Next came his shirt, which he ripped from his body, sending buttons flying everywhere. And without losing steam he jerked his belt through the loops and tossed it in the air to land on the other side of the room.

Without a belt his jeans shifted low on his hips, and she couldn't keep her eyes from moving from his face to his chest to trace the trail of hair that tapered from his chest down his abdomen to disappear beneath the waistband of his jeans.

And then there was what he was packing between those muscular thighs of his. She had seen it, touched it and tasted it. And what made her body tingle all over was knowing it was hers.

She studied Bane's face and saw the intensity etched in his features. A few more steps and he would have made it to the bed. And to her. It seemed the room was quiet; nothing was moving but him and he was a man with a purpose.

By the time he reached her she was a ball of desire, and his intoxicating scent—a mixture of aftershave and male—wasn't helping matters. Her head began spinning and she could actually feel her nipples tighten hard against her sweater, and the area between her legs throbbed mercilessly.

"Do you know what I love most about you?" he asked her in a low, husky voice.

"No, what?" She was barely able to get the words out.

"Every single thing. I can't just name one," he said, gazing down at her. "And do you know what I was thinking while standing there watching you sit on this bed?"

"No, what were you thinking?" He was asking a lot of questions and she was providing answers as best she could. Her mind was struggling to keep up and not get distracted by the masculine physique standing directly in front of her. Shirtless, muscular and sexy as sin.

"I was thinking that I should be on this bed with you."

"No problem. That can be arranged. Join me."

She watched his eyes darken. "If I do, you know what's going to happen."

"Yes, but we're making up for lost time, right?"

"Right."

"In that case." She slowly scooted back on the bed. "Join me," she invited again.

In an instant he was bending over to remove his shoes and socks. Straightening, his hands moved to the snap of his jeans and she watched as he pulled his jeans and briefs down his legs.

When he stood stark naked looking at her, he said, "You got too many clothes on, Crystal."

A smile touched her lips. "Do I?"

"Yes."

She chuckled. "And what, Bane Westmoreland, are you going to do about it?"

Hours later Crystal opened her eyes and adjusted to the darkness. The only light she could see was the one streaming in through the bedroom door from the living room. The bed was huge but she and Bane were almost on the edge, chest to chest, limb to limb. She didn't want to wake him but she needed to go to the bathroom.

He wasn't on top of her but he might as well have been. With his thigh and leg thrown over hers, he was definitely holding her hostage. When she tried untwining their limbs to ease away from him, his eyes flew open.

"Sorry, didn't mean to wake you."

He stared down into her eyes and she stared back into his. They were sleepy, drowsy, satisfied. He tightened his hold on her. "And where do you think you're going?"

"The bathroom."

"Oh."

He released his tight hold on her and rolled to the side. "Don't be gone too long. I'll miss you."

She smiled when he closed his eyes again. She quickly searched for her clothes but didn't see them anywhere and didn't want to turn the lamp on to look for them further. So she decided to cross the room in the nude, something he'd done plenty of times.

Moments later after coming out of the bathroom, she decided to go through her luggage to find something to put on. Their bags were just where they'd left them, not far from the door. She was able to see in the light coming from the sitting room, so it didn't take her long to open her luggage and pull out one of her nightgowns. After slipping it on she noticed the satchel Bane had given her.

Not feeling sleepy, she decided now would be a perfect time to read. Opening the satchel, she saw Bane had placed the letters and cards in stacks so she could read them in order. He had also banded them together and labeled them. She grabbed the ones marked My First Year.

She decided to sit on the sofa in front of the fireplace. Using the remote, she turned it on and the bright glow and the heat gave her a warm cozy feeling.

Settling on the sofa with her legs tucked beneath her, she opened the first letter and began reading...

Crystal,

I made it to the navy training facility in Indiana. The other recruits here are friendly enough but I miss my brothers and cousins back home. But more than anything, I miss you. A part of me knows I need to do this and make something of myself for you, as well as for myself, but I'm not sure I can handle our separation. We've never been apart before, and more than once I wanted to walk out and keep walking and return to Denver and confront your parents to find out where they sent you. I want to let them and everyone know you are my wife and that I have every right to know where you are.

But on those days I feel that way, I know why I am enduring the loneliness. It's for you to reach the full potential that I know you can reach. You are smart. Bright. And you're also pretty. I want you to make something of yourself and I promise to make something of myself, as well.

Not sure if you will ever read this letter but I am hoping that one day you will. Just know that you will always have my heart and I love you more than life itself and I'm giving you space to come into your own. And the day I return we will know the sacrifice would have been for the best.

Love you always,
Your Bane

Crystal drew in a deep breath and wiped a tear from her eye. *Her Bane.* Putting the letter back in the envelope, she placed it aside and picked up a Valentine's Day card. She smiled after reading the poem and when she saw how he'd signed the card, "Your Bane" once again, she felt her heart flutter in her chest.

She kept reading all the cards and letters in the stack. In them he told her how his chief had noted how well he could handle a gun, and how he could hit a target with one eye closed or while looking over his shoulder. "Show-off," she said, grinning as she kept reading. His extraordinary skill with a weapon was what had made him stand out so much that his chief had brought it to the attention of the captain who had recommended him for the SEAL program.

She also noted that although her birthday and their wedding anniversary were the same day, he'd bought her separate cards for each. By the time she had finished the first stack she felt she knew how that first year had gone. His first year without her. He had been suffering just as much as she had. He had missed her. Yearned for her. Longed for her. She felt it in the words he'd written to her, and she could just imagine him lying down at night in his bunk and writing her. He'd told her about the guys he'd met and how some of them had become friends for life.

Crystal was halfway through reading the second stack of cards and letters when she heard a sound. She glanced up and saw Bane standing in the doorway.

"You didn't come back. And I missed you."

At that moment all she could think about was that the man standing there was *her Bane*. Putting the stack of cards and letters aside, she eased to her feet and crossed the room to him. They had been through a lot, were still going through a lot, but through it all, they were together.

When she reached him she wrapped her arms around his waist and said the words that filled her heart. "I love you, Bane."

"And I love you." He then swept her off her feet and into his arms. "I'm taking you back to bed."

"To sleep?" she asked.

"No."

She smiled as he carried her back into the bedroom. Once there he eased her gown off her and tossed it aside before placing her back in bed. "I began reading your letters and cards," she said when he joined her there. "Thank you for sharing that period of time with me. And I kept something for you, as well. A picture journal. I'll give it to you when we get to Alaska."

He stroked a hand down her thigh. "You're welcome, and thanks for keeping the journal for me."

And then he leaned down and kissed her and she knew that like all the other times before, this was just the beginning.

Nineteen

"I can't believe this place," Crystal said, after entering the cabin and glancing around.

Bane knew what she meant because he could barely believe it, either. The cabin was huge, but it wasn't just the size. It was also the location and the surroundings, as well as how the cabin has been built with survival in mind.

They had arrived in Kodiak, Alaska, a few hours ago after spending another full day in North Carolina. They had been Garth's guests on his private jet owned by Outlaw Freight Lines. Garth's three brothers—Cash, Sloan and Maverick—had met them at the tiny airport. Their brother Jess, who was running for senator of Alaska, was currently on the campaign trail and their sister, Charm, had accompanied their father to Seattle on a business trip. Garth had joked that it was business for their father and a shopping expedition for their sister.

As far as Bane was concerned, Garth hadn't been lying when he'd said that there was a strong resemblance between him and Cash. The similarity was uncanny in a way. And the similarities between the Westmorelands and the Outlaws didn't end there. In fact, Sloan closely resembled Derringer, and Maverick favored Aidan and Adrian. The Outlaws had easily accepted their biological connection to the Westmorelands, but according to Garth, their father had not. He was still in denial and they didn't understand why.

After making a pit stop at Walker's ranch to drop off Bailey and Walker, Garth and his brothers had driven them on to the Outlaw cabin, which was deep in the mountains and backed up against the Shelikof Strait, a beautiful waterway that stretched from the southwestern coast of Alaska to the east of Kodiak.

"Let us show you around before we leave," Garth said. He and his brothers led them from room to room, and each left Bane and Crystal more in awe than the last. And then the Outlaw brothers showed them the movable wall that led to an underground tunnel. It was better than what Bane had expected. It was basically a man cave with living quarters that included a flat-screen television on one of the walls. The sofa, Bane noted, turned into a bed. The pantry was filled with canned goods. Then there was the gun case that probably had every type of weapon ever manufactured.

"Our grandfather was a gun collector," Sloan Outlaw explained. "Our father didn't share his passion so he gave them to us to get rid of. He has no idea we kept them. As far as we were concerned, they were too priceless to give away."

"Of course, over the years we've added our own favorites," Maverick said, grinning, pointing to a .458 caliber Winchester Magnum, a very powerful rifle. "That one is mine. Use it if you have to."

A short while later, after the tour of the cabin ended, they had returned to the front room. Bane looked over at Cash, the cousin whose identity he would assume for a while. "Hope I'm not putting you out, man."

Cash smiled. "No problem. I need a few days away from Alaska anyway. A couple of friends and I are headed for Bermuda for a few days. Hate how I'll miss all the action."

The plan was to lead the group looking for Crystal to assume that she was in the cabin with Cash, an old college friend. But in order for that plan to work, in case someone went digging, the real Cash Outlaw needed to go missing for a while.

Oakwood would be calling in the morning to give Bane the final plans and let him know when word of Crystal's whereabouts would be leaked so they could be on guard and get prepared. The DOD already had men in place around the cabin. They had been there when Bane and the group arrived. Other than Garth, no one had noticed their presence, since they blended in so well with the terrain.

A short while later Bane and Crystal were saying goodbye to everyone. After Bane closed the door behind him, he looked across the room at Crystal. He thought she was holding up pretty damn well for a woman who in the next twenty-four hours would be the bait in an elaborate trap to catch her would-be kidnappers. As soon as the DOD purposely leaked her whereabouts, it would set things in motion.

"I like them."

He saw her smile. "Who?"

"Your cousins."

"And what do you like about them?" he asked, moving away from the door toward her.

"For starters, how quick they pitched in to help. They didn't have to offer us the use of this place."

"No, they didn't. Garth and his brothers paid a visit to Colorado the week before Thanksgiving to meet the Denver Westmorelands and from there they headed south to visit with the Atlanta Westmorelands. Dillon told me I would like them when I met them and I do."

He drew her into his arms. "If we pull this off we'll owe them a world of thanks. This place is perfect, and not just because of the underground tunnel. There's also the location, the seclusion. I can see someone hiding out here, and I'm sure the people looking for you will see it, too."

"I wonder when Oakwood will send his men," she said thoughtfully, looking up at him.

Bane chuckled. "They're already here."

Surprise appeared on her face. "What? Are you sure?"

"Pretty much. I haven't seen them but I can feel their presence. I noticed it the minute we pulled up in the yard. And because Garth is an ex-Marine, he did, too."

"He said something to you about it?"

Bane shook his head. "He didn't have to. He knew what to look for." Bane didn't say anything for a minute and then he said, "Nothing can happen to you, Crystal. I won't allow it. Do you know what you mean to me?"

She nodded and reached up to place her arms around his neck. "Yes, I know." And she really did. Reading those cards and letters had left her in awe at the magnitude of his love for her.

"Good." And then he leaned down and captured her mouth with his.

* * *

Later that night, just as before, Crystal untangled herself from Bane and slid out of bed. At least she tried. But Bane's arms tightened around her. "Where are you going?"

"To read. I'm on stack three now."

He rolled over in bed so they could lie side by side. "Interesting reading?"

"I think so," she said. "It means a lot knowing you were thinking about me." Reading those cards and letters, especially the letters, had helped her to understand that he loved being a navy SEAL and that his teammates were his family, as well.

"I always thought about you," he said huskily. He rubbed her cheek. "Sleepy?" he asked her.

"No. I plan to read, remember? So let me go."

"Okay, just as long as you're where I can see you."

"I'll just be in the living room."

He shook his head. "Not good enough. I want you in here with me."

She was about to argue with him, remind him the cabin was surrounded by the good guys, but instead she said, "Okay, I'll read in bed if you're sure I won't disturb you."

"I'm sure. I'm wide-awake, as well."

He released her. After slipping back into the gown that he'd taken off her earlier, Crystal padded across the room to pull the third stack out of the satchel.

While getting the cards and letters, she pulled out the photo album she had packed. Going back to the bed, she handed it to him. "Here. This is my gift to you."

Bane took it. "Thanks, baby." He then got into a sitting position and began flipping through the photo album. He came across their marriage license and smiled. When she saw his smile, she said, "We were so young then."

"Yes," he agreed. "But so much in love."

"We still are," she said, settling into position beside him. In amiable silence, he turned the pages of the photo album while she read his cards and letters. "This is your high school graduation picture?" he asked.

She glanced up from reading the letter to look over at the photograph he was asking about. "Yes. And all I could think about that day was that because of you, I had done it. I had gotten the very thing I thought I hadn't wanted and was actually pretty happy about it."

He looked at several more pictures, and when he came to her college graduation picture he said, "Isn't it weird that Cash was there on campus at the same time you were?"

"Yes. I can't imagine what my reaction would have been had I ran into a guy on campus who reminded me of you. So personally, I'm glad our paths didn't cross."

She was about to go back to reading her cards and letters when Bane's cell phone went off. He reached for it. "This is Bane."

Crystal tried reading his expression while he talked with the caller but she couldn't. The only clue she had that he was angry was the way his chin had tightened. And then when he asked the caller in an angry tone, "How the hell did that happen?" she knew something had made him furious. A few moments later he ended the call and immediately sent several text messages.

"What's wrong, Bane?"

He looked over at her and paused before saying anything, and she figured he was trying hard to get his anger in check. "That was Oakwood. Someone in his department screwed up."

He threw his head back as if to get his wrath under control and said, "Your location has already been leaked. The only good thing is that whoever they suspected as the mole took the bait, and he and his men are headed here believing that you're hiding with Cash."

"And the bad thing?" she asked, knowing there was one.

Bane drew in a deep fuming breath. "Whoever this guy is, he's evidently pretty high up there at Homeland Security. He contacted the person in charge of Oakwood's men and gave an order to pull out because a special task force was coming in to take over."

Crystal frowned. "Are you saying Oakwood's men are no longer outside protecting us?"

"That's exactly what I'm saying. But I don't want you to worry about anything. I got this," Bane said, getting out of bed and slipping on his jeans. "What I need for you to do is to go and get in the tunnel below."

"Is that where you'll be?"

"No," he said, picking up his Glock and checking his aim. "I might need to hold things down for a while. Oakwood ordered the men to return and hopefully they'll be back soon."

Crystal didn't want to think about what could happen if they didn't. Bane expected her to be hiding out below, where she would be safe, while he single-handedly fought off the bad guys until help arrived. "I prefer staying up here with you. I may not be as good a shot as you, but thanks to you I'm not bad."

He frowned. "There's no way I can let you stay here with me."

"I don't see why not," she said, sliding out of bed to begin dressing, as well. "To be honest with you, I feel pretty safe."

He shook his head. "And why are you feeling so safe?"

She looked over at him and a smile spread across her lips. "Because I'm not here with just anyone protecting my back. I'm here with Badass Bane."

Twenty

A short while later, Crystal studied the arsenal of Bane's personal weapons spread out on the table and glanced over at him. "I thought a person couldn't travel on a plane with one weapon, much less a whole suitcase full of them."

He met her gaze. "They can't."

She lifted a curious brow. "Then, how did you get through the security checkpoint when you flew to Dallas?"

"I didn't. Bailey figured I might need them and brought them with her to the cabin. I'm glad she did. And there was no problem bringing them with me on Garth's private plane."

Crystal watched how he checked each one out, making sure there was enough ammunition for each. It was close to one in the morning. "You have some awesome teammates, Bane. I enjoyed reading about them, and they have been here for you. For us. Throughout this ordeal. I can't wait to meet Coop. You mentioned him a lot in your letters."

She noticed Bane's hands go still, and when she glanced into his face she saw pain etched in his features. "Bane? What is it? What's wrong?"

He looked at her. "You won't get a chance to meet Coop, Crystal. We lost him during one of our covert operations."

"Oh, no!" She fought back tears for a man she'd never met. But in a way she had met him through Bane's letters and knew from what he'd written that he and Coop shared a special bond. "What happened?"

"I can't give you the details but it was a setup. I'm not sure how it was done but he was taken alive. Then a few days later they sent our CO Coop's bloody clothes and military tag to let us know what they did to him."

She wrapped her arms around Bane's waist. "I am so sorry for your loss. After reading your letters I know what a special friendship the two of you shared."

Bane nodded. "Yes, he was a good friend. Like a brother. I'm sorry you didn't get to meet him."

Hearing the sadness in his words, Crystal leaned up on tiptoe and pressed her lips to his. It was a quick kiss, because they didn't have much time and the situation wouldn't allow anything else. She released him, took a step back and glanced at the clock on the wall. "That's strange."

"What is?"

"I'm surprised no one has called. I would think Oakwood would be keeping tabs on us, letting us know what's going on or how close those people are to here." When Bane didn't say anything she studied his features. "You noticed it, too. Didn't you?"

"Yes, I noticed it and I think I know the reason."

"Why?"

"Someone blocked any calls coming in or out of here. Whoever did it assumes they have us cornered, but I was able to text Walker and the Outlaws right after talking with Oakwood to apprise them of what's going on. I have every reason to believe they are on their way if they aren't here already." He looked down at her. "I'm asking you again to go down below, Crystal."

"Only if we're down there together."

She heard his deep breath of frustration before Bane said, "Then take this," and passed her one of the smaller handguns off the table. "Not that you should need to use it," he added. She inserted it into the pocket of her jacket.

At that moment the light in the room flickered a few times before going completely out, throwing the entire house into darkness. "Bane?"

"I'm here," he said, wrapping an arm around her.

She jumped when suddenly there was a hard knock at the door.

"Seriously? Do they think we plan on answering it?" Bane said in an annoyed tone.

"But what if it's Walker or the Outlaws? Or even Oakwood?"

"It's not," he said. "Too soon to be Oakwood. And as far as Walker and the Outlaws, we agreed to communicate by a signal."

"What kind of signal?"

"The sound of a mourning dove's coo. I didn't hear the signal so you know what that means."

She nodded. Yes, she knew what that meant.

Bane wished like hell that Crystal had done what he'd said and gone down below. He needed to concentrate and wasn't sure he could do that for worrying about her.

Suddenly a loud voice that sounded as if it came through a megaphone blared from outside. "Mr. Outlaw. Miss Newsome. We are members of the Department of Homeland Security. We're here to take Miss Newsome to safety."

"Like hell," Bane whispered in a growl. "Those bastards expect us to just open the door and invite them inside in total darkness. They figure we're stupid enough to fall for that?"

"If you don't respond to our request," the voice continued, "we will assume the two of you are in danger and will force our way in."

Your decision, Bane thought. *Bring it on*.

"You think they really will force their way in?" Crystal asked softly.

"That's evidently their plan, so let's get prepared," he said, lowering her to the floor with him. At that moment his cell phone vibrated in his pocket. Someone had gotten past the block. He quickly pulled the phone out and read the text message from Walker. 5 of them.

"Somehow Walker got through the block to let me know there are five men surrounding the cabin. At least that's all they see. There might be others."

"At least Walker and the Outlaws are here."

"Yes, and they know to stay low and not let their presence be known unless something serious goes down. We need to get the ringleader."

"So for now it's five against two."

He frowned. "I want you to stay down, Crystal. They won't do anything that will harm you since you're valuable to them. That means they'll try to get inside to grab you."

Suddenly there was a huge crash. It sounded like the front door caving in. "Shh," Bane whispered. "Someone just got inside."

* * *

Male voices could be heard from another room. "Miss Newsome, let us know where you are. We know you think you're safe here with Cash Outlaw, but we have reason to believe he can't be trusted. We need to get you out of here and get you to safety."

Multiple footsteps could be heard going from room to room, which meant more than one man had gotten inside. Suddenly the lights came back on. "Stay down," Bane ordered her as he moved to get up from the floor.

"Not on your life." The moment she eased up with Bane, who had his gun drawn, two men entered the room with their guns drawn, as well. Bane shoved her behind him.

"Miss Newsome? Are you okay?" one of the men asked. Both were dressed in camouflage. One appeared to be well over six feet and the other was five-nine or so.

"I'm fine," she said, poking her head from around Bane to size up the two men. Both looked to be in their forties, with guns aimed right at Bane. He in turn had his gun aimed right at them.

"Then, tell your friend to put his gun down," the shorter of the two men said.

"Why can't the two of you put yours down?" Crystal retorted. She tried to block from her mind the sudden thought that this was how things had played out in the dream she'd had a few nights ago.

"We can't. Like we told you, Homeland Security has reason to believe he's dangerous."

As far as Crystal was concerned, that wasn't an understatement. She could feel the anger radiating off Bane. "Who are you?" she asked the one doing all the talking.

"We're with Homeland Security," the taller man said.

"I want names."

She could tell from his expression that he was getting annoyed with her. "I'm Gene Sharrod, head of the CLT division, and this is Ron Blackmon, head of DMP."

"You're both heads of your divisions. I'm impressed. Why would the top brass personally come for me?"

"The people after you want you for insalubrious reasons. Reasons that could be a threat to our national security."

"I got the note."

"Yes, and we believe you did the right thing by disappearing like it told you to. But now we're here to handle things and keep you safe."

Crystal lifted her chin. "How did you know what the note said?" She could tell from the look on the man's face that he realized he'd just made a slip.

"Let's cut the BS." Bane spoke up in an angry voice. "Bottom line is she isn't going anywhere."

"You aren't in any position to say anything about it, Mr. Outlaw," the shorter of the two men said with a sneer. "In case you haven't noticed, there are two guns aimed at you so I suggest you drop yours."

"And I suggest the two of you drop yours," Bane responded tersely, looking from one man to the other.

The taller man had the audacity to snicker. "Do you honestly think you can take the both of us down, Outlaw?"

A cocky smile touched Bane's lips. "I know I can. And the name isn't Outlaw. Cash Outlaw is my cousin. I'm Brisbane Westmoreland. Navy SEAL. SE348907. And just so you know, I'm a master sniper. So be forewarned. I can blow both your heads off without splattering any blood on that sofa."

The shorter man seemed taken aback by what Bane

had said, but Crystal could tell by the look that appeared in the taller man's eyes that he thought Bane was bluffing.

"Trust me," she said. "He's telling the truth."

The taller man's eyes darkened in anger. "We're not leaving here without you."

"Wanna bet?" Bane snarled. "My wife isn't going anywhere with either of you."

"Wife?" Sharrod asked, shocked.

"Yes, his wife," Crystal confirmed, holding up the finger of her left hand, where her diamond ring shone brilliantly.

"I'm tired of talking," Bane said. "Put your damn guns down now."

Blackmon narrowed his gaze at Bane. "Like Sharrod said. You're in no position to give orders."

Suddenly shots rang out and before Crystal could blink, Bane had shot the guns right out of both men's hands. "I am now," Bane said easily.

The two men bowed over, howling in pain. One of them, Crystal wasn't sure which one, claimed one of his fingers had gotten shot off. Then they heard the mourning dove coo just seconds before Walker, Bailey and Garth stormed into the room with their own guns drawn.

"You guys okay?" Bailey asked, rushing over to them, while Walker and Garth went over to the two men, who were wailing at the top of their lungs, sounding worse than babies. "Sloan and Maverick are outside taking care of the men who came with these two."

"You're going to regret this, Outlaw…Westmoreland, or whatever your name is," Blackmon snarled. "Homeland Security is going to nail your ass. This is treason. You are betraying your country."

"No, I think the two of you are betraying yours," Oakwood said, charging in. "Gene Sharrod and Ron Blackmon, you are both under arrest. Get them out of here," he told his men as they rushed forward.

"We need medical treatment," Blackmon screamed, holding his bloodied hand when agents came to grab him.

Bane frowned. "Better be glad it was just your hands and not your damn heads like I threatened to blow off. So stop whining."

After Oakwood and his agents had taken both men out the door, Bane turned to Crystal and frowned. "I told you to stay down."

She reached up to caress the angry lines around his jaw. "I know, but you forgot what you also said."

"What?"

"That we were in this together."

And then she leaned up to place a chaste kiss on his lips, but he evidently had other ideas and pulled her into his arms and deepened the kiss. She wrapped her arms around him and returned the kiss, not caring that they had an audience.

When one of the men cleared his throat, they broke off the kiss and Bane whispered against her moist lips, "Come on, Mrs. Westmoreland. Let's go home."

Twenty-One

A week later

Crystal hadn't meant to awaken Bane. But when he shifted in bed and slowly opened sleepy eyes that were filled with a heavy dose of desire, she saw he was now wide-awake.

She knew of no other man who could wake up ready to make love after going to bed the night before the same way. But then, hadn't he warned her that as far as the intensity of their lovemaking was concerned, this was just the beginning?

"Good morning," he said in that deep, husky voice that she loved hearing.

She smiled. "And good morning to you, too, Bane."

And as far as she was concerned, it was a good morning, especially after that phone call they had received yesterday. According to Oakwood, Sharrod had caved in under pressure and told them everything, including the location where those other two chemists were being held. By now the two men had been reunited with their families.

She glanced around the cabin. Their cabin. Bane had built it years ago for her as their secret lovers' hide-away. Now it was her home. Originally it had just one large room with a bathroom, but last year Bane had instructed Riley to hire someone to add a kitchen nook and a sitting area and to enlarge the bathroom. His sister Gemma, who was an interior decorator, had put her signature on it both before and after the renovations. There was an iron bed in the bedroom with colorful curtains that matched the bedspread.

The sitting room was the perfect size, just large enough for a sofa, a chair and a table. And she loved the fireplace that provided such great heat on those really cold days and nights. There was also a flat-screen television on the wall. Bane told her that he had begun spending his days and nights here whenever he came home. For that reason, he had installed internet services and didn't have to worry about missing calls due to his phone being out of range. Now he could send and receive phone calls just fine.

Already plans had been made to build the house that would become their permanent home. It wouldn't be far from here on Bane's Ponderosa, the name of the spread he had inherited. They would start looking at house plans next week. The one thing they did know was that whatever house they built would have to be large enough for all the kids they planned to have one day.

She had gotten around to reading all his cards and letters, and if she could have loved him even more than she already did, she would have. He had poured out his heart, his soul and his agony of a life without her in it. She needed no further proof that she was loved deeply by the man who was meant to be hers always, just as she was meant to be his.

Yesterday she and Bane had visited her parents' property. Property that was now hers. The place was deserted and badly in need of repairs. However, they'd decided not to make any decisions about what they would do with it for now.

In a way the five years of separation had done what it was meant to do. It had helped them grow into better people. She definitely saw a change in Bane. He could still be a badass when he needed to be, but there was a calmness about him, a discipline, self-control and purpose that hadn't always been there before. He'd always loved her and his family. And now he loved his country with just as much passion.

And his family was wonderful. She was enjoying getting to know the ladies his brothers and cousins had married. She had always been a loner, and for the first time in her life she was feeling part of the family.

Because Crystal had lost a lot of her things in the fire, Pam had organized a welcome-home party for her and Bane where she had received a lot of gift cards. It just so happened they were all from the ladies' favorite places to shop.

And then there was the Westmoreland family tradition. Every other Friday night, the Westmorelands got together at Dillon's place. The women would do the cooking and the men would arrive hungry. Afterward, the men took part in a poker game and the women did whatever they pleased. Usually they planned a shopping expedition. Tonight would be Crystal's first

Westmoreland Family Chow Down, and she was looking forward to it.

Bane shifted his position in bed and Crystal was instantly aware of the erection poking against her backside. Instinctively, she scooted back to bring her body
closer to his. All that desire bottled up inside him was
beginning to affect her, as well. "What happens when
you get tired of me?"

"I won't. You're in my blood, baby. And in my soul.
And especially here," he said, taking her hand and placing it on his chest, right against his heart.

His words touched her deeply. And it didn't help matters that he was staring down at her, seducing her with
those gorgeous hazel eyes. "Oh, Bane." At that moment
she wanted him. "Make love to me."

"It will be my pleasure."

Later that evening Crystal sat beside Bane at the
dinner table at Dillon's home, surrounded by Bane's
brothers, cousins and their spouses. And then there were
the children. A lot of children. Beautiful children who
were the joy of their parents' lives. Seeing them, spending time with them, made her anxious to have a child
of her own. A baby. Bane's baby.

Dillon had made a toast earlier to her and Bane, officially welcoming her to the family and telling them
how proud he and the family were of them, and their
strong and unwavering commitment to each other. He
also gave them his blessings, just as he'd known his
parents would have done, for a long and happy marriage. His words had almost brought tears to her eyes
because she felt she was truly a part of this family. The
Westmoreland family.

A short while later, when dinner was over and the

women were clearing off the table as the men geared up for a card game, Bane's cell phone rang. "It's my CO," he said, quickly pulling his phone out of his jeans pocket. "Excuse me while I take this."

She felt a hard lump in her throat. She knew Bane was on military leave until March. Had something come up where his CO was calling the team together for an assignment? It was three weeks before Christmas. Besides that, it was their first week together without all the drama. Crystal wasn't sure how she would handle it if he had to suddenly leave.

You will handle it the same way any SEAL wife would, an inner voice said. *You will love him, support him and be there with open arms when he returns*. She was suddenly filled with an inner peace, prepared for whatever came next.

"What is it, Bane?" Dillon asked.

Crystal, like everyone else, turned to gaze at Bane when he returned to the dining room. There was a shocked look on his face. Although it had been Dillon who asked the question, Bane met Crystal's gaze and held it.

"That was my CO. He wanted to let me know he got a call from the Pentagon tonight that Coop is alive and is being held prisoner somewhere in Syria."

"Your friend Coop?" Crystal asked, getting up out of her seat and crossing the room to Bane.

"Yes. And the CO is getting our team together to go in and get Coop, and any other hostages they're holding, out of there."

She nodded. "When will you be leaving?" she asked softly.

He placed a hand on her shoulder. "I'm not. The CO just wanted me to know. He's aware of our situation and what we went through last week. He's letting me know he's exempting me from this mission if that's what I want."

Crystal studied Bane's features. And not caring if they had an audience listening to their every word, she said, "But that's not what you really want, is it?"

He rubbed his hand down his face. "Doesn't matter. It's three weeks before Christmas. There's no telling when I might return. I might not make it back until after the holidays, and I wanted to spend every single day with you."

"And I with you. But you *must* go," she said, not believing she was actually encouraging him to do so. "Coop is your best friend."

"And you are my wife."

A smile touched her lips. "I'm also the wife of a SEAL. So things like this are to be expected. I know it and I accept it. I will be fine until you get home, and if you don't make it back by Christmas, I won't be alone. For the first time, Bane, thanks to you I have a family," she said, glancing around the room. "I have a big family."

"Yes, you do," Dillon said, joining the conversation. "And whenever Bane has to go out on covert operations we will be here for you."

"Thanks, Dillon." Crystal returned her gaze to Bane. "So go, Bane, and be the dedicated and fierce SEAL that you are. The one you were trained to be. Be careful and do everything in your power to bring Coop home."

Bane stared at her for a long moment before he reached out and pulled her to him and held her close. And then he leaned down and kissed her with all the love she actually felt. The love she knew was there and had always been there between them. Suddenly she was swept off her feet and into big, strong arms.

"Bane!"

Holding her tight, he headed for the door. "We're going home," Bane said over his shoulder as his whole family watched them. "Crystal and I bid you all a good night."

Twenty-Two

Christmas Eve

"And you're sure you don't want to spend the night at our place, Crystal? You're more than welcome."

Crystal smiled at her brother-in-law when he brought the car to a stop in front of the cabin. "Thanks, Dillon, but I'll be okay."

"I promised Bane I would look out for you."

"And you have. I really do appreciate the invitation, but I'm fine."

She knew she would be a lot better if Bane called, but neither she nor his brothers and cousins had heard from him since he'd left three weeks ago. He had told them that no one knew how long this operation would take. She just hoped he was safe and all was going well.

In the meantime she had tried staying busy. Bane had wanted her to look at house plans while he was gone, and she had helped Pam at her acting school in town. Jason's wife, Bella, had invited her for tea several times, and there had been a number of shopping trips with the Westmoreland ladies. There had been the annual Westmoreland charity ball. It was her first time attending one and she wished Bane could have been there with her. But it had been good seeing the Outlaws again.

And she had been summoned to the nation's capital last week. Dillon, Canyon and their wives had gone with her. She'd had to give a statement about Sharrod and Blackmon. No one had asked about Bane's whereabouts and she figured they knew it was classified information.

The director of Homeland Security had told her of the value of her research and that someone would be contacting her soon. They wanted her, along with the other two biochemists, to come work for the government to perfect their research while she completed her PhD. She promised she would give it some thought but refused to make any decisions until Bane returned.

"I used to worry about Bane whenever I figured he was out on one of those operations," Dillon said softly to her as he unbuckled his seat belt. "But then I figured it didn't pay to worry. Besides, we're talking about Bane, the one person who can take care of himself. If we should be worried about anyone, it's those who have to come up against him."

Crystal smiled, knowing that was true. She had seen how Bane had handled Sharrod and Blackmon. He had been confident, cool and effective, even when it had seemed the odds had been stacked against him.

"Bane will be okay, Crystal," Dillon said when she didn't respond to what he'd said.

She nodded and absently touched the locket she still wore around her neck. "I hope so, Dillon."

"Don't just hope. Believe."

Her smile spread. "Okay, I believe."

"Good."

He got out of the car and came around to open the door for her. "You will be joining us for Christmas breakfast in the morning and then later a special Westmoreland Holiday Chow Down tomorrow night, right?"

"Yes, I'm looking forward to it."

"The Outlaws will be arriving about noon along with Bailey and Walker and some of the Atlanta Westmorelands."

She had gotten the chance to meet Charm Outlaw before she and Bane had left Alaska. Charm and her father had been returning from their business trip. The woman was as beautiful as she was nice. However, Crystal thought the father of the Outlaws had been reserved, as if he'd rather them not be there. Bane had explained that the old man was having a hard time accepting the fact that his father had been adopted.

"You know the drill," Dillon said, grinning when they reached the door of the cabin.

"Yes, I know it." Because she was living in a secluded area, the men in the family refused to let her drive home alone. They either drove her back home or followed behind her in their car to make sure she got there safely. And then before they would leave, she'd have to give a signal that everything was okay by flashing the window blinds.

"Good night, Dillon."

"Good night. Do you need a ride to my place in the morning?"

"No, thanks. I'll drive."

She opened the door to go inside the house and was glad she'd left the fireplace burning. The cabin felt warm and cozy. She was about to turn and head for the window to flash the blinds when she saw a movement out the corner of her eye. She jerked around.

"Bane!"

She raced across the room and was gobbled up in big, strong arms and kissed by firm and demanding lips. It seemed as though the kiss lasted forever as their tongues tangled and mingled, and they devoured each other's mouths. Finally, he broke off the kiss. "I missed you, baby."

"And I missed you," she said, running her arms all over him to make sure he was all in one piece. His skin was damp, he smelled of aftershave and he was wearing his jeans low on his hips. It was obvious he'd just gotten out of the shower.

"Why didn't you let me know you were coming home tonight?"

A smile touched his lips. "I wanted to surprise you. The mission was a success, although it was damn risky at times. They were keeping Coop and two other American prisoners secluded up in the mountains. Getting up there was one thing and getting them out alive was another. It wasn't easy but we did it, and all returned home safely. No injuries or casualties."

He paused a moment and said, "Coop was glad to see us and they didn't break his spirit, although they tried. He said what kept him going was believing that one day we would come rescue him. And we did. He and the others were taken to Bethesda Hospital in Maryland to get checked out."

Crystal was about to open her mouth to say something when there was a loud pounding at the front door. "Oops. That's Dillon. He brought me home and I forgot to flash the blinds to let him know I was okay," she said, racing across the room to open the door.

"Crystal, are you okay? When you didn't flash the blinds I—" Dillon stopped talking when he glanced over her shoulder and saw his brother. "Bane!"

The two men exchanged bear hugs. "Glad to see you back in one piece," Dillon said, grinning as he looked his baby brother up and down.

Bane pulled Crystal to his side and planted a kiss on her forehead. "And I'm glad to be back, too."

"I'll let the family know you're home. And I guess we won't be seeing you bright and early tomorrow morning for breakfast as planned, Crystal," Dillon said, his grin getting wider.

"No, you won't," Bane answered for her. "My wife and I are sleeping in late. We will try to make it for dinner, however."

Dillon chuckled. "Okay." He then looked at his watch. "It just turned midnight on the East Coast. Merry Christmas, you two."

"And Merry Christmas to you, Dillon," Crystal said, cuddling closer in her husband's strong arms. And in that moment she knew that for her this would be the merriest because she had her Bane. It would be their first Christmas spent together as man and wife.

As soon as the door closed behind Dillon, Bane tightened his embrace and looked down at her. "I like the tree and all the decorations."

She glanced over at the Christmas tree she'd put up a couple of weeks ago. What was special about it was that it had come right off Bane's Ponderosa. Riley had chopped it down for her. She'd had fun decorating the tree and had even trailed Christmas lights and ornaments along the fireplace mantel. "Thanks."

And then Bane pulled her even closer into his arms. "I've already placed your gift under the tree, baby."

She glanced over her shoulder and saw the huge red box with a silver bow. She looked back at him, feeling like a kid on Christmas morning. "Thanks. What's in it?"

He chuckled. "You get to open it in the morning." He leaned down and placed a kiss on her lips. "Merry Christmas, sweetheart."

She reached up and wrapped her arms around his neck. "And merry Christmas to you, Bane."

And then their mouths connected, and she knew this was still just the beginning. They had the rest of their lives.

Epilogue

Valentine's Day

"I would like to propose a toast to the newlyweds," Ramsey Westmoreland said, getting everyone's attention and holding up his champagne glass. "First of all, we didn't ever think you would leave us, Bay, but we know you'll be in good hands living in Alaska with Walker. We're still going to miss you showing up unannounced, letting yourself into our homes and eating our food."

"And getting all into our business," Derringer hollered out.

Ramsey chuckled. "Yes, she did have a knack for getting all in our business. But I think we can safely say we wouldn't have wanted it any other way. I know Mom and Dad are smiling down on us today, happy for their baby girl."

He paused as if to compose himself before he continued, "And, Walker, she's yours now and I'm going to tell you the same thing I told Callum when he married Gemma, and Rico when he married Megan. You can't give her back. You asked for her, flaws and all, so deal with it."

Everyone laughed at that. Ramsey then raised his champagne glass higher. "To Walker and Bailey. May you have a long and wonderful marriage, and watch out for the bears." The attendees laughed again as they clicked their glasses before drinking their champagne.

Dillon then stepped up to stand beside Ramsey. The wedding had been held inside the beautiful garden club in downtown Denver. Riley's wife, Alpha, who was an event planner, had done her magic. The wedding theme had been From This Day Forward, and since it was Valentine's Day the colors had been red and white.

"No, I'm not giving Walker and Bailey another toast," Dillon said, grinning. "With so many members of the family gathered here together, I want to take this time to welcome our cousins, the Outlaws of Alaska. Your last names might be Outlaw but you proved just how much Westmoreland blood ran through your veins when you gave Bane and Crystal your protection when they needed it the most. And all of us thank you for it. Our great-grandfather Raphel would be proud. And that deserves another toast."

Crystal felt Bane's arms tighten around her waist. What Dillon had said was true. The Outlaws had come through for them during a very critical time. Their last names might be Outlaw, but they looked and carried themselves just like Westmorelands.

Later, she saw Dillon and Ramsey talking to Garth and Sloan and couldn't help but notice how the single women at the wedding were checking them out. With all the Denver Westmoreland males marked off the bachelor list, it seemed that the single ladies were considering the Outlaws as hopefuls. Evidently the thought of moving to Alaska didn't dissuade them one bit.

"What's this I hear about the two of you moving to Washington?" Senator Reggie Westmoreland approached to ask. He had his beautiful wife, Olivia, by his side.

Bane smiled. "It will be just for a little while, after Crystal graduates in May with her PhD. She will be working at that lab in DC for six months and I was offered a position teaching SEAL recruits how to master a firearm."

"That's great! Libby and I will have to invite the two of you over once you get settled."

Jess Outlaw walked up to join them. Because he had been out on the campaign trail when they were in Alaska, the first time Bane and Crystal had met him had been when the Outlaws had joined the Westmorelands for Christmas.

"And I hope to see you soon in Washington, as well," Reggie said to Jess.

Jess smiled. "I hope so. The race is close and has begun getting ugly."

"Been there before," Reggie said. "Hang in there and stick to your principles."

Jess nodded. "Thanks for your advice, and thanks so much for your endorsement."

A smile spread across Reggie's lips. "No thanks needed. We are family. Besides, I reviewed your platform, and it's a good one that could benefit the people of your state. I think in the end they will see that."

"Let's hope so," Jess said.

A few moments later Crystal found herself alone with Bane. Coop was doing fine and had visited them in Westmoreland Country a few times. So had Nick, Flipper and Viper. Flipper had personally delivered to her the items that he and his brother had removed from her house before the fire.

She had gotten to know all of Bane's team members and thought they were swell guys. And she had met their wives, as well. But Flipper, Viper and Coop were single and swearing to stay that way. Since the three were extremely handsome men, she couldn't wait to see just for how long.

"Did I tell you today how much I love you?" Bane leaned down to ask her, whispering close to her ear.

"Yes," she said, smiling up at him. "But you can tell me again."

"Gladly. Crystal Gayle Westmoreland, I love you very much. With all my heart."

She reached up and caressed his cheek as she thought about all they'd endured over the years. A lot had changed, but the one thing that had remained constant had been their love. "And I love you, too, Bane. With all my heart."

And then they kissed, sealing their words and their love. Forever.

* * * * *

"We have challenges in front of us. I'd like to focus on them without. . . complications."

That part wasn't the whole truth, but it was certainly true enough.

It didn't matter. No more kissing. That was the rule and she was sticking to it.

"Caitlyn. You focus on your challenges your way, and I'll focus on my challenges my way."

"What's that supposed to mean?" she whispered, afraid she wasn't going to like the answer.

Antonio looked at her. "It means I'm going to kiss you again. You'd best think of another argument if you don't want me to."

* * *

Triplets Under the Tree
is part of Mills & Boon Desire's number 1
bestselling series, Billionaires and Babies:
Powerful men. . .wrapped around
their babies' little fingers.

TRIPLETS UNDER THE TREE

BY
KAT CANTRELL

Published in Great Britain 2015
by Mills & Boon, an imprint of Harlequin (UK) Limited,
Eton House, 18-24 Paradise Road, Richmond, Surrey, TW9 1SR

© 2015 Kat Cantrell

ISBN: 978-0-263-25288-0

51-1215

Harlequin (UK) Limited's policy is to use papers that are natural, renewable and recyclable products and made from wood grown in sustainable forests. The logging and manufacturing processes conform to the legal environmental regulations of the country of origin.

Printed and bound in Spain
by CPI, Barcelona

Kat Cantrell read her first Mills & Boon novel in third grade and has been scribbling in notebooks since she learned to spell. What else would she write but romance? She majored in literature, officially with the intent to teach, but somehow ended up buried in middle management in corporate America, until she became a stay-at-home mum and full-time writer.

Kat, her husband and their two boys live in north Texas. When she's not writing about characters on the journey to happily-ever-after, she can be found at a soccer game, watching the TV show *Friends* or listening to '80s music.

Kat was the 2011 Mills & Boon So You Think You Can Write contest winner and a 2012 RWA Golden Heart Award finalist for best unpublished series contemporary manuscript.

To Diane Spigonardo.
Thanks for the inspiration.

Prologue

Near Punggur Besar, Batam Island, Indonesia

Automatically, Falco swung his arm in an arc to block the punch. He hadn't seen it coming. But a sense he couldn't explain told him to expect his opponent's attack.

Counterpunch. His opponent's head snapped backward. *No mercy.* Flesh smacked flesh again and again, rhythmically.

The moves came to him fluidly, without thought. He'd been learning from Wilipo for only a few months, but Falco's muscles already sang with expertise, adopting the techniques easily.

His opponent, Ravi, attacked yet again. Falco ducked and spun to avoid the hit. His right leg ached with the effort, but he ignored it. It always ached where the bone had broken.

From his spot on the sidelines of the dirt-floored ring,

Wilipo grunted. The sound meant more footwork, less jabbing.

Wilipo spoke no English and Falco had learned but a handful of words in Bahasa since becoming a student of the sole martial arts master in southern Batam Island. Their communication during training sessions consisted of nods and gestures. A blessing, considering Falco had little to say.

The stench of old fish rent the air, more pungent today with the heat. Gazes locked, Falco and Ravi circled each other. The younger man from a neighboring village had become Falco's sparring partner a week ago after he'd run out of opponents in his own village. The locals whispered about him and he didn't need to speak Bahasa to understand they feared him.

He wanted to tell them not to be afraid. But he knew he was more than a strange Westerner in an Asian village full of simple people. More than a man with dangerous fists.

Nearly four seasons ago, a fisherman had found Falco floating in the water, unconscious, with horrific injuries. At least that was what he'd pieced together from the doctor's halting, limited English.

He should have died before he'd washed ashore in Indonesia and he certainly should have died at some point during the six-month coma his body had required to heal.

But he'd lived.

And when he finally awoke, it was to a nightmare of physical rehabilitation and confusion. His memories were fleeting. Insubstantial. Incomplete. He was the man with no past, no home, no idea who he was other than angry and lost.

The only clue to his identity lay inked across his left pectoral muscle—a fierce, bold falcon tattoo with a scarlet banner clutched in its talons, emblazoned with the word *Falco*.

That was what his saviors called him since he didn't remember his name, though it chafed to be addressed as such.

Why? It must be a part of his identity. But when he
pushed his memory, it only resulted in his fists primed to
punch something and a blinding headache. Every waking
moment—and even some of those dedicated to sleep—he
heard an urgent soul-deep cry to discover why he'd been
snatched from the teeth of a cruel death. Surely he'd lived
for a reason. Surely he'd remember something critical to
set him on the path toward who he was. Every day thus
far had ended in disappointment.

Only fighting allowed him moments of peace and clarity as he disciplined his mind to focus on something other
than the struggle to remember.

Ravi and Wilipo spoke in rapid Bahasa, leaving the
Westerner out of it, as always.

Wilipo grunted again.

That meant it was time to stop sparring. Nodding, Falco
halted, breathing heavily. Ravi's reflexes were not as in-
stantaneous and his fist clipped Falco.

Pain exploded in his head. *"Che diavolo!"*

The curse had spit from his mouth the moment Ravi
struck, though Falco had no conscious knowledge of Italian. Or how he knew it was Italian. The intrigue saved
Ravi from being pulverized.

Ravi bowed apologetically, dropping his hands to his
sides. Rubbing his temples, Falco scowled over the late
shot as a flash of memory spilled into his head.

White stucco. Glass. A house perched on a cliff, overlooking the ocean. *Malibu.* A warm breeze. A woman with
red hair.

His house. He had a home, full of his things, his memories, his life.

The address scrolled through his mind as if it had always been there, along with images of street signs and impressions of direction, and he knew he could find it.

Home. He had to get there. Somehow.

One

Los Angeles, California

At precisely 4:47 a.m., Caitlyn bolted awake, as she did every morning. The babies had started sleeping through the night, thank the good Lord, but despite that, their feeding time had ingrained itself into her body in some kind of whacked-out mommy alarm clock.

No one had warned her of that. Just as no one had warned her that triplets weren't three times the effort and nail-biting worry of one baby, but more like a zillion times.

But they also came with a zillion times the awe and adoration.

Caitlyn picked up the video monitor from her nightstand and watched her darlings sleep in their individual cribs. Antonio Junior sighed and flopped a fist back and forth as if he knew his mother was watching, but Leon and Annabelle slept like rocks. It was a genetic trait they shared with Vanessa, their biological mother, along with her red hair. Antonio had hair the color of a starless night, like his father.

And if he grew up to be half as hypnotically gorgeous as his father, she'd be beating the women off her son with a Louisville Slugger.

No matter how hard she tried, Caitlyn couldn't go back to sleep. Exhaustion was a condition she'd learned to live with and, maddeningly, it had nothing to do with how much sleep she got. Having fatherless eight-month-old triplets wreaked havoc on her sanity, and in the hours before dawn, all the questions and doubts and fears crowded into her mind.

Should she be doing more to meet an eligible man? Like what? Hang out in bars wearing a vomit-stained shirt, where she could chat up a few victims. "Hey, baby, have you ever fantasized about going all night long with triplets? Because I've got a proposition for you!"

No, the eligible men of Los Angeles were pretty safe from Caitlyn Hopewell, that was for sure. Even without the ready-made family, her relationship rules scared away most men: you didn't sleep with a man unless you were in love and there was a ring on your finger. Period. It was an absolute that had carried her through college and into adulthood, especially as she'd witnessed what passed for her sister Vanessa's criteria for getting naked with someone—he'd bought her jewelry or could get her further in her career. Caitlyn didn't want that for herself. And that pretty much guaranteed she'd stay single.

But how could she ever be enough for three children when, no matter how much she loved them, she wasn't supposed to be their mother? When she'd agreed to be Vanessa's surrogate, Caitlyn had planned on a nine-month commitment, not a lifetime. But fate had had different plans.

Caitlyn rolled from the king-size bed she still hadn't

grown used to despite sleeping in it for over a year. Might as well get started on the day at—she squinted at her phone—6:05 a.m. Threading her dark mess of curls through a ponytail holder, she threw on some yoga pants and a top, determined to get in at least twenty minutes of Pilates before Leon awoke.

She spread out her mat on the hardwood floor close to the glass wall overlooking the Malibu coastline, her favorite spot for tranquility. There was a full gym on the first floor of Antonio and Vanessa's mansion, but she couldn't bear to use it. Not yet. It had too much of Antonio stamped all over it, what with the mixed martial arts memorabilia hanging from the walls and the regulation ring in the center.

One day she'd clean it out, but as much as she hated the reminders of Antonio, she couldn't lose the priceless link to him. She hadn't removed any of Vanessa's things from the house, either, but had put a good bit away, where she couldn't see it every day.

Fifteen minutes later, her firstborn yowled through the monitor and Caitlyn dashed to the nursery across the hall from her bedroom before he woke up his brother and sister.

"There's my precious," she crooned and scooped up the gorgeous little bundle from his crib.

Like clockwork, he was always the first of the three to demand breakfast, and Caitlyn tried to spend alone time with each of her kids while feeding them. Brigitte, the babies' au pair, thought she was certifiable for breast-feeding triplets, but Caitlyn didn't mind. She loved bonding with the babies, and nobody ever saw her naked anyway; it was worth the potential hit to her figure to give the babies a leg up in the nutrition department.

The morning passed in a blur of babies and baths, and just as Caitlyn was about to return a phone call to her lawyer that she'd missed somewhere along the way, someone pounded on the front door.

Delivery guy, she hoped. She'd had to order a new car seat and it could not get here fast enough. Annabelle had christened hers in such a way that no bleach in existence could make it usable again and, honestly, Caitlyn had given up trying. There had to be some benefits to having custodial control of her children's billion-dollar inheritance.

"Brigitte? Can you get that?" Caitlyn called, but the girl didn't respond. Probably dealing with one of the kids, which was what she got paid well to do.

With a shrug, Caitlyn pocketed her phone and padded to the door, swinging it wide in full anticipation of a brown uniform–clad man.

It wasn't UPS. The unshaven man on her doorstep loomed over her, his dark gaze searching and familiar. There was something about the way he tilted his head—

"Antonio!" The strangled word barely made it past her throat as it seized up.

No! It couldn't be. Antonio had died in the same plane crash as Vanessa, over a year ago. Her brain fuzzed with disappointment, even as her heart latched on to the idea of her children's father standing before her in the flesh. Lack of sleep was catching up with her.

"Antonio," the man repeated and his eyes widened. "Do I know you?"

His raspy voice washed over her, turning inside her chest warmly, and tears pricked her eyelids. He even sounded like Antonio. She'd always loved his voice. "No, I don't think so. For a moment, I thought you were—"

A ghost. She choked it back.

His blank stare shouldn't have tripped her senses, but all at once, even with a full beard and weighing twenty pounds less, he looked so much like Antonio she couldn't stop greedily drinking him in.

"This is my house," he insisted firmly with a hint of wonderment as he glanced around the foyer beyond the open door. "I recognize it. But the Christmas tree is in the wrong place."

Automatically, she glanced behind her to note the location of the twelve-foot-high blue spruce she'd painstakingly arranged in the living room near the floor-to-ceiling glass wall facing the ocean.

"No, it's not," Caitlyn retorted.

Vanessa had always put the tree in the foyer so people could see it when they came in, but Caitlyn liked it by the sea. Then, every time you looked at the tree, you saw the water, too. Seemed logical to her, and this was her house now.

"I don't remember you." He cocked his head as if puzzled. "Did I sell you this house?"

She shook her head. "I…uh, live here with the owners."

The Malibu mansion was actually part of the babies' estate. She hadn't wanted to move them from their parents' house and, according to the terms of Vanessa's and Antonio's wills, Caitlyn got to make all the decisions for the children.

"I remember a red-haired woman. Beautiful." His expression turned hard and slightly desperate. "Who is she?"

"Vanessa," Caitlyn responded without thinking. She shouldn't be so free with information. "Who are *you*?" she demanded.

"I don't know," he said between clenched teeth. "I remember flashes, incomplete pictures, and none of it makes sense. Tell me who I am."

Oh, my God. "You don't know who you are?" People didn't really get amnesia the way they did in movies. Did they?

Hand to her mouth, she evaluated this dirty, disheveled

man wearing simple cotton pants rolled at the ankles and a torn cotton shirt. It couldn't be true. Antonio was dead.

If Antonio *wasn't* dead, where had he been since the plane crash? If he'd really lost his memory, it could explain why he'd been missing all this time.

But not why he'd suddenly shown up over a year later. Maybe he was one of those con men who preyed on grieving family members, and loss of memory was a convenient out to avoid incriminatory questions that would prove his identity, yet he couldn't answer.

But he'd known the Christmas tree was in the wrong place. What if he was telling the truth?

Her heart latched on to the idea and wouldn't let go.

Because— Oh, goodness. She'd always been half in love with her sister's husband and it all came rushing back. The guilt. The despondency at being passed over for the lush, gorgeous older Hopewell sister, the one who always got everything her heart desired. The covert sidelong glances at Antonio's profile during family dinners. Fantasies about what it would be like if he'd married her instead of Vanessa. The secret thrill at carrying Antonio's babies because Vanessa couldn't, and harboring secret dreams of Antonio falling at her feet, begging Caitlyn to be the mother of his children instead.

Okay, and she'd had a few secret dreams that involved some…carnal scenarios, like how Antonio's skin would feel against hers. What it would be like to kiss him. And love him in every sense of the word.

For the past six years, Caitlyn had lived with an almost biblical sense of shame, in a "thou shalt not covet thy sister's husband" kind of way. But she couldn't help it—Antonio had a wickedly sexy warrior's body and an enigmatic, watchful gaze that sliced through her when he turned it in her direction. Oh, she had it bad, and she'd never fully reconciled because it was intertwined with guilt—maybe she'd wished her sister ill and that was why the plane had crashed.

The guilt crushed down on her anew.

Tersely, he shook his head and that was when she noticed the scar bisecting his temple, which forked up into his dark, shaggy hair. On second thought, this man looked nothing like Antonio. With hard lines around his mouth, he was sharper, more angular, with shadows in his dark eyes that spoke of nightmares better left unexplained.

"I can't remem—you called me Antonio." Something vulnerable welled up in his gaze and then he winced. "Antonio Cavallari. Tell me. Is that my name?"

She hadn't mentioned Antonio's last name.

He could have learned the name of her children's father from anywhere. Los Angeles County tax records. From the millions of internet stories about the death of the former UFC champion and subsequent founder of the billion-dollar enterprise called Falco Fight Club after his career ended. Vanessa had had her own share of fame as an actress, playing the home-wrecking vixen everyone loved to hate on a popular nighttime drama. Her red hair had been part of her trademark look, and when she'd died, the internet had exploded with the news. Her sister's picture popped up now and again even a year later, so knowing about the color of Vanessa's hair wasn't terribly conclusive, either.

He could have pumped the next-door neighbor for information, for that matter.

Caitlyn refused to put her children in danger under any circumstances.

Sweeping him with a glance, she took as much of his measure as she could. But there was no calculation. No suggestion of shrewdness. Just confusion and a hint of the man who'd married her sister six years ago.

"Yes. Antonio Cavallari." Her eyelids fluttered closed for a beat. What if she was wrong? What if she just wanted him to be Antonio for all the wrong reasons and became the victim of an elaborate fraud? Or worse—the victim of assault?

All at once, he sagged against the door frame, babbling in a foreign language. Stricken, she stared at him. She'd never heard Antonio speak anything other than English.

Her stomach clenched. Blood tests. Dental records. Doctors' exams. There had to be a thousand ways to prove someone's identity. But what was she supposed to do? Tell him to come back with proof?

Then his face went white and he pitched to his knees with a feeble curse, landing heavily on the woven welcome mat.

It was a fitting condemnation. Welcoming, she was not.

Throat tight with concern, she blurted out, "Are you okay? What's wrong?"

"Tired. Hungry," he stated simply, eyes closed and head lolling to one side. "I walked from the docks."

"The docks?" Her eyes went wide. "The ones near *Long Beach*? That's, like, fifty miles!"

"No identification," he said hoarsely. "No money."

The man couldn't even stand and, good grief, Caitlyn had certainly spent enough time in the company of actors to spot one—his weakened state was real.

"Come inside," she told him before she thought better of it. "Rest. And drink some water. Then we can sort this out."

It wasn't as if she was alone. Brigitte and Rosa, the housekeeper, were both upstairs. He might be Antonio, but that didn't make him automatically harmless, and who knew what his mental state was? But if he couldn't stand, he couldn't threaten anyone, let alone three women armed with cell phones and easy access to Francesco's top-dollar chef's knives.

He didn't even seem to register that she'd spoken, let

alone acknowledge what he'd surely been after the whole time—an invitation inside. For a man who could be trying to scam her, he certainly wasn't chomping at the bit to gain entrance to her home.

Hesitating, she wondered if she should help him to his feet, but the thought of touching him had her hyperventilating. Either he was a strange man, or he was a most familiar one, and neither one gave her an ounce of comfort. Heat feathered across her cheeks as her chaste sensibilities warred with the practicality of helping someone in need.

He swayed and nearly toppled over, forcing her decision.

No way around it. She knelt and grabbed his arm, then slung it across her shoulders. The weight was strange and, oddly, a little exhilarating. The touch of a man was alien, though, no doubt—she hadn't gone on a date in over two years. Her mind went blank as he slumped against her.

Looping her own arm around his waist, she pushed up with her legs, grateful for the core strength she'd developed through rigorous Pilates, both before and after the babies were born.

Gracious. He smelled like three-day-old fish and other pungencies she hesitated to identify—and she'd have sworn babies produced the worst stench in the world.

The man hobbled along with her across the threshold, thankfully revived enough to do so under his own power. When she paused in front of the pristine eggshell-colored suede sofa in the formal living area, he immediately dropped vertically onto the cushions without hesitation. Groaning, he covered his eyes with his arm.

"Water," he murmured and lay still as death.

And now for the second dilemma. Leave him unattended while she fetched a glassful from the wet bar across the foyer in Antonio's study? It wasn't that far, and she was being silly worrying about a near comatose man posing some sort of threat. She dashed across the marble at breakneck pace, filled the glass at the small stainless-steel sink and dashed back without spilling it, thankfully.

"Here it is," she said to alert him she'd returned.

The arm over his eyes moved up, sweeping the long, shaggy mane away from his forehead. Blearily he peered at her through bloodshot eyes, and without the hair obscuring his face, he looked totally different. Exactly like Antonio, the man she'd secretly studied, pined over, fantasized about for years. She gasped.

"I won't hurt you," he muttered as he sat up, pain etching deeper lines into his face. "Just want water."

She handed it to him, unable to tear her gaze from his face, even as chunks of matted hair fell back over his forehead. Regardless of her immense guilt over his presumed identity, she couldn't go on arguing with herself over it. There was one way to settle this matter right now.

"Do you think you're Antonio?" she asked as he drank deeply from the glass.

"I…" He glanced up at her, his gaze full of emotions she couldn't name, but those dark, mysterious eyes held her captive. "I don't remember. That's why I'm here. I want to know."

"There's one way." Before she lost her courage, she pointed to her chest over her heart as her pulse raced at the promise. "Antonio has a rather elaborate tattoo. Right here. Do you?"

It wouldn't be impossible to replicate. But difficult, as the tattoo had been commissioned by a famous artist who had a unique tribal style.

Without breaking eye contact, he set his water glass on the side table and unbuttoned his shirt to midchest. *Unbuttoned his shirt*, as if they were intimate and she had every right to see him unclothed.

"It says Falco. What does it mean?" he asked.

The truth washed through her even before he drew his

shirt aside to reveal the red-and-black falcon screaming across his pectoral muscle. Her gaze locked on to the ink, registering the chiseled flesh beneath it, and it kicked at her way down low with a long, hot pull, exactly the way she'd always reacted to Antonio.

She blinked and refocused on his face. The sight of his cut, athletic torso—sun browned and more enthralling than she'd ever have expected—wouldn't fade from her mind.

That tattoo had always been an electrifying aspect of his dangerous appeal. And, oh, my—it still was.

"It means that's proof enough for me to know you're Antonio." She shut her eyes, unable to process the relief flooding through his gaze. Unable to process the sharp thrill in her midsection that was wholly erotic…and felt an awful lot like trouble. Stunning, resplendent, *forbidden* Antonio Cavallari was alive. "And we have a lot of hurdles in front of us."

Everything in her world had just slid off a cliff.

The long, legal nightmare of the past year as she'd fought for her right to the babies had been for nothing. Nearly two years ago, she'd signed a surrogacy agreement, but then a year ago Vanessa and Antonio had crashed into the South China Sea. After months of court appearances, a judge had finally overturned the rights she'd signed away and given her full custody of her children.

Oh, dear Lord. This was Antonio's home. It was his money. *Her children were his.* And he had every right to take them away from her.

Two

Antonio—he rolled the name around on his tongue, and it didn't feel wrong like Falco had. Before Indonesia, he'd been called both Antonio and Falco by blurry-faced people, some with cameras, some with serious expressions as they spoke to him about important matters. A crowd had chanted *Falco* like a tribal drum, bouncing off the ceiling of a huge, cavernous arena.

The headache nearly flattened him again, as it always did when he tried too hard to force open his mind.

Instead, he contemplated the blushing, dark-haired and very attractive woman who seemed vaguely familiar but not enough to place her. She didn't belong in his house. She shouldn't be living here, but he had no clue where that sense came from. "What is your name?"

"Caitlyn. Hopewell," she added in what appeared to be an afterthought. "Vanessa is—was—my sister." She eyed him. "You remember Vanessa but not me?"

"The redhead?" At Caitlyn's nod, he frowned.

No, he didn't remember Vanessa, not the way he remembered his house. A woman with flame-colored hair haunted his dreams. Bits and pieces floated through his mind. The images were laced with flashes of her flesh as if he'd often seen her naked, but her face wouldn't quite clarify, as though he'd created an impressionist painting of this woman whose name he couldn't recall.

Frustration rose again. Because how was it fair that he knew exactly what an impressionist painting was but not who *he* was?

After Ravi had knocked loose the memories of his house, Antonio had left Indonesia the next morning, hopping fishing boats and stowing away amidst heavy cargo containers for days and days, all to reach Los Angeles in hopes of regaining more precious links with his past.

This delicate, ethereally beautiful woman—Caitlyn—held a few of these keys, and he needed her to provide them. "Who is Vanessa to me?"

"Your wife," she announced softly. "You didn't know that?"

He shook his head. Married. He was *married* to Vanessa? It was an entire piece of his life, his persona, he'd had no idea existed. Had he been in love with her? Had his wife looked for him at all, distraught over his fate, or just written him off when he went missing?

Would he even recognize Vanessa if she stood before him?

Glancing around the living room for which he'd instantly and distinctly recalled purchasing the furnishings—without the help of anyone, let alone the red-haired woman teasing the edges of his memory—he asked, "Where is she?"

"She died." Grief welled up across her classical features. The sisters must have been close, which was probably why

Caitlyn seemed familiar. "You were both involved in the same plane crash shortly after leaving Thailand."

"Plane crash?" The wispy images of the red-haired woman vanished as he zeroed in on Caitlyn. "Is that what happened?"

Thailand. He'd visited Thailand—but never made it home. Until now.

Eyes bright with unshed tears, she nodded, dark pony-tail flipping over her shoulder. "Over a year ago."

All at once, he wanted to mourn for this wife he couldn't remember. Because it would mean he could still experience emotions that stayed maddeningly out of reach, emotions with clinical definitions—love, peace, happiness, fulfillment, the list went on and on—but which had no real context. He wanted to feel *something* other than discouraged and adrift.

His head ached, but he pressed on, determined to unearth more clues to how he'd started out on a plane from Thailand and ended up in a fishing village in Indonesia. Alone. "But I was on the plane. And I'm not dead. Maybe Vanessa is still alive, too."

Her name produced a small ping in his heart, but he couldn't be certain if the feeling lingered from before the crash or if he'd manufactured it out of his intense need to remember.

Hand to her mouth, Caitlyn bowed her head. "No. They recovered her...body," she murmured, her voice thick. "They found the majority of the fuselage in the water. Most of the forty-seven people on board were still in their seats."

Vivid, gory images spilled into his mind as he imagined the horrors his wife—and the rest of the passengers—must have gone through before succumbing to the death he'd escaped.

"Except me."

For the first time, his reality felt a bit like a miracle in-

stead of a punishment. How had he escaped? Had he unbuckled himself in time to avoid drowning or had he been
thrown free of the wreckage?

"Except you," she agreed, though apparently it had
taken the revelation of his strange falcon tattoo to convince her. "And two other passengers, who were sitting
across the aisle from you in first class. You were all in the
first row, including Vanessa. They searched for survivors
for a week, but there was no trace."

"They were looking in the wrong place," he growled.
"I washed up on the beach in Indonesia. On the south side
of Batam Island."

"I don't know my geography, but the plane crashed into
the ocean near the coast of Malaysia. That's where they
focused the search."

No wonder no one had found him. They'd been hundreds of miles off.

"After a month," she continued, "they declared all three
of you dead."

But he wasn't dead.

The other two passengers might have survived, as well.
Look for them. They might be suffering from memory loss
or ghastly injuries. They might be frightened and alone,
having clawed their way out of a watery crypt, only to face
a fully awake nightmare. As he had.

He had to find them. But he had no money, no resources—
not at this moment anyway. He must have money, or at least
he must have had some once. The sum he'd paid for this
house popped into his head out of nowhere: fifteen point
eight million dollars. That had been eight years ago.

Groaning, he rubbed his temples as the headache grew
uncontrollable.

"Are you okay?" Caitlyn asked.

Ensuring the comfort of others seemed to come naturally to this woman he'd found living in his house. His sister-in-law. Had she always been so nurturing?

"Fine," he said between clenched teeth. "Is this still my house?"

He could sell it and use the proceeds to live on while he combed the South China Sea.

Caitlyn chose that moment to sit next to him on the couch, overwhelming him with the light scent of coconut, which, strangely, made him want to bury his nose in her hair.

"Technically, no. When you were declared dead, it passed to your heirs."

"You mean Vanessa's?" Seemed as if his wife's sister had made out pretty well after the plane crash. "Are you the only heir? Because I'm not dead and I want my money back."

It was the only way he could launch a search for the other two missing passengers.

"Oh." She stared at him, her sea-glass-blue eyes wide with guilt and a myriad of other emotions he suddenly wished to understand.

Because looking into her eyes made him feel something. Something good and beautiful and he didn't want to stop drowning in her gaze.

"You don't remember, do you?" she asked. "Oh, my gosh. I've been rambling and you don't even know about the babies."

Blood rushed from his head so fast, his ears popped.

"Babies?" he croaked. Surely she didn't mean babies, plural, as in more than one? As in *his* babies?

"Triplets." She shot him a misty smile that heightened her ethereal beauty. Which he wished he could appreciate, but there was no way, not with the bomb she'd just dropped. "And by some miracle, they still have a father. You. Would you like to meet them?"

"I…" A father. He had children? Three of them, apparently. "They're really mine?" Stupid question, but this was beyond—he shook his head. "How old are they? Do they remember me?"

"Oh, no, they weren't born yet when you went to Thailand."

He frowned. "But you said Vanessa died in the plane crash. Is she not their mother?"

Had he cheated on his wife with another woman? Catholic-school lessons from his youth blasted through his mind instantly. Infidelity was wrong.

"She's not," Caitlyn refuted definitively. "I am."

Guilt and shame cramped his gut as he eyed Caitlyn. He'd cheated on his wife with his *sister-in-law*? The thought was reprehensible.

But it explained the instant visceral reaction he had to her.

Her delicate, refined beauty didn't match the obvious lushness of the redhead he'd married. Maybe that was the point. He really preferred a dark-haired, more classically attractive woman like Caitlyn if he'd fathered children with her.

"Were we having an affair?" he asked bluntly. And would he have a serious fight to regain control of his money now that his mistress had her hooks into it?

Pink spread across her cheeks in a gorgeous blush, and a foreign heaviness filled his chest, spreading to heat his lower half. Though he couldn't recall having made love to her before, he had no trouble recognizing the raw, carnal attraction to Caitlyn. Obviously, she was precisely the woman he preferred, judging by his body's unfiltered reaction.

"Of course not!" She wouldn't meet his gaze, and her blush deepened. "You were married to my sister and I would never—well, I mean, I did meet you first and, okay, maybe I thought about…but then I introduced you to Vanessa. That was that. You were hers. Not that I blame you—"

"Caitlyn."

Her name alone caused that strange fullness in his chest. He'd like to say it again. Whisper it to her as he learned what she tasted like.

She glanced up, finally silenced, and he would very much like to understand why her self-conscious babbling had caused the corners of his mouth to turn up. It was evident from the way she nervously twisted her fingers together that she had no concept of how to lie. They'd never been involved. He'd stake his life on it.

He cleared his raspy throat. "How did the children come to be, then?"

"Oh. I was your surrogate. Yours and Vanessa's. The children are a hundred percent your DNA, grown in my womb." She wrinkled her nose. "That sounds so scientific. Vanessa couldn't conceive, so I volunteered to carry the baby. Granted, I didn't know three eggs were going to take."

She laughed and he somehow found the energy to be charmed by her light spirit. "So Vanessa and I, we were happy?"

If only he could remember her. Remember if they'd laughed together as he vaguely sensed that lovers should. Had they dreamed together of the babies on the way, planning for their family? Had she cried out in her last moments, grief stricken that she'd never hold her children?

"Madly in love." Caitlyn sighed happily. "It was a grand story. Falco and the Vixen. The media adored you guys. I'll go ask Brigitte, the au pair, to bring down the babies."

Reality overwhelmed him.

"Wait." Panicked all of a sudden, he clamped down on her arm before she could rise. "I can't… They don't know me."

He was a father. But so far from a father, he couldn't

fathom the idea of three helpless infants under his care. What if he broke one? What if he scared them? How did you handle a baby? How did you handle *three*?

"Five minutes," she said calmly. "Say hello. See them and count their fingers and toes. Then I'll have Brigitte take them away. They'll get used to you, I promise."

But would he get used to them? "Five minutes. And then I'd like to clean up. Eat."

Breathe. Get his bearings. Figure out how to be Antonio Cavallari again before he had to figure out how to be Antonio Cavallari plus three.

"Of course. I'm sorry, I should have thought of that." Dismay curved her mouth downward.

"There is no protocol when the dead come back to life," he countered drily and smiled. Apparently he'd found a sense of humor along with his home.

His head spun as Caitlyn disappeared upstairs to retrieve the babies and Brigitte, whoever that was. A few minutes later, she returned, followed by a young blonde girl pushing a three-seated carriage. Everything faded away as he saw his children.

Three little heads rested against the cushions, with three sets of eyes and three mouths. Wonder and awe crushed his heart as he drank in the sight of these creatures he'd had a hand in creating.

"They're really mine?" he whispered.

"Really, really," Caitlyn confirmed at normal volume, her tone slightly amused.

She picked up the one from the first seat and held him in the crook of her arm, angling the baby to face him. The blue outfit meant this was his son, didn't it?

"This is Leon." Her mouth quirked. "He's named after my father. I guess it's too late to ask if that's okay, but I thought it was a nice tribute to Vanessa's role in his heritage."

"It's fine."

Antonio was still whispering, but his voice caught in his throat and he couldn't have uttered another sound as his son mewled like a hungry cat, his gaze sharp and bright as he cocked his head as if contemplating the secrets of the universe.

His son. Leon.

Such a simple concept, procreating. People did it every day in all corners of the world. Wilipo had fourteen children and as far as Antonio could tell, never thought it particularly miraculous.

But it *was*.

This little person with the short baby-fine red hair was his child.

"You can say hello," Caitlyn reminded him.

"Hello." His son didn't acknowledge that Antonio had spoken, preferring to bury his head in Caitlyn's shoulder. Had he said the wrong thing? Maybe his voice was too scratchy.

"He'll warm up, I promise." She slid Leon back into the baby seat and picked up the next one.

The pink outfit filled his vision and stung his eyes. He had a daughter. The heart he could have sworn was already full of his son grew so big, he was shocked it hadn't burst from his rib cage.

"This is Annabelle. I always wanted to have a daughter named Annabelle," Caitlyn informed him casually, as if they were discussing the weather instead of this little bundle of perfection.

"She has red hair, too," he murmured. "Like her brother."

Her beautiful face turned up at the sound of his voice and he got lost in her blue eyes.

He had a very bad feeling that the word *no* had just vanished from his vocabulary, and he looked forward to spoiling his daughter to the point of ridiculousness.

"Yes, she and Leon take after Vanessa. Which means Annabelle will be a knockout by the time she's fourteen. Be warned," she said wryly with a half laugh.

"I know martial arts," he muttered. "Any smarmy Romeo with illicit intentions will find himself minus a spleen if he touches my daughter."

Caitlyn smirked. "I don't think a male on the planet would come within fifty yards of Annabelle if they knew you were her father. I was warning you about *her*."

With that cryptic comment, she spirited away his daughter far too quickly and replaced her with the third baby, clad in blue.

"This is Antonio Junior," Caitlyn said quietly and moved closer to present his other son. "He looks just like you, don't you think?"

Dark hair capped a serious face with dark eyes. Antonio studied this third child and his gut lurched with an unnatural sense of recognition, as if the missing pieces of his soul had been snapped into place to form this tiny person.

"Yes," he whispered.

And suddenly, his new lease on life had a purpose.

When he'd set off from Indonesia to find his past, he'd never dreamed he'd instead find his future. A tragic plane crash had nearly robbed these three innocent lives of both their parents, but against all odds, Antonio had survived.

Now he knew why. So he could be a father.

As promised, Caitlyn rounded up the babies and sent them upstairs with Brigitte so Antonio could decompress. Brigitte, bless her, didn't ask any more questions about Antonio's presence, but Caitlyn could tell her hurried explanation that he'd been ill and unable to travel home hadn't satisfied the au pair. Neither would it be enough for the hordes of media and legal hounds who would be snapping at their heels soon enough.

The amazing return of Antonio Cavallari would make worldwide headlines, of that she was sure. But first, he needed to rest and then see a discreet doctor. The world didn't have to know right away. The household staff had signed nondisclosure agreements, and in Hollywood, that was taken so seriously, none of them would ever work again if they broke it. So Caitlyn felt fairly confident the few people who knew about the situation would keep quiet.

She showed him to the master suite, glad now that she'd never cleaned it out, though she'd have to get Rosa to pack up Vanessa's things. It was too morbid to expect him to use his former bedroom with his late wife's clothes still in the dresser.

"I'll send Rosa, the housekeeper, up with something to eat," she promised and left him to clean up.

She wandered to the sunroom and pretended to read a book about parenting multiples on her e-reader, but she couldn't clear the jagged emotion from her throat. Antonio's face when he'd met his children for the first time... It had been amazing to see that much love crowd into his expression instantly. She wished he could have been there in the delivery room, to hold her hand and smile at her like that. Tell her everything would be okay and he'd still think she was beautiful even with a C-section scar.

Except if he *had* been there, he'd have held Vanessa's hand, not hers, and the reality squelched Caitlyn's little daydream.

The babies were his. It wouldn't take long for a judge to overturn her custody rights, not when she'd signed a surrogacy agreement that stated she'd have no claim over the babies once they were born.

But the babies were hers, too. The hospital had listed her name on their birth certificates as their mother—who else would they have named? She'd been their sole parent for nearly eight months and before that, carried them in her womb for months, knowing they weren't going home with Vanessa and Antonio as planned, but with her.

It was a mess, and more than anything, she wanted to do what was best for the babies. Not for the first time, she wished her mother was still alive; Caitlyn could use some advice.

An hour later, Antonio reappeared.

He filled the doorway of the sunroom and the late-afternoon rays highlighted his form with an otherworldly glow that revealed the true nature of his return to this realm—as that of an angel.

She gasped, hand flying to her mouth.

Then he moved into the room and became flesh and blood once again. But no less beautiful.

He'd trimmed his full beard, revealing his deep cheekbones and allowing his arresting eyes to become the focal point of his face. He'd swept back his still long midnight-colored hair and dressed in his old clothes, which didn't fit nearly as well as they once had, but a man as devastatingly handsome as Antonio could make a bedsheet draped over his body work.

Heat swept along her cheeks as she imagined exactly that, and it did not resemble the toga she'd meant to envision. *Antonio, spread out on the bed, sheet barely covering his sinewy, drool-worthy fighter's physique, gaze dark and full of desire...for her...* She shook her head. That was the *last* thing she should be thinking about for a hundred reasons, but Antonio Junior, Leon and Annabelle were the top three and she needed to get a few things straight with their father. No naked masculine chests required for that conversation.

"You look...different," she squawked.

Nice. *Tip him off that you're thinking naughty thoughts.*

"You kept my clothes?" He pointed to the jeans slung low on his lean hips. "And my shaving equipment?"

All of which he apparently remembered just fine as he'd slipped back into his precrash look easily. Antonio had always been gorgeous as sin, built like a lost Michelangelo sculpture with a side of raw, masculine power. And she was still salivating over him. A year in Indonesia hadn't changed that, apparently.

She shrugged and tried to make herself stop staring at him, which didn't exactly work. "I kept meaning to go through that room, but I thought maybe there would be something the babies would want. So I left it."

"I'm glad you did. Thank you." His small smile tripped a long liquid pull inside and she tamped it down. Or she almost did. It was too delicious to fully let it go.

Serious. Talk. Now, she told herself sternly.

"I had a gym," he said before she could work up the courage to bring up item one on her long list of issues. "Did you leave it alone, too?"

"It's untouched."

"I need to see it. Will you come with me?"

Surprised, she nodded. "Of course."

Was it wrong to be thrilled he'd asked her to be with him as he delved into his past?

Well, if that was wrong, it was probably just as wrong to still have a thing for him all these years later. If only she hadn't given up so easily when she'd first met him— it was still one of her biggest regrets.

But then, her relationship rules didn't afford much hope unless a man was interested enough to hang around for the long haul. She'd thought maybe Antonio might have been, once upon a time. The way he'd flirted with her when they'd met, as though he thought she was beautiful, had floored her…and then Vanessa had entered stage left, which had dried up his interest in the chaste sister.

She followed him as he strolled directly to the gym, mystified how he remembered the way, and halted next to him as he quietly took in the posters advertising his many fights, his championship belts and publicity shots of himself clad in shorts and striking a fierce pose.

There was something wicked about staring at a photo of Antonio half clothed while standing next to the fully dressed version, knowing that falcon tattoo sat under his shirt, waiting to be discovered by a woman's fingers. *Her* fingers. What would it feel like?

Sometimes she dreamed about that.

"Do you remember any of this?" she asked as the silence stretched. She couldn't keep thinking about Antonio's naked chest. Which became more difficult the longer they stood there, his heat nearly palpable. He even smelled like sin.

"Bits and pieces," he finally said. "I didn't know I had martial arts training. I thought I was remembering a movie, because I wasn't always in the ring. Sometimes I was outside the ring, watching."

"Oh, like watching other fighters? Maybe you're remembering Falco," she offered. "The fight club."

He shook his head as if to clear it. "I feel as if I should know what that is."

He didn't remember Falco, either? Antonio had lived and breathed that place, much to Vanessa's dismay on many occasions. Her sister had hoped to see her husband more often once his time in the ring was up, but the opposite had proved true.

Caitlyn led him to a picture on the wall, the one of him standing with two fighters about to enter the ring. "Falco is your MMA promotional venue. You founded it once your career ended. That's where you made all your money."

"When did I stop fighting?"

"It wasn't long after you and Vanessa got married. You don't remember that, either?" When he shook his head, she told him what little she knew about his last fight. "Brian

Kerr nearly killed you. Illegal punch to the back of your head and you hit the floor at a bad angle. Knocked you out. You were in the hospital unconscious for two days. That's probably why your amnesia is so pronounced. Your brain has sustained quite a bit of trauma."

Really, he should have already been checked out by a competent doctor, but he'd refused when she'd mentioned it earlier. It wasn't as if she could make him. Caitlyn had no experience with amnesia *or* a powerful man who wouldn't admit to weakness.

Deep down, she had an undeniable desire to gain some experience, especially since it came wrapped in an Antonio package.

He stared at the picture for a moment. "Falco is the name of my company," he announced cautiously as if testing it out. "It's not *my* name."

Her heart ached over his obvious confusion. She wanted to help him, to erase that small bit of helplessness she would never have associated with confident, solid Antonio Cavallari if she hadn't seen it firsthand.

"Falco was your nickname when you were fighting. You transferred it to your promotional company because I guess it had some sentimental value." Not that he'd ever discussed it with her. It was an assumption everyone had made, regardless.

"What happened to my company while I was missing?"

Missing—was that how he'd thought of himself? She tried to put herself in his place, waking up with few memories, in a strange place, with strange people who spoke a different language, all while recuperating from a plane crash and near drowning. The picture was not pretty, which tugged at her heart anew.

"I, um, have control over it." And it had languished like the bedroom and his gym.

What did she know about running an MMA promotional company? But she couldn't have sold it or tried to step into his shoes. In many ways, his place in the world had been on accidental hold, as if a higher power had stilled her hand from dismantling Antonio's life. It had been here, waiting for him to slip back into it.

His expression hardened and the glimpse of vulnerability vanished. "I want control of my estate. And my company. Do whatever you have to do to make that happen."

The rasp in his voice, which hadn't been there before he got on that plane, laced his statement with a menacing undertone. He seemed more like a stranger in that moment than he had when he'd first appeared on her doorstep, unkempt and unrecognizable.

It was a brutal reminder that he wasn't the same man. He wasn't a safe fantasy come to life. And she wasn't her sister, a woman who could easily handle a man like Antonio—worse, she wasn't the woman he'd picked.

"It's a lot to process, I realize," she said slowly as her pulse skittered out of control. This harder, hooded Antonio was impossible to read, and she had no idea how to handle this unprecedented situation. "But you just got back to the States. You don't even remember Falco, let alone how to run it. Why don't you take a few days, get your bearings? I'll help you."

The offer was genuine. But it also kept her in his proximity so she could figure out his plans. If she got a hint that he was thinking about fighting her for custody of the triplets, she'd be ready. She was their mother, and this man—who was still very much a ghost of his former self—was not taking away her children.

Three

Antonio shifted his iron-hard gaze from the pictures on the wall to evaluate Caitlyn coolly, which did not help her pulse. Nothing in her limited experience had prepared her to face down a man like Antonio, but she had to make him agree to a few ground rules.

"You cannot fathom what I've been through over the past year," he stated firmly. "I want nothing more than to pick up the pieces of my life and begin the next chapter with these new cards I've been dealt. I need my identity back."

Which was a perfectly reasonable request, but executing it more closely resembled unsnarling a knotted skein of yarn than simply handing over a few account numbers. This was one time when she couldn't afford to back down.

Caitlyn nodded and took a deep breath. "I understand, and I'm not suggesting otherwise. The problem is that a lot of legalities are involved and I have to look out for the interests of the children."

His gaze softened, warming her, and she didn't know what to do with that, either.

"I'm thinking of the children, as well."

"Good. Then, it would be best to take things slowly. You've been gone for a long time and the babies have a routine. It would be catastrophic to disrupt them."

He pursed his lips. "If you're concerned that I might dismiss the nanny, I can assure you I have no intention of doing so. I couldn't care for one child by myself, let alone three."

Her stomach jolted and she swallowed, gearing up to lay it on the line. "You won't be by yourself. I'll still be here."

If only her voice hadn't squeaked, that might have come across more definitively. Besides, she was still breast-feeding and didn't plan to stop until the triplets were a year old. She was irreplaceable, as far as she was concerned.

"You're free to get back to your life," he said with a puzzled frown. "There's no reason for you to continue in your role as caretaker now that I've returned."

"Whoa." She threw up a palm as the back of her neck heated in a sweaty combination of anger and fear. "Where did you get the idea that I'm just a caretaker? The babies are *mine*. I'm their mother."

Nothing she'd said thus far had sunk in, obviously.

Antonio crossed his arms and contemplated her. "You said you were the surrogate. A huge sacrifice, to be sure, but the children would have been mine and Vanessa's. You've been forced to care for them much longer than anyone has a right to ask. I'm relieving you of the respon-sibility."

Her worst nightmare roared to life, pulsing and seeth-ing as it went for her jugular.

"No!" A tear rolled down her face before she could stop it as she tried to summon up a reasonable argument against the truth in his words. "That's not what happened. I care

for them because I love them. They became mine in every
sense when I thought you and Vanessa were both gone. I
need them. And they need me. Don't take away my babies."

A sob choked off whatever else she'd been about to say.
The one and only time she'd ever tried to fight for something, and instead of using logic and reason, she'd turned
into an emotional mess.

Concern weighted Antonio's expression as he reached
out to grasp her hand in a totally surprising move. His fingers found hers and squeezed tightly, shooting an unexpected thrill through her that she couldn't contain. Coupled
with the emotional distress, it was almost overwhelming.

"Don't cry." The lines around his eyes deepened as he
heaved a ragged sigh. "I don't know how to do this."

"But you don't have to know," she countered, clinging
to his hand like a lifeline. "That's what I'm trying to tell
you. Don't change anything. It's Christmastime and we're
family, if nothing else. I'll stay here and continue to care
for the babies, then we can spend this time figuring it out
together. After the first of the year, maybe the path will
seem clearer."

Please, God.

Relief coursed through her as he slowly nodded. "I want
to be as fair as possible to everyone. If you don't have a
life to get back to, then it makes sense for you to stay here.
At least until January."

"This *is* my life."

Or at least it was now, since she'd given up her job as
an accountant. She had no desire to be anything other than
the mother she'd become over the past year. And now she
had until the first of January to find a way to stay in that
role. If Antonio decided his children would be better off in
another arrangement, she had little to say about it.

What would she do without the family she'd formed?

"Caitlyn, I appreciate what you've done." His dark eyes

sought hers and held, his gratitude genuine. "You stepped into my place to care for my children. Thank you."

That he recognized her efforts meant the world to her. He was a good man, deep inside where brain trauma couldn't touch. As she'd always known.

She nodded, still too emotional to respond, but the sentiment gave her hope. He wasn't heartless, just trying to do the right thing.

Somehow, Antonio had to recognize that *she* was the right thing for the children and then the two of them could figure out how to be co-parents. After learning how to handle triplets, that should be a walk in the park.

The next two days passed in a blur. When Caitlyn had mentioned legalities, Antonio had half thought it was an excuse to avoid giving up control of his money. But she'd vastly understated the actuality. An avalanche of paperwork awaited him once the man who'd been his lawyer for a decade became convinced Antonio had really returned from the dead.

Funny how he'd instantly recognized Kyle Lowery the moment his lawyer's admin had ushered Antonio and Caitlyn into the man's office. His memory problems were inconsistent and frustrating, to say the least.

Antonio's headache persisted and grew worse the more documents Kyle's paralegal placed in front of him. The harsh lights glinting from the gold balls on the Christmas tree in the corner didn't help. Antonio wished he could enjoy the spirit of the season.

But Christmas and family and all of the joy others seemed to associate with this time of year meant little to him. Caitlyn had told him that his parents had died some time back, which probably explained why he remembered them with a sense of distance, as if the scenes had happened long ago.

After many more stops and an interminable number of hours, he had: a temporary driver's license, a temporary bank card, a promise of credit cards to come, a bank teller who'd fallen all over herself to give him access to his safe-deposit box…and a dark-haired enigma of a woman who'd stuck to his side like glue, determined to help him navigate the exhausting quagmire reentering his life had become.

Why was she still here?

Why did her presence make him so happy? She somehow made everything better just by being near him. And sometimes, she looked at him a certain way that burrowed under his skin with tingly warmth. Both had become necessary. Unexpectedly so.

He studied her covertly at lunch on the third day after he'd pounded on the door of his Malibu house, delirious and determined to find answers to the question marks in his mind.

What he'd found still hadn't fully registered. Caitlyn was an amazing woman and his kids were surprising, funny little people. Together, they were a potent package. But how did that make sense? She wasn't their biological mother.

While Antonio absently chewed on a thick sandwich designed to put back some of his lost weight, Caitlyn laughed at Leon as he shoved his food off his tray to the floor below.

She'd insisted on the triplets sitting at the table when the adults had meals, even though the babies ate little more than puree of something and bits of Cheerios. Antonio wouldn't have thought of having infants join them, but with the additions, eating became something more than a routine. It was a chance to spend time with his children without expectation since Brigitte and Caitlyn handled everything.

Secretly, he was grateful Caitlyn hadn't skipped through

the door the moment he'd given her the out. In the hazy reaches of his mind, he had the distinct impression most women would have run very fast in the other direction from triplets. He couldn't understand Caitlyn's motivation for staying unless she thought she'd get a chunk of his estate as a thank-you. Which he'd probably give her. She deserved something for her sacrifices.

"Your turn."

Antonio did a double take at the spoon in Caitlyn's outstretched hand and blinked. "My turn to what?"

"Feed your daughter. She won't bite you." Caitlyn raised her brows and nodded at the spoon. "Of the three, Annabelle is the most laid-back about eating, so start with her."

Since he couldn't see a graceful way to refuse, he accepted the spoon and scooted closer to the baby's high chair, eyeing the bowl of…whatever it was. Orange applesauce?

Scowling, he scooped some up and then squinted at the baby watching him with bright eyes. How was he supposed to feed her with her fingers stuck in her mouth?

"Come on, open," he commanded.

Annabelle fluttered her lashes and made an uncomplimentary noise, fingers firmly wedged where the spoon was supposed to go.

He tried again. "Please?"

Caitlyn giggled and he glanced at her askance, which only made her laugh harder. He rolled his shoulders, determined to pass this one small test, but getting his daughter to eat might top the list of the most difficult things he had to do today.

Antonio had learned to walk again on the poorly healed broken leg that the Indonesian doctor had promised would have to be amputated. He'd defied the odds and scarcely even had a limp now. If he could do that, one very small person could not break him.

He tapped the back of Annabelle's hand with the edge of the spoon, hoping that would act as an open sesame, but she picked that moment to yank her fingers free. She backhanded the spoon, flinging it free of Antonio's grip. It hit the wall with a *thunk*, leaving a splash of orange in a trail to the floor.

Frustration welled. He balled his fists automatically and then immediately shoved them into his lap as horror filtered through him. His first instinct was to fight, but he had to control that impulse, or else what kind of father was he going to be?

Breathing rhythmically, he willed back the frustration until his fists loosened. Better.

His first foray into caring for his kid and she elected to show him her best defensive moves. Annabelle blinked innocently as Antonio's scowl deepened. "Yeah, you work on that technique, and when you've got your spinning backhand down, we'll talk."

Spinning backhand. The phrase had leaped into his mind with no forethought. Instantly other techniques scrolled through his head. *Muay Thai.* That had been his specialty. His "training" with Wilipo had come so easily because Antonio should have been teaching the class as the master, not attending as the student.

Faster now, ingrained drills, disciplines and defense strategies exploded in his mind. Why now instead of in his gym, surrounded by the relics of his former status as a mixed martial arts champion?

The headache slammed him harder than ever before and the groan escaped before he could catch it.

"It's okay," Caitlyn said and jumped up to retrieve the spoon. "You don't have to feed her. I just thought you might like it."

"No problem," he said around the splitting pain in his temples. "Excuse me."

He mounted the stairs to his bedroom and shut himself away in the darkened room, but refused to lie on the bed like an invalid.

Instead, he sank into a chair and put his head in his hands. This couldn't go on, the rush of memories and the headaches and the inability to do simple tasks like stick a spoon in a baby's mouth without becoming irrational.

But how did he change it?

Coming to LA was supposed to solve everything, give him back his memories and his life. It had only highlighted how very far he had yet to go in his journey back to the land of the living.

An hour later, the pain was manageable enough to try being civilized again. Antonio tracked down Caitlyn in the sunroom, which seemed to be her favored spot when she wasn't hanging out with the babies. Her dark curls partially obscured the e-reader in her hands and she seemed absorbed in the words on the screen.

"I'll visit a doctor," he told her shortly and spun to leave before she asked any questions. She'd been after him to see one, but he'd thus far refused, having had enough of the medical profession during his months and months of rehabilitation in Indonesia.

No doctor could restore his memories, nor could one erase the scars he bore from the plane crash.

But if a Western doctor had a way to make his headaches go away, that would be stellar. He had to become a father, one way or another, and living in a crippling state of pain wasn't going to cut it.

"I'll drive you." She followed him into the hall. "Just because you have a driver's license doesn't mean you're ready to get behind the wheel. We'll take my—"

"Caitlyn." He whirled to face her, but she kept going, smacking into his chest.

His arms came up as they both nearly lost their balance

and somehow she ended up pinned to the wall, their bodies tangled and flush. His lower half sprang to attention and heat shot through his gut.

Caitlyn's wide-eyed gaze captured his and he couldn't have broken the connection if his life depended on it. Her chest heaved against his as if she was unable to catch her breath, and that excited him, too.

"Caitlyn," he murmured again, but that seemed to be the extent of his ability to speak as her lips parted, drawing his attention to her mouth. She caught her plump bottom lip between her teeth and—

"Um, you can let go now," she said and cleared her throat. "I'm okay."

He released her, stepping back to allow her the space she'd asked for, though it was far from what he wanted to do. "I'm curious about something."

Nervously, she rearranged her glossy hair, refusing to meet his eyes. "Sure."

"You said that you introduced me to Vanessa. How did you and I meet?" Because if he'd ever held Caitlyn in his arms before, he was an idiot if he'd willingly let her go.

"I was Rick's accountant." At his raised brows, she smiled. "Your former manager. He'd gone through several CPAs until he found me, and when I came by his house to do his quarterly taxes, you were there. You were wearing a pink shirt for a breast cancer fund-raiser you'd attended. We got to talking and somehow thirty minutes passed in a blur."

Nothing wrong with her memory, clearly, and it was more than a little flattering that she recalled his clothing from that day.

"And there was something about me that you didn't like?" Obviously, or she wouldn't have matched him up with her sister. Maybe she'd only thought of him as a friend.

"Oh, no! You were great. Gorgeous and gentlemanly." The blush that never seemed far from the surface of her skin bloomed again, heightening the blue in her eyes. "I mean, I might have been a little starstruck, which is silly, considering how many celebrities I've done taxes for."

That pleased him even more than her pink-shirt comment, and he wanted to learn more about this selfless woman who'd apparently been a part of his life for a long time. "You're an accountant, then?"

"Not anymore. I gave up all my clients when...Vanessa died." She laughed self-consciously. "It's hard to retrain my brain to no longer say 'when Antonio and Vanessa died'."

The mention of his wife sent an unexpected spike of sadness through his gut. "I don't remember being married to her. Did you think we'd be a good couple? Is that why you introduced us?"

All at once, a troubling sense of disloyalty effectively killed the discovery mode he'd fallen into with Caitlyn. He had no context for his relationship with Vanessa, but she'd been his wife and this woman was his sister-in-law. He shouldn't be thinking about Caitlyn as anything other than a temporary mother to his children. She'd probably be horrified at the direction of his thoughts.

"Oh. No, I mentioned that she was my sister and you asked to meet her. I don't think you even noticed me after that. Vanessa is—was—much more memorable than me."

"I beg to differ," he countered wryly, which pulled a smile out of her. "When I close my eyes, yours is the only face I can picture."

Apparently he couldn't help himself. Did he automatically flirt with beautiful women or just this one?

More blushing. But he wasn't going to apologize for the messed-up state of his mind or the distinct pleasure he'd discovered at baiting this delicate-skinned woman.

He'd needed something that made him feel good. Was that so wrong?

"Well, she was beautiful and famous. I didn't blame you for wanting an introduction. Most people did."

"Famous?" Somehow that didn't seem like valid criteria for wishing to meet a woman.

Caitlyn explained that Vanessa starred on *Beacon Street*, a TV show beloved by millions of fans, and then with a misty sigh, Caitlyn waxed poetic about their fairy-tale wedding. "Vanessa wanted a baby more than anything. She said it was the only thing missing from your perfect marriage."

He'd heard everything she'd said, but in a removed way, as if it had happened to someone else. And perhaps in many respects, it had. He didn't remember being in love with Vanessa, but he'd obviously put great stock in her as a partner, lover and future mother of his children.

Part of his journey apparently lay in reconciling his relationship with the woman he'd married—so he could know if it was something he might want to do again, with another woman, at some point in the future. He needed to grieve his lost love as best he could and move on.

Perhaps Caitlyn had a role in this part of his recovery, as well. "I'd like to know more about Vanessa. Will you tell me? Or is it too hard?"

She nodded with a small smile. "It's hard. But it's good for me, too, to remember her. I miss her every day."

Launching into an impassioned tribute to her sister, Caitlyn talked with her hands, her animated face clearly displaying her love for Vanessa. But Antonio couldn't stop thinking about that moment against the wall, when he'd almost reached out to see what Caitlyn's glossy hair felt like. What might have happened between them all those years ago if he hadn't asked Caitlyn to introduce him to Vanessa?

It was madness to wonder. He would do well to focus

on the present, where, thanks to Caitlyn, he'd forgotten about his headache. She'd begged him to allow her to stay under his roof and, frankly, it was easy to say yes because he needed her help. Incredible fortune had smiled on him since the plane crash, and he couldn't help feeling that Caitlyn was a large part of it.

Four

Instead of taking Antonio to the doctor, Caitlyn arranged for the doctor to come to the house the following afternoon. Antonio needed his space for as long as possible, at least until he got comfortable being in civilization again—or at least that was Caitlyn's opinion, and no one had to know that it fit her selfish desire to have him all to herself.

As a plus, Caitlyn wouldn't have to worry about wrestling Antonio into the car in case he changed his mind about seeing a doctor after all. Not that she could have. Nor did she do herself any favors imagining the tussle, which would likely end with Antonio's hard body pinning her against another wall.

Recalling yesterday's charged encounter had kept her quite warm last night and quite unable to sleep due to a restless ache she had no idea how to ease. Well, okay, she had *some* idea, but her sensibilities didn't extend to middle-of-the-night visits to the sexy man down the hall. One did not simply walk into Antonio's bedroom with the intent of hopping into bed with him, or at least *she* didn't. Risqué nighttime shenanigans were Vanessa's style, and her sister had had her heart broken time and time again as a result. Sex and love were so closely entwined that Caitlyn was willing to wait for the commitment she'd always wanted.

Nor did she imagine that Antonio was lying awake fantasizing about visiting Caitlyn anytime soon, either. They were two people thrown together by extraordinary circumstances and they both had enormous, daunting realities to deal with that didn't easily translate into any kind of relationship other than…what? Friends? Co-parents? Trying to figure it out was exhausting enough; adding romance to the mix was out of the question.

Especially since Antonio could—and likely would—have his pick of women soon enough. A virgin mother of triplets, former accountant sister-in-law didn't have the same appeal as a lush, redheaded actress-wife combo, that was for sure.

The doctor buzzed the gate entrance at precisely three o'clock. Antonio ushered the stately salt-and-pepper-haired physician into the foyer and thanked him for coming as the two men shook hands.

All morning, Antonio had been short-tempered and scowling, even after Caitlyn told him the doctor was coming to him. Caitlyn hovered just beyond the foyer, unsure if she was supposed to make herself scarce or insist on being present for the conversation in case the doctor had follow-up instructions for Antonio's care.

Vanessa would have been stuck to Antonio's side. As a wife should. Caitlyn was only the person who had made the appointment. And she'd done that just to make sure it happened.

"Caitlyn," Antonio called, his tone slightly amused, which was a plus, considering his black mood. "Come meet Dr. Barnett."

That she could do. She stood by Antonio, but not too close, and exchanged pleasantries with the doctor.

"I saw you fight Alondro in Vegas," the doctor remarked with an appreciative nod at Antonio. "Ringside. Good match."

Antonio accepted the praise with an inclined head, but his hands immediately clenched and his mouth tightened; clearly, the doctor's comments made him uncomfortable. Because he didn't remember? Or had he lost all context of what it meant to be famous? Either way, she didn't like anyone making Antonio uncomfortable, let alone someone who was supposed to be here to help.

"Can I show you to a private room where you can get started?" Caitlyn asked in a no-nonsense way.

"Of course." Dr. Barnett's face smoothed out and he followed Caitlyn and Antonio to the master bedroom, where Antonio had indicated he felt the most at home in the house.

Score one for Caitlyn. Or was it two since a medical professional was on the premises?

She started to duck out, but Antonio stopped her with a warm hand on her arm. "I'd like you to stay," he murmured. "So it will feel less formal."

"Oh." A bit flummoxed, she stared up into his dark eyes. "It won't be weird if the doctor wants you to...um... get undressed?"

On cue, her cheeks heated. She'd blushed more around this man in the past few days than she had in her whole life.

His lips quirked and she congratulated herself on removing that dark scowl he'd worn all day. Too bad his new expression had come about because he likely found her naïveté amusing.

"It will only be weird if you make it weird." His head tilted as he contemplated her. "What kind of doctor's appointment do you think this is?"

She scowled in return. "I'll stay. But only if you stop making fun of me."

He winked. *Winked.* "I solemnly swear. Provided you stop saying things that are funny."

"And," she continued as if he hadn't tried to be charming and slick, when, in truth, it fluttered her heart to be so firmly in the sights of Antonio's weapons of choice. "I'll stay if you'll be perfectly honest with the doctor. If you aren't, I will be."

At that, he smiled. "Then, you'll definitely have to see me undressed."

"For what reason?" she hissed with a glance at the doctor, who was pretending not to listen to their far-too-loud discussion. Did Antonio have zero sense of propriety?

"Otherwise, how will you know what to say about my badly healed broken leg?" Antonio responded innocently and laughed as Caitlyn smacked his arm. Over his shoulder, he called, "Dr. Barnett, can we start out dressed or shall I strip immediately?"

Dr. Barnett cleared his throat. "We'll talk first and then I'll take some vital signs. A more…ah…thorough examination will only become necessary pending the outcome of our discussion. Ms. Hopewell is free to excuse herself at that point."

Even the doctor sounded as if Caitlyn's lack of experience around naked men was cause for hilarity. She firmed her mouth and sank into the chair Antonio indicated in the sitting area, which was thankfully far from the bed, then crossed her arms. *Men.*

And speaking of pigheaded males—why was she just *now* finding out Antonio had suffered a broken leg? It probably needed to be reset and it must pain him something awful and…it wasn't her business. She'd gotten him in front of a doctor; now someone with a medical degree could talk sense into the man, who apparently thought he'd turned immortal.

Dr. Barnett settled into a wing-back chair with a clipboard he'd pulled from his bag of tricks. After a quick back-and-forth with the patient to determine Antonio's age, approximate height and weight, the doctor took his heart rate and peered into his throat.

"Now, then." The doctor contemplated Antonio. "Ms. Hopewell indicated that you have trouble remembering your past. Can you tell me more about that?"

"No," Antonio said smoothly, but Caitlyn heard the obstinacy in his voice. "You're here because I have headaches. Make them go away."

Caitlyn frowned. *That* was the thing he was most worried about?

The doctor asked a few pointed questions about the nature of Antonio's pain, which he refused to answer. Dr. Barnett pursed his lips. "I can write you a prescription for some heavy-duty painkillers, but I'd like to do a CT scan first. I'm concerned about your purported memory loss coupled with headaches. I'd prefer to know what we're dealing with before treating the symptoms."

"No tests. Write the prescription," Antonio ordered and stood, clearly indicating the appointment was over whether the doctor wished it to be or not. "Ms. Hopewell misrepresented the nature of the medical care I need."

Caitlyn didn't move from her chair. "How long will the CT scan take? Will you get results immediately or will it only lead to more tests? Will you also look at his leg?"

Someone had to be the voice of reason here.

"It doesn't matter, because that's not the problem," Antonio cut in with a scowl. "I'm not sick. I'm not an invalid, and my leg is fine. I just need something to make my headaches manageable."

Dr. Barnett nodded. "Fine. I'll write you a prescription for a painkiller, but only for enough pills to get you through the next few days. If you go to the radiology lab and get the CT scan, I'll give you more."

"Blackmail?" Antonio's lips quirked, but no one would mistake it for amusement. "I'll just find another doctor."

"Perhaps." Dr. Barnett shrugged. "Hollywood is certainly full of dishonest medical practitioners who will write prescriptions for just about anything if someone is willing to pay enough. Just keep in mind that many of those someones wind up in the morgue. I will never be a party to putting one of my patients there."

That was enough to convince Caitlyn she'd selected the right doctor, and she wasn't going to stand by and let Antonio destroy an opportunity to get the help he needed, not when he had three very good reasons to get better the medically approved way. "Dr. Barnett, please write the prescription for the amount of pills you think is appropriate and leave me the information about the radiology lab. We'll discuss it and get back to you."

Antonio crossed his arms, his expression the blackest it had been all day, but thankfully he kept his mouth closed instead of blasting her for interfering.

The doctor hastily scrawled on his pad and tore off the top page, handing it to Caitlyn with a business card for the radiology lab. She saw him out and shut the front door, assuming Antonio had stayed holed up in his room to work off his mood.

But when she turned, he was leaning against the wall at the other end of the foyer, watching her with crossed arms and a hooded, hard look. His expression wasn't as black as it had been, but somehow it was far more dangerous.

Startled, she backed up against the door, accidentally trapping her hands behind her. Feeling oddly exposed, she yanked them free and laced her fingers together over her abdomen, right where a strange sort of hum had started.

"I'm not getting a CT scan," he said succinctly. "I didn't ask you to call the doctor so you could railroad me into a bunch of useless tests. I had enough of doctors in Indonesia who couldn't fix me."

She shook her head, not about to back down. This was too important. "But what if the tests help? Don't you want to get your memory back?"

"Of course." A hint of vulnerability flitted through his gaze and the hum inside her abdomen sped up. "There's only one thing that's helped with that so far and it wasn't a doctor."

The atmosphere in the foyer pressed down on her, almost agonizing in its power. She couldn't think when he was like this, so focused and intense, funneling all of his energy toward her. It woke up her nerve endings and they ruffled under the surface of her skin, begging her to move with a restless insistence. But move where?

"What helps?" she asked softly, afraid of spooking him. She couldn't predict if he'd leave or advance on her and, at this point, she couldn't say which she'd prefer.

"Fighting." The word reverberated against the marble, ringing in her ears.

She gasped, hand flying to her mouth. Surely he didn't mean actual fighting. As if he intended to return to his former sport.

"I need to get in the ring again," he confirmed, his dark gaze on hers, searching for something she couldn't give him. Pleading with her to understand. "I have—"

"No," she interrupted as her stomach dropped. "You can't. You have no idea what's going on inside your skull and you want to introduce more trauma? Not a good idea."

He'd only returned to civilization a few days ago, broken on the inside. He needed…something, yes, but it wasn't picking up his former MMA persona as if no time had passed. As if he was still whole and healthy. As if he had nothing important to lose.

"This is not your call, Caitlyn," he said gently. Too gently. He'd already made up his mind. "This is my life, my head. I'm a fighter. It's what I do."

She stared up at him, and the raw emotion swimming through his eyes took her breath. "You haven't been a fighter for a long time, Antonio. You're a businessman now."

That was the man she knew well, the safe, contained version of Antonio. When he'd quit his MMA career to manage what went on in the ring for other fighters, it was the best of both worlds. Antonio still had all the outer trappings of his lean fighting physique, which—*let's be honest*—was wickedly delicious enough to get a nun going, but he'd shed the harsh brutality of Falco.

She liked him as a businessman. Businessmen were constant, committed. The way she'd always thought of Antonio. If he wasn't that man, who was he?

"I might have been before the crash, but I don't remember that part of me." Bleakly, he stared off into the distance and her heart plummeted. "That Antonio might as well be dead. The only Antonio *I* know is the one who lives inside my heart, beating against the walls of my chest, alive but not *whole*. That Antonio screams inside my head, begging to be free of this web of uncertainty."

God, how poetically awful and terrible. Her soul ached to imagine the confusion and pain he must experience every minute of every day, but at the same time, she thrilled in the knowledge that he'd shared even that small piece of himself.

His gaze snapped back to hers and she'd swear on a stack of Bibles he hadn't moved, but his heat wrapped around her, engulfing her, and she was powerless to stop it from affecting her. She wanted to step back, quickly. As fast as her legs could carry her. But he'd backed her against the wall…or she'd backed herself against the wall by starting this madness. By assuming she could convince a man who'd survived a plane crash to see a doctor.

Madness.

Because her body ached for Antonio to step into that scant space between them, which felt uncomfortably slight and yet as massive as the ocean that had separated him from his old life.

She wanted to support him. To care for him. To help him reenter his life in whatever way made sense to him. Who was she to say he shouldn't be in the ring again? Vanessa hadn't liked him fighting, either, but her sister had held many weapons in her arsenal that might have prevented the man she'd married from doing something dangerous.

Caitlyn had nothing.

"Please understand." He held her captive without words, without touching her at all, as his simple plea burned her throat. "I have to unleash my frustration on an opponent who can take it. Who's trained for it. Before I take it out on someone else."

Her teeth caught her lip and bit down as his meaning sank in. He sought a healthy outlet for his confusion, one that was familiar to him. Why was that so bad?

She'd been trying to keep him away from the media, away from his former employees and business partners, who might ask uncomfortable questions he couldn't answer. Perhaps she'd worried unnecessarily. Most likely, he'd be firmly in the public eye for the rest of his life, whether she liked it or not, and she couldn't keep him to herself forever. It was ridiculous to even pretend they could hide away in this house, even for a few days.

And then he reached out, encompassing her forearm with his palm. "I need you—" He swallowed and faltered.

"I need you in my corner, Caitlyn. I don't have anyone else."

Wide-eyed, she covered his strong fingers with hers. Reassuringly, she squeezed, reveling in the contact as warmth flooded the places where their skin touched. *She* was comforting *him* in what was clearly a difficult conversation for them both.

He needed her. More important, he needed her to validate his choices, no matter how crazy they seemed.

A little awed by the realization, she nodded because speaking wasn't an option as he rested his forehead on hers, whispering his gratitude. She closed her eyes against the intimacy of the thank-you, feeling as if she'd just fought an exhausting battle, only to look up and see the opposing general's second flank swarming the battlefield.

"I'll take you to Falco," she promised, her voice croaking, and wished she only meant she would take him to the building housing the empire he'd founded called Falco Fight Club. But she suspected she would really be taking him back to his former self, when he *was* Falco, a champion fighter who regularly took blows to the head.

God help her for enabling this lunacy.

Caitlyn insisted on driving to Falco, and Antonio humored her only because his pounding head had blurred his vision. Slightly. Not enough to give the doctor's ridiculous CT-scan idea any credence. He'd had plenty of brain scans in the past and the final one had ended his career.

He'd given up trying to understand why he could recall the last CT scan he'd endured, but couldn't remember the woman he'd been married to for—what? Four or five years? He didn't even know. He couldn't even fully picture her face, just bits of it in an insane collage.

They picked up Antonio's prescription on the way, but he waited to take a pill since the warning said the medication might make him drowsy. He definitely wanted to be alert for this first trip to his place of business.

The building came into view and Caitlyn pointed at it, saying Antonio had bought the lot and built Falco from the ground up, approving the architect's plans, surveying the drywall as it went up and hand selecting the equipment inside.

He waited for some sense of recognition. Pushed for it with widened eyes and a mostly empty mind. But the simple glass and brick looked like hundreds of other buildings in Los Angeles.

Falco Fight Club. The red-and-black letters marched across the brick, signifying this as the headquarters for the global MMA promotional company Antonio had founded. Under the name, a replica of the falcon tattoo on Antonio's pectoral had apparently been worked in as Falco's logo.

He briefly touched the ink under his shirt. This was part of his past, and likely his future as well, though he knew nothing about the business side of Falco. Nor did he have a driving desire to reclaim the helm…not yet.

He was here for what happened inside the ring.

Grimly, he climbed from the Range Rover Caitlyn drove more carefully than a ninety-year-old priest, and hesitated, suddenly fearful at crossing the threshold. What if he climbed into the ring and none of his memories came back? What if Caitlyn was right and additional trauma to his head actually caused more problems? He was a father now; he had other people to think about besides himself.

Caitlyn's presence wrapped around him before she slipped her smooth hand into his. It felt oddly…right to have her by his side as he faced down his past. She didn't say a word but stood with him as he surveyed the entrance, silently offering her unconditional support, even though she'd been adamantly against him fighting.

Somehow, that made his unsettling confusion acceptable. No matter what happened inside Falco Fight Club, he'd found his old life, and after a year of praying for it, he'd count his blessings.

The falcon emblem on his chest mirrored the one on the bricks in more ways than one—both decorated a shell housing the soul of Antonio Cavallari, and somewhere inside lay the answers he sought. He wouldn't give up until he had reclaimed *all* of his pieces.

"Is the company still in operation?" he asked, wishing he'd unbent from his bad mood enough to ask the question in the car. But his headache had grown worse as the day wore on, and he was weary of dealing with pain and questions and the blankness inside his head.

She nodded. "I get monthly reports from the interim CEO, Thomas Warren. He's been running it in your stead, but I have no idea if he's doing a good job or not. I was hoping you'd want to take over at some point, but I think everyone would understand if you didn't do so right away."

"Do they know?" He inclined his head toward the building, and even that renewed the pounding at his temples. Maybe he should take a painkiller anyway. It might dull the embarrassment and frustration of not knowing who "they" were.

She squeezed his hand and let it go, then shoved hers into her pocket. He missed the feel of her skin on his instantly and almost reached for her but recognized the wisdom in not appearing too intimate in public.

"Thomas called me yesterday after your lawyer gave him the heads-up that you were back," she said. "But I didn't tell him anything other than to confirm it was true, which was all he asked. I didn't know how much you'd planned to divulge."

"Thanks." He didn't know, either, but the truth would likely come out soon enough when Antonio stepped in-

side and had to be led around his own building like a
blind person.

"Antonio." She hesitated for a moment. "I've been trying to shield you from the media, but you should know
that coming to Falco is probably going to trip their radar.
You should be prepared for a full onslaught at any time."

*A crush of people, cameras, microphones, babbling.
The chants of "Falco, Falco, Falco."* The montage was
the clearest yet of elements from his past. The memory
washed over him, or rather it was a blend of several memories bleeding together, of him leaving the ring to follow
his manager as Rick pushed through the crowd.

With the images came the expected renewed headache.
The increased pounding and pressure wasn't so difficult
to deal with if it came with new memories. But it was a
brutal trade-off.

"I…" He'd been about to say he was used to reporters
and cameras. But then he realized. The media wouldn't
be interviewing him about his latest bout with Ramirez
or Fuentes. He wasn't a fighter anymore.

Instead, the media would ask him painful questions,
like, "Why don't you remember your wife?" and "What
did you do for a whole year while you were gone?"

They might even ask him something even more difficult to answer, like, "How does it feel to find out you're a
father after all this time?" Would the media want to crack
open his life and take pictures of his children? He didn't
want the babies exposed to anyone who didn't necessarily
have their best interests at heart.

Caitlyn had been *shielding* him from the media. As if
she wanted to protect him. It snagged a tender place inside, and he had no idea what to do with that.

"I shouldn't have come here," he muttered and turned
to climb back into the Range Rover.

Fight or flight. The more he delved into his past, the

more appropriate the name Falco became. Seemed as if Antonio was constantly poised to use his talons or his wings, and he didn't like it. But he had no idea how to change it, how to achieve a happy medium where he dealt with life in a healthy way.

"Wait."

Caitlyn stopped him with a warm hand on his shoulder and the area under her palm tingled. Did all women affect him so greatly, or just this one?

Aggravated because he couldn't remember, Antonio moved out of her reach but paused before sliding into the passenger seat.

"I wasn't trying to talk you out of going inside," she said, concern lacing her tone. Enough so that he turned to face her. "This is important to you, and I think you need to do it. Five minutes. We'll walk around, say hello and then leave. The press won't have time to congregate in that length of time if you'd prefer not to be accosted."

"And then what?" he asked far more sharply than he'd intended, but she didn't flinch. "The hurdles will still be there tomorrow and the next day."

And he didn't just mean the press. All at once, the uphill battle he faced to reclaim his memories, coupled with the constant physical pain, overwhelmed him.

"That will be true whether you take this step or not." She held out her hand for him to clasp, as if she'd known exactly what he needed.

Without hesitation, he slid his hand into hers and held it, wordlessly absorbing her energy and spirit, and it calmed him instantly. Miraculously.

"Walk with me." She pulled him away from the car and shut the door. "I'll do all the talking. If you want to spar with someone, the training facility is adjacent to the administrative offices. I'm sure one of the guys would indulge you in a round. There's always a ton of people either in the rings or strength training on the gym equipment."

"How do you know so much about my company?" he asked as he let her lead him toward the door, his pulse hammering in his temples. From nerves, trauma, the silky-sweet scent of Caitlyn? He couldn't tell. Maybe it was all three.

"I spent time here occasionally over the past year." A shadow passed through her expression. "I've brought the babies a couple of times, hoping to infuse your heritage into them. Silly, I know. They're too young to understand it."

She laughed and he felt an answering tug at his mouth. How did she do that? He'd been all set to command her to drive away as fast as she could, and when he got home, he'd probably have barred himself in his room to indulge in a fit of bad temper. Instead, Caitlyn had gotten him across the parking lot and pulled a smile from him, as well.

All in the name of physically, mentally and spiritually guiding him through a place she hadn't wanted him to go.

What an amazing, beautiful, selfless woman. The mother of his children. There was nothing temporary about her role; he saw that now. Her love for them shone through in every action, every small gesture.

Caitlyn Hopewell was his children's mother, and it was an odd addition to her attractiveness. But there it was.

That ever-present sense of disloyalty squelched the warmth in his chest that had bloomed at the sound of Caitlyn's laugh. Caitlyn was sensual and beautiful and likely that meant her sister'd had those qualities, as well. But why couldn't he remember being so outrageously attracted to Vanessa? Why couldn't he remember her touch the way he could recall with perfect clarity what Caitlyn's hand felt like on his shoulder? Surely he'd fallen for Vanessa for a myriad of reasons, especially if he'd married the redheaded sister instead of the dark-haired one. His late wife's attributes and personality must have eclipsed Caitlyn's.

But he couldn't fathom how, not when innocently thinking about Caitlyn caused a burn in his gut he couldn't explain away. It was pure, sensual attraction that he wished to explore.

How was he supposed to move past his relationship with Vanessa and potentially have a new one—especially if the woman was Caitlyn—when thinking about moving on caused a wretched sense of unfaithfulness?

Five

Antonio stepped through the glass doors to Falco with a silent sense of awe. The reception area held a hushed purpose, as if to say important matters happened between these walls, and it hit him oddly to imagine he owned all of this, had made it happen, had created this company himself through his own ingenuity and resolve.

White marble stretched under his feet, edged with red and black. Framed promotional pictures lined the walls on both sides, similar to the ones in his home gym, featuring fierce-faced fighters with raised gloves or crossed arms sporting bulging biceps. Many wore enormous title belts with distinctive, rounded shields in the center, proclaiming the fighter a world champion.

His own face stared back at him from three of the frames, one each for his three welterweight titles. The memory of posing for the shots crowded into his head, crystal clear.

But he couldn't remember picking out the marble under

his feet or the lot under the foundation or ever having walked into this building before today. It was becoming evident that his most severe memory loss encompassed the events that had happened after that final knockout Caitlyn had spoken of, the one that had ended his fighting career.

Perhaps the CT scan wasn't such a far-fetched next step. If there was something in his brain locking up his memories of that period, shouldn't he explore options to remove the block? Of course, he barely remembered Vanessa and he didn't remember Caitlyn at all, though he'd clearly known them both prior to his career-ending coma. So nothing was guaranteed.

After all, none of the Indonesian doctors had helped. Nothing had helped. And he hated hoping for a cure that would eventually amount to nothing.

In deference to the holidays, the reception area held a small decorated tree, and holly boughs covered nearly every surface. A classic Bing Crosby tune filtered through the sound system and he recognized it, of course, because his brain retaining Christmas songs made perfect sense. The receptionist looked up from her desk, blonde and perky, smiling with genuine happiness when she saw Antonio.

"Mr. Cavallari!" She shook her head, her wide-eyed gaze searching his face. "It's as if the past year never happened. I can't believe it. You look exactly the same."

Antonio nodded, because what else would he do when he couldn't remember this woman's name, though he'd probably hired her.

"Hi, Mandy," Caitlyn said smoothly, as if she'd read his mind. "Antonio would like to see what you've done with the place in his absence. I assured him that Thomas and his stellar team kept things in order, but there's nothing like an in-person tour, right?"

Rescued again. Antonio squelched the gratefulness

flooding his chest, because how long could Caitlyn's savior superpowers actually last? It was a fluke anyway. There was no way she'd picked up on his distress. They barely knew each other and besides, her ability to read his mind had to be flawed; *he* didn't even know what was in his head most of the time.

"Of course." The receptionist—Mandy—smiled at Caitlyn and picked up the phone on the desk to murmur into it, then glanced up again. "Thomas will be here momentarily to show you around. Glad you're…um…*here*, Mr. Cavallari."

Here, meaning not dead. That was definitely a plus and cheered him slightly. "Thanks, Mandy. I plan to be around for a long time."

A man with a graying crew cut wearing an expensive, tailored suit bustled into the reception area. *Thomas.*

A memory of the two of them standing in nearly this same spot popped into Antonio's head, from Thomas's first day on the job. Relief stung the back of Antonio's throat. His memories were in there somewhere. It just took the right combination of criteria for them to battle to the forefront.

Thomas Warren was flanked by a couple of younger men in sweatpants and hoodies. Fighters. They wore almost identical expressions with a slight menacing edge, and they both leaned into the room, fists lightly curled as if preparing to start swinging.

Antonio recognized the stance instantly—he'd entered thousands of rooms that way. Still did, even now. Or perhaps he'd only picked it up again recently. Had he lost that ready-to-fly edge in the past few years, only to regain it after awakening to a blank world where simply entering a room brought on a barrage of questions and few answers?

These were the pieces of Antonio Cavallari he hoped to recover inside this building.

"Thomas." Antonio held out his hand to the older man, who shook Antonio's hand with a critical once-over.

"It's true." The interim CEO of Falco Fight Club narrowed his gaze, mouth slightly open as he fixated on Antonio's face. "I guess you can call me a doubting Thomas because I really didn't believe it until I saw you for myself. Come, let me show you the improvements we've made in your…ah, absence."

Seemed as if everyone was going to stumble over the proper verbiage to explain they'd assumed Antonio had died in the plane crash. He didn't blame them; he didn't have any clue what you were supposed to say, either.

"Let's put pretense aside," Antonio said before he'd fully determined what he planned to say. "You thought I was dead and spent the past year accordingly. I may disagree with some, or even all, of your decisions, but I fail to see how I could find fault with them. You did what you thought was right and I have no intention of walking in here to undo everything you've done."

Thomas's eyebrows rose. "Fair enough. It is an unprecedented situation and I appreciate that we might both need to maintain flexibility."

Thomas inclined his head and indicated Antonio should follow him into the interior of the building.

The two fighters fell in behind as well, and Antonio had the distinct sense the men were either intended as intimidation or accessory. It didn't matter which; either one was as laughable as it was baffling.

The short tour generated little in the way of jogging his memories, but the visit to Falco itself had already yielded a valuable harvest. Antonio had the unique opportunity to appreciate what he'd built using his own fortitude and business savvy as he surveyed it for what was, for all intents and purposes, the first time.

The vast influence of Falco unrolled before him as he

learned of his vision for bringing glory back to the sport
of mixed martial arts with a promotional powerhouse that
had no ties to a media conglomerate. Untainted by corporate politics or the need for a healthy bottom line, Antonio
had pushed boundaries, opening MMA to unconventional
fighting disciplines, training some of the most elite fighters in the world and gaining entry to off-the-beaten-path
venues. Most important, he'd insisted all his fighters be
allowed to compete for titles based on their records, not
handshake promotional deals.

And he'd been wildly successful, beyond anything he'd
envisioned when Caitlyn mentioned Falco was where he'd
made all his money. When he'd asked Thomas to show him
the books, his eye had shot straight to the profit line, as if
he'd last glanced at a balance sheet yesterday. The number of decimal places couldn't be right, and Antonio had
nearly chalked it up to a clerical error until he glanced at
the rest of the line items.

Not a mistake. Billions of dollars flowed through his
company. It was dizzying. He should have paid more attention to the balances of his accounts when Caitlyn had
transferred control of his estate back to him at his lawyer's
office the other day.

No wonder Caitlyn hadn't taken the first opportunity to
get out of Dodge when he'd offered to relieve her of baby
duty. He could easily give her eight or nine figures for her
trouble and never think twice about it, which was probably what she was hoping for. She seemed to genuinely
care about the children, but everyone wanted something,
and that something tended to be money.

"I want to see the training facility," Antonio announced
abruptly.

"Absolutely." Thomas led the way to the adjacent building.

Energy bolted through his body as he anticipated climbing between the ropes. That had been his sole purpose in coming here and it had thus far been eclipsed by a slow slide back into Businessman Antonio.

Which didn't seem as bad as it once might have.

Maybe part of his journey lay in coupling both halves of his soul—the fighter and the suit—under one banner. But it wouldn't be today. He needed to get his wits about him, what few remained, and the ring was the only place where he'd experienced any peace in the past year.

As he entered the training facility, Antonio's lungs hitched as his eye was drawn to the equipment closet, to the three rings, one with a regulation metal cage surrounding it, to the workout area. Exactly where he'd known they would all be placed. Because he truly remembered, or because he'd modeled the layout on another facility from before the career-ending knockout?

Eager to find out, he strode through the cavernous room, drawing the attention of the muscled men—and surprisingly, a few women—engaged in various activities. One by one, weights drifted to the ground and sparring partners halted, gloves down, as they stared at him.

"That's right," he called to the room at large. "I've arisen from my watery grave. Who's brave enough to go a round with a ghost?"

"Cavallari, you sly dog." A grinning Hispanic male, early twenties, jogged over from his spot at a weight bench and punched Antonio on the arm as if he'd done it often. "They told us you were dead. What have you been doing, hiding out to get back in professional shape without any pressure? Smart."

What a ridiculous notion. Ridiculously brilliant. Maybe he'd adopt it as his easy out if the media did start harassing him about his whereabouts over the past year.

"Hey, Rodrigo," Caitlyn called, and when Antonio

glanced at her, she winked, and then murmured under her breath, "Rodrigo was a good friend. Before."

When they got home, he'd treat her to the most expensive bottle of wine in his cellar. And then when she was good and looped, he'd carefully extract her real agenda.

No matter how much she seemed to love his kids, no one did nice things without a motive. He wanted to know what hers was.

"Are you my volunteer?" Antonio jerked his head at the nearest ring, eyes on his potential sparring partner.

"Sure, boss." Rodrigo shadowboxed a couple of jabs at Antonio's gut. "Like old times. Just go easy on me if your secret training put you out of my league."

Rodrigo's grin belied the seriousness of the statement— did he not believe Antonio had actually trained over the past year or did he assume that regardless, they'd still be matched in skill? Apparently, they'd sparred before and had been on pretty equal ground.

"Likewise," Antonio commented, mirroring Rodrigo's grin because it felt expected. Honestly, he had no idea how they'd match up. He couldn't wait to find out.

Something inside rotated into place, as if two gears had been grinding together haphazardly, and all at once, the teeth aligned, humming like a well-oiled machine.

His headache had almost receded and if God had been listening to his pleas at all, the next few minutes would knock loose a precious memory or two.

Before long, Antonio had slipped into the shorts Caitlyn had insisted he bring from home. She watched him face off against Rodrigo in the large ring, both men barechested and barefoot. It hadn't taken the office grapevine but about five minutes to circulate the news that Antonio Cavallari was both back and in the ring. Nearly everyone from FFC's administrative building had crowded into the training facility and around the cage with expectant faces, murmuring about Antonio's return.

You couldn't have pried most of the women's gazes from Antonio with a crowbar, Caitlyn's included, though she at least tried to hide it. But he was magnificent, sinewy and hard, with that fierce tattoo so prominent against his golden body. His still-longish hair was slicked back from his forehead, highlighting his striking eyes as they glittered like black diamonds.

Apparently she liked him as a fighter just as much as she liked the savvy businessman. Maybe more. Her raw reaction at the sight of Antonio in the ring was powerful and uncomfortably warm. Hot, even. And far lower than seemed appropriate in public.

It was shameful. Shameful to be so affected by her sister's husband, shameful that she'd carried a yet-to-be-extinguished torch for Antonio all of these years. Most shameful of all was that at least half of his appeal lay in his primal stance as he waited for an opening to do bodily harm to another human. She'd always thought of him as the perfect man—committed, beautiful, steady. And it frightened her to be so attracted to him for purely carnal reasons.

But she couldn't stop the flood of elemental longing any more than she could explain how over-the-top sexy the man had become once he slipped into his glory in the ring.

She'd never seen him fight live. Once he and Vanessa had hooked up, she'd spent a lot of time feeling sorry for herself and as little time as possible around the two of them. It was too hard to be reminded that he'd picked the glamorous Hopewell sister instead of the quiet, unassuming one. Not that she blamed him; most men had overlooked Caitlyn in favor of Vanessa, and Caitlyn had never been bitter about it. Until Antonio.

She'd spent the entirety of their marriage hiding her hurt and disappointment and jealousy, the entirety of their re-

lationship wishing she could have her sister's marriage...
and then the past year feeling guilty and sick about the
uncharitable thoughts she'd had.

Now she just wanted to feel as if she didn't have to
apologize for being alive when her sister wasn't. For being
a woman affected by a prime specimen of man as he engaged in physical combat. Was that so wrong?

The men circled each other, trash-talking. Suddenly,
Antonio lashed out in a blur of intricately executed moves,
both beautiful and lethally graceful. Her breath caught as
she drank in the visual panorama. Antonio's body moved
fluidly, as if it had been made specifically for this purpose,
and it was stunning to behold.

In enabling him to return to the ring, she'd unwittingly
exposed herself to a piece of his soul that was the opposite of harsh, the opposite of brutal. It was breathtaking.

Caitlyn blinked as Rodrigo hit the mat without having
lodged one defense.

Violence was unfolding before her very eyes and the
only thing she'd noticed was how exquisitely Antonio had
executed it. Something was very wrong with her.

The crowd murmured as Rodrigo shook his head and
climbed to his feet, rubbing his jaw.

"Lucky shot, boss," he grumbled.

Not that she had any basis for judgment, but Caitlyn
didn't think so. As the men went at it again, Antonio's superior skill and style couldn't be mistaken, even by an un-
trained eye such as hers. Rodrigo landed a couple of shots,
but the younger man called a halt to the match after only
a few more minutes, breathing heavily. Caitlyn grimaced
at his split lip.

Rodrigo and Antonio shook hands and the crowd slowly
dispersed, many of them stopping to welcome Antonio
back or clap him on the shoulder with a few congratula-
tory words about his performance.

Caitlyn hung back, remaining as unobtrusive as possible while Antonio excused himself to shower and change. No one was paying attention to her anyway, which she considered a blessing as long as her insides were still so unsettled. This whole Falco Fight Club experience had shown her something about herself that she didn't understand and didn't know what to do with.

Antonio returned. His gaze cut through the crowd and locked on to hers, his eyes dark with something untamed and unnameable and she shivered. It was as if he knew exactly where she was in the crowd. And exactly what she'd been thinking about while watching him fight.

Her cheeks heated and she blessed his distance because, hopefully, that meant he couldn't tell. But the distance disappeared as he strode directly to her.

Though clothed, his potency hadn't diminished in the slightest. Because she knew what his hard body looked like under his crisp white shirt and slacks. Heat rolled between them and his gaze fell to her mouth for a moment as if he was thinking about dropping a kiss there.

Her lips tingled under his scrutiny. Madness. She'd fallen under some kind of spell that caused her imagination to run away with her, obviously.

"I'm ready to go home," he murmured and the moment broke apart. "I've had enough for one day."

"Sure," she managed to get out around the tight, hot lump in her throat.

Goody. Now they could cram themselves into a tiny Range Rover for the drive home, where his masculine scent would overpower her, and she'd spend the drive reminding herself that no matter how sexy he was, the complications between them were legion.

Which was exactly what happened. She gripped the wheel, white-knuckling it onto the main street and, thankfully, Antonio fell silent.

Too silent. He'd just reentered his old world in the most immersive way possible. She desperately wanted to ask him about it.

Had he remembered any of Falco? All of it? What had it felt like for him to get in the ring again? Antonio hadn't fought professionally in years and, as far as Caitlyn knew, Vanessa had forbid him from even messing around with the guys in the ring because she feared he'd get hurt again.

Part of Caitlyn wondered if she'd helped facilitate his return to Falco because it was something her sister never would have done. As if it was some kind of sick contest to see if Antonio would realize Caitlyn was the better woman for him.

But she had no idea how to navigate the heavy vibe in the Range Rover, so she kept her mouth shut and let the silence ride.

When they got home, she followed him into the house from the garage, unable to stand the silence any longer. "How's your head?"

That was a safe enough topic, wasn't it?

He paused in the kitchen to get a glass of water and gulped the entire thing down before answering. "It hurts."

She leaned a hip on the granite countertop as close to him as she dared and crossed her arms over her still-unsettled insides. "Why don't you take a painkiller and rest."

"Because I'm not ninety and waiting around to die," he said shortly, then frowned. "Sorry, I don't mean to snap."

The line between his eyebrows concerned her and she regretted not encouraging him to talk to her while they'd been in the car. Her own uncertainties weren't an excuse to be selfish. "It's okay. You've had a difficult day."

His gaze latched on to hers and he surveyed her with a focused, hooded expression that pulled at something deep in her core. In or out of the ring—didn't matter. He exuded a primal energy that she couldn't stop herself from reacting to, and it was as frightening as it was thrilling.

The way Antonio made her feel had nothing to do with the safe, nebulous fantasy she'd carried around in her heart for years. *That*, she understood. The raw, ferocious draw between them, she didn't.

"Difficult?" he repeated. "Really? What gives you that impression?"

"Uh…because you're snapping at me?" When the corners of his mouth lifted, she smiled involuntarily in return. "It couldn't have been easy to get into the ring today in front of all your colleagues. How long has it been since you last went a round?"

"A couple of weeks. I trained six hours a day in Indonesia over the past few months. It was part of my rehabilitation."

"Oh, you never mentioned that." And why would he? She wasn't his confidante. But she'd kind of hoped he saw her in that role, as someone he could turn to, who would be there for him in a confusing world.

"It wasn't worth mentioning." A smile still played with his lips and she couldn't tear her gaze from his mouth as he talked. "Indonesia was about survival. Only. I fight— then and now—because I have to."

The confessions of his deepest self were as affecting as watching him fight had been. She wanted more but was afraid of what it might mean to get it. "I remember you said you needed to get in the ring to blow off frustration. Did it work?"

"Partially," he allowed. "I need a more skilled partner."

"Yes, even I could see that Rodrigo was outmatched."

A blanket of intimacy settled around them as a full, genuine smile bloomed on his face, and she reveled in it.

Brigitte bustled into the kitchen at that moment, shattering the mood. "Oh, you're back. Grand. Do you want to spend time with the babies before dinner?"

Taking a guilty step backward, Caitlyn tore her gaze from Antonio to focus on the au pair. "Um, yes. Of course."

She always played with the babies before dinner while Brigitte helped the chef, Francesco, put the children's meal together. What was wrong with Caitlyn that she hadn't noticed the time? Well, duh—Antonio was what was wrong with her.

"They're in their cribs waiting for you," Brigitte said sunnily and went to the fridge to pull out covered bowls of premashed fruit and veggies.

"Come with me." Caitlyn put a hand on Antonio's arm before she thought better of it. Heat prickled her palm and she snatched it back. "It'll be fun. Low pressure."

Fun, plus an excuse to stay in his presence under the pretense of guiding his steps toward fatherhood—but with the added distance the babies would automatically create.

Then she remembered his headache. "You don't have to if you'd rather be alone. I don't want to push you into a role you're not ready for."

"I'd like to," he said, surprising her.

He followed her upstairs and into the nursery. Leon stood in the center of his crib, both chubby hands gripping the edge to support his wobbly legs as he yowled like a wet cat. Annabelle sat with her back to the room banging one of the crib slats with a rattle while sweet Antonio Junior lay on his back staring at the mobile above his crib.

"There you go," Caitlyn murmured to their father. "This is a perfect encapsulation of your children's personalities. Leon does not like being forced to do something and he isn't a bit hesitant to tell you how unhappy he is. He'll be the first to learn how to climb out of his crib, mark my words. God help us then."

"Why?" Antonio eyed first his son and then Caitlyn as

she boosted Leon from his crib and into her arms, which predictably, quieted down his protests.

"Because then he'll be a holy terror, climbing out in the middle of the night while we're asleep." She nodded to the baby. "Would you like to hold him?"

"Yes," he said decisively and then his brows drew together as Caitlyn handed over the baby. "Do I have to do anything?"

"Nothing special, just make sure he feels secure."

She laughed as Leon peered up at his father suspiciously, as if trying to figure out whether he was okay with this new person. They'd learn the verdict in about two seconds.

Thankfully, Leon waved his fist around, which was his way of saying things were cool. Antonio's gaze never left his son's face, and his clear adoration shot straight through Caitlyn's heart with a painful, wonderful arrow.

Caitlyn spun to busy herself with Antonio Junior before the tears pricking at her eyelids actually fell in a mortifying display of sentiment. It was just a dad with his kid. Why should it be so tender and meaningful?

There were so many reasons locked up in that question, she could hardly start answering it—but first and foremost, because it was her kid, too, one she'd created with this man in a most unconventional way, sure, but that didn't make it any less powerful to watch the two interact.

Then there was the compelling contrast between this tender version of Antonio and the fierce warrior he'd been in the ring. The dichotomy created an even more compelling man, and he was already so mesmerizing, she could hardly think.

Antonio Junior hadn't made a sound since they'd entered the room, so Caitlyn checked on him as she often did, just to be sure he was still breathing. He'd always been quiet, carrying the weight of the world on his shoulders, and it bothered her that he'd adopted such a grave demeanor.

He definitely took after his father in that respect, where Leon was a demanding prima donna like Vanessa.

"That's my serious little man," she crooned to Antonio Junior and slid her fingertips across his fine dark hair as he refocused his gaze from the mobile to Caitlyn.

The sheer beauty of her child nearly took her breath. She'd always thought he looked like Antonio, but it had been an academic observation based on memory and expectation—they both had dark hair and dark eyes; of course the comparisons would come.

"Is he serious?" Antonio asked with genuine curiosity.

"Very. He's also quiet. Annabelle would probably be content to sit in her crib until the cows came home as long as she could make noise," Caitlyn called over her shoulder and, dang it, her voice caught on the emotion still clogging her throat. She cleared it, hoping Antonio had been too caught up in Leon to notice. "That's her favorite thing. Noise. She likes it best when she can bang on something and then imitate the noise with her voice and, trust me, she practices a lot."

"I don't mind," Antonio said softly, and she sensed him come up behind her long before she heard his quiet intake of breath. He peered over her shoulder into Annabelle's crib. "Hi, there, sweetheart."

Annabelle tipped her head up to focus on her father, her upside-down face beaming. "Gah."

"Is that her imitation of banging the rattle?" Antonio asked with a laugh. "Because she should practice some more."

"No, that's how she says hello."

Caitlyn's throat tightened again, which was silly when she was only explaining her children's quirks. But their father didn't know any of these things—because he'd been lost and alone half a world away while she'd lived in his house, cared for his children and spent his money. She wanted to make that up to him as best she could.

"Come on, you big flirt." Caitlyn hoisted Annabelle out of the crib and set her on the soft pink blanket already spread out on the nursery floor. "I realize pink is clichéd for a girl, but I thought Annabelle needed girlie things with two brothers."

"You don't have to justify your choices." Antonio crouched down on the blanket and settled Leon next to his sister. "I'd be the last person to tell you you're doing it wrong, and even if I have a conflicting opinion, I'd prefer to talk through it, not issue countercommands. You've done the best you can, and it couldn't have been easy to do it alone."

"It wasn't." One tear spilled over before she could catch it. "I worried every day that I wasn't enough for them."

Antonio glanced up from his perch on the fluffy pink blanket, which should have looked ridiculous but didn't in the slightest. "You've been amazing. More than enough. Look at how perfect these babies are. Healthy, happy. What more could you have provided?"

"A father," she whispered. And somehow the fates had granted that wish in the most unexpected, flawless way possible. "They deserve two parents."

A shadow passed over his face. "And for now, that's what they have."

For now? Was that a cryptic comment about the future of her place in this family?

"No matter what happens, I will always be their mother," she stated firmly, and if only her voice hadn't cracked, it might have sounded as authoritative out loud as it had in her head.

They needed to talk about the future, but she was afraid to bring it up, afraid to overload him with one more thing he didn't want to deal with, afraid he was only letting her stay because it was Christmas and she'd begged him not to kick her out.

But she had to get over it and go to the mat for her children. If anyone could understand the bone-deep need to fight for what you wanted, it would surely be Antonio.

"Yes," he said quietly. "You *are* their mother."

And that took the wind out of her sails so fast, she couldn't breathe. "Okay, then."

She'd have to bring up the future another time, after she'd recovered from all of this.

Six

Antonio's headache persisted through dinner, but he couldn't stomach the idea of taking the pills now that he actually had them. He'd lost so much of his past; losing his present to drowsiness held little appeal. Instead, he bided his time until Caitlyn and Brigitte put the babies to bed and then he cornered Caitlyn in the sunroom.

He hoped she wouldn't mind the interruption. It was time to dig into what Caitlyn wanted from him in exchange for the role she'd played thus far in his life and the lives of his children. And did she see a continued role? If so, what role did she envision for herself?

The sun had set long ago and Caitlyn read by low lamp-light. He started to say her name but the words dried up on his tongue. Something inside lurched sweetly, as confusing as it was intriguing. Silently, he watched her, loath to alert her to his presence until he was good and finished sating himself on her ethereal beauty.

But she glanced up almost instantly, as if she'd sensed

him. He knew the feeling. There was an undeniable draw between them, and he'd bet every last dollar that she felt it, too. Maybe it was time to dig into that as well, and find out what role *he* wanted her to play.

"Have a glass with me?" He held up the uncorked bottle of wine he'd judiciously selected from his extensive wine cellar.

"Um, sure." Her fair skin bloomed with that blush he liked far more than he should. But what had brought it out? He had a perverse need to find out.

Which seemed to be the theme of this nighttime rendezvous. He'd barely scratched the surface of what made Caitlyn Hopewell tick, and exposing her layers appealed to him immensely.

Antonio poured two glasses of the deep red cabernet and handed one to Caitlyn, then settled into the other chair, separated from hers by a small wooden end table. For a moment, he watched the moonlight dance on the silvery surf so beautifully framed by the wall of glass opposite the chairs.

"I bought this house specifically for the view from this room," he commented instead of diving right in. "It's my favorite spot."

"Mine, too," Caitlyn agreed quietly.

"I figured. This is where I find you most often." He sipped his wine, rolling it around on his tongue as the easy silence stretched. For once, Caitlyn didn't seem determined to fill the gap with nervous chatter.

It was nice to sit with no expectations and not worry about his missing memories. His headache eased the longer he watched the waves crash on the shore below.

"Did you have something on your mind?" she blurted out and then sighed. "I mean, other than the regular stuff, like becoming a father and having amnesia and learning to live in civilization again and—"

"Caitlyn." He touched the rim of his glass to hers in silent apology for the interruption, but he wasn't really sorry. He liked that she gave him so many opportunities to say her name. "I wanted to have a bottle of wine with you. As you pointed out, if nothing else, we're a family by default. Nothing wrong with acting like one."

She didn't relax. "Except we're not a family, not really. You were all set to send me on my way until I convinced you to let me stay through the holidays. Then what, Antonio? I need to know what you plan to do."

Nothing like laying it on the line. Apparently, the easy silence hadn't been so easy for her. If she wasn't keen on a social drink, they didn't have to play nice. Shame. He'd have preferred to have the wine flowing before getting to the reason he'd tracked her down.

But clearly, her ability to read him wasn't a fluke, as he'd assumed earlier today.

"I'm not sure," he said carefully. "It's not January yet and I have a lot to consider. Tell me what you'd like to see happen."

Her fingers gripped the stem of the wineglass until her nail beds turned white. "That's difficult to answer."

Because she didn't want to come right out and say that on the first of January, she'd take a wire transfer with nine zeros tacked onto the end? "Then, maybe you can answer this for me. Why did you rescue me at Falco so many times today? It was as if you could read the room and tell exactly when I was floundering."

"Oh, um…" Her eyebrows drew together as her gaze flew to his face, searching it, and unexpected rawness sprang into the depths of her eyes. "I don't know. It was painfully obvious when you didn't remember someone. I hated that you were uncertain."

That rawness—it nearly eviscerated him with its strength. What did it mean? He had no context for it, not with her, not with any woman. And he wanted to know if it signified the same intense desire to explore each other, the way it did in him.

The draw between them grew tighter as he contemplated her. "Obvious?"

"Well, probably not to everyone," she corrected quickly. "To me anyway. I was, uh…paying attention."

Her gaze traveled down his body, and she didn't try to hide it, probably because she had no idea how to play coy. Heat flared in his loins as he became extremely aware of how the lamp highlighted the curves under her clothes. "I never thanked you for paying such close *attention*. I'm curious, though. What do you hope to gain from helping me?"

"Gain?" She cocked her head, confusion evident. "I'm helping you navigate your life because you need me. You told me so. I want to help."

"Why?"

"Because I like the fact that you need me!" Her eyelids flew shut and she shook her head. Leaping to her feet, she backed away. "I didn't mean to say that."

"Caitlyn." He'd upset her, and he didn't like the way it snagged at his gut to be responsible for the distress around her mouth and eyes.

He'd much rather be responsible for the raw intensity he'd glimpsed a moment ago.

When he slid from his chair and approached her, she stood her ground despite the fact that her body was poised to flee.

"Wait," he murmured. "What did you mean to say?"

She wouldn't meet his gaze. "I meant to say that the children are my first priority."

No, there was more here, more she didn't want to say, more she didn't want him to discover—and that unidentified something called to him.

Instinct alone guided his hand to her chin and he tipped

her head up to evaluate her stricken expression. "Mine, too. That's why I ask these questions. I want to know whether you're helping me in hopes of a nice payout. Or some other, yet-to-be-determined motive."

"Really, Antonio?" Fire flared in her blue eyes, surprising him in its intensity. "Do you have any context for what being a mother means? What it means to me personally?"

Her lips curled into a harsh smile and he couldn't stop watching her, fascinated by the physical changes in her as she schooled him. Even more surprising, she didn't pull away but pushed her chin deeper into his grip.

"Leon, Annabelle and Antonio Junior are my *children*," she continued, her voice dipping lower with each impassioned word. "Just as much as they're yours. More so. I carried them in my womb and I've raised them. I could do it on an accountant's salary and would have if the judge hadn't granted me conservatorship of their inheritance. Keep your money. This is about love."

Love. A nebulous notion that he should understand but didn't.

With that one word, the atmosphere in the sunroom shifted, growing heavier with awareness. Her body leaned toward his, bristling with vibrancy. No longer poised to flee but to fight.

It reached out and punched him with a dark thrill. She wasn't backing down. She was prepared to meet him halfway, taking whatever he dished out. But what would she do with it?

"Hmm." The sound purred from his throat as he slanted her chin a touch higher. "Let's examine that. What do you know about love?"

More important, did she know the things he wanted to learn?

"I know enough," she retorted. "I know when I look at those babies, my heart feels as if it's about to explode with so many wonderful, terrible emotions. I know what it feels like to lose my sister to an early death and sob for days and days because I can't ever tell her I love her again."

Yes, that tightness in his chest when he'd gazed at his own flesh and blood encapsulated in a tiny person for the first time. It *was* wonderful and terrible. And inexplicably, that decided it. She was telling the truth about her motives, and all interest in grilling her over them evaporated.

Now his agenda included one thing and one thing only—Caitlyn and getting more of her soft skin under his fingers.

Love for a child he understood, but it wasn't the full extent of the kind of love possible. The kind of love he must have had for Vanessa. *That* was the concept that stayed maddeningly out of reach. "What about love for a man? Romantically."

"What, as if you're going to prove my motives are ugly because I've never been in love?" Fiercely, she eyed him. "I know how it feels to want a man to tell you he loves you. You want it so badly that you can't breathe. You want him to touch you and kiss you. It hurts deep down every second that you don't get it. And when you do get it, you want it to last forever."

Electricity arced between them and he ached to close the distance between them, to give her everything on her checklist, right here, right now.

"Is that what you wanted to hear?" she said, her chest rising and falling with quickened breath. "Love is equal parts need and commitment. What do *you* know about love?"

"Nothing," he growled, and instantly, the reality of it crushed through his chest.

The love that she'd painted with her impassioned speech—he wanted that. Wanted to know that he *could* feel like that. But love grew over time, over shared experiences, over shared memories.

He'd been robbed of that when he crashed in the ocean. But he had a chance to start over with someone else, to move on from the past he couldn't reclaim.

This nighttime interlude had started out as a way to get her to explain her motives, but instead, she'd uncovered his. Everything he wanted was right here, gripped in his hand. So he took it.

Hauling Caitlyn forward, he fused his mouth to hers. Hungrily, desperately, he kissed her, and his body ignited in a firestorm of sensation. Her mouth came alive under his, taking and giving with each stroke, matching him in the power of her appetite. He soared into the heavens in the most intense flight he'd ever experienced.

His eyes slammed shut as he savored the tight, heated pulls in his groin that could only be eased by burying himself in this woman, body and soul. *More.* He worked her mouth open and her tongue met his in the middle in a perfect, hot clash of flesh. Her eagerness coursed through him, spurring him on, begging him to take her deeper.

His mind drained of everything except her. He felt alive in the most elemental way, as if he'd been snatched from the jaws of hell for this moment, this woman.

Scrabbling for purchase, he slid his arms around her, aligning her with his body and dragging her into the most intimate of embraces. She clung to his shoulders and the contact sparked through his shirt. The contrast of her soft curves sliding against his brutally hardened torso and thighs drove him wild with sharp-edged need.

So frustrating. Too many clothes in the way. His fingertips explored her automatically, mindlessly, craving her. He wanted every millimeter of her beautiful skin exposed, wanted to taste it, feel it, rake it with his gaze and incite that gorgeous blush she could never seem to stop.

The kiss abruptly ended. Caitlyn tore out of his arms, hair in wild disarray from his questing fingers. Chest heaving, she stared at him, eyes limpid and heated.

And then she fled without a word.

Still mortified over her brazen behavior, Caitlyn curled in a ball on her bed, praying none of the babies would wake up tonight. Praying that Antonio didn't take her display of wantonness as an invitation to knock on her door. Because she didn't know if she'd open it. Or never come out.

She'd kissed her sister's husband. And the guilt was killing her—almost as much as the fact that she wouldn't stop herself from doing it again.

That kiss had rocked her to the core.

And shattered all her harmless fantasies about what it might be like to kiss Antonio.

The gap between imagination and reality was so wide, she couldn't see across it. Never would she have imagined her body capable of feeling such raw *need*. Or such a desire to let Antonio take her further into the descent of sensual pleasure, a place she'd never gone with any man.

The way he made her feel scared her, no doubt. But she scared herself even more. She was afraid of her own impaired judgment. If she gave in to that swirl of dark desire—which had seemed like a very real possibility when Antonio had taken her into his arms—what happened then? Was Antonio gearing up for a marriage proposal? She had no idea how any of this worked. Where his thoughts were on the matter. How you even brought up such important subjects as commitment and love when a man had done nothing more than kiss you.

She needed these questions answered before she let these confusing new feelings brainwash her. The confusion was made even worse by the fact that it was *Antonio* on the other end of the equation. A different, harder, sexier, more over-the-top Antonio, who wasn't necessarily the man he'd been. She had no idea how to handle any of this.

And while she'd long ago accepted that she was already half in love with him, he hadn't professed any such thing to her. Sex was a big deal and until she knew he got that, no more kissing. Otherwise, she might find herself on the wrong side of a broken heart—as she'd always feared.

Along with a guilty conscience she couldn't shake, it was too much.

So they'd just have to pretend that scorching, mind-altering kiss had never happened.

By morning, she'd figured out that was impossible. The long, need-soaked night had not been kind.

Today's goal: get Antonio into a public place so he couldn't entice her again.

When he entered the breakfast nook, fresh from the shower, her heart did a crazy, erratic dance. It was sinful how perfect he was, how well his shoulders filled out a simple T-shirt, how his sinewy arms made her want to run her fingertips across them. Those arms... They'd held her expertly last night as he'd treated her to the most passionate kiss of her life.

How did the sight of him muddle her insides so much?

"Good morning," he murmured, his gaze full of knowledge.

"Hi," she squeaked in return. What did that dark, enigmatic look mean? That he remembered the taste of their kiss and wanted more?

Or was that a classic case of projection since that was what *she* was thinking? Would he even bring up the kiss, or was he of the same mind that it was better to forget about it?

Quickly, she tore her gaze from his and concentrated on her...oatmeal. At least that was what she vaguely recalled she'd been eating before he'd waltzed in and stolen her ability to use her brain.

"Would you like to go Christmas shopping with me today?" she asked and winced at the desperation in the question. As if she was dying to spend the day in his company instead of the truth—public places were her new best friend.

He pursed his perfect lips, which made it really hard not to stare at them. *Oatmeal*. She put her head down and shoveled some in her mouth.

"I'd like that," he said easily. "Will we shop for the children? Or are they too young for gifts?"

"Oh, no. It's their first Christmas. I planned to shower them with presents and lots of brightly wrapped boxes. You know how kids only like to play with the boxes? I thought it would be fun to have empty boxes as well as toys. Of course, I came up with all of that before you returned, so if it's too extravagant—"

"Caitlyn."

She didn't look up. Didn't have to in order to know she was rambling again. Her name was like a code word. Anytime she heard it, it meant *shut up*.

With a soft rush of cloth, he crossed the breakfast nook, pausing by her chair. He tilted her chin to force her to meet his gaze. The way he'd done last night, but this morning, she didn't have the fuel of righteous indignation to keep her semisane. Caught in the grip of his powerful presence, she watched him, unable to look away or breathe. His fingers were like live electrical conduits, zapping her skin with energy, and she was pretty sure the heat had climbed into her cheeks.

"Let's just go shopping, okay?" he asked. "Money is not subject to discussion today."

"Oh. Um, really?" That certainly wasn't the tune he'd

been singing last night. "I told you, I don't want your money, nor am I okay with treating you like a blank check."

She *had* said that, hadn't she? The atmosphere last night had been so vibrant and intense, there was no telling what she'd actually communicated now that she thought back.

"I believe you. So let's be clear. I'm paying. You are shopping." His smile broadened as she opened her mouth. "And not arguing," he added quickly before she could interrupt.

"So you don't have my name in your head next to a little check box labeled 'gold digger' anymore?" she asked suspiciously.

He shook his head and dropped his hand, which she instantly wished he'd put back simply because she liked his touch.

"I'm sorry. I was less than tactful last night. We still have the future to sort out, but I'm less concerned about that today than I was yesterday. I'm willing to see what happens."

"You know I'm breast-feeding the babies, right?" she blurted out, and yeah, that heat was definitely in her cheeks.

His gaze narrowed, but to his credit, he didn't outwardly react to such an intimate topic. "All three of them?"

She scowled. "Yes, all three of them. Why in the world would I be selective?"

For some reason, that amused him. "I wasn't suggesting you should be. Forgive my surprise. It just seems like a huge undertaking. Though, admittedly, my understanding of the mechanics is limited."

Yeah, she'd bet he understood breasts better than most men. "It's a sacrifice, for sure, but one I'm more than willing to make. But the point is, I can't just stop. So there's not a lot of room for seeing how it goes. I'm their mother, not an employee."

He nodded. "I'm beginning to see that point more clearly."

At last. There was no telling if he'd actually softened his stance or whether she could explain her feelings any better now than she'd thus far been able to. But the time seemed right to try.

She shut her eyes for a beat and laid it on the line. "Well, thank you for that. You asked me last night what I envision and honestly, I see us co-parenting."

"You mean long-term?" Even that didn't ruffle his composure, which, hopefully, meant it wasn't too far out of a suggestion in his mind.

"Forever. They're my children," she said simply. "I want to shop for Annabelle's prom dress, see them graduate from college, be there when they get married. The works. There's not one single thing I'd agree to miss."

His silence wasn't very reassuring. Finally, he nodded once. "I don't know how to do that. But I'm willing to talk about it after the holidays, like we agreed. It will give us time to think about what that looks like."

Breath she hadn't realized she was holding whooshed out. It was something. Not the full-bore yes she'd have preferred but more than she'd had five minutes ago.

"That's great. Thank you. It means a lot to me."

"It means a lot to me that you're willing to be their mother." His dark, hooded expression sought hers and held again and she shivered under the intensity. "They need a mother. Who better than the one who carried them for nine months?"

"That's exactly what I've been trying to tell you," she said and wished she could have pulled that off with a smirk, but it probably just sounded grateful.

"Let me eat some breakfast and we'll go shopping." He smiled as Francesco hustled into the breakfast nook, carrying a bowl of oatmeal and some coffee with two teaspoons of sugar, milk and a shot of espresso, the way Antonio liked it.

Not that she'd memorized his likes and dislikes over the years, but she found it interesting that his coffee preference hadn't changed even through the nightmare of amnesia.

"I'll drive," she told him. "Unless your headache is better?"

"It's not as bad today." He glanced at her. "I took a painkiller last night. Figured it was the only way I'd get to sleep after you ran out on me."

Amusement danced through his gaze along with a hint of heat that she had no trouble understanding. And on cue, there came the stupid blush. "I'm sorry. That was juvenile."

"Why did you take off, then?" Casually, he spooned up some oatmeal as if the answer didn't matter, but she caught the tightness around his mouth.

"It was too much," she said carefully. And honestly. "We have a lot of challenges in front of us. I'd like to focus on them without…complications."

That part wasn't the whole truth, but it was certainly true enough.

"That's a good point." Antonio polished off his breakfast without fanfare and without arguing.

Caitlyn frowned. Was she that easy to resist?

It didn't matter. No more kissing. That was the rule and she was sticking to it.

She stood and moved toward the door of the breakfast nook, hoping it didn't appear too much as if she was running away again, but Antonio confused her and she wanted to find a place where she could breathe for a few minutes. "I'll be ready to go shopping in about thirty minutes, if that's okay."

"Caitlyn."

She paused but didn't turn around.

"You focus on your challenges your way, and I'll focus on my challenges my way."

"What's that supposed to mean?" she whispered, afraid she wasn't going to like the answer.

"It means I'm going to kiss you again. The complications aren't great enough to stop me. You'd best think of another argument if you don't want me to."

Seven

The Malibu Country Mart at Christmastime might not have been the smartest choice for keeping her distance from Antonio. For the fourth time, the crush of holiday shoppers forced them together, and for the fourth time, his thigh brushed Caitlyn's hand.

She snatched it back before considering how telling a gesture it was.

Of course, his parting comment at breakfast had obviously been designed to throw her off balance, so alerting him to the fact that he'd succeeded shouldn't be that big of a deal.

"There's Toy Crazy," she squawked and cleared her throat, pointing with her still-tingling finger. "Let's hit that first."

Antonio nodded without comment about her affected voice, bless him, and they walked in tandem to the store.

A Salvation Army bell ringer called out season's greetings as they passed, and the holiday decor added a cheer-

ful mien to the shopping center that Caitlyn wished she
could enjoy. She loved Christmas, loved the holiday spirit
and had been looking forward to the babies' first experience with the festivities.

Now everything with Antonio was weird and uncertain
and she hated that. For so long she'd dreamed of having
a relationship with him, and nothing had happened like
she would have thought. *He* was nothing like she would
have thought, so different than the man he'd been before
the crash. Darker, fiercer Antonio wasn't the tame businessman her sister had married, and Vanessa was far more
suited to handle this version of the man than Caitlyn was.

Antonio had flat-out told her he was going to kiss her
again. What did she do with that? How did she come up
with a better argument than "It's complicated"? Especially
when there wasn't a better argument.

"After you," Antonio murmured and allowed Caitlyn to
enter the toy store ahead of him, then followed her closely
as they wandered into the fray.

Dolls and rocking horses and toy trains dominated
the floor space, jockeying for attention amidst the shoppers. Caitlyn grabbed a cart and jostled through the aisles
in search of the perfect toys for their children. True to
his words at breakfast, Antonio didn't allow her to look
at prices, and insisted she put everything in the cart she
wanted.

Somewhere along the way, the sensual tension faded
and the task became fun. They were just two parents
picking out presents for their kids: swapping suggestions,
agreeing with each other's ideas, nixing the toys that one
of them felt wasn't age appropriate—mostly Caitlyn took
on that role, especially after Antonio joyfully picked out
remote-control cars for Leon and Antonio Junior. Honestly. The boys couldn't even walk yet.

Before long, the cart overflowed and Caitlyn had shared

more smiles with Antonio than she'd expected, given yesterday's kiss.

"I don't think anything else will fit," she announced.

"Then, I suppose we're finished." Antonio nodded toward the front of the store. "Unless you want to get another cart and keep going."

She laughed. "No, I think this is enough to spoil three children rotten."

Antonio smiled and pushed the cart toward the register. He'd manhandled it away from Caitlyn about halfway through without asking, insisting it had grown too heavy for her to maneuver. How could she argue with chivalry?

After they paid and Caitlyn got over her sticker shock, she let Antonio carry the umpteen bags.

But she didn't make it two feet toward the door. Antonio nearly plowed into her when she stopped. 'Twas the season to spend money as if it was going out of style, but it was also the season to spread good cheer to those who wouldn't be waking up to their parents' overindulgence.

"I just remembered that I wanted to donate something to Toys for Tots." Caitlyn picked up a Barbie doll and a GI Joe action figure located near the register. "I'll pay for this out of my own money."

Antonio's brows drew together. "What's Toys for Tots?"

He didn't remember Toys for Tots? Amnesia was such a strange beast, constantly surprising her with the holes it had created in Antonio's mind. Her heart twisted anew as she imagined how difficult his daily life must still be.

"It's a charity sponsored by the US Marines that gives toys to underprivileged kids. Not everyone has a billionaire for a father," she joked. "I like to donate every year, but I selfishly got caught up in my own children this year and nearly forgot."

His expression flickered with a dozen inexplicable emotions.

"Wait here," he instructed. "I'll be right back."

Mystified, she watched him thread back through the crowd and say something to the girl behind the register. Wide-eyed, she nodded and called to another worker. They spoke furiously to each other and then the second worker came alongside the first to speak to Antonio. He handed her something and then returned to Caitlyn's side with a small smile.

"Sorry, but you can't use your own money to buy toys for the kids without fathers."

Kids without fathers. That wasn't what she'd said, but he'd interpreted the term *underprivileged* in a way that had affected him, obviously. And many of the Toys for Tots recipients probably *didn't* have fathers.

"Don't argue with me," she told him sternly. "I didn't say anything about you paying for the babies' gifts, but this is something for me to do on my own."

"I don't mean I don't want you to. I mean, you can't. I bought out the whole store," he explained, and didn't even have the grace to look chagrined.

"You…what?"

"I told the clerk that she should check out the people already in the store and I'd buy whatever was left." He looked downright gleeful. "So we're going to hang out until they clear the store and then she's going to run my credit card."

Her heart thumped strangely. "That's…extravagant. And generous. What brought that on?"

He shrugged. "I don't think I've ever done anything for others before. That charity event you mentioned, the one where I wore the pink shirt. On the day we met," he prompted, as if she'd ever forget. "I did that because it was part of my contract. Not because I believed in the cause. I'm a father now. It means something to me and I want to be a better person than I was."

Tears pricked her eyes and she fought to keep them from falling. "You already are, Antonio."

Somehow her hand ended up in his and he squeezed it tight. "You're the one who brought it up."

What, as if she had something to do with Antonio's beautiful gesture? "Not so you could unload an entire toy store on the marines!"

He laughed and it rumbled through her warmly. *This* was what she'd dreamed of all those lonely nights when she imagined what it would be like to have a relationship with Antonio. Here they were, holding hands, standing near each other, and it was comfortable. Nice.

Not desperate and sensual and dark the way that kiss had been. Which one was the real Antonio?

His thumb stroked her knuckle and heat curled through her midsection. Okay, so he had the capacity to be both, which wasn't an easy thing to reconcile.

"I'll call someone to pick up the toys after the customers are gone and arrange for everything to be taken to the drop-off location," he said.

Yeah, there was nothing wrong with that part of his memory—he had no trouble recalling how to be large and in charge. And she hated that she found that shockingly attractive, too. As much as his generosity and his warrior-like persona and the way he was with the babies.

Who was she kidding? *All* of him was attractive.

When they got home, she spent an hour with the babies feeding them, which was time with her children that she treasured. They wouldn't breast-feed forever and while it had its challenges, such as having to use a breast pump after she'd had wine with Antonio the other night, she would be sad when this special bonding period was over.

Brigitte took over when Caitlyn was finished and they chatted for a few minutes. Leon was teething and making his displeasure known. Brigitte made a few suggestions and they agreed to try a different approach.

Should they include Antonio in discussions about the children's care? Caitlyn hadn't even thought to ask him but she really should. That was what being co-parents was all about.

She went in search of him and found him in his gym. Shirtless. And putting his hard body through a punishing round of inverted push-ups. Muscles bunched as he lowered himself to the ground and back up. His torso rippled and his skin glistened with his effort.

Dear Lord. A more exquisitely built man did not exist anywhere in the world.

Her mouth dried up. She couldn't peel her eyes from his body. Watching him put a burn in her core that ached with unfulfilled need. Somehow, the fact that he didn't know she was there heightened the experience, heating her further.

What was she *doing*?

She backed away, horrified to be gawking like a teenager. Horrified that she'd allowed herself to have a carnal reaction to Antonio.

"Caitlyn."

She glanced up. He'd climbed to his feet and stood watching her with a slightly amused expression. His torso heaved with exertion, and the falcon on his pectoral seemed poised to fly off his chest with each breath.

"Did you want something?" he asked, eyebrows raised.

So many things… "Uh—"

Wide-eyed, she watched him approach and speaking wasn't much of an option. His masculinity wrapped around her in a sensual cloak that settled heavily along her skin, warming it.

"Maybe you wanted to work out with me?" he asked, his head cocked in contemplation.

He was too close. Her body woke up in thrumming anticipation.

"I…um…do Pilates." *What did that have to do with anything, dummy?* She could still lift weights or something in Antonio's company, couldn't she? She shook her head. What was she thinking? That wasn't even why she'd tracked him down.

He reached out and toyed with a lock of her hair, smoothing it from her cheek, letting his fingers trail across her throat as he tucked the strand behind her back.

"Maybe you're here to deliver that argument we talked about earlier?" he murmured.

"Argument?"

Her mind went blank as Antonio's hand slipped from her shoulder to her waist. His naked chest was right there, within her reach. Her fingertips strained to trace the ink that bled into his skin, branding him as Falco. A fierce bird of prey.

"Against me kissing you. If you've got one, now would be the time to say your piece."

She glanced up into his eyes and the typhoon of desire swirling in their dark depths slammed through her. That sensual flare—it was desire *for her*.

She was his prey. She should be frightened. She was… and yet perversely curious what *would* happen next if she let things roll.

"We're, uh… That is…" She yelped as his arm slid around her waist, tugging her closer.

Her breasts brushed his bare torso, and even through her clothes, the contact ignited her already tingling core, flooding her with damp warmth.

"Caitlyn," he murmured. "Don't deny this. Hush now, and let me kiss you."

And before she could blink, he cupped her chin and lifted her head, bringing her mouth to his in one expert shot. The touch of his lips sang through her and she fell into Antonio, into the dark need, into her own pleasure.

Hot and hungry, he kissed her, hefting her deeper in his arms so their bodies snugged tight. She couldn't stop herself from spreading a palm on his heated flesh, right across his heart. Where the falcon lived.

His tongue coupled with hers, sliding against hers with rough insistence, and the sparks it generated ripped a moan from her throat.

Her core liquefied. No man had ever made her feel like this, so desperate and incomplete, as if she'd never be whole without him. She wanted…more. Wanted things she had little concept of. Wanted him to teach her about the pleasure she sought but hadn't yet realized.

Antonio gripped her shirt at the waist and pulled it from her pants before she could protest. Suddenly, his fingertips slid up her spine, magic against her bare flesh. She reveled in it, losing herself in his touch. He palmed her rib cage and thumbed one breast through her bra. Her core throbbed in time with her thundering pulse. Her head lolled backward as he mouthed down her throat to suck at the hollow of her shoulder blade, his unshaven jaw scrubbing her sensitive skin, heightening the pleasure tenfold.

That questing thumb worked its way under her bra and the shock of his rough, insistent touch against her nipple rocketed through her with a spike of dangerous lust.

"Antonio," she croaked and somehow got a grip on his wrist to pull it free from her clothing. "That's too far. It's too much. I can't—"

She bit off the rest—she sounded exactly like the inexperienced virgin she was. She peeled her hands from his chest and tore out of his grip.

"Don't run away," he commanded quietly. "Not this time. I enjoy kissing you. I want to make love to you. But you keep stopping me. Why?"

Afflicted, she stared at him, totally at a loss. "You want to…"

She couldn't even say that out loud. *He wanted to sleep with her.* Of course he did; she'd led him on like a wicked temptress who was perfectly prepared to strip naked right there in his gym and go at it on the floor.

This was her fault. She had no clue how to handle a man like Antonio, who was built like a woman's fantasy come to life. Who probably thought of sex as the next logical step in this type of attraction. No wonder she was screwing this up.

"I'm not like that," she said firmly. "I don't run around sleeping with people indiscriminately."

Something dangerous whipped through his expression. "I'm not 'people' and I object to being classified as such. You're cheapening what's happening between us. Also, I don't think that's the reason. You're afraid to be intimate with me."

He was offended. And disappointed in her. It scratched at her insides painfully. He'd cut through her surface protests to find the truth of her uncertainty. The realization that he understood her so well, even better than she'd understood her reticence, coated her throat, turning it raw.

"Yes," she whispered. "I need space."

She left the gym and he didn't try to stop her. Good. She needed to sort out her confusion. Antonio wasn't some random guy who'd love her and leave her, and of course he'd seen right through that excuse. Good grief, he had *commitment* written all over him—it was a huge part of his appeal.

Still was, but the physicality of her attraction far eclipsed it. Somehow. He'd brought out a part of her she'd never known existed. Around Antonio, she became a sensual, carnal woman that she didn't recognize, who liked his fierce side, his raw masculinity. Who wanted to delve into the pleasures of his touch with no regard to the emotional connection she thought she'd valued above anything else. And it scared her.

Because she didn't want to be like Vanessa. And yet, Caitlyn craved the type of relationship her sister had had with Antonio. It was a paradox, one she didn't know how to resolve.

Antonio had offered himself up on a silver platter. And she never dreamed she'd be fighting herself over whether to accept.

Antonio gave Caitlyn her space.

It was the last thing he wanted to do, but he had enough wits about him to recognize that Caitlyn required delicacy. Not his forte. But he'd learn it to get what he wanted.

The long night stretched, lonely and uncomfortable. The enormous four-poster bed would fit five people, but there was only one person he wanted in it. He had the vague sense that he must have slept in this bed with Vanessa, but he didn't think of his late wife at all. Instead, his vivid fantasies involved a dark-haired beauty who'd tied him up in knots.

Twice.

The first kiss had floored him. The second kiss had thrown him into a whole other level of senselessness. What had started as a way to help him move on from his marriage had exploded into something far more intriguing than he'd dreamed. When he kissed Caitlyn, her essence crawled inside him, haunting him. Pleasing and thrilling at the same time.

He wanted more. So much more. He shifted, unable to find a comfortable position, and the too-soft mattress doubled as a torture device. His half-aroused state didn't help.

The next morning, he bought a town car and hired a full-time driver to shuttle him back and forth to Falco. He still didn't feel comfortable driving, not with the head-aches that sometimes cropped up out of the blue. Navigation sometimes tripped him up as well, especially while trying to get to a place he didn't remember. His house—no problem. Falco wasn't on the approved list of memories his brain had apparently created.

Fighting was his only outlet for the constant frustrations. And his opportunities for it were limited.

Once at Falco, he first arranged for a private detective to start searching for the remaining two unaccounted-for passengers from his flight to Thailand. He gave the highly recommended man one instruction—spare no expense. If those two people were out there, Antonio would help them get back their lives.

Then he spent the afternoon with Thomas untangling legalities. They worked through the brunt of it until Antonio thought his head would explode with details and pain. This office job was where he belonged, where he'd built a company out of the ashes of his first love.

He didn't want it.

In reality, Antonio longed to climb back in the ring. The business side of this promotional venue he'd created didn't call to him as it once must have. Some aspects felt comfortable and familiar, though he didn't have conscious memories of strategy and balance sheets. Surely sitting behind his desk and monitoring his empire had once made him supremely happy.

As Thomas gathered up his paperwork, Antonio swiveled the high-backed chair toward the window, which overlooked a landscaped courtyard with a wishing-pool fountain in the center. He must have enjoyed this view often, as Caitlyn mentioned that he'd been a workaholic, often clocking eighty-hour weeks.

"Thomas, what would it take to get me back in rotation?" Antonio asked without taking his gaze off the gurgling fountain. Not only was it a shocking request in and of itself, but worse, the man who owned an MMA promotional company should probably know the answer already.

"You want to fight again?" Thomas kept any surprise from his tone, which Antonio appreciated. "As a contender? Or just exhibition?"

His mouth quirked involuntarily. "It's not worth doing if you're not going for the title."

The ins and outs of being a professional fighter he had no problems remembering. The pain and the training and the brutal conditioning…all worth it for a shot at glory.

But Antonio had underlying reasons. Reasons why he was a fighter in the first place. It was a part of him, an indelible piece of his makeup that even a near lobotomy of his memory couldn't extricate.

Thomas cleared his throat. "Well, you certainly proved the other day that you're in good enough shape for it. But you stopped fighting for a reason. What's changed?"

"*I* have. Make it happen."

After Thomas left, restlessness drove Antonio to the training facility, where several people called out greetings, none of whom he recognized, and without his mind-reading guide to assist, there was no chance he'd come up with names. If only Caitlyn hadn't requested her space, he'd have gladly brought her with him.

Trainers worked with fighters of all shapes and sizes, some in the rings, some at the bags. Along with the grunts and slaps of flesh, a sense of purpose permeated the atmosphere. Falco had been born out of Antonio's love of mixed martial arts, but he felt far more comfortable in this half of it than in the CEO's office.

He watched a couple of heavyweights duke it out in the circular-cage ring. Round, so one fighter couldn't force the other into an inescapable corner as so often happened in traditional boxing. MMA strove to even the playing field, to create fairness. The two heavyweights sparred under the watchful eye of a middle-aged man who moved with the fighters gracefully and knowledgeably. A former fighter, clearly, and Antonio liked his coaching style instantly.

Both men in the ring were good and they likely practiced together often. But one was better, with a stellar command of his body and a force of will the second man couldn't match.

Even without clear memories of planning or creating this place, Antonio recognized that he'd spared no expense when purchasing and maintaining the equipment. He'd also managed to attract world-class athletes and trainers, who'd sustained his company while he'd been in Indonesia.

Everyone here had come to improve their technique, to become better fighters, to win. Including Antonio. What happened in the ring made sense, followed a set of rules, a flow. The discipline and repetition settled him and allowed his damaged mind to take a breather.

"Who wants a piece of me?" he called.

"I'm up for it, if you are, old man."

Slowly, Antonio turned to face one of Thomas's right-hand men. A dark gray hoodie partially obscured the younger man's face, but his slight smirk beamed brightly from the depths.

The fighter vibrated with animosity, and Antonio's radar blipped. The man didn't like him. Dirty fight. Excellent. Darkness rose inside him and he didn't squelch it.

He'd been itching for this since his last round with Ravi in Punggur Besar. Rodrigo hadn't matched even a tenth of Antonio's skill and the fight had left him unsatisfied. Plus, Antonio and Rodrigo must have been friendly at some point in the past and that alone had caused Antonio to hold back.

There would be no holding back required with this matchup.

Antonio let his gaze travel down the length of his opponent and snorted his derision. "Hope your moves back up your mouth."

"Only one way to find out."

"What do they call you?" His real name was irrelevant, but the nicknames fighters adopted often gave clues about their style, their mind-set.

"Cutter." The insolent lift of his chin revealed eyes so light blue, they were almost colorless. "Because you're gonna walk away with my cuts all over your face."

Or in some cases, when you were good at reading your competition, nicknames revealed their weaknesses. Cutter was arrogant. Overconfident. Eager to prove himself against the legendary Falco.

Of course, Antonio had known all of that the moment Cutter had labeled him "old man." And this punk was about to be schooled on what age meant for a man's technique and skill.

In minutes, Antonio and Cutter had suited up and squared off. Antonio sized him up quickly now that his opponent wasn't hiding under shapeless clothing. Muscular but not too bulky. Blond hair shaved close to his scalp. Viking-style tattoos across his torso and wrapped around his biceps. Feral sneer firmly in place. Nothing to differentiate him from the dozens of other fighters in his age and weight class—which was probably what pissed Cutter off the most.

The metal cage gleamed around them, providing a safe backdrop for the two men to tear each other up, no holds barred. No chance of being thrown from the ring...and no chance of escape.

There was nowhere to hide and nowhere to run. And blood would be spilled before long.

The younger man feinted and went low. Amateur. Antonio circled away and spun to catch him off guard with a sideways kick to his hip.

Cutter's retribution came in a series of attacks that kept Antonio busy deflecting. Duck. Spin. Feint. The rhythm became comfortable. Mindless.

In a split second, Antonio found a hole. *Attack*. His opponent was a lightweight, so Antonio had a few pounds on him, which he used ruthlessly to force Cutter against the fence. Going for the man's mouth was a no-brainer.

Antonio's fist connected and Cutter's flesh separated. The scent of blood rolled over him.

Cutter sprang forward with an amazing show of strength, fury lacing his expression and weighting his punches. A lucky cuff caught Antonio across the temple before he could block.

Pain exploded in his head, blurring his vision. Images of Vanessa's red hair ricocheted through his consciousness. Images of her in various scenarios. The two of them shouting at each other. Of her talking. Laughing. Of Antonio with her, skin bared, his hand on her flesh, mouth on hers.

Something about the memories pricked at him, sitting strangely. Something wasn't right. He couldn't—

He had no time to think.

Show no weakness. Blindly, he circled away, trying to give himself a moment to let his mind clear. The moment he regained his faculties, he went on the offensive. Uppercut, double kick. *No mercy*.

Often two fighters left the ring shaking hands. MMA was more gentlemanly than outsiders would assume. That wasn't the case in this ring.

In moments, it was finished. Antonio wiped the trickle of blood leaking into his right eye. Cutter lay crumpled on the mat, groaning.

Endorphins soared through his body like bullets. Memories of his wife crowded his mind. The metallic scent of blood stung his nose and he craved more.

"Anyone else want a go at me?" Antonio challenged.

No one volunteered.

Eight

Antonio sneaked into the house and closed himself off in his bedroom to clean up before anyone saw him. Anyone, meaning Caitlyn. The split skin near his eyebrow wasn't life threatening but it wasn't pretty, either. Nor was he good company, not with adrenaline still swirling through his body like a tornado.

A long, hot shower gave him decompression time, allowing him to force back the base urge to smack something again and again. Once he got going, it was hard to shut it off.

But he couldn't live in the ring. He had to find a balance between the need to fight and the rest of his life. Until he could, what kind of father would he be? How could he willingly expose his children to that?

Someone knocked on his bedroom door as he exited the bathroom, toweling off his damp hair. For modesty's sake, he draped the towel over his lower half and pulled open the door.

"Hi." Caitlyn's eyes strayed to his torso, lingered and cut back up again quickly. Pink bloomed in her cheeks.

He loved that blush, and with his body already caught in an adrenaline storm, it set off fireworks. His groin filled, primed for a whole different sort of one-on-one. Not a good combination when in the company of a woman who'd asked for space.

But then, she was also a woman who'd sought him out— in his bedroom. Maybe she'd gotten her space and was done with it.

Her eyebrows drew together as she focused on his face. "What happened? You're bleeding."

"I ran into something." He shrugged as her gaze narrowed. "Another guy's fist. I went to Falco this afternoon."

Her expression didn't change. "Do you need antiseptic? A Band-Aid?"

He bit back a smile. "No self-respecting fighter walks around with a Band-Aid on his face. Thanks for the concern, but it doesn't hurt."

It didn't hurt because his body was still flying on a postmatch trip that ignored the pain of a cut. Instead, he was solely focused on the ache caused by Caitlyn's nearness. She was exactly what his queued-up body craved.

"Come in," he murmured thickly and held the door open wider.

She shook her head, eyes wide. "I don't think that's a good idea."

Oh, it was a very good idea. Obviously she thought so, too, or she wouldn't have knocked on his door. "Then, why *are* you here, Caitlyn?"

The question seemed to confuse her. She bit her lip and it drew his gaze to her mouth, causing him to imagine replacing her teeth with his.

She glanced away and cleared her throat. "I, uh, meant

to talk to you about something, but I didn't realize you'd be…undressed."

"Didn't you?" He cocked his head. "That's what generally happens behind closed doors. Here, let me demonstrate."

But when he reached for the towel, intending to drop it and see where it led, she squeezed her eyelids shut. "No, no! That's okay. I get the point. I shouldn't have come to your bedroom, not after you'd just come back from Falco. I didn't realize you'd gone there, but you didn't come down for dinner, and I was worried and you're hurt and…this was a mistake."

Caitlyn whirled as if about to flee. Again.

Antonio shot out his hand to grip her arm before she took a step. "Caitlyn. Stop running away."

He needed her in a raw, elemental way. In other, more emotional ways he couldn't fully grasp. He didn't think it was one-sided, and the longer this back-and-forth went on, the clearer it became that they needed to deal with it head-on.

Smoothly, he turned her around to face him, searching her gaze for clues to her constant caginess. Confusion and something else skated through her expression.

"Come inside," he pleaded again.

If only he could get her on this side of the threshold, he'd feel less as if he was losing a grip on his sanity. If only he could get her to understand he was desperate to explore things he didn't fully grasp, things only she could teach him because she was the only woman he wanted.

"I can't." Her eyes were huge and troubled and her gaze flicked to the wound near his eyebrow. "I'm…scared."

The admission pinged through him, drawing blood with its claws of condemnation. He dropped his hand from her arm, flexing his raw fist, which smarted from connecting with bone in Cutter's face. Antonio lived and breathed to inflict bodily harm on other human beings, and she saw that about him.

She'd needed space because the falcon inside him frightened her. It *should* scare her.

He'd forced her to watch him fight the other day, forced her to remain in his presence now with evidence of his brutal nature plain as day on his face. Practically forced her into his room so he could have his carnal way with her because of his own selfish desires.

But she didn't leave when he let go. She had every right to. She deserved someone gentle and kind.

"I won't hurt you," he said brusquely, and cleared his throat. He'd done nothing to assure her otherwise. "I hate that you think I might."

Her rounded gaze flew to his and the glint of moisture nearly undid him.

"I'm not scared of *you*," she corrected, but her voice cracked halfway through. "Never of you. I…"

She swallowed and he watched the delicate muscles of her beautiful throat work. If she wasn't scared of him, what was it? And why was it so difficult for her to articulate?

"Then, tell me," he commanded softly, and reached out to grasp her hand in his so he could draw her forward. Almost over the threshold. She didn't resist, but neither did she rush. "What's going on in your mind when I do this?"

Slowly, he took her hand and placed it flat on his chest, over his thundering heart. Her touch nearly drove him to the carpet, but he locked his knees, sensing that if he could keep his wits about him, paradise might be within their reach.

Mute, she stared at her splayed hand under his. Her fingertips curled slightly as if she wanted to grip harder but couldn't.

"It's like granite," she whispered. "That's what I think

about. So hard. But underneath lies something so amazing."

"What?"

"You. Antonio." His name fluttered from her throat on a half groan and the sound almost broke him open.

"You say that as if my name is poetry." It was just a simple name. But one he'd sought in the reaches of his messed-up mind for so long. Hearing it on her lips… It was an elemental thrill.

He was Antonio. And yet not. Because he couldn't fully remember all of the parts that created the whole.

"*All* of you is poetic," she murmured, and drew in a ragged breath. "The way you walk, the way you hold your children. How you move in the ring. I couldn't stop watching you and it was, um…nice."

"You liked watching me fight?" The idea was ludicrous. But her dreamy smile spoke volumes.

"I didn't think I would, but it was amazing." She sighed, a breathy sound that hardened him instantly. "Watching you execute those perfect moves, your body so fluid and in such harmony. It's like a perfect song lyric that when you hear it for the first time, it climbs inside your heart and lives there."

His own breath came more quickly as he stared at her with dawning comprehension. "You have feelings for me."

That was what he'd seen in her expression, what he couldn't quite grasp. It was a wondrous, blessed revelation. As obvious all at once as the sun bursting over the horizon to announce daytime. But he had no context for how he felt. And he wanted to.

Blinking slowly, she bit her lip again and nodded. "I've tried not to. But I can't help it."

A hundred questions rocketed through his mind, but he stuck with the most important.

"Then, why?" he asked hoarsely. "Why do you run away? Why are you so scared of what's happening?"

"I…" She glanced off and the moment of honesty, of her raw confession, started slipping away.

Desperate not to lose it, he cupped her face in both hands and brought it to his, a breath away. "What, Caitlyn? Tell me. Please. I'm losing my mind here. And I don't have much left to lose."

His wry joke earned him a watery smile.

"I'm scared of *me*," she whispered. "I want…things. Things I barely understand. It's like in all the fairy tales where they tell the girl not to touch the spindle or not to eat the apple. I never understood why they couldn't help themselves. Because I never understood what it meant to truly *desire* something. Or someone. Until you. I don't know what to do."

She wanted him. And that made all the difference.

"There's only one right answer to that."

He leaned into the space between them and laid his lips on hers for a scant second, kissing her with only a thousandth of the passion he wished he could unleash. But didn't because she wasn't fully inside the room.

Once she stepped over the threshold, all bets were off.

Pulling back with an iron will that could only be developed by years of ruthless training, he evaluated her. "Do you like kissing me?"

"Yes," she murmured. "More than I should."

"Then, come inside. Let me kiss you. Let me give you that experience you described. Let me be the man who touches you and loves you."

He wanted that—badly. Wanted to feel her skin next to his, to feel alive alongside her. To feel as if the things she spoke of were more than just words but concepts his soul recognized.

Her eyes closed and her lips pursed as if in invitation,

as if she yearned for him to kiss her again. But then her eyes blinked open and she swallowed. Hard.

"I need to tell you something else." Her gaze sought his and held. "I've never had a lover before."

Antonio's expression didn't waver, bless him. "You're a virgin?"

Caitlyn nodded. Her tongue was stuck to the roof of her mouth, glued there by nerves and who knew what else—three or four of the seven deadly sins, most likely.

"That explains a lot. I'm sorry you didn't trust me with that fact sooner. That's why you asked for space." His chiseled lips turned down. "I didn't give it to you."

Her heart fluttered. Antonio had the patience of Job.

"You did," she corrected hurriedly. "You've been perfect. I'm the problem. That's what I've been trying to tell you. I don't have any experience at…you know. And I'm nervous. You're this beautiful, wonderful man with all these expectations about being with me, probably because I've led you on, and I'm… Well, I'm not Vanessa, that's for sure—"

"Caitlyn." The quirk of his eyebrow rendered her speechless, as he'd probably intended. "Are you trying to tell me that you think I'll compare you unfavorably to Vanessa?"

"Uh…" Clearly, yes wasn't the right answer. But it was the only one she had. "She was so gorgeous, with a body men salivated over. She knew how to please a man in bed, too, which she liked to brag about. It's hard to imagine following that."

His quick smile knocked her off-kilter. Was it *that* funny?

"Isn't it ironic, then," he mused, "that I can't remember Vanessa?"

"At all?" He couldn't remember his wife, the one he'd

ended his career for, whose babies he'd wanted to have so badly, he'd agreed to surrogacy?

Her gaze flicked to the year-old scar disappearing into his hairline. What kind of whack to the head had he endured that his memories were that insubstantial? It must have been vicious.

"Some." His tone grew somber. "I see flashes of her red hair and remember bits and pieces, like her laugh. It's all jumbled in my head. Sometimes it's her face and sometimes her body. But I don't remember being in love with her. I feel so disconnected from her, as if she wasn't real. I don't remember feeling like you said I should, as if I want to be with her so badly I can't breathe."

The despondency in his voice caught in her chest and made it hurt. "I'm sorry, Antonio. I didn't realize you hadn't regained your memories of her. That must be very difficult."

"What's difficult is that I want to move on." His lashes lowered and he speared her with that dark, enigmatic glance that set her blood on low simmer. "I want to be in the here and now, not stuck dwelling on the past I can't remember. I've found someone new, someone I *do* want so badly I can't breathe. I want to love her and fulfill her and let her do the same to me. But I can't seem to get her into my arms."

"Me?" she whispered.

Heat climbed into her cheeks, on cue. *Duh*. Of course he meant her. But her brain wasn't working quite right. Too busy filtering through the divine idea that Antonio wanted to love her.

"Yes, you." His thumb feathered across her hot cheek. "I not only can't compare you to Vanessa, I don't want to. I want what's possible now, for as long as we have together. I want to learn about the kind of love that you talked about. Teach me."

"How can I teach you anything? I'm not the one with experience."

His gorgeous lips turned upward into a killer smile. "I'm not the one with any experience I can remember. In a way, this will be the first time for both of us."

For some reason, that appealed to her. Immensely.

He didn't remember Vanessa and wanted to learn everything about love, sex, relationships over again. It was like the slate being wiped clean—Caitlyn could make this experience anything and everything she could imagine, be as wicked in his arms as she wished and wrap it up in a beautiful emotional connection that could last an eternity.

He'd come back from the dead a different person, and she'd often dwelt on the darker changes. It had never occurred to her that amnesia would be a positive in this one case.

Except he'd been born with a body designed for pleasure, and just as he'd not forgotten how to breathe, he likely hadn't lost any knowledge of how to make a woman quiver with desire. She couldn't do the same to him, no way.

"Are you sure this is what you want? With me? I mean, you might not precisely remember Vanessa, but you have to recall other women." *Shut up.* Nobody brought up former lovers on the brink of becoming the next one. She sighed. "See. I'm a big mess. That's so not attractive, I realize."

He glanced down at the two feet of space between them. "We've been standing in this doorway for ten minutes now, and for nine minutes and fifty-five seconds of it, I've been in danger of losing this towel due to the serious arousal you've caused me. Stop worrying so much about things that don't matter. Don't deny us any longer, Caitlyn."

He stepped aside, opening the doorway for her to enter if she chose.

This was it. Her opportunity to grab what she'd longed for. To put her guilt to rest and finally become a full-fledged, sexually realized woman at the hands of a master. A man who was probably the great love of her life, the only one she might ever love.

And his pretty speech about learning how to love at *her* hands surely meant he was open and willing to returning her feelings. He'd loved Vanessa, had married her and obviously yearned to have that sort of connection again. The sort of connection Caitlyn had dreamed of.

It was all within her reach.

Yet she hesitated, long enough for his eyebrows to rise.

What would happen if she stepped over the threshold, signaling to Antonio that she was ready to embark on a romantic relationship, and if it didn't work out? How would she co-parent their children with a broken heart? The past few years had been difficult enough when she'd revered him from afar. How much harder would it be to actually love and be loved by a man like Antonio, only to lose him because she wasn't the kind of woman who could handle him?

And what if he cut her out of her children's lives in retribution?

This was why she never got very far in a relationship with any man, including Antonio when she'd first met him. She was terrified of what came *after* she opened herself body and soul to someone.

As she let her gaze rest on his bare torso, on that glorious inked falcon, she wanted to let him melt her resistance.

Because it would be impossible to walk away.

She took a breath to calm her racing heart, which didn't work, and walked into Antonio's bedroom.

Nine

The door clicked shut behind her and Caitlyn froze.

She was inside a man's bedroom. She wouldn't leave it a virgin. She'd been saving herself for the right man, a man she was ready, willing and eager to love forever, and here he was…but this wasn't the safe fantasy she'd harbored for years. Was she *really* ready for this?

Oh, my. Antonio was going to see her naked, with her C-section scars and ridiculously shaped breasts that had served as a milk source for three hungry mouths for months.

Nearing full-blown panic, she tried to suck in a deep, calming breath. And choked on it as she thought back to getting dressed this morning. What underwear had she put on?

"Caitlyn."

She whirled. Antonio leaned against the door, arms crossed over his cut torso, towel dipping dangerously low. Her mouth went sticky and she averted her gaze. Then shifted her gaze back because, dang it, *surely* it was okay to look at him if they were about to make love. Maybe it was even expected. Part of foreplay.

"Do you want a glass of wine?" he asked casually.

"To drink?" When he laughed, she thought about punching him but would probably only hurt her hand. Mortified, she scowled. "I didn't know what you meant! Maybe it's some kind of sex thing, like you want me to pour it on you and lick it off."

His eyebrows rose and he treated her to a thoroughly wicked once-over. "Would you? Lick it off?"

The image of her tongue swirling over the ink on his chest popped into her mind and she couldn't shake it. As she imagined the taste of his golden skin melded with fruity red wine, her insides contracted. "Maybe. *Was* it a sex thing?"

He shrugged, a smile still playing about his expressive mouth. "As much as I want you right now, it could be. Seems a little messy, though. Let's save that for another time."

"How many times do you envision there being?"

"A thousand." His expression darkened carnally as if he was imagining each time individually and it was hot. "The things I want to do to you, to experience with you, might very well take a lifetime."

She couldn't blink, couldn't look away. Couldn't quite believe the sincerity ringing from his voice. She rubbed at the ache in her chest as she internalized that she'd heard precisely what he'd meant for her to hear. "A lifetime?"

Of course, it was what she'd yearned for. But it was another thing entirely to hear it from Antonio's mouth.

He tilted his head quizzically. "You aren't the kind of person who sleeps around indiscriminately. Neither am I. I want to be with you from now on. Awake, asleep. In bed, out of bed. Which part is confusing you?"

"All of it. Starting with 'hi' when I first knocked on the door," she muttered.

"So that wasn't a good subject, obviously. Here's what we're going to do instead," he said decisively, because of course he could read her like a book. "We're going to have a glass of wine. Then we're going to take this as slowly as you want to."

"Why?" Could she have sounded more suspicious? He was saying all the right things and she was botching this.

"The wine is to relax you," he explained, not seeming at all bothered by her lack of decorum. "Actually, both parts are to relax you. And both parts get me where I want to be. Inside you. Anticipation will make it sweeter, so I'm quite happy with the idea of taking my time. I've got a whole night and I'm not afraid to use it."

Dumbfounded, she let him lead her to his sitting area overlooking the coastline and sank onto the love seat he pointed to. Apparently, Antonio was botchproof. Good thing. She'd probably do ten more things to increase her mortification level before the night was through.

He selected a bottle of red wine from the rack on the wet bar and pulled the cork. Since his back was to her, she watched his bare torso unashamedly. Too quickly, he returned with two glasses full of deep red wine, handed her one and settled in next to her on the love seat. Clad in a towel.

It should be weird. He was completely naked underneath the terry cloth, which gaped at his thigh, revealing the muscular stretch of leg that led to his…good parts.

He glanced at her and then followed her line of vision. "Curious?"

Yes, wine was a fantastic idea. The alcohol needed to be swimming through her bloodstream, not sitting in a glass untouched. She gulped as much as she could get down, for fortification.

Because, oh, yes, she was curious. Burning with it.

"I've never seen a naked man before," she croaked.

Not enough wine, obviously, if she was still going to utter gems like that.

"Not even in pictures?"

She shook her head. "I'm a novice. I tried to tell you."

Antonio set down his glass on the side table with a hard click and then took her free hand in his. "Listen to me, because I don't want there to be any confusion about this."

Heart hammering in her throat, she stared at him as something tender sprang into his gaze.

"It means everything to me that no other man has ever touched you. That I get to be the first. It's an honor and I intend to treat it as such. You should never feel as if you have to apologize for this gift you're giving me."

"I...um." What did you say that *that*? "Okay."

That must have been the magic word. His thumb brushed over her knuckles and he let go of her hand to run his fingertips over the back of her wrist.

And kept going up her bare arm, watching her with that dark intensity as he touched her. Without a word, he took the glass from her suddenly nerveless fingers and set it next to his. A breath later, his mouth descended and took hers in a slow, deliberate kiss that melted her bones.

His sweet lips... They molded hers, explored. Slowly, as promised.

"Wait," he murmured, and his heat left her as he rose to click off the lights. Moonlight poured in from outside the glass, illuminating the love seat and throwing the rest of the room into shadow.

Antonio returned with the comforter from his bed and a couple of small squares that she eyed curiously until she realized what they were. Condoms. This had just turned real and her throat closed.

He spread the comforter in front of the floor-to-ceiling

window and stretched out on it, beckoning her to join him. "Just to set the mood."

But the sight of Antonio bathed in the glow from the moon froze her completely. He was beautiful, mystical. Too perfect to be real. She just wanted to soak him in, to gorge herself on his splendor.

He seemed to sense her thoughts and lay still, allowing her to gaze at him as much as she wanted. The scar marking the location of his once-broken leg forked up his calf, as seductively savage as the rest of him.

After an eternity, he reached for his towel and held it in both hands, poised to take it off. "Do you want to see all of me?"

Too numb to speak, she nodded, but before she could properly school her expression or her thoughts or her... anything, the towel fell away and... *Oh, my.* He was utterly divine in all his glory, hard everywhere, with a jutting erection she'd felt when he'd kissed her in the gym, but never in a million years would she have thought it would look like *that.*

She couldn't stop drinking him in. And he didn't seem to be in a hurry to stop her.

"By the way," he murmured, "you know you're going to do this for me in a minute, right?"

"Do what?" Then she clued in. "You mean lie in front of the window naked so you can stare at me?"

A wolfish smile bloomed on his face. "Let me know when you're ready."

"I don't think I'll ever be ready for that," she muttered.

He flipped onto his hands and knees and crawled to her, kneeling between her legs. "Then, I'll have to fix that. Because I want to see you in the moonlight. I want to watch your face as I make love to you. And you will most definitely need to be naked for that."

With exquisite care, he cupped her face with both hands and brought her lips to his.

This kiss was nothing like the one a minute ago, when there'd still been a towel and some modesty between them. There was nothing but Antonio between her legs, and when his mouth claimed hers in a scorching kiss, he palmed the small of her back and shoved her to the edge of the couch, almost flush with his body. Close, so close, and she arched involuntarily, seeking his heat.

His tongue plunged toward hers, possessing her with his taste, with his intoxicating desire. Moaning, she slid her arms around his strong torso, reveling in the feel of his sleek, heated skin under her palms. A small movement forward, just the slightest tilt of her hips, and his erection would brush her center.

And she ached for that contact. Desire emboldened her and she strained for it.

When it came, she gasped. He must have sensed her instant need for more because he pressed harder, rubbing in small circles. Heat exploded at her core and her head tipped back in shock.

He followed the line of her throat with his luscious lips, laving the tender skin expertly until he got a mouthful of her blouse. She nearly wept as his mouth lifted.

"I'm going to take this off," he murmured and fingered the first button for emphasis. "Okay?"

She nodded, appreciative that he respected her nerves enough to ask. Plus, she was very interested in getting his magic mouth back on her skin. "Seems fair. You're not wearing a shirt."

His warm chuckle had a hint of wicked that shuddered through her. Now, *that* was delightful.

"I'm not wearing anything. If you want to talk about fair…"

"You know what, you're right."

This imbalance *wasn't* fair. She stood quickly without thought of his proximity, and it was a testament to his superior balance that she didn't bowl him over.

He sat back on his muscular haunches, completely at ease in his own skin. She wanted to be that confident. To feel as if she belonged here, able to handle a man as virile and gorgeous as Antonio. There was only one way. She had to get over this virgin hump and take this night—her destiny, her *pleasure*—into her own hands. It wasn't Antonio's job to lead her through this.

He desired her. It was in his expression, in his words. In the hard flesh at his center. What purpose did it serve to protect her maidenly modesty? None.

She wanted him to take her in the basest sense. *Now*. And she wanted it to be hot. Sinful. Explosive. He could make that happen, she had no doubt. But he was holding back. She could feel it.

"I'm ready," she announced, and though her hands shook, she slipped the first button on her blouse from its mooring.

His eyelids lowered a touch as he watched her move on to the next button. "Ready?"

Third button. Fourth. "For you to see me. In the moonlight."

Heat flared in his expression and he hummed his approval. The sexy sound empowered her. Last button.

She slipped the blouse from her frame, gaze glued to his, and let it float from her fingers. That wasn't so bad. The clasp on her bra was a little harder to undo even though it was in front, and she couldn't even blame that on being a novice; she'd definitely taken her bra off a million times in her life, but never in front of a man, and this was it—the first time a man would see her bare breasts—and suddenly, the clasp came apart in her hands.

Well, that was the point, wasn't it?

Nothing left to do but shed the hideous nursing bra. In retrospect, stripping out of it probably increased her sexiness quotient. She dropped it on the ground near her blouse and fought the urge to cover herself when Antonio's heavy-lidded gaze swept her with clear appreciation.

"You might want to hurry," he muttered, hands clenched on his thighs as he looked up at her from his prone position. "I'm about to lose my mind."

"Really?" That sounded...lovely. "Am I making you crazy?"

The thought pleased her. Imagine. Caitlyn Hopewell was driving a man insane with a slow striptease. It practically made her giddy.

He groaned. "Completely. You're killing me. If you had any idea how much I want to—" He shook his head, teeth gritted. "Never mind. You take this at your pace. I'll be the one over here practicing my patience."

"No. Tell me. What do you want to do?" She fingered the clasp on her jeans, toying with it the way she imagined a more experienced woman might do. "I might let you."

"Oh, yeah?" he growled. "Lose those pants and let's rumble, my darling."

The endearment rolled through her and left a whole lot of heat and pleasure in its wake. "I like it when you talk to me like that."

"You do, huh?" Amusement curled his lips upward. "Not well enough, since you're still dressed."

"Well, you still haven't told me what you want to do." The curiosity was killing her. So she shoved off her pants, careful to take her nonsexy underwear along for the ride, and kicked them both away.

She couldn't get more naked. With the moon as the only source of light, her flaws weren't as noticeable and the lines of her postpregnancy body smoothed out. And that was when it dawned on her—that had been the whole purpose of lights-out. Was there nothing that the man missed?

Antonio worshipped her with his gaze and she let him, keeping her arms by her sides. The way he looked at her made her feel beautiful. As though she had nothing to hide.

"Now then. Tell me," she commanded, proud that her voice didn't waver. "What sorts of wicked activities do you have in store? Because I've waited a lifetime to be thoroughly ravished and I'm a little anxious to get started."

Groaning, Antonio tried to keep his faculties about him as he surveyed the very tempting woman on display before him wearing nothing but moonlight and a smile.

Blood and adrenaline pounded through his veins. He'd kept a very tight hold on his body since he'd opened the bedroom door. Caitlyn had just pushed him to the brink with a unique mix of innocence and friskiness that belied her lack of experience.

He hadn't expected it to be such a turn-on.

Or for her to systematically break down his resistance until he held on to his self-control by the barest edge. He wanted her more fiercely than he'd ever wanted anything—including his memories. His muscles strained to pounce. To possess. To claim. To relentlessly drive her to the threshold of madness the way she'd driven him.

But he couldn't because Caitlyn deserved something special for her first time. She deserved someone gentle. Restrained. Refined.

She had to make do with Antonio Cavallari instead.

"I…" He nearly swallowed his tongue as Caitlyn sauntered toward him, invitation in her eyes that he couldn't misread even in the pale light. "My intentions are to make love to you. There's nothing wicked about that."

The hard floor beneath the comforter ground into his knees, but he couldn't have moved if his life depended on it. He should have prepared better for this, changed out the furniture. Caitlyn's first experience with sex should happen in a bed, but he refused to make love to her in the same place he'd been with another woman. Whether he could remember it or not. It was a matter of principle.

"Why not? What if I want wicked?" she murmured and halted directly in front of him, then folded her legs under her to mirror his pose. Knee to knee. She pierced him with a gaze far too knowing for a woman of her innocence. "Listen to me so there's no confusion about this, Antonio. I watched you in the ring and it was brutal. But it was beautiful at the same time. Like you. It was an unsettling, thrilling experience. There's probably something wrong with me that I like the primal part of you. But I don't care."

Without hesitation, she traced the falcon tearing across his flesh, watching him as she touched him, and he sucked in a breath as his skin pulsed under her fingers.

"I want Falco," she said simply. "And Antonio. I'll only have one first time. Make it memorable. Give me all of it and don't hold back."

His iron will dissolved under the onslaught of her sensuous plea. With equal parts desperation and need, he hauled her into his arms and fell into her, into the innocence that called to him. Not to destroy, but to absorb. She was perfectly whole and exquisite and the shattered pieces of his soul cried out for her.

Hungrily, he kissed her, twining her body with his so he could feel her. His skin screamed for more of the sweet friction against hers. He palmed her heavy breasts, which filled his hands and then some. They were gorgeous, full, with huge nipples that his mouth strained to taste.

Unable to wait, he sucked one between his lips. She gasped and her back arched instantly. *Yes.* Amazingly responsive, as he'd fantasized. He moved to the other breast, and the sensation of his tongue curling around her hard nipple had him pulsing with need.

The groan ripped from his throat and he murmured her name as he eased her back against the comforter. Moonlight played with her features as she lay there, exactly as he'd envisioned, and it was almost too much to take in. The mother of his children. His savior. Soon to be lover.

He needed her. Needed to be inside her, with her, loving her. But first things first. He bent one of her legs back and knelt to swirl his tongue at her center.

She froze and made mewling sounds in her throat.

"Shh, my darling," he murmured and kissed her inner thigh. "You asked for wicked." He kissed the other and opened her legs farther. "Close your eyes and imagine me in the ring. What about it excited you?"

"You were so graceful," she murmured. "Like an apparition. But so very real and raw. It made me hot. All over."

"Like this?"

Slowly, he touched her again with the tip of his tongue. She shuddered but didn't tense up this time. He went a little farther, lapping a little harder. Her hips rolled and she sighed in pleasure.

"That's right, sweetheart. Lie still, think about me and let me taste you." He cupped her hips and tilted her up to his lips to feast.

She thrashed under his onslaught, but since her shudders brought her center closer and closer each time, he took full advantage of it instead of scolding her for doing the opposite of lying still. Honey gathered under his tongue a moment before she cried out.

Her climax went on and on and his own body throbbed in response, aching for a release in kind inside this woman.

Shaking with the effort, he managed to roll on a condom without breaking it—a minor miracle, given that he couldn't precisely remember the technique—and stretched out next to her to take her into his arms.

"Ready?" he asked hoarsely, shocked he could speak at all.

"There's more?" Since the question was laced with wry humor, he hoped that meant she was kidding.

"Oh, yes, there's more," he said fiercely. "I'm dying to show you."

She feathered a thumb across his lips, sparking sensation to the point of pain. "Show me, Antonio."

More roughly than he'd intended, he nudged a knee between her thighs and rolled, poised to thrust with all his pent-up energy. But he held back at the last second, somehow, and kissed her with every ounce of that longing instead. When she responded with a throaty moan that he felt in his groin, he couldn't wait. He pushed as slowly as he could into her center.

She wasn't on board with slow.

Her hips rose up to meet him, accepting him, encouraging him, and with a groan, he sheathed himself completely. Then forced his muscles to pause, though every fiber of his being screamed to let loose, to drive them both to completion with frenzied coupling.

He sought her gaze. "Tell me it's okay."

She nodded and let out a breath, her eyes shining as she peered up at him, hair a dark mass around her ethereal face. *She* was the apparition, a heavenly body trapped on this plane, and he'd been lucky enough to find her.

"It doesn't feel like I would have thought," she commented.

That made two of them.

Emotion he couldn't name wrenched at his heart, threatening to pull it from his chest. *Love*. He wanted it to be love, to know that he could feel such things and wasn't irreparably damaged.

But the sense he had of his previous experiences didn't match this. Not even close. This was so much bigger, so overwhelming. What if he *was* damaged? What if his memories never returned? How would he know if he was loving Caitlyn the way she deserved?

"You feel amazing," she murmured. Experimentally, she wiggled her hips. "What does it feel like to you?"

Her innocent movements set off a riptide of heat. "Let's compare notes later."

Settling her firmly under him, he began to move, rendering them both speechless. She arched against him, nails biting into his shoulders, those perfect, full breasts peaked against his torso.

Thrust for thrust, she met him, never retreating, never yielding. *More. Faster.* His body took from hers and she gave endlessly. Palming her rear, he changed the angle. Reversed the dynamic so he was doing the giving. Spiraling her higher into the heavens where she'd already taken him.

He needed to discharge, to explode. But he couldn't… not yet. He tasted blood on his lip where he'd bitten down with the effort to hold back. Animalistic sounds growled from his throat as he bent one of her legs back to go deeper still.

Exquisite pleasure rolled over him, and he needed more. Relentlessly, he rolled his hips to meet hers, and when she tightened around him with a small moan, he lost control.

Groaning as he spilled his release, he collapsed to the side, rolling her with him as he lost all feeling in his extremities.

In the aftermath, they lay together, and he gently spooned her into his body to hold her tightly. She snuggled in willingly with a small sigh of contentment.

He let her essence bleed through him as he lay with his eyes shut, absorbing her. If he never had to move from this spot, it would be too soon.

An instant later, he cursed his own selfishness. "Can I get you anything?"

What did you give a woman who had just offered up her virginity? Diamond earrings? A washcloth? She was likely bruised and raw. It wasn't as if he'd been gentle, not the way he'd pretended he was going to be.

"I'm fine, thanks. Don't you dare move." She wiggled closer to him. "Your body heat feels good against my sore muscles."

"I should have gone slower." Remorse crashed through his breastbone. He'd taken her innocence like the brute that he was. "I'm sorry I hurt you."

"Don't you dare apologize. Some of it hurt, but in a good way. It was amazing. Perfect. Beautiful. Everything I've ever dreamed of." Threading her fingers through his, she raised his hand to her lips. "Thank you for that."

Emotion clogged his throat and he swallowed against it, fighting to keep himself level.

The things she made him feel... He wished he could understand them. Could draw on his past to make sense of the swirl in his belly when he looked at her. But he couldn't.

All he knew was that Caitlyn was a miracle. Everything he'd prayed to find when he'd set off from Indonesia in search of his life.

He stroked her side and with moonlight spilling over them both, he murmured the million-dollar question. "Why me? Of all the men in the world you could have chosen for your first experience."

"I always wanted it to be you," she said slowly. "Well, not *always*. Vanessa was...rather free with her affections, even back in high school. I didn't like how broken up she always was after, and I vowed to save myself for the right man. The first moment I met you, I had this strange shock of recognition, like *there you are*."

His hand stilled. "The first moment? You mean the pink-shirt meeting?"

She nodded and her hair brushed his chin. "After that, no other man could compare. I've had a crush on you for a long time."

"Even while I was married?" It should have seemed wrong, but it thrilled him for some reason. Caitlyn had been saving herself for *him*, even through his marriage to someone else. It spoke to her constancy and devotion, and it humbled him.

"I didn't say I was a saint. I had a lot of mixed feelings about it. You know, I cried for almost two days straight when they came to tell me the plane had crashed. I thought I'd lost you forever," she whispered brokenly.

In the long pause, he gathered her in his arms and held her as close as physically possible as his heart thumped in tandem with hers.

While he'd been lost and alone, Caitlyn had been here in his house, mourning him. He'd thought no one cared. But she had. She still did.

It was a far better gift than her virginity.

Ten

The next morning, Caitlyn awoke at dawn, stiff and sore from a night sleeping on the floor entwined with Antonio. And every inch of her body felt glorious.

Antonio had kissed her soundly before sending her off to her own room, presumably to keep the rest of the household in the dark about the new relationship that had bloomed between them. She showered under the hottest stream of water she could stand, letting the water ease her aches. Her thoughts never strayed far from the sexy man down the hall.

He might even be in his own shower, naked, with water sluicing down his gorgeous body. Feeling a little scandalous, she allowed the image to play through her mind... because she could. She knew what every inch of that man's flesh looked like, thank you very much.

She'd slept with Antonio. Her sister's husband, whom she had always coveted. There was probably a special place in hell for a woman who did that. And she hated to admit that she'd loved every second of it.

When she emerged, steam had obscured the mirror. She wiped it with a towel and stared at herself in the glass. Odd. She didn't look any different than she had yesterday morning, and it was a bit of a shock to see her same face reflected back at her.

By all rights, there should be *some* external mark to account for the rite of passage she'd undertaken. What, she couldn't say. But a man had loved her thoroughly last night. He'd filled her body with his, tasted her intimately, brought her to a shuddering climax. Twice. It was an earth-shaking event worthy of distinction. Maybe she should get a tattoo to commemorate the experience.

A dove on her breast, maybe.

Silly. She was already picking out matching tattoos after sleeping with a man one night.

But it had been so incredible. Now she totally got why he'd said he planned to do it a thousand more times. Once could never be enough.

She'd just pretend he'd never been married to Vanessa. Block it out and never think about it. Vanessa was gone, and Caitlyn and Antonio deserved to move on. Together. It wasn't a crime.

At breakfast, the babies played with their bananas and Cheerios as always, Brigitte chattered up a storm as she did every morning and Caitlyn sat in her usual spot at the table. But the secret looks Antonio shot her gave everything a rosy, sensual glow, and she was very much afraid she was grinning at him like a besotted fool.

Perhaps she should be more covert if the goal was to keep their relationship on the down low.

"Caitlyn and I are going shopping today," Antonio announced out of the blue when everyone finished eating.

"We are?" Did they have some Christmas presents to

buy that she'd forgotten about? "It's two days until Christmas. The stores will be insane."

"I believe I have adequately demonstrated my ability to dispense with holiday crowds," he countered with a smirk.

"So that's your solution to everything now? Just buy out the whole store?"

"When I find something that works, I stick with it. You might consider thanking me for that." His dark gaze flickered with promise, and yesterday, such innuendo might have made her blush, but she was a worldly woman now. So she stuck her tongue out at him instead.

Brigitte watched all of this with unabashed fascination, probably interpreting the exchange in the wrong way. "Well. You two have *fun*."

Or the right way, depending on how you looked at it.

Antonio herded her into the Range Rover, and she dutifully drove, navigating through the paparazzi outside the gate. She wasn't used to all of this. The cameras had camped out there ever since the first time Antonio had gone to Falco.

As always, Antonio ignored them. Oh, his lawyer and Thomas Warren had fielded a ton of questions on Antonio's behalf, but he wasn't in a hurry to take that part of his life back. He liked his privacy, which suited Caitlyn fine.

Once they were clear of the knot of people and vans, she asked, "What are we shopping for?"

"Bedroom furniture."

She glanced at him askance and flicked her gaze back to the road immediately. "Because there's something wrong with the furniture you already have?"

"Yes. It's Vanessa's," he explained quietly, oblivious of the sword he'd just stuck through her abdomen. "Every stick of furniture in that room will be gone by the time we return. I already arranged it. Help me pick out something new."

Oh. So that was why they'd slept on the floor. He didn't

want to sleep with Caitlyn in the bed he'd shared with his wife. He'd probably considered it the height of betrayal.

Her throat burned with sudden unshed tears. "That's..."

There were no words to explain the hard twist of her heart. Vanessa had been his wife first, and there was nothing she could do to change that. After all, Antonio hadn't chosen her when he'd had the opportunity. Caitlyn was the backup sister.

And Antonio had done something unbelievably considerate in removing the remnants of his first marriage. He'd told her last night that he wanted to move on. She couldn't blame him for choices he'd made either before the crash or after.

He deserved a fresh start after the horrors he'd endured. If he wanted new bedroom furniture because the old pieces had belonged to his first wife, she'd help him redecorate once a week until he was happy. And keep her mouth shut about how hard it was on her to constantly recall that she was living her sister's life by default.

A clerk approached them the moment they stepped into the hushed store. Expensive plank flooring and discreet lighting lent to the moneyed atmosphere, and the high-end pieces on display even smelled expensive. It would be a Christmas miracle if Antonio walked out of here with a full bedroom set for less than fifty thousand dollars.

"What are you looking for today?" the salesclerk asked politely. "A new sofa to accommodate extra party guests, perhaps?"

"We're in need of new bedroom furniture," Antonio said as Caitlyn did a double take.

What was this "we" stuff?

"Absolutely, sir." The clerk eyed them both. "Can you give me an idea what style you might be looking for? Art deco, maybe? American heritage or contemporary?"

"Caitlyn, did you have a particular style in mind?" Antonio asked, and put a palm to the small of her back as if she had every right to be included in the decision. As if they were a couple shopping for furniture together.

"I, um…don't know what you'd like," she admitted, which seemed ridiculous to say when she'd not only studied him surreptitiously for years, she'd also just had sex with him. Shouldn't she know what he liked?

"I'd like something that puts a smile on your face." The look he gave her curled her toes and rendered her speechless. To the clerk, he nodded and said, "Show her everything and make sure she's given the opportunity to pick colors and such. I assume you do custom orders."

Dollar signs sprang into the clerk's eyes. "Of course. Down to the throw pillows. Please call me Judy. And you are?"

"This is Ms. Hopewell," Antonio said smoothly. "And she's the star of this show. She doesn't walk out of here without an entire bedroom set. When she's finished picking what she wants, you let me know and I'll pay for it."

"Excuse us a moment." Caitlyn pulled Antonio to the side. "What are you doing?" she whispered hotly. "I can't pick out your bedroom furniture. It's too…"

Intimate. Fast. Expensive.

"I want you to," he insisted. "After all, you're going to be using it."

She shut her eyes for a moment as she envisioned exactly what he meant by that. "But it's not going to be *mine*. I have a bedroom."

"Not anymore." Antonio's eyebrows drew together as her eyes widened. "I'm messing this up, aren't I? I should have talked to you about this at home. I want you to move into my bedroom. Permanently."

Warmth spread through her abdomen. The staff would know instantly that they were together, so maybe he *didn't* intend for their relationship to be a secret.

But what *was* their relationship? She knew he was the committed sort—it wasn't a surprise that he wanted something permanent. But it would be nice to have specifics. She'd never done this before. Was this his subtle way of asking her to be his girlfriend? Or was this the precursor to a marriage proposal?

Yes. Yes. Yes. No matter what he was asking, the answer was yes.

This definitely wasn't the time nor the place to hash this out, but she couldn't be upset. He wanted her to be a part of his life. Permanently. There was no possible way to misinterpret *that*. Who cared what label they slapped on it? Her heart flipped over and back again, unable to find the right spot in her chest now that everything she'd ever dreamed for herself had fallen in her lap.

He took her hand and squeezed it. "Help me make it a place we can be together without shadows of the past."

Her unsettled heart climbed into her throat as the sentiment crashed through her happiness. If only new furniture could actually achieve that.

She could never be rid of Vanessa's shadow. She was living her sister's life, the one Vanessa couldn't live because she'd died. A life Caitlyn never should have had, despite desperately wanting it. The enormous burden of guilt settled over her anew.

And the worst part was, she couldn't even tell Antonio how she felt, because he definitely didn't need an extra layer of guilt. He couldn't even *remember* Vanessa and it weighed on him.

This was going to go down far worse than the toy store. Picking out a forty-dollar toy for their children didn't carry a million heavy implications the way picking out furniture did.

"Please." Antonio's plea slid through her. "I need to feel as if I'm not still adrift and alone. I need you."

She shut her eyes and let Antonio bleed through her. This wasn't just about furniture. *Nothing* in their interaction was surface level. Or simple. Regardless, there was no point in acting as if there was a choice here. She lacked the strength—or the desire—to deny him anything.

"Okay." She blew out a breath and turned back to the expectant clerk. "I'm ready."

Panic ruffled her nerves. This was so far out of her realm of experience. She was shopping for furniture with a man. With Antonio.

But he was holding her hand and smiling at her as though she'd just given him the world's best Christmas present. She couldn't let her guilt or the circumstances ruin this. She couldn't let him down.

"Right this way." Judy escorted her to the left, already chattering about fabric and colors and who knew what.

At the end of the day, she'd be sleeping in Antonio's bed. Honestly, who cared what the furniture looked like when her full attention would be firmly fixed on the amazing, sensitive man lying on the next pillow?

As dawn broke through the glass wall overlooking the pounding Malibu surf, Caitlyn curled around Antonio's slumbering form and watched him breathe. The way she'd done yesterday morning. Because it could never be enough. He didn't get any less beautiful, and it was her God-given right to gawk at the man she was sleeping with, wasn't it?

His sooty lashes rested above his cheekbones and his lips pursed as if he was dreaming about kissing her. Funny, that was exactly what she'd dreamed about, too.

So she indulged them both and kissed him awake. "Merry Christmas."

His dark eyes blinked open and he smiled sleepily. "Is it already the twenty-fifth? I lost track."

"We've been busy."

Once she'd gotten over herself, the redecoration effort had consumed them both as they'd laughed and argued good-naturedly over the style and placement of the purchases. Then Antonio had gotten started on artwork, perusing gallery upon gallery until he'd found precisely what he wanted.

Late last night, they'd tossed the final teal pillow onto the couch in the sitting area and declared it done. The finished product looked nothing like the former space. Vanessa's taste had run to heavy and ornate baroque. Caitlyn had selected more simple lines and colors: a four-poster bed with simple square posts. A compact dresser in espresso-colored wood with silver pulls. Teal and dark brown accents.

It had been a magical, breathless few days. But as she'd suspected, Antonio was the best thing in the room. Every day was Christmas, as far as she was concerned.

Antonio rolled onto his side and pulled her into his arms. "Then, Merry Christmas to you, too."

She snuggled into his warm body. "We don't have to get up right away, do we?"

"Not for years and years. The kids won't know about Santa until they're, like, three or four, right?"

She loved it when he talked like that, as if they were a family who would be together forever, come what may. He hadn't mentioned the word *marriage*. But she hoped that was where they were headed.

"Ha. We'll be lucky if they aren't up at 5:00 a.m. next year, pounding down the stairs on their little toddler feet to see what Santa brought."

With a gleam in his eye that was impossible to misread, he winked. "Then, we better make good use of our one bye year."

So slowly she thought she might weep, he took her lips

in a long kiss that set off a freight train of heat through her blood.

It was so much more powerful to know what this kind of kiss led to as she fell into the sensual pleasure of his lips thoroughly claiming hers. His tongue was hot and rough and she reveled in the shock of it invading her mouth. Thrilled in it. Because while it mated with hers, it was so unbelievably arousing to recall that he'd also tasted her intimately with that same tongue.

His thigh slid between her legs, insistent and tight against her core. She moaned and arched into the pleasure as sparks exploded under his ministrations. Silently, she urged him on, riding his muscular thigh with small rolls of her hips. She needed…more. But she didn't have to tell him because he seemed to know instinctively what she wanted, as if he could read her mind.

He replaced his thigh with one strong hand and instantly, he found her sensitive bud, rolling it between his fingers as if he'd been born to touch her exactly in this way.

She gasped and her eyelids fluttered shut as waves of heat broke over her skin like the surf on the shore below their window. The man must have a deal with the devil. How else could he be so beautifully built, so incredibly successful at both of his chosen professions *and* be so *good* at making her feel like this?

Murmuring flowery Italian phrases like a prayer against her lips, he touched her intimately and pleasured her until she feared her skin would incinerate and leave her in ashes. Then he trailed his lips down her throat and set that magic mouth on one of her incredibly sensitive breasts. As soon as he curled his hard tongue around a nipple, she detonated like the Fourth of July.

The climax overwhelmed her, tensing her muscles and sending shooting stars across her vision.

"Antonio," she whispered. Or screamed. Hard to tell

when her entire body sang his name so loudly, it deafened her.

"Yes, my darling. I'm here." He rolled her to her back and covered her with his unbelievable body, resting his weight on his forearms so he wouldn't crush her.

But it was far too late to prevent that. As he positioned himself to slide into her, joy burst open inside her chest and streamed through her entire body. Oh, she'd been crushed, all right.

Crushed by the overwhelming sensations of being completely, fully in love. That desperation of wanting him from afar—that wasn't love. That was infatuation, and there was no comparison.

Antonio filled her to the hilt, and she rocked her hips to draw him deeper still, a technique she'd discovered by accident last night. And judging by his answering groan, he approved of it just as much this morning as he had last night.

She shut her eyes and savored the fullness of him as he shifted to hit her sweet spot. A sigh escaped her lips. Perfection. Was it always like this, like being touched physically and spiritually at the same time? Or did she and Antonio have a bond other people never experienced?

It was an academic question because she'd never know. This was the only man she'd ever love. The only man she'd ever be intimate with. She trusted him fully, knew he'd be there for her, steadfast and strong. Waiting for him had been worth it. She couldn't imagine being with anyone else like this, opening her body and her heart to another person in this beautiful expression of their love.

His thrusts grew more insistent, more urgent, and she bowed to meet him, taking pleasure, giving it until they came together one final time in a shuddery dual climax that left her boneless and replete.

They lay in each other's arms, silent but in perfect harmony until her muscles regained enough strength for her to move. But she didn't go very far. She pillowed her head on his shoulder and thanked whatever fates had seen fit to grant her this second chance to be with Antonio.

As he'd done yesterday morning, Antonio flipped on the wall-mounted flat-screen TV to watch the news. Habitual, he'd told her when she asked, since returning from Indonesia—to break the silence.

"You don't need that noise anymore," she said and grabbed the remote with every intention of powering it off again.

But in the split second before she hit the button, the news anchor mentioned Antonio's name.

"What are they saying?" He sat up against the headboard and focused his attention on the newscast.

"…the identity of the anonymous donor who had the entire inventory of a toy store delivered to Toys for Tots." The blonde on the screen smiled as a photo of Antonio appeared next to her head. "It will be a merry Christmas indeed for thousands of local children who have this secret Santa to thank. Antonio Cavallari made headlines recently by returning to LA after being presumed dead in a plane crash over a year ago—"

"They shouldn't have tracked down who donated those toys." Antonio frowned. "It was anonymous for a reason."

The newshounds had finally scented Antonio's story due to his generous gesture, which, as he pointed out, should have remained anonymous. He could have paraded around naked in front of Falco and generated less interest apparently, but the one thing he hadn't wanted advertised was what had garnered coverage. The nerve.

A photo of Vanessa flashed on the screen and she flipped the channel. The guilt was bad enough. She didn't need her sister staring at her from beyond the grave. "Enough of that."

But Antonio wasn't even looking at the TV. His gaze was squarely on Caitlyn. "You're very good for me, you know that?"

He tucked a lock of her hair behind her ear and then lifted the long strands from her neck to press a kiss to her throat. She shuddered as he gathered her closer, fanning the ashes of their lovemaking, which apparently hadn't fully cooled.

"I have something for you," he said, his lips sparking against her skin.

"And it's exactly what I wanted," she murmured, arching into his mouth, silently encouraging him to trail those lips down her throat.

It could never be enough. He could touch her every minute of every day, crawl inside her ten more times before they left this bed, and she'd never reach the saturation point.

He laughed and reached behind him to pull a long, flat box from the bedside dresser drawer.

Entranced by the possibilities, Caitlyn ripped off the green foil wrapping paper and lifted the lid. A silver chain lay on the velvet interior.

Antonio withdrew it from the box and held it up so she could see the silver-filigreed initial charms hanging from it. "There's an *A*, an *L* and another *A*."

"Oh," she breathed as her heart surged. "One for each of the babies."

He fingered an *A* and tilted it so the light glinted off the polished white stone set in the center. "When I was in Indonesia, I trained in a makeshift dirt ring. Oftentimes, when we sparred, we'd uncover rocks buried in the soil. I carried one in my pocket when I left in search of where I belonged. It was symbolic of what I hoped I'd find when I got to America. Myself, buried beneath the layers of damaged memories."

Speechless, she stared at him as her pulse pounded.

"I had the jeweler cut and polish my stone. Each letter holds a fragment of it." His gaze far away and troubled, he set the *A* swinging with a small tip of his finger. "If Vanessa had been carrying the babies, they would have died along with her."

True. And horrifying. She'd never thought about her decision to be their surrogate in quite that way. When Vanessa had asked her, Caitlyn had agreed because she loved her sister, but honestly, the thought of getting to carry Antonio's baby had tipped the scales. It had been a win-win in her book, but the reality had so much more positives wound up in that she couldn't feel guilty about it any longer.

He bunched the chain in his fist and drew the covers back from her naked form. She was too emotional to do anything but watch. He knelt to lay his lips on her C-section scars for an eternity, and then his dark gaze swept upward to fixate on her. "My children are a piece of me that I never would have had without you. I cannot ever repay you for what you've given me. This is but a small token."

Tears splashed down her face unchecked as Antonio leaned up to hook the chain around her neck. Everything inside swelled up and over, pouring out of her mouth.

"I love you," she choked out.

She didn't care if he didn't say it back. Didn't care if the timing was wrong. Didn't care if it was only the emotion of the moment that had dragged it out of her. It was the pure honest truth, and she couldn't have held back the tide of her feelings even with a dam the size of Asia.

His gaze flicked to hers and a wealth of emotions swam through his dark eyes. "I wish I could say the same. I'd like to. But it would be unfair."

She nodded and a few more tears splashed down on the teal comforter she'd painstakingly selected. His heart still belonged to Vanessa. It was a poetic kind of justice for her sister. And for Caitlyn, truth be told.

"It's okay. I'm not trying to pressure you. But I thought you should know how I feel."

He gathered her close and held her as if he never planned to let go. "Yet another gift you've given me without expectation of anything in return. You're an amazing woman, Caitlyn."

She laid her cheek over the falcon and listened to his heartbeat. He just needed time to get over Vanessa. She'd *help* him get over her so that strong, beautiful heart could belong to Caitlyn forever. And then she'd be complete.

"Let's go spend Christmas with our family," Caitlyn suggested, and Antonio's rumbled agreement vibrated against her cheek.

The day after Christmas, Antonio couldn't stand his own company any longer and the only solution for his foul mood was to go to Falco. Without Caitlyn.

She sent him off with a kiss and nary a backward glance, as if she really had no clue he was about to lose his mind. Seemed as if he'd done a spectacular job keeping his doubts and trepidation to himself.

He had to do something different to regain his memories. It wasn't fair to Caitlyn that she was stuck in a relationship with a man who had no concrete memories of his marriage and therefore no guideposts to help him move on.

He wanted to. Desperately. He'd hoped finally getting Caitlyn into his arms would do the trick. Instead, all he'd accomplished was to make things worse.

She was in love with him. And the way he felt about her—*wonderful and terrifying emotions* was a stellar way to describe it. When he looked at her, it was as if every star in the sky shined all at once, lighting up the darkness. *She* was his star. The only constellation in his life that would ever make sense. Because he'd done exactly what he'd set out to do. He'd created new memories, new experiences with her.

Surely this was love.

But he'd been in love with Vanessa, or so Caitlyn had told him. Why couldn't he remember her clearly? It seemed wrong to tell Caitlyn about his feelings, his fledging certainty that he was in love with her, too, to promise her any sort of future, when he'd done the same with Vanessa... only to lose all consciousness of that relationship.

What if he did that to Caitlyn one day? What if he got in the ring with Cutter again and the next blow to his head erased his memories of her?

He couldn't stand the thought.

At Falco, he sat in the chair behind his desk. It was a sleek behemoth with a front piece that went all the way to the ground, hiding his lower half from view to visitors. Why had such obscurity appealed to him? He had no idea, but Caitlyn had told him he'd selected it along with all of the other furniture in the office.

Perhaps he'd shopped for furniture with Vanessa, too, as he'd done with Caitlyn. He yearned for his relationship with Caitlyn to feel special and unique. But how would he know either way?

This frustration was useless, and nothing he'd done thus far today came close to handling his memory problems differently. So he picked up the phone and scheduled the CT scan for the following week after the holidays.

It might not help, but he couldn't live in this fog of uncertainty any longer. He'd promised Caitlyn they would talk about the future after the first of the year and he'd been entertaining the notion of taking her to someplace she'd enjoy for New Year's Eve, like Paris or Madrid. Just the two of them.

Antonio pulled the ring box from his pocket and flipped

the lid. The fifteen-karat diamond dazzled like a perfect, round star against the midnight velvet. The moment he'd seen it in the case as he'd waited for the jeweler to retrieve Caitlyn's custom-made necklace, he'd known. That was the ring he wanted on Caitlyn's finger forever, as a physical symbol that she belonged to him and he needed her. He imagined her eyes filling with all that sweet, endless emotion as she realized he was asking her to marry him.

But he couldn't ask her until he exorcised the ghost of his first wife.

He pushed away from the desk and strode outside to get some fresh air. Street sounds and the ever-present sting of smog and pollution invaded what little serenity he might have found outdoors.

A flash of red hair in his peripheral vision put a hitch in his gut. An otherworldly sense of dread overwhelmed him.

Slowly, he turned to see a woman approaching him, a quizzical, hopeful slant to her expression. Long legged, slim build, beautiful porcelain face, fall of bright red hair to her waist.

Vanessa.

Oh, God. *It was his wife.* In the flesh. A million irreconcilable images flew through his head as he stared at her. Pain knifed through his temples.

"Antonio," she whispered, her voice scratchy and trembling. She searched his gaze hungrily. "I saw the news report and couldn't believe it. I had to find you, to see you for myself."

"Vanessa," he croaked, and his throat seized up.

She recoiled as if he'd backhanded her across the face. "What is that, a joke?"

"You're supposed to be dead. Caitlyn told me they found your body."

Caitlyn. Horrified, he stared at the redhead filling his vision. Caitlyn was the mother of his children, his lover.

She lived in his house, in his heart…and there was no room for Vanessa. How could this be *possible*?

"I'm not Vanessa, Antonio. What's going on? It's me." Confusion threw her expression into shadow when he shook his head. "Shayla."

The name exploded in his head. Across his soul. *Shayla*.

Laughing, moaning, murmuring his name—dozens of memories of her scrolled through his mind. Her body twining with his. Her full breasts on unashamed display, head thrown back as she rode him, taking her pleasure as if she had done it often, as if she had a right to use his body.

And of course she *had* done it often.

Shayla. His mistress. Vanessa—his wife.

The images in his head of the redheaded woman were so jumbled and nonsensical because he'd had incomplete, fragmented memories of *two different women*.

Eleven

A swirl of nausea squeezed Antonio's stomach as his eyes shut against the shocking revelation. He couldn't look at her, couldn't take the idea that he'd been intimate with her.

He'd been carrying on an affair with this woman. Cheating on his wife with her.

It was repulsive. Wrong. Not something he'd ever have imagined himself doing.

But clearly, that hadn't always been his opinion of adultery.

Gagging against the bile rising in his throat, he turned away from Shayla's prying, too-familiar gaze.

"What's the matter?" she asked. "Aren't you happy to see me? Vanessa is gone and we can finally be together."

"I don't…" *Remember you.* But it was a lie. He remembered her all too well.

Oblivious of his consternation, she put a manicured hand on his arm. He fought the urge to shake it off because it wasn't her fault he'd forsaken his marriage vows.

His skin crawled under her fingers.

He yanked his arm away and her hand fell to her side as hurt clouded her expression.

"I'm sorry," he said roughly, as pain ice-picked through his skull. "Things are not like you assume."

She cocked her head. "I don't understand what's wrong. You're alive and it's a miracle. Why didn't you call me? I've thought you were dead for over a year. Do you have any idea what I've gone through?"

His short bark of laughter startled them both. "Shayla, I—" God, he couldn't even say her name without wanting to cut out his tongue. Swallowing, he tried again. "I have amnesia."

It was the first time he'd uttered that word out loud. And oddly, naming it, *owning* it, diminished its power. Not completely, but his spine straightened and he nodded at her stunned flinch.

"Yes, you heard correctly," he told her a bit more firmly. "The plane crash dumped me on the shore of an island in Indonesia with few memories. I only found my way home a few weeks ago."

"You don't remember me." Her expression caved in and tears shimmered in her eyes. "Of all the things… I thought we'd pick up where we left—I mean, Vanessa is dead. When I heard you'd survived the crash, I figured you—"

"I remember you," he broke in. "But I didn't until I saw you."

As he'd remembered his lawyer and Thomas. But he hadn't remembered Caitlyn. Or Rodrigo. Which led to the most important question—

Would he remember Vanessa if he saw *her*?

A perverse need to know overtook him.

"I'm sorry," he told the tearful redhead before him, determined to get home and discover what else he could extract from the sieve in his brain. "There's nothing here for you any longer. I'm not in love with you and I never will be."

She laughed bitterly. "Funny, that's almost exactly what you said before you left to go to Thailand. Except you were talking about Vanessa at the time. Didn't stop you from running off on your lovers' retreat."

The words blasted through his head, but in his voice as he said them to Shayla one night.

I'm not in love with her and I never will be. There's nothing left for me in that cold, empty house. The Malibu house. He'd meant the one he'd shared with Vanessa. The one he now shared with Caitlyn and his children.

He'd told Shayla he wasn't in love with Vanessa. Truth? It might explain why he couldn't recall what that had felt like. Or had it been something he'd told his mistress to string her along?

After all, he'd gone to Thailand with Vanessa. Had fathered children with her. All while conducting a hot-and-heavy affair with this woman.

What kind of man did such things? When he'd come to LA to find out who he was, he'd never imagined he'd discover such dishonesty and selfishness in his past. Who had he *been* before the crash?

Some aspects, like being a fighter, he didn't have to question. That was a part of him. Was being an adulterer part of him, too? A part he couldn't remove any easier than he could stop fighting? He owed it to himself, his children and Caitlyn to learn everything he could about what kind of person Antonio Cavallari had been. So he could chart a course for the kind of man he wanted to be in the future.

"I'm sorry," he repeated. "I have to go. Please don't contact me again. Our relationship, whatever it was, is over."

"Yeah." She sighed. "It has been for more than a year. I mistakenly assumed we had a second chance this time.

A real one. You were never going to divorce Vanessa, not with the baby on the way."

That resonated. Divorce wasn't something the man he *knew* he was deep inside would tolerate. "No, I wouldn't have. And turns out there were three babies. Triplets."

Her smile was small but genuine. "Congratulations. Didn't see that coming. Vanessa was smarter than I would have given her credit for. That's triple the amount of child support if you ever did divorce her. I wish I knew how she'd pulled that off."

Child support. A fight with Vanessa where that term had been launched at him like a grenade... The details slammed through his head. Shayla's name had come up. Vanessa was furious because he'd sworn he'd end things with "that woman," but he apparently hadn't. Then Vanessa had taunted him with the pregnancy, saying it was insurance. Against what?

He couldn't remember that much of the conversation.

"The triplets were an accident," he assured her. "A happy one."

She nodded and he watched her walk away, then strode to the town car so the driver could take him home, where he would get some answers to the mysteries locked in his mind, once and for all.

Once he got into the house, he disappeared into the media room to queue up episodes of the TV show Vanessa had starred in. He should have done this weeks ago. Why hadn't he?

He'd told himself it wouldn't do any good. That his memories of Vanessa were so scattered and fragmented that seeing her wouldn't help. It was a lie, one he'd convinced himself of for his own self-preservation.

Vanessa walked onto the sixty-inch screen as his pulse thundered in his throat. Slim, redheaded, with delicate features. The way she held herself, something about her demeanor, was horribly familiar...because she looked like a redheaded version of Caitlyn.

Pain knifed through his temples, throbbing in tandem with his pulse.

His memories of Shayla and Vanessa split instantly. Distinct and whole, the snippets of scenes and his interactions with each woman flooded his consciousness. He let them flow despite the enormous shock to his system, absorbing, reliving. And he didn't like the realizations that followed.

Maybe he hadn't wanted to remember either his wife or his mistress. Maybe he'd known subconsciously that he didn't deserve someone as innocent as Caitlyn and he'd suppressed his memories on purpose to avoid facing the dark choices he'd made before the crash.

Grief clawed at his throat.

He had to tell Caitlyn. She should know what kind of man he'd been. What kind of man he still was. Amnesia hadn't made him into someone different. Just someone who didn't remember his sins.

He powered off the TV and sat on the plush couch in full darkness for an eternity, hating himself. Hating his choices, hating that he couldn't remember why he'd made them. Because that was part of the key in moving toward the future—understanding the past.

The door to the media room opened and Caitlyn's dark head poked through. "Hey, I didn't know you were back, but I saw the car and—"

"Come in," he commanded unevenly. "Please."

She was here. Might as well lay it all on the line. The hordes of paparazzi hanging out at Falco had likely snapped a picture of his conversation with Shayla, and he'd rather Caitlyn hear about it from him.

She came into the room, reaching for the lamp switch. He caught her arm before she could turn it on. Dark was appropriate.

"What's wrong?" she asked, concern coating her voice.

It was a painful, unintentional echo of Shayla's question. Apparently, they could both read him well. Better than he could read himself. "I need to talk to you."

How did you approach such a subject? He hadn't dishonored *her*. But she'd likely be outraged on her sister's behalf. Regardless, she had to know the truth.

"Sure." She perched on the couch, her features barely discernible in the faint light from the still-open door. He could sense her, smell her light coconut shampoo, and his heart ached to bury himself in her, no talking, no specters of the past between them.

But he'd probably never touch her again. She deserved better than he was capable of giving her.

"I...ran into someone today. A woman. From before the crash. I...remembered her."

"That's great!" Caitlyn's sweet voice knifed through him.

"No, it's not. I was having an affair with her," he said bluntly. Harshly. But there were no punches to be pulled here, no matter how difficult it was to keep swinging.

"An affair?"

Her confusion mirrored his but must have been ten times worse because she'd only just learned of it. He'd had hours to reconcile how truly sinful he was.

"Yes. A long-standing one, apparently." Remorse nearly overwhelmed him.

She grew quiet and he wished he hadn't insisted on no lights. Was she upset? She should be. But the darkness left him only his own guilt for company.

"I don't understand," she finally said. "You and Vanessa were happy. You were in love."

"I wasn't. Happy," he clarified. "Or in love."

That was perhaps the most painful realization of all. His confusion about love stemmed wholly from not ever having been in love before. When his memories of Vanessa resurfaced, he'd recognized the truth Shayla had revealed. He hadn't loved Vanessa.

He couldn't compare how he felt now to the past because there was nothing to compare it to. His feelings for Caitlyn were unprecedented.

And he was most definitely in love with her.

Otherwise it wouldn't be breaking his heart to tell her who he was, deep down inside where he couldn't change it.

"Why didn't you get a divorce, then?" Her voice had grown faint, as if she'd drawn in on herself.

"I don't know," he admitted quietly. "Too Catholic, maybe. And there was a baby on the way. I'm still missing huge pieces of my memories of the past, pieces I might never recover."

They lapsed into silence and he ached to bridge it, but this was an unprecedented situation, too. She should be allowed to react however she wanted.

"Did Vanessa know?" Her voice cracked and he realized she was crying as she sniffled quietly.

His gut twisted, and her pain was far worse than the pain he'd caused himself. She was hurting. More than he would have anticipated. Of course he hadn't thought this would go over well, but he'd expected her to be angry, not injured. His nails dug into his palms as he struggled to keep from touching her, comforting her. He was the source of her hurt, not the solution.

"She knew." And he wished he understood the dynamics of his marriage, why Vanessa would have stayed in a marriage where her husband didn't love her and was having an affair with another woman. He didn't even remember if she'd professed to love him. "I'm sorry to drop this on you with no warning. It's not how I envisioned this going between us."

They should have been talking about the trip he'd hoped to surprise her with, the imminent marriage proposal.

"It's a lot to take in, Antonio." Her voice fractured again on the last syllable of his name. "I don't know what to say."

Frustration and grief and anguish rose up inside, riling his temper as he tried to reconcile how to get through this, how to move forward when all he wanted was to hear her say it was okay, that she still loved him. That it didn't matter who he'd been. "Say how you feel. Are you mad at me? Hurt? You want to punch me?"

"I feel as if I don't know you. Commitment isn't important to you like it is to me. I wish I'd never slept with you," she admitted on a whisper that turned his whole body cold. "I can't deal with all of this. Not right now."

She slid to her feet and left the media room with a rush of quiet sobbing.

His guiding star had left him in the dark, and he felt further away from finding himself than ever. Ironic that he'd spent so long fighting to remember and now all he wished for was the ability to forget.

Dry-eyed, Caitlyn fed the babies. It was the only accomplishment she could list for the afternoon.

She rocked Annabelle, staring blindly at the wall as she tried to quiet the storm of misery zinging through her heart. If only she could crawl into bed and shut out the world, she might figure out how to get through this.

But she couldn't. Children still needed to be fed no matter what pain had just ripped a hole in your chest. Christmas decorations still had to be put away, leaving an empty hole where the holiday cheer had been. Life went on, oblivious of how one simple phrase had destroyed her world.

I was having an affair with her.

For years, Caitlyn had envied her sister's marriage. For

years, Caitlyn had lived with her unrequited feelings for Antonio. *For years*, she'd suffered crippling guilt over both.

And it was all a lie.

Her sister's marriage had been a sham. The strong, beautiful commitment she'd imagined was an illusion. The man she'd thought so steadfast and constant? An adulterer. Antonio wasn't perfect in the way she'd thought he was, and her guilt had been all for nothing.

Nothing. That guilt certainly hadn't served to keep her out of Antonio's bed. Oh, no, she'd hopped right into his arms with practically no resistance. She'd given her virginity to a man who thought so little of marriage vows that he couldn't honor them. Who thought so little of love that he hadn't considered it a necessity when choosing a wife.

It was reprehensible.

And none of it made *sense*. The awful words pouring out of Antonio's mouth: the admission that he hadn't been in love with Vanessa, the affair, the reasons for not divorcing—they didn't mesh with the man she'd fallen in love with.

She'd known Antonio for seven years. Was she really such a bad judge of character that she could love a man who'd treated her sister like that? How could she forgive any of this?

She wished she could cry. But everything was too numb.

After the babies had been fed, she slumped in the rocking chair as Leon, Annabelle and Antonio Junior crawled around on a blanket in the center of the nursery. It had been only a couple of hours since Antonio had told her. But it felt like a year.

"May I come in?"

Her gaze cut to the door. As if her thoughts had conjured him, Antonio stood just inside it, his expression blank.

For an instant, her heart lurched as she drank him in. Apparently, nothing could kill the reaction she still had to him. A sobering realization. As was the fact that he hadn't tracked her down with some magical solution to the giant cloud over them now, as much as she might wish that such a thing existed. No, he was here because they always played with the babies before dinner. It had become a ritual all five of them enjoyed, and he would still want to spend time with his children no matter what else happened.

Life went on. And they were co-parents of small children. Forever.

"Of course you can come in," she said. "This is your house."

He winced and she almost apologized for the bitter tone. But she didn't have the energy and she wasn't all that sorry. The old Caitlyn would have apologized. The old Caitlyn always had a kind word for everyone and lived in a rosy world of rainbows and unicorns, obviously.

All that had gotten her was devastated and broken-hearted. Why hadn't someone warned her that a commitment had absolutely nothing hidden inside it to guard against being hurt? Actually, it was worse because then you had to figure out how to live with your hurt.

Antonio crouched on the blanket and handed Leon a rattle, murmuring encouraging words as his son crawled toward it. Annabelle hummed as she explored the perimeter of the blanket and Antonio Junior lay on his back in the center of the room, examining the ceiling with his unique brand of concentration.

Not so unique, actually. His father had that same ability to hone in on something and it was nearly hypnotic.

She tamped down the tide of sheer grief. Antonio wasn't who she thought he was. He hadn't been probably since the beginning. She had to get past it, forgive him and get over her disappointment so they could move on. Didn't she?

The clock on the wall ticked loudly, marking off second after interminable second. They bled into a minute, then another. The silence stretched, heavy and thick. But this was how it had to go. They'd play with the babies and eat dinner. Then what? They shared a bedroom. Would they get ready for bed and lay next to each other with the silence and the big letter *A* for *affair* creating an invisible boundary between them?

"I can't do this." She was on her feet, hands clenched in tight fists, before she fully registered moving. "It's like waiting for the executioner's ax to fall."

Antonio glanced up at her, his mouth set in a hard line. It ruined the beauty of his face. He was obviously as miserable as she was. She hated that she noticed and hated even more that she apparently still cared.

"What is? Hanging out with our kids?"

"No. This." She swirled a taut hand in the air to encompass the room at large, but she meant the two of them and the big question marks surrounding their relationship, how they moved forward, all of it. "I can't do this with you. I'm not Vanessa. I won't put up with affairs and I'm not okay with it."

She'd yearned for her sister's life and now she had it. The whole kit and caboodle. Clearly she needed to be more careful what she wished for. Yet it was such a suitable penance. She bit back hysterical laughter.

"I'm not asking you to be okay with it," he countered quietly with a glance at Annabelle who had pulled up on her crib with a loud squeal of achievement. "*I'm* not okay with it. And you should know, it wasn't affairs. Just one. I told her not to contact me anymore. I don't want anything to do with her."

Did he honestly expect any of that to make a *difference*?

"I need to move back into my own bedroom." Her throat hitched as she said the words and she wished she could take them back, but it was the smartest move for her sanity. "I can't be with you anymore, not like we were."

And there it was. She'd held this man in her arms, cradled him with her body, loved him, slept with him, tasted him. Never in a million years would she have imagined she'd be the one to call off their relationship. In the end, she'd been painfully spot on—she wasn't the right kind of woman for Antonio Cavallari.

Grimly, he crossed his arms. "What will we be like, then?"

She shook her head blindly. "Parents. Roommates. I don't know. I just know I can't sleep in that bedroom. I can't—"

A sob broke through, ending whatever she'd been about to say. Head bowed, she buried her head in her hands, squeezing her eyes shut. She sensed Antonio's presence as he approached, but he didn't touch her.

She wished he would. Wished they were still in a place where he could comfort her. But was glad he didn't. It would only confuse things.

"Caitlyn."

She blinked up at him through watery eyes.

His dark gaze zeroed in on her, overwhelming her with unvoiced conflict and soul-deep wounds. Even now, with these irreparable ruptures between them, she could read him.

"Will you fight me for custody of the children?" he asked softly.

She gasped. "What? Why in the world would I do that?"

"What kind of father could I possibly be?" Resolute and stoic, he stared her down. "I have an uncontrollable urge to decimate other men in the ring. I have amnesia. I defiled my marriage with a tasteless affair. Any judge would grant your petition to take my children and likely award you as much money as you ask for to raise them. If I were you, I would have already taken steps to remove them from my influence."

"Antonio." Her chest constricted as she searched his ravaged expression. "None of that makes you a bad father. Your children need you."

I need you.

But she bit it back. She needed the man she'd *thought* he was, the one who made her feel treasured because he'd chosen her. Because of all the people in his life he could have reached out to, he'd taken her hand and asked her to stand with him when he had gone to Falco the first time. He'd asked her to see the doctor with him. He'd been alone and frightened and he hadn't wanted anyone else but her.

Then he'd destroyed her trust by morphing into someone else. Someone who didn't respect and honor marriage the way she did. Who hadn't loved his wife.

If he couldn't love Vanessa, what hope did Caitlyn have that he could ever feel that way about her? And she wouldn't settle for anything less than a man's love. Yet, how could she trust him if he *did* say that he loved her?

It was a vicious cycle, one she couldn't find a way to break, no matter how many times she went over it in her head. All this time, she'd thought he couldn't tell her he loved her because his heart still belonged to Vanessa. The reality was…indescribable.

Antonio glanced at the babies, and all the love she knew he felt for them radiated from every pore of his being. He was capable of love. Just not loving her.

"No, I need *them*," he said. "As long as you're not going to take them from me, I can handle anything else."

It was a strange reversal of some of their earlier conversations, when she'd been terrified he'd find a way to dismiss her from her children's lives. She knew what that clawing, desperate panic felt like and it softened her. More than she'd have liked.

A harder, more cynical person might have taken the information he'd laid out and run with it, ensuring that she got exactly what he said—custody and Antonio's money. It would be a fit punishment for his crimes.

But she wasn't that person, and as she stood close enough to touch him, close enough to smell his heady masculine scent, her heart twisted.

She still loved him. Nothing he'd said to her today could erase that.

"I will never take your children from you," she promised and her voice cracked. "But I can't have a romantic relationship with you. We have to figure out a way to live together as parents and nothing else. Can we?"

He stepped back, hands at his sides and his beautiful face a mask. "I'll respect whatever decision you make."

Her heart wept over his matter-of-fact tone, as if he had no interest in fighting for her. But what would she have said if he told her no, that it was totally unacceptable to end their relationship? That he loved her and wanted her in his bed, come hell or high water?

She'd have refused.

So here they were. Parents. And nothing else.

That made her want to weep more than anything else that had happened today.

Twelve

Antonio stood outside Caitlyn's old bedroom at 1:00 a.m., hands on the wood, listening to her breathe. God, this separation was an eternal hell.

After two days of staying out of her way, he was done with it.

She was awake and lying there in despair. He could sense it. Her essence had floated down the hall to him on a whisper of misery, and he'd caught it easily because he'd been lying awake in his own bed in similar turmoil.

His headaches had grown worse since they'd been apart, and his pillow still smelled like Caitlyn even after ten washings. She haunted him, asleep or awake. Didn't matter. She was so close, yet so far, and his body never quite got used to the fact that she wasn't easily accessible any longer. He still rolled over in the night, seeking her heat and the bone-deep contentment that came with touching her.

Only to come up empty-handed and empty hearted. The

only thing in life that made sense was gone, and it hurt worse than any physical pain he'd ever endured.

The pounding in his temples wouldn't ease no matter how many rounds he went in the ring at Falco. He'd even resorted to a pain pill earlier that evening, to no avail.

The only thing that ever worked to take away his headache was Caitlyn.

He pushed the door open and stepped inside her room. She didn't move, but the quick intake of her breath told him she knew he was there.

"I can't sleep," he said inanely.

Her scent filled his head, pulsing through it with sweet memories, and it was worse than being in his lonely bed without her. This was too close. And not close enough.

It was maddening.

"I'm sorry." Her voice whispered across his skin, raising the hair. "But you can't come in here in the middle of the night."

"This is my house," he growled as his temper got the best of him. It was the wrong tactic; he knew that. But she was killing him. "I need to talk to you."

"Can't it wait?"

It was a reasonable request for one o'clock in the morning. "No, it can't. Please, Caitlyn. What can I say, what can I do? I'm sorry. I hate that I did something so inexcusable. Can't you get past it?"

"I don't think so." The quiet words cut through him. "We don't have the same views on commitment, and that's not something that I can get past. You told me you believed in forever and I believed you. Now I can't trust you, and without that, what kind of relationship would we have? I'm not like Vanessa."

Why couldn't she see that he didn't want her to be like Vanessa? At one point in time, he'd liked a certain kind of woman, clearly. But he didn't remember why and didn't want to.

He wanted Caitlyn.

And she didn't want him. Because of something he'd done a long time ago. Something he couldn't undo. Something that haunted him, something he hated about himself. He'd surgically extract whatever she objected to if he could. If it would make a difference.

But it wouldn't, and this was one fight he lacked the skill to win.

Without another word, he left her there in the dark because he couldn't stand the space between them any longer. Couldn't stand that he didn't know what to do.

He had to change her mind. She was everything to him and he needed her. Loved her.

For the first time in his life, he was pinned against the fence, strength draining away, and his opponent was too big to overcome.

But he refused to go down for the count. He needed to do something big and drastic to win her back. But what?

After a long night of tossing and turning, Caitlyn gave up at 5:00 a.m. She'd slept in this bed pre-Antonio for over a year and had never thought twice about it. A few days in paradise, also known as the bedroom down the hall, and suddenly there was no sleep to be had in this old room.

And she wasn't fooled into thinking it was the mattress. Her inability to sleep had everything to do with the black swirl of her thoughts and the cutting pain in her chest after shutting down Antonio's middle-of-the-night plea. Closing her eyes only made it worse.

Caitlyn padded to the sunroom and tried to get in the mood for Pilates before Leon woke up. But all she could think about was the first time Antonio had kissed her. He'd backed her up against a wall, literally and figuratively, in this very room, demanding she tell him about love. So she'd spilled her heart and turned the question back to him, expecting a profound tribute straight from the poetry books. An ode to his late wife about his devotion and the wonders of their marriage.

What do you know about love? she'd asked.

Nothing, he'd returned.

She'd assumed he didn't remember love and stupidly thought he was asking her to help him. But really, he'd meant he'd never loved Vanessa. How awful it must have been for her sister, to be stuck in a loveless marriage with a man who wouldn't divorce her solely because of the baby on the way. Instead, he'd forced her to put up with his infidelity.

How had Vanessa done it? How had she woken up each morning, her mind ripe with the knowledge that her husband had been intimate with another woman? Unrequited love was something Caitlyn had a special empathy for. Had her sister cried herself to sleep at night, the way Caitlyn had over the past few days? Why hadn't Vanessa told her what was going on?

Inexplicably, she wished her sister was here so she could bury her head in Vanessa's shoulder and weep out all her troubles. Which was the worst kind of juxtaposition. If Vanessa was alive, Caitlyn's troubles would be nonexistent. She'd still be laboring under the false premise that marriage, commitment, love and sex were all tied up with a big, magnificent bow.

Leon woke up early. While Caitlyn fed him, her mind wandered back to Vanessa and it suddenly hit her that her sister's possessions sat tucked away in the attic. Her sister might be gone, but Caitlyn could still surround herself with Vanessa. Maybe it would help ease Caitlyn's bruised and battered soul.

She turned the babies over to Brigitte, who bundled

them up for a ride in the triple-seated stroller, and then escaped to the attic. *Attic* might be a little grandiose of a term—it was really a small, unfinished room above the second floor, accessible by a narrow staircase next to the linen closet.

Caitlyn hadn't been in here for over a year, not since she'd moved the bulk of Vanessa's things after the plane crash. A coating of dust covered the items farthest from the entrance. The boxes near the front had been placed there recently and weren't as grimy. Shortly after Antonio had returned, Caitlyn had asked the housekeeper to pack up the rest of her sister's things.

Sitting down cross-legged, she opened the nearest untaped box. Clothes. She pulled out one of her sister's silk blouses and held it to her cheek. The heavy, exotic perfume Vanessa had favored wafted from the fabric. All at once, Caitlyn recalled the last time she'd smelled it, when she'd been four months pregnant and had come to say goodbye before Vanessa and Antonio left for Thailand.

Tears slid down her face and she suspected the majority of them were because she missed Antonio. Not Vanessa. Apparently, her shame knew no bounds, but he'd been so lost last night. She'd wanted to tell him she wished there was a way to get past it, too. But she couldn't see it.

The clothes weren't helping. Pushing that box to the side, she dived into the next one, which was full of Vanessa's toiletries, including two small, jeweled bottles of her perfume. Caitlyn pulled them out to give to Annabelle. The perfume would likely not last that long, but the bottles were encrusted with real semiprecious stones and the pair would be a lovely keepsake for their daughter.

Perhaps the children she shared with Vanessa were actually the answer Caitlyn had been seeking about how she was supposed to find the strength to live in the same house with Antonio. Had Vanessa considered the babies a good enough reason to stay with her husband despite the emotional pain he'd caused her? Leon, Annabelle and Antonio Junior were certainly the reason why Caitlyn was still here after all. She couldn't imagine not waking up each day and seeing the faces of her kids. It was worth the sword through her heart every time she saw their father to get daily access to her children.

Maybe it had also been worth it to Vanessa to keep her family intact. Maybe that was why she hadn't pressed for a divorce and stayed with Antonio even after she found out about his affair.

Drained, Caitlyn rested her head on the box. Her weight threw it off balance and it tumbled to spill its contents into her lap.

A leather-bound book landed on top. It looked like an old-fashioned journal. Curious, Caitlyn leafed through it and recognized her sister's handwriting.

"Sept 4: Ronald doesn't think the Paramount people will consider me for the lead in *Bright Things*. The role is too opposite from Janelle. I should fire him, but he's my third agent in two years. Ugh. I really want that movie!"

Interesting. Caitlyn wouldn't have considered Vanessa the type to record her innermost thoughts, especially not in written form when her sister had been so attached to her smartphone, but here it was, in blue pen. With all of the email hacking and cloud-storage security breaches that plagued celebrities, Vanessa might have felt paper had a measure of privacy she couldn't get any other way. Feeling a little voyeuristic, Caitlyn read a few more entries at the beginning and then skipped ahead.

Wow, she hadn't realized how much Vanessa had wanted to move on from Janelle, the character she'd played on the prime-time drama *Beacon Street*. Her sister had never said anything about how trapped she'd felt.

It kind of stung to find out Vanessa hadn't confided in

Caitlyn about her career woes. Or much of anything, apparently. The journal was full of surprises. Caitlyn would have said they were pretty close before the crash, but obviously Vanessa had kept a lot of things hidden.

Antonio's name caught her eye and she paused mid–page flip.

"I told Antonio about Mark. He totally freaked out, worse than I expected. Simple solution to the problem, I told him. If he'd just stop this ridiculous nonsense about reviving his glory days in the ring, I'd agree to stop seeing Mark. Which won't be hard. He's nowhere near as good as Antonio in bed, but I had to do something to get my stupid husband's attention!"

Caitlyn went cold, then hot.

Her sister had been having an affair, too?

Dread twisted her stomach inside out as she flipped to the beginning of the entry. It was dated over two years ago. Well before Vanessa had approached Caitlyn about being a surrogate. Her sister's marriage problems had extended that far back?

She kept reading entry after entry with slick apprehension souring her mouth.

"Antonio is still really upset about Mark. He demanded I quit *Beacon Street*. I laughed. As if I'd ruin my career for him just so my darling husband didn't have to watch me on-screen with the man I'm sleeping with? Whatever."

And then a few pages later: "Antonio is so horrible. Not only is he still talking about fighting again—which I will not put up with!—he's found what he thinks is the best way to get back at me for Mark. He's having an affair with a woman who looks like me. On purpose. It's so juvenile. He's so not the type to be this vindictive. But I left him no choice, he said in that imperious voice that never fails to piss me off."

Antonio had started his affair in retaliation for Vanessa's. It didn't change how she felt about infidelity, but it changed how she felt about her sister. And her sister's views on marriage, which clearly didn't mirror Caitlyn's.

Information overload. Wave after wave of it crashed over her. So Antonio had wanted to get back in the ring even before the crash—did he remember that?

Her throat and eyes both burning uncontrollably, Caitlyn forced herself to read to the end. Without checking her strength, she threw the leather-bound confessional at the wall, unable to hold the evidence of how little she'd actually known her sister.

She'd walked into this attic hoping to find some comfort for the task ahead of her—living with a man she loved but couldn't fathom how to trust—and instead found out her sister hadn't been sitting around pining for her husband. In fact, Vanessa had had skeletons of her own in her closet.

Hot, angry tears coursed down Caitlyn's face, and she couldn't stop the flood of grief. Didn't want to. Nothing was as she'd thought. Vanessa had pushed Antonio into the arms of another woman first by forbidding him from doing something he loved and then punishing him via a romance with her costar. It didn't make Antonio's choices right, but against everything Caitlyn would have expected, she had sympathy for him nonetheless.

It was too much. She sank into a heap and wept.

She registered Antonio's presence only a moment before he gathered her into his arms, rocking her against his strong chest. Ashamed that her soul had latched on to his touch like a greedy miser being showered with gold, she clung to him as he murmured her name. She cried on his expensive shirt and he didn't even seem to notice the huge wet spot under her cheek.

His fingers tangled in her hair as he cupped her head gently, massaging with his strong fingers. Tiny needles of awareness spiked through her skin, energizing her with the power of his sweet touch, but she ignored it. He didn't speak and somehow that made it okay to just be, no words, no excuses, no reasons to shove him away yet again.

When the storm passed, she peeked up at his blank expression. "Where did you come from? I didn't think you were home."

"I just got back," he said gruffly. "I…heard you and I couldn't stay away. I know you can take care of yourself, but I needed to check on you. Don't say I should have left you alone and let you cry because that was not going to happen."

"It's okay. I'm glad you found me."

"I doubt that's true when I'm the reason you're crying."

His arms dropped away and she missed them, almost calling out for him to encompass her again with that blanket of serenity. But she didn't. There was still so much unsaid between them. So much swirling through her heart that she could hardly think.

She shook her head. "Not this time. Vanessa—" her deep breath fractured on another half sob "—was sleeping with her costar. Mark—"

"Van Allsberg." Antonio's expression wavered between outrage and bleak resignation. "I remember now. I didn't until you said his name. I almost got in the car to drive to his house and take him apart for touching my wife. How did you find out?" he asked quietly as he sat back on his heels.

"She wrote in a journal." Bitterness laced her tone involuntarily. Vanessa had been very free with information when the page was her only audience. "I read it. It was illuminating."

Caitlyn's chest hurt as she watched the pain filter through his entire body anew, as if he was experiencing it for the first time. And perhaps amnesia was like that, continually forcing Antonio to relive events he should have been able to put behind him. Distance didn't exist for him the way it did for other people, who could grow numb to the pain—or deal with it—over time.

Unwittingly, she'd forced him to do the same by jumping on the self-righteous bandwagon, lambasting him for an affair that had happened a long time ago when in reality, she'd known nothing of the difficulties in his marriage. She'd been judge, jury and executioner without all of the facts.

She stared at the exposed beams of the ceiling until she thought she could talk without crying. "Her affair was your punishment for daring to express your interest in fighting again."

"I… It was?" Frustration knitted his features into an unrecognizable state. "I thought…"

His anguish ripped through her, and before she could list the hundreds of reasons why it was a bad idea, she grabbed his hand, holding it tightly in hers as if she could communicate all her angst through that small bit of contact.

"You made mistakes, Antonio. But there were extenuating circumstances."

It didn't negate the sacredness of marriage vows, but it did throw a lot of light on how Antonio's choices had come about.

"That's no excuse," he bit out savagely. "There *is* no excuse. That's why I can't forgive myself."

That speared through her gut and left a gaping wound in its wake.

His distress wasn't faked. Cautiously, she searched his face, his body language, and the truth was there in every fiber of his being. He clearly didn't think the affair was okay now, despite having thought differently back then.

Not only had the affair happened a long time ago, she'd refused to take into account that Antonio wasn't the same person he'd been while married to her sister. As many times as she'd noted he was different, in this, she'd convicted him of being the same.

Amnesia had taken pieces of his memory, and perhaps what was left had reshaped him. Could she find a way to trust the Antonio who had returned to her from the grave and allow the old one to stay buried?

"Antonio." He didn't look at her, but she went on anyway. "You should know something. She said you talked her into going to Thailand as a way to reconnect. You wanted to try again, just the two of you."

He nodded. "I don't remember. But I'm glad that Vanessa died knowing that I was committed to her."

That gelled with the Antonio she'd always known. A man who valued commitment, who despite the rockiness of his marriage had wanted to try again. "I'm sorry I dredged up all of this pain again."

He huffed out an unamused half laugh, scrubbing his face with his free hand. "You don't have to apologize. I remember so little about Vanessa in the first place. Hell, practically everything I know is from things you've told me. So the fairy tale you painted wasn't true. That's actually easier to deal with than the reverse."

"The reverse?"

With a small smile, he stared at the dusty attic floor between them. "That Vanessa was the love of my life but I would never remember what that felt like. That I'd never be able to move on until I properly mourned our relationship. Now I know all I had with her was a dysfunctional marriage that I can put behind me. The future seems a lot brighter knowing that the best relationship of my life is yet to come."

The cloud of pain seemed to lift from his features as he spoke, and she couldn't look away from his expression. It was fresh, beautiful, hopeful.

His strength was amazing and it bolstered hers. "I like the sound of that."

He tipped up her chin and feathered a thumb across her cheek. Lovingly. She fell into his gaze, mesmerized, forgetting for a moment that things were still unsettled between them. Then it all crashed down again: the disappointment, the heartache. The sense that they'd both cleansed a lot from the past but the future still had so many question marks.

Did she have what it took to put the affair behind her, as he seemed to want her to? As he seemed to do so easily himself?

"Caitlyn," he murmured and hesitated for an eternity, his gaze playing over her face as if he couldn't make up his mind what to say. Finally, he sighed. "I'm miserable without you. Can't sleep, can't eat. I deserve this purgatory you've cast me into, but you have to know that our relationship isn't going down without a fight."

"I'm miserable, too." She bowed her head. "But part of that misery is because I don't know how I'm supposed to feel about all of this. The revelations in Vanessa's journal don't change anything. Marriage is a sacred thing. Sex is, too. I have a hard time trusting that you truly believe that. I have a hard time trusting that if you and I fall into a rough spot in the future, you won't console yourself with another woman."

It was the old adage: once a cheater, always a cheater. Except she'd never thought she'd be wondering how true it was. People could and did change all the time, especially when presented with the best kind of motivation. Just look at her—she'd never envisioned being a mother, and it had taken a huge mind-set change to prepare for it.

He winced and nodded. "I deserve that, too. So that's why I went to Falco this morning and spent hours locked in a room with Thomas Warren and the other executives to hash out the details required to sell Falco Fight Club."

"You…what?" She couldn't catch her breath.

"I want it gone." Grimly, he sliced the air with a flat palm. "It's a brutal, bloody sport. I've got kids now, and limiting their exposure to MMA is always in the back of my mind. But that's not the reason I want to sell."

Sell. The word reverberated in her heart and nearly made her sick.

"Antonio! You can't sell Falco." It would be akin to her announcing she wanted to sell one of the babies. It was lunacy. "That place is a part of you. I watched you fight. You love it. It's as if you were born to be in the ring."

"Exactly. I sign everyone's paychecks. Who's going to tell me no if I say I want to get back into rotation? As long as I own Falco, I have a guaranteed path into the ring."

"You're not making any sense. All of that sounds like a *good* thing. If you want to get in the ring again, I won't stop you. I'll support it," she countered fiercely. "I'm not Vanessa."

Caitlyn would never be so daft as to forbid Antonio to return to the ring if that was what he wanted. Love didn't bind a man's wings and then selfishly expect him to fall in line.

"No, you're not." He knelt on one knee and cupped her face in his hands, holding her steady as he treated her to a beautiful, tender smile. "That's why I'm selling. I want to show you that I can stop fighting. Don't you see? If I can shut off such a deep-seated piece of my soul, I can also remove the part that believed infidelity was okay."

Her eyelids flew shut as she processed that. "Why would you do that just for me?"

"It wasn't just for you. I need to prove it to myself, too." His smile faltered. "As hard as it's been to live without you, it's been even harder to live with myself, knowing that I have the capacity to do something so wrong. This is the only way I can come to you again and ask you to reconsider being with me. How else could you believe me when I say I'd never have an affair again? I needed to prove in a concrete way that I love you."

Stricken, she stared at him as tears spilled over and splashed down her face.

He'd done this for her, as a gesture to show that he loved her. That she could give him another chance and she could trust him because he'd truly changed.

And he *had* changed. She'd recognized that from the very beginning.

He wasn't the same Antonio. It was blatantly, wonderfully obvious that he'd become someone else. Someone better, stronger, who knew the meaning of love to a far greater degree than she did.

He'd fought the demon of amnesia to find his family and fought to regain a foothold in his life. Antonio had been nothing but brutally honest with Caitlyn from day one, and just as he'd been honest about his affair, she could trust that he was telling the truth that he'd never do that to her. Perhaps she should look within for the root of her issues.

She'd feared for a long time that she wasn't woman enough, strong enough or just plain *enough* for a powerful, complex man like Antonio. Because she wasn't Vanessa and couldn't be like her sister.

But the dynamic between Caitlyn and Antonio would never follow the same path as his first marriage because her relationship with Antonio had no parallel to the one he'd had with her sister. He loved *Caitlyn*, enough to do something crazy like sell his company, which he'd never have considered for Vanessa.

No, she wasn't Vanessa, who had no clue how to love a man like Antonio. Caitlyn did.

Antonio was a fighter. And so was she.

"No," she said firmly. "I refuse to stand by and let you do this. It's not necessary."

"Then, what can I do, Caitlyn?" Frustrated, he started to drop his hands, but she snatched them back and threw her arms around him.

"You can love me." His embrace tightened and she melted into it as all her reservations vanished. "Forever. That's what I want."

She loved Antonio, and forgiveness was a part of that. She wouldn't withhold it a moment longer.

He murmured her name, his lips in her hair as he shifted her more deeply in his lap. "You've already got that. You should ask for the moon because I would give it to you."

"You're more than enough. You're all I've ever wanted."

Antonio stood with her in his arms and navigated the narrow stairway from the attic with all the grace and finesse she'd come to expect from such a magnificent man.

Caitlyn silently said goodbye to her sister and left the past in the dusty attic where it belonged. She had the family of her dreams and she'd never let it go again.

Epilogue

The announcer took the mic and announced, "And by unanimous decision, the winner is Antonio Cavallari!"

With his name buzzing in his ears, Antonio raised his aching hands to the roaring crowd in a classic fighter's victory pose, but his gaze only sought one face—Caitlyn's. The lights of the packed arena blinded him, as did the trickle of blood from his eyebrow, but he ignored it all until he located her in her usual ringside spot.

His wife of six months shot him that sexy, sleepy smile that had replaced her maidenly blush. Sometimes he missed that blush, but not very often, because she backed up the smile with abandon behind closed doors. He grinned back. He couldn't wait to get her alone later. But it would have to wait because a hundred people wanted a piece of the new welterweight champion.

After an hour of interviews, in which he was asked over and over again the secret to revitalizing his career, and then showering through the pain of his cuts and bruises and Thomas Warren's incessant chatter about another champion coming out of Falco, Antonio finally threaded through the animated crowd to press up against Caitlyn's back.

Exactly where he wanted to be.

She leaned into him, and he slipped his arms around her. The silk of her blue dress felt like heaven under his battered hands, but her skin would feel even better, and he let all his desire for her surge through his veins because she could take it. Later, she would beg for him to love her, meet him in his urgency. Because she was his missing piece, and without her, he'd still be wandering through the confusion inside his head, trying to figure out where he belonged.

"Congratulations," she murmured and turned her head to press a kiss to his throat. "How does it feel to be the king of the comeback?"

"Feels as if it's been too long since you were naked," he grumbled in her ear, careful not to say it too loudly when Brigitte was only a few feet away with the babies.

The au pair had one hand on the three-seated stroller, expertly splitting her attention between her charges and the young featherweight fighter engaging her in conversation. Matteo Long was a rising star in Antonio's empire, and his children's caregiver could do worse.

Caitlyn had continually insisted the kids should be immersed in their father's world so they could learn for themselves the artistry and discipline of Antonio's passion. The fact that she truly understood what made him tick was yet another reason he loved his wife completely.

And his love for her and his children had finally gotten him into a doctor's office to get that CT scan. That had led to more tests and procedures that had eventually uncovered the medical reason for Antonio's headaches— and a solution. He rarely had them these days, which was a blessing for an athlete going after a title.

His private detective hadn't turned up evidence of other survivors from the plane crash. So Antonio had let that quest go—his own amazing story was enough.

Turning in his arms, Caitlyn fingered the chain around her neck where she wore his wedding band while he was in the ring and undid the clasp. Encircling the band, she slid it on his finger and said, "Till death do us part."

It was a ritual they performed often, reminiscent of their wedding ceremony. A tactile reminder of their love, commitment and marriage vows. He'd insisted on it.

Not that he needed any reminders. He still hadn't fully regained his memories from before the crash and had accepted that he likely never would. Odd flashes came to him at strange times, but it didn't matter what his brain resurfaced.

Caitlyn was the only woman he could never forget.

* * * * *

MILLS & BOON®

Desire™

PASSIONATE AND DRAMATIC LOVE STORIES

A sneak peek at next month's titles...

In stores from 18th December 2015:

- **Twin Heirs to His Throne** – Olivia Gates *and*
  Nanny Makes Three – Cat Schield

- **A Baby for the Boss** – Maureen Child *and*
  Pregnant by the Rival CEO – Karen Booth

- **That Night with the Rich Rancher** – Sara Orwig *and*
  Trapped with the Tycoon – Jules Bennett

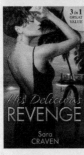

'High drama and lots of laughs'
—*Fabulous* magazine

Fed up with disastrous internet dates and
conflicting advice from her friends, Ellie Rigby
decides to take matters into her own hands.
Instead of looking for a man for herself, she's
going to start a dating agency where she can
use her extensive experience in finding
Mr Wrong to help others find their Mr Right.

Well, that is until a match with one of her clients,
charming, infuriating Nick, has her questioning
everything she's ever thought about love…

MILLS & BOON

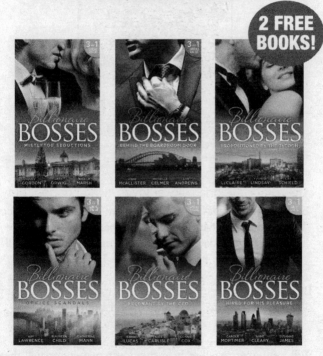

Don't miss Sarah Morgan's next Puffin Island story

The No. 1 bestselling author

Sarah Morgan

Some kind of Wonderful

'The perfect book to curl up with' *Heat*

Brittany Forrest has stayed away from Puffin Island since her relationship with Zach Flynn went bad. They were married for ten days and only just managed not to kill each other by the end of the honeymoon.

But, when a broken arm means she must return, Brittany moves back to her Puffin Island home. Only to discover that Zach is there as well.

Will a summer together help two lovers reunite or will their stormy relationship crash on to the rocks of Puffin Island?

MILLS & BOON®

Want to get more from Mills & Boon?

Here's what's available to you if you join the exclusive **Mills & Boon eBook Club** today:

✦ *Convenience – choose your books each month*
✦ *Exclusive – receive your books a month before anywhere else*
✦ *Flexibility – change your subscription at any time*
✦ *Variety – gain access to eBook-only series*
✦ *Value – subscriptions from just £3.99 a month*

So visit **www.millsandboon.co.uk/esubs** today to be a part of this exclusive eBook Club!

MILLS & BOON®

Why shop at millsandboon.co.uk?

Each year, thousands of romance readers find their perfect read at millsandboon.co.uk. That's because we're passionate about bringing you the very best romantic fiction. Here are some of the advantages of shopping at www.millsandboon.co.uk:

* **Get new books first**—you'll be able to buy your favourite books one month before they hit the shops

* **Get exclusive discounts**—you'll also be able to buy our specially created monthly collections, with up to 50% off the RRP

* **Find your favourite authors**—latest news, interviews and new releases for all your favourite authors and series on our website, plus ideas for what to try next

* **Join in**—once you've bought your favourite books, don't forget to register with us to rate, review and join in the discussions

Visit **www.millsandboon.co.uk**
for all this and more today!